THE ROCHEFORTS

THE ROCHEFORTS

A Novel

CHRISTIAN LABORIE

All rights reserved, including without limitation the right to reproduce this book or any portion thereof in any form or by any means, whether electronic or mechanical, now known or hereinafter invented, without the express written permission of the publisher.

This is a work of fiction. Names, characters, places, events, and incidents either are the product of the author's imagination or are used fictitiously. Any resemblance to actual persons, living or dead, businesses, companies, events, or locales is entirely coincidental.

The origin of denim, the fabric used in jeans, has been the subject of controversy. The author sides with the many historians who say denim came from the French city of Nîmes. The roles played by the fictional characters in this novel are entirely imaginary and should not be compared with people who really existed.

First published in France as *Les Rochefort* by Presses de la Cité, an imprint of Place des Editeurs

Copyright © 2012 by Presses de la Cité, an imprint of Place des Editeurs

Cover design by Neil Alexander Heacox

978-1-5040-0077-2

Publishers Square
12 Avenue d'Italie
75627 Paris Cedex 13
France
www.publishers-square.com

Distributed by Open Road Integrated Media, Inc.
345 Hudson Street
New York, NY 10014
www.openroadmedia.com

THE ROCHEFORTS

Prologue

1

The Man in Black

Nîmes, January 1898

The night sky was pitch black. The air was freezing, and the darkness absorbed all noise. Nîmes was plunged into the heart of a harsh winter, the kind that rarely happened more than once in a decade. The amphitheater was frozen under the dull glow of the moon. Church steeples rose up like giant crosses in a gloomy, unmoved sky. The world was petrified. Yet the narrow streets and wide boulevards were not covered in snow. The dry, icy winds had swept everything away, even the nauseating stench that usually rose from the seedier parts of town.

Only the hungriest of the light-footed night cats dared to venture under the streetlamps. Their mournful mewing died out in the basement windows where they sought refuge. Occasionally, a stealthy shadow brushed the walls and slipped into a mysterious alcove. On other nights, beauties in the brothels entertained disloyal husbands, men passing through, and soldiers on leave. But now even the brothels showed little signs of life.

Nestled in the hilltops, Nîmes jealously guarded its secrets, which were sealed in the thick walls of its ancient ruins. Centuries after the end of Roman rule, the city's upper class had made Nîmes a center of prosperous industry and trade. Several dynasties had taken root, achieving renown in finance, textiles, and the wine trade. As a result, opulent homes were numerous, despite a certain modesty imposed by the Protestant ethic.

A carriage coming from the train station broke the silence of the night. Hooves hammered the cobblestones. Their clip-clop echoed eerily between the walls of the sleeping houses. The vehicle, entirely covered in black leather, turned onto the Avenue Feuchères, heading toward the esplanade. It went around the amphitheater and climbed the Boulevard Victor-Hugo before pulling up to the curb a hundred or so yards from the Maison Carrée. A few seconds later, a man stepped down nimbly. He was dressed in black and wore a wide-brimmed hat. He tied the horse to a railing and walked to the rear door of a mansion. Nobody answered. Showing no signs of impatience, the man used the bronze knocker a second time.

The pounding drew the attention of an elderly fellow living across the way, an insomniac for whom the night was bad company. Curious, he approached his window, candlestick in hand, just in time to see the man in black disappear into the mansion.

"What is it?" grumbled his wife, torn from a deep slumber.

"Nothing. Go back to sleep. A coach stopped across the way."

"And?"

"And nothing. A strange man got out. Then he disappeared."

"Come back to bed."

A few minutes later, the man in black reappeared. Under his arm, he carried a large basket wrapped in dark cloth. He carefully placed the basket in the carriage, untied the horse, and climbed into his seat. At a crack of the whip, the animal started moving.

The man then drove the carriage around the outside of the city at a slow trot, as if he didn't want to wake up the sleeping residents. The coach turned onto the Arles road, and only then did the driver crack his whip three times to pick up the pace. With its nostrils giving off steam in the icy air, the animal obeyed and galloped into the shadows.

Behind the convent walls, the Sisters of Charity prepared for Matins. The chapel bells rang three times to remind them of the day's first duty. In the strictest silence, they left their cells and walked along the cloister ambulatory with their hands together and their heads down in prayer.

Before starting the liturgy, the mother superior always counted her flock to make sure no one was still lost in Morpheus's arms. Although there weren't many nuns, Sister Angela felt compelled to check, just as she counted the children at the orphanage every morning. She ran the institution with a firm hand.

The outside world accessed the chapel via a windowless vestibule that had a small door fitted with an elaborately carved grate. Sister Angela jealously guarded the keys, as if they opened the way to heaven. In her God-fearing eyes, however, the door did not lead to heaven, but to a world of temptation, covetousness, and sin—Satan's world. Girls who entered the convent with the intention of taking their vows seldom used this door again. Once in the convent, they stayed, and most of them had taken their vows years earlier.

A second door led to a large slightly sloped hallway that was completely dark. The smell of incense and wax wafted from the chapel into this passageway after every service. It had seeped into the woodwork and impregnated the walls and ceiling. Sister Angela considered it a purifying bath for the young souls crossing the threshold for the first time. At the end of the hallway, a final door opened to another world, one offering redemption to those beings who had begun their sorry lives on earth in the gravest of sin: that of not being wanted.

There were nearly sixty Sisters of Charity orphans. Some were the bastards of highborn families. Others were poor children abandoned by hard-pressed mothers and fathers. The parentage of still others was entirely unknown. They all carried the misery of the world on their frail shoulders. Yet the world knew nothing of their existence. The nuns gave them a basic Christian education. Girls learned domestic work—sewing, cooking, and cleaning—while the boys tended the convent orchards and vegetable garden. The boys and girls crossed paths only in the chapel, where they attended daily Mass, and the classroom. They were not allowed to communicate or even look at each other. When they left their near-monastic existence, the orphans were expected to face the world without straying from the Lord's sacred path.

At the time, the city of Nîmes had no secular orphanage. As a result, the convent orphanage was at capacity, and the sisters were always worried that they would have to turn away a homeless child.

When the Matins liturgy ended, the nuns would return to their cells in silence to delve into Bible reading, contemplation, and supreme communion with God. Then, after a frugal breakfast, they would set about their respective tasks. Some were assigned to housework, others to gardening. Those with the most education taught the orphans, and still others were responsible for administrative duties. The day was punctuated by periods of group prayer and the daily office—Lauds,

Prime, Terce, Sext, None, Vespers, and Compline—which occupied them from predawn until deep into the night.

Sister Agnes was the last to pass before the mother superior as the nuns made their way back to their cells. When five knocks on the vestibule door echoed throughout the entire chapel, the young novice stopped and turned to Sister Angela. "Who could that be at this hour?" she said, looking worried.

Sister Angela maintained her stoic calm. At her age, nothing disturbed or frightened her. She lifted her left index finger to her lips, signaling silence.

Three more knocks resounded.

"Go see," the mother superior said to Sister Agnes.

Sister Agnes didn't move. She was scared to death. "You want me to . . . "

"Yes," Sister Angela answered tersely. "You heard me. Go see. Open the grate, and see who it is. The devil is not going to jump out at you."

"Oh, Mother!" Turning pale, Sister Agnes signed herself three times.

"What are you waiting for? Go on, child. Toughen up."

The novice did as she was told. She crossed the chapel, her hands hidden in the sleeves of her ample white habit. She mouthed a prayer. Fear made her muddle the words.

Once in the vestibule, she waited a few seconds, holding her breath. She listened. On the other side of the door, she heard breathing. Whether it was a man or a woman, she could not tell. Her hand shaking, she reached for the grate. But a strange black vision stopped her. She felt as if she were about to face the devil himself. At this hour, it would never be a lost soul seeking charity. She quickly signed herself again. Her entire being trembled. This was the first time since she had entered the convent that Sister Angela had tested her, and her old fears haunted her.

Since the age of thirteen, Sister Agnes had battled nightmares and hellish visions. Her parents had consulted all the professors at the university. None had found any effective remedy for her anguish. Religion was her only refuge. In church, her soul could rise and her spirit could pull free of its heavy burden. That was why, at the age of eighteen, Agnes de Boisdèvre had entered the convent to lead a reclusive life dedicated to God and her fellow sisters. With the Sisters of Charity, she recovered the calm and inner peace that her fragile soul needed. The regimented simplicity of her new life in a realm divorced from the world gave her the stronger ramparts she needed against the psychoses she interpreted as clear signs of evil.

Still hesitating, she looked over her shoulder. At the back of the chapel, the mother superior stared at her. In her black habit, she looked like a shadow from beyond the grave. Her eyes were two steely slivers. Sister Angela pointed at the door, wordlessly telling her to do as instructed.

Sister Agnes gathered her courage and slowly slid the grate open. To her great surprise, she saw nobody on the other side, only the fading glow of a lamp. "Who's there?" she asked, her voice quavering.

She heard footsteps. Then two piercing eyes appeared in the opening.

"Finally," came a man's voice. "I didn't think anyone was there. I was going to leave."

"What do you want?" the novice said, still filled with fear.

"To see the mother superior."

"Why do you want to see the mother superior?"

"It's personal. Let me in."

"I cannot open the door without permission. This is a convent. No man can enter without authorization."

"So go get the mother superior, please."

"Sir, do you realize what time it is, that you are disturbing us in the middle of the night?"

"Charity keeps no hours, for God's sake."

Sister Agnes made the sign of the cross again. "Um, let me go see."

"Hurry! It's freezing. And what I have for you is fragile."

Sister Agnes closed the grate, gathered herself, and went back to inform Sister Angela. It's just a beggar, she said to herself as reassurance.

"So?" the mother superior asked.

"A man is asking to see you, Mother."

"At this time of the night?"

"That is what I said, but he insisted. He said charity keeps no hours."

"You did well, my child. You overcame your fear. I wanted to test you. I know that nighttime terrifies you. Do not forget that God is with you in everything you do, day and night. He is your greatest support. Go in peace now. Pray and ask Our Lord to enlighten your spirit so that you will no longer be afraid of the shadows. I will take care of this visitor."

"Thank you, Mother."

As Sister Agnes walked away, she looked over her shoulder. The mother superior was standing in front of the grate. She looked like a sentinel. The novice had a fleeting apprehension that the mother superior might be trying to keep the devil himself from entering.

At the door, the stranger leaned in close and spoke at length. After long minutes of negotiations, Sister Angela sighed and threw up her arms. She allowed the man in black to enter. He was carrying the basket that he had slipped into the carriage. He set it down on the cold marble tiles and handed Sister Angela a purse and a letter. The mother superior read the letter. Then she stuffed both the purse and the letter into the folds of her habit.

The man talked a few more minutes and turned around and left.

Through her cell window, Sister Agnes heard the horse break into a gallop. She tried to return to reading the Epistle of the Corinthians, which she had been studying for two days, but her mind was elsewhere. It was as if the visitor had taken possession of her thoughts. So she abandoned the Bible on its lectern and kneeled on the prie-dieu at the foot of her bed. She took refuge in prayer.

At the following office, she couldn't resist giving Sister Angela a questioning glance. The mother superior let nothing show. When dawn had illuminated the hills, and light had chased away the shadows of the night, Sister Angela went to see Sister Agnes in the study, where she was preparing a catechism lesson for the orphans she taught.

"Last night, my child, you heard nothing and saw nothing. Nobody came to our door." The mother superior's tone was firm.

The novice was surprised and nearly offended at the idea of having to commit the sin of lying, but she didn't dare contradict her mother superior. "Mother, I didn't see or hear anything."

"Very good, my child. I know I can count on your discretion."

That afternoon, while she was spending time with the other novices, Sister Agnes learned what had happened during the night. "This morning, we received a gift from heaven," Sister Theresa, who cared for the youngest orphans, joyfully announced. "A real little angel sent by the Lord."

"This morning? Are you sure?" Sister Agnes said.

"Yes. Not more than an hour ago, Sister Angela called me into her office to present our newest border: a baby who is just a few days old. Her mother was poor, lost, and completely distraught. She didn't have the means to raise the child decently without a husband, money, or work. It pained her to leave her child with us. Sister Angela told me all about it."

"A baby? A young mother?" Sister Agnes couldn't believe it.

"Yes. That's what Sister Angela told me when she gave me the little angel to care for."

As she had promised, Sister Agnes didn't say a word about what she had seen. She pretended to be surprised and happily welcomed the abandoned child.

"It's true that a tiny angel has come to us from heaven," she told Sister Theresa. "It's so cute! Is it a girl or a boy?"

"A boy."

"He is so little, so vulnerable."

"The cherub was just born."

"Barely born, and misfortune has already struck."

Sister Agnes understood that abandonment wasn't the child's only misfortune. While charity was abundant in the orphanage, affection was not. In this place, one did not find happiness shining in the eyes of the children. François de Boisdèvre, Sister Agnes's father and a benefactor of the orphanage, hadn't hidden the truth from his daughter when she decided to take her vows.

"The Sisters of Charity are saints," he had told her. "Their self-denial is limitless. Their generosity is immeasurable. They care for our good city's lost children with devotion that is only equaled by their love for the Lord. But they are disciplined and devoid of sentimentality. This does not mean they are insensitive to the suffering of the world. Their calling proves the opposite. These children have hard lives ahead of them and must be prepared. You can love them and guide them along the Lord's path. Pity, however, will only cripple them. Do not allow yourself to fall prey to it."

Sister Agnes approached the newborn's cradle and leaned over the child. "What is his name?" she asked her fellow novice.

"Vincent Janvier."

"Is that his real name?"

"No, his mother had not yet given him one. Since she gave him to us on Saint Vincent's Day, and we are the month of January, Sister Angela registered him under the name Vincent

Janvier, born on January 20, 1898, two days before he came to us."

Sister Agnes pretended to believe Sister Theresa's story but privately wondered why the mother superior had stamped this new border's arrival with a seal of lies.

2

A Marriage of Reason

The Rochefort household was in mourning. Large black sheets covered the ornate façade of the mansion, which had been one of the most notable in Nîmes for two generations. A chapel had been set up in the small sitting room. The body of the deceased, visible underneath a veil of tulle, lay in a coffin made of the finest oak. Bronze and silver candelabras gave off subdued lighting, making the atmosphere all the gloomier. A profusion of floral wreaths and sprays attested to the sympathy of acquaintances and relatives. Loved ones took turns keeping vigil so that the poor soul would not be alone on its mysterious passage to the beyond, and receiving condolences from visitors, friends, and neighbors touched by the misfortune that had fallen upon one of the city's foremost families.

The deceased was the daughter of Anselme and Elisabeth Rochefort. The eldest of four children, she was only eighteen at the beginning of 1898, when death carried her away. All the family's close friends and relatives knew of her kindness. Catherine Rochefort had been a cultivated, joyful girl, always helpful and mindful of others' needs. But she had sometimes given the impression that she could not share in the happiness that she lavished on others.

The Rocheforts were expecting their fifth child when Catherine died. Some said that God was trying to compensate for what the unfortunate parents had lost when He had called Catherine. Elisabeth was due to give birth in the spring and had sworn that this would be her last child. She was nearly forty years old and felt she had fulfilled her wifely duty. Furthermore, the doctors had warned her about getting pregnant again. "You would be putting your life and the future child's life in danger."

As for Anselme Rochefort, he had always prided himself on his lineage, and at forty-eight, he felt as spritely as an oak sapling. "I'm made of strong wood," he liked to boast to those who tried to warn him against overindulging.

Only his wife could attest to his manly fervor, but decorum kept her from alluding to it among her friends. They knew, however, that the poor woman suffered her husband's hotheadedness, and the man did very little to hide his infidelity.

Anselme Rochefort came from a line of industrialists who had made their fortune in textiles. During the golden age of silk production in the Cévennes region of France, an ancestor, Simon Rochefort, had opened his first mill in the Gardon d'Anduze valley, where he had been born. He quickly became rich and purchased a large property—the Clos du Tournel—where mulberry trees provided quantities of silkworm cocoons. His descendants multiplied and consolidated the family fortune until a disease called pebrine infected the silkworms. That was during the Second Empire. It was in the same year that Louis Pasteur was asked to eradicate the silkworm disease that Anselme Rochefort's father, Charles-Honoré, decided to settle in Nîmes and open a cotton mill and weaving workshops.

Charles-Honoré Rochefort had felt the wind changing. Without sacrificing his silk production, which Pasteur's research had saved, he launched into the production of a fabric that a certain American manufacturer, Levi Strauss, had started importing at the end of the 1850s. The name of the fabric came from the Italian *"blu di Genova,"* a dye made from indigo and wood. The term was then used to designate a very durable indigo-dyed serge—or twill—produced in Nîmes as early as the sixteenth century and exported to Genoa for use by the Genoan marines.

The industrialist managed to build a substantial business for himself in a booming market. He expanded his factory, hired more people, and built trade with Levi Strauss, who was using the twill weave from Nîmes to make pants for farmers, railway builders, and forty-niners. Rochefort's success enabled him to buy a mansion on par with the wealthiest homes in the city.

Charles-Honoré had come from a family of landholders, and he had deep roots in the Cévennes region. He had inherited the family home with its many acres spread across the towns of Anduze and Tornac. A sharecropper worked the land, focusing almost entirely on winegrowing. Charles-Honoré loved to visit his land, and his cellars produced wine that was abundant, if not the highest quality. Winegrowing in the region had changed over the years. Some growers lacked the scruples of the past and were mass producing. In addition, diseases such as phylloxera and mildew had affected the yield.

In Nîmes, Charles-Honoré Rochefort used his well-established fortune to weave networks of friends and relations, which made him an influential man. The prefect and the bishop had seats at his table. He had connections at the city hall and a pew reserved for the family at the Saint Castor Cathedral, although he didn't attend regularly. His wife, Hortense, represented him at Sunday Mass.

Charles-Honoré passed for an opportunist in Nîmes society. He was a Bonapartist during the Second Empire. Afterward, he admitted missing those heady days of economic liberalism. He adhered to the republic but without any real conviction.

Charles-Honoré and Hortense had one son, Anselme. He was his father's single great hope of ensuring that his work continued. When Anselme came up for military duty in the middle of the war against Prussia, rather than risk losing his heir, Charles-Honoré used his connections to keep him out of the conflict.

At twenty, Anselme was a fickle young man who was more interested in pursuing life's pleasures, especially his lady friends, than tending to his studies at Montpellier law school. His teachers barely knew him.

Charles-Honoré was aware of his son's faults and finally forced him to face facts. "Either you get serious and come help me at the factory so that you can take my place one day, or I'll send you off to the army to fulfill your duty."

Considering the options, Anselme didn't hesitate. As he didn't have the courage to go fight on the front or the discipline to apply himself at school, he accepted his father's offer. He dropped his law studies and returned to Nîmes.

When Charles-Honoré died unexpectedly five years later, Anselme found himself at the head of a prosperous company at the mere age of twenty-five. Unfortunately, an economic crisis loomed, and Anselme lacked pugnacity. Little by little, the fine business Charles-Honoré had left him declined. By the time Anselme's mother died, he had been forced to close several production lines, fire half his employees, sell off a silk mill, and mortgage part of his real-estate assets.

That was when he decided to take action.

Anselme had not only inherited his father's fortune, but also managed to maintain the man's network of relations and friends. Although they did not help him as his business declined, their doors were still open to him. Anselme was not a man burdened with scruples, and so he set out to cement an alliance with a wealthy heiress.

"I have no choice," he said to Mr. Lambert, his business attorney, the night his mother was buried. "I must form an alliance with a large wealthy family."

"You are harboring illusions," his attorney answered. "Considering your finances, nobody will agree to give their daughter in marriage. You discredited yourself. And the once fine business you inherited from your father is on its way down. You do not have your father's business acumen."

"You are wrong, Lambert. I will prove it. In a little while, you will be hearing about Rochefort Industries once again."

Stinging from his attorney's skepticism, Anselme focused on changing his situation. He began frequenting the stylish salons, showed up more than ever at the theater, and gave multiple invitations to dine in the tarnished glitter of his mansion. Scandalmongers did not refrain from spreading the rumor that the Rochefort heir was looking for a charitable soul to keep his business afloat.

One evening, a friend, Pierre Duponteil, introduced him to a young woman whose beauty was only equaled by the sadness written on her face.

It was during a charity ball given by members of the Montalban family, who were prosperous wine traders. All of Nîmes's high society was gathered around the government representative. His presence demonstrated that the authorities were determined to calm any fears regarding moves toward increased laicism in education. Indeed, the government, prodded by statesman Jules Ferry, had just agreed to two measures. One ordered the dissolution of the Society of Jesus, and the other required unauthorized congregations to apply for the right to teach within a period of three months. Most of the guests were Catholic, and they were concerned.

Pressed with questions, the prefect tried to minimize the ramifications of the measures.

Anselme Rochefort had little interest in ups and downs of this sort. That night, he only had eyes for the beauty his friend Duponteil had pointed out to him. Her name was Eleanor Letellier. She was twenty years old.

Duponteil took him aside. "If you want my opinion, you should be quick to remove that weeping beauty from the lustful gaze of those vultures. If you handle it right, she could get you out of your predicament."

"Tell me more. I'm curious now."

"Of course you've never heard of her. Eleanor Letellier is the sole survivor of a very wealthy couple who moved to the region just three years ago. Her parents bought an estate just outside Uzès in the hopes of spending their final days in the sun. Unfortunately, they were never able to do that. They took a trip to Egypt to celebrate the beginning of their new life, and they never returned. Vanished. Nobody knows what happened. They were declared dead after more than a year of searching led only to the discovery of their travel trunks and a witness who suggested they were the victims of desert pillagers. After losing her parents at such a young age, she also lost her fiancé. It's like bad luck is pursuing her."

"Her fiancé?"

"Yes, a handsome captain in the colonial army, killed in an ambush in Algeria just a month ago."

"So she has no family left?"

"No. She is alone and inconsolable. You get my drift. If you marry her, you marry her fortune."

Anselme didn't need any more encouragement. However, he did show concern. "Her loss is recent. Don't you think it's a little early for her to be involved with someone else?"

"In her state, I don't think so."

"What do you mean? That seems rather mysterious."

"She's not showing yet, but soon the curves will betray what she's concealing."

"Do you mean . . . "

"Exactly. You understand me. She is pregnant and not married."

"How do you know that? What secrets are you privy to?"

"I know Eleanor's best friend. She's the one who told me."

"What do you know about the captain?"

"Not much. His name was Lavalette, and he came from a long line of soldiers, some of whom made names for themselves in the Battle of Fontenoy, then during the First Empire, and later under Napoléon III. He had bad luck and was killed the day after he learned he was going to be a father."

"So, Miss Eleanor will soon be an unwed mother, which is hardly acceptable in her milieu."

"Would you be opposed to proposing marriage in her state?"

"Do you think she would accept? It may be a little premature."

"In her situation, she doesn't have a choice. She needs to give her child a father as quickly as possible."

Anselme Rochefort let his friend introduce them. Eleanor Letellier agreed to have a glass of Champagne with them. Then Duponteil slipped away, leaving Anselme and Eleanor alone, away from the other guests.

Two months later, they were married in a discreet ceremony. Rochefort had had no trouble convincing the young woman. He was ten years her elder with the self-possession she needed. He could offer rest for her soul when it was still bleeding from the two severe blows. In reality, Eleanor was a wreck and far from feeling any love for her new beau. She accepted Rochefort's proposal out of despair, without really being aware of what she was getting into.

"I will give you the love you deserve," Anselme had told her. "In return, I won't ask you to love me the same way you loved before. I won't strive to replace the man who made your life a paradise on earth. But with time, I'm sure you will be able to love again. And when you are, you will discover who I really am. I will be here for you, loyal and devoted, as I am now."

Eleanor had noticed that her close friends were distancing themselves. In high society, single mothers were outcasts, as if they were solely responsible for their sin. So with no family or true friends, she was already feeling abandoned, and her wealth was no solace.

When Rochefort said he would be a real father for her child, she fell into his arms. She let her dammed-up feelings burst, and she poured out her heart.

Immediately after the ceremony, Anselme took Eleanor to Taillades, one of his country houses, to shelter her from any gossips.

"I have a little home near La Bastide," he had told her. "The pure mountain air will renew you. You'll be calm there as you wait for your child. I'll visit regularly and will be by your side on the big day. La Bastide's doctor is a friend. He'll let me know in time."

Catherine was born six months later, and Eleanor remained in Taillades for nearly a year. When friends asked where his wife was hiding, Anselme responded, "I am keeping her from those who envy me. I know more than one who would lure my new wife and ravish her as soon as I wasn't looking."

People joked that Rochefort was jealously guarding his wife like some precious treasure.

Eleanor returned to Nîmes when Catherine was a few months old. Anselme had already announced Catherine's birth, so nobody found it strange that she returned with a baby. By this time, Anselme was no longer seeing anyone from Eleanor's old circle. Pierre Duponteil was the only one he still talked with, and he had agreed to keep the secret. So Catherine was welcomed as Anselme and Eleanor's daughter, and nobody dug deeper.

A year went by.

Eleanor supported her husband financially. He proved to be a good husband and an attentive father. His factories' finances improved, and people began referring to Rochefort Industries as a sound business. For that matter, bankers no longer hesitated to lend Anselme the money he needed to invest, as his wife's assets served as a guarantee.

No fool, Anselme knew he owed the restoration of his business to his wife. And everyone knew that Eleanor was the sole heir to the Letellier fortune, handed down from a line of industrialists who had drawn their wealth from ironworks in the Creusot region.

"Beware," his attorney had warned. "Whatever you get from your wife, you will owe her as long as she is alive. Use her financial support wisely, but succeed by your own means. You'll need to put your accounts in order to safeguard what you have acquired since your marriage. You don't want anyone to take that away."

"Who would want to do that? You're losing it, Lambert."

"Who knows what could happen. You're never safe from a bad stroke of luck."

Anselme Rochefort did not feel more vulnerable because he was dependent on his wife's money. "It's a temporary situation," he concluded.

Anselme and Eleanor passed for a model couple. Their hospitality equaled their generosity to local charities. Anselme avoided being seen at high-society events and public ceremonies. He preferred to maintain his relationships in the privacy of his sitting room, which he had refurbished in a more contemporary style to please his wife.

Eleanor, however, brooded. Even with her daughter at

her side, she was increasingly anxious. Sadness was written all over her face. She did honor her husband's private receptions with her presence, but she barely spoke and just smiled at the compliments she received for her elegance and beauty.

Several times, Anselme had found her crying, her daughter held tight against her chest. Mrs. Combe, the nurse who cared for little Catherine, reported that her mistress asked to be alone with the child more and more often. "It's like she's afraid someone will take the girl from her."

"Has she said anything that could explain this?"

"No, sir. Madame doesn't say what she thinks in front of the help."

"Haven't you noticed anything, some detail that could be useful?"

The nurse seemed to hesitate. "Just, well, once when she was holding Catherine, she said, 'My darling, if only your father were still alive.' I didn't really understand. I thought I heard it wrong, but she said it again."

Anselme didn't want to betray any emotion in front of a servant. "You must have misunderstood. She must have said, 'If only my father were still alive.' She's still very affected by her father's death."

"You must be right, sir." The nurse wouldn't dare to contradict her master, but inside, she was certain she had heard his wife's words correctly.

In the days that followed, Eleanor's sadness became more worrisome. Nothing made her smile. Her face was pale and expressionless. With empty eyes, she stared into the distance. She pushed away her food, and her face grew gaunt, her complexion sallow, the first signs of anemia.

Anselme understood the real reason of her despair and did not question her. He would simply discuss daily business to distract her from her inner torment.

One night, he couldn't control himself anymore. "Eleanor,

you have to do something," he blurted out. "I know what's making you so sad. You have to turn the page."

Eleanor looked at her husband with eyes full of distress. But her voice was a monotone. "What do you know about love, my friend? You married me out of self-interest. You parade me around as if I were your finest conquest. Before we got married, you told me that time would help me forget, and I would learn to love you. That hasn't happened. Time has eroded, erased, and destroyed the real, sublime love that I once experienced. Time hasn't given birth to anything close to that love."

"You're talking nonsense, my dear. You are too upset to see things as they are. Why don't you go rest at our house in La Bastide or the one in Anduze if you prefer. It's not as far away. It is peaceful there. Your taste for life will return. Take our daughter. She will take your mind off your troubles."

"*Our* daughter, you say? Catherine is *my* daughter. Don't claim her like you're claiming my money."

"Eleanor, calm down. Mrs. Combe will go with you. She'll watch over Catherine. And you. I'll let the tenant know, so he can prepare the Clos du Tournel for you."

As Anselme gave instructions, Eleanor went off to her room.

Several hours went by.

Around eight in the evening, when it was time for dinner, Anselme sent Suzon, a servant, to tell Eleanor that dinner was ready. Suzon knocked on the door several times, with no response. The servant informed her master. "Madame isn't answering, sir. She's locked in her room."

Anselme went upstairs, knocked softly, and asked his wife to come down. When she didn't respond, he pounded on the door. "Eleanor, say something, would you!"

Anselme called the butler, Marcellin, and ordered him to break open the door.

The room was pitch black. Eleanor lay on her bed, in peace, a letter in her hand and a flask overturned on the bedside table.

Anselme rushed to her side, rubbed her cheeks, and lifted her eyelids. "It's too late," he stuttered. "The poison has already taken effect."

Tears clouded his vision as he read the letter.

> I can't do it anymore. I've gone to join the man who gave me so much, who showed me more than anyone else ever could. I'm sorry. I never knew how to love you. Take care of Catherine as though she were your own daughter. Love her like you loved me. Adieu. Eleanor

Twenty months after his marriage, Anselme Rochefort was a widower. Rather than tumble into despair, he reacted immediately. Hadn't Eleanor Letellier left him her huge fortune, along with her daughter, who was just a little over a year old?

In Saint Castor Cathedral, the priest stood before Catherine Rochefort's coffin and began his sermon. Memories of his first unhappy marriage came back to Anselme. It had started off well but had ended quickly and tragically. Eleanor's image came back to him, as if to reproach him for not having kept his promises. Eighteen years had passed since that short period in his life when he had made his business comeback. But he could still hear her last words and see the good-bye letter she had written in despair before her death.

Had he taken good care of Catherine? Had he been the father he swore he would be when he married Eleanor? Had he done what she had asked in that letter? Had he really loved her?

These questions gnawed at him and distracted him during the funeral, after which *his* daughter, Catherine, would be buried in the family vault that the Rocheforts had pompously erected on the central drive of the local cemetery.

At his side, Elisabeth—his second wife—knew that doubt and remorse were preying on her husband. They had shared a life for nearly fifteen years now. Their children were sitting to her right. Weren't they proof of the love he had always shown her? Just like the baby who was already kicking inside her?

Elisabeth mourned Catherine as though she were her own daughter. In reality, wasn't she?

She squeezed her husband's hand to confirm her feelings. He did not react. He was lost in thoughts of his past.

3

A Large Family

Eleanor's death didn't seem to affect Anselme Rochefort to any great extent. He went right back to work. His close friends were primarily concerned for Catherine, deprived of her mother at such a vulnerable age. Those who were charitable acknowledged that she was lucky to have a father like Anselme, because she would never want for anything material. The nurse, Mrs. Combe, continued to take care of Catherine as she had when Eleanor was alive. She was even more attentive to the poor child now. The gossips said that Rochefort's bed would not be empty for long. His past and his taste for young ladies led them to believe that Eleanor Letellier would be replaced quickly.

To tell the truth, Anselme Rochefort was focused entirely on his factories. The money that had allowed him to restore his business had come from the Letellier fortune. Until he was called before the notary for confirmation that he was the sole heir to those resources, he wanted to be extremely careful. Only when his finances were safe could he relax.

Mr. Labert reassured him. "What has been invested is yours for good. The papers, deeds, treasury bonds, and claims are all in order and cannot be questioned. It is all in your name."

"And in the future?" Rochefort asked. "We need to think about the future. I have financial obligations. And to stay competitive, I'll need to invest more. Without my wife's money, we can't manage."

"Your wife had no family left. You are the sole heir. You have nothing to worry about. My dear Rochefort, you are saved. You are now free to do as you like."

Contrary to what those closest to him had predicted, Anselme remained alone and behaved like a respectable widower. He never appeared in public with lady friends and rarely participated in society parties. He didn't give the impression of being overwhelmed with sorrow, but he was clearly subdued.

"Everything's fine, thank you," was his only answer to prying questions. "I don't have a moment's rest between my daughter and the mills."

Some people—mostly women—began to heap praise on the unfortunate man with a young child to care for.

"Little Catherine is so lucky to have such a devoted father," Eleanor's former friends said.

In reality, Anselme had never considered the child his own. In the evening, when he returned from work, he rarely stopped in to see her and never asked Mrs. Combe if the girl had everything she needed. When Catherine came down with childhood diseases such as measles and mumps, he let the nurse handle the doctor's visits.

So the child was growing up without her mother or any real paternal presence.

When Catherine began to babble, it took her a long time to say the word "papa." Mrs. Combe did her best. She always talked about Anselme, explaining what he did and saying he would soon be back from the factory or it would not be long before he took her to La Bastide, their house in the mountains, or the Clos du Tournel, their house near the river. Catherine was a bright child. She listened attentively and rattled off question after question. Her curiosity was limitless. But she refused to call Anselme "papa," as if even at her age she understood that he was a man living under the same roof but was not a real father.

"It will come," Mrs. Combe would say. "You need to be patient with children. Losing a mother is devastating. When she's old enough to understand what you are doing for her, she'll recognize you as her father, and in her heart you will supplant the mother she never had. Everything will fall into place."

At the age of three, Catherine finally said the word the nurse was so desperate to hear. "Will Papa be home soon?"

That evening, Mrs. Combe hurried to announce the news to her master, who barely showed any emotion. He did not become any more paternal.

Rochefort Industries was prospering and promised to do even better. Production at his cotton weaving and silk mills was at capacity. The twill he manufactured was competitive with others made in the city. Exports to the United States were turning a substantial profit, and even more heartening, those exports were no longer responsible for the lion's share of the business's revenue. Mr. Lambert, who was taking on a larger role as the company's legal representative, advised establishing a trading house in Genoa, Italy, the city where the Nîmes twill had earned its fame, and possibly additional ones in New York and San Francisco.

Anselme thought those ideas were too enterprising. "I know I'm not the only manufacturer on the jeans market and not the largest either. I prefer to wait before investing capital abroad. If there were an international crisis, nothing could ensure the safety of our investments."

"You're being too careful, Rochefort."

"My youthful mistakes made me wiser, my dear Lambert. Let me remind you of your own words. You criticized me for not being as good a businessman as my father. Isn't that what you told me when I wanted to form a merger with the woman whose dowry bailed me out?"

"I didn't want to hurt you, Rochefort, just warn you so you would make the best business decisions. That is what you are doing, and I'm very happy about it."

"So I'm going to surprise you a second time."

Lambert was wary of decisions his most important client made without consulting him. "What is this plan that you haven't told me about?"

"As far as I know, I'm not obliged to share my private life with you, Lambert!"

"Rochefort, don't be so touchy. I just want what's best for you. More precisely, what's best for your business so that Rochefort Industries maintains its good name. You owe it to your ancestors."

"It's not about the business, Lambert."

"What is it then?"

"I'm going to remarry."

The lawyer looked surprised and then seemed reassured. "Getting married again! Well, that is good news. May I ask who the lucky young lady is?"

"Absolutely. I'm going to marry Elisabeth Langlade."

"Langlade? From the Langlade family that heads up the largest civil engineering company in the region?"

"Exactly. She is the youngest of their four children. Their only daughter."

"You keep your cards close, don't you?"

"Our families have known each other for a long time. I maintained the good relations my grandfather had with the family patriarch, who founded the company. Old Joseph. His son, Eugène, Elisabeth's father, was a friend of my father's. He's the one who hinted that our families had much to gain by joining together."

"So he offered his daughter up in marriage. With a fine dowry, I suppose."

"I can't hide anything from you, my dear Lambert. But I must say that Elisabeth has enough charm and other qualities to make one forget the dowry."

"How old is this charming young lady?"

"Twenty-five."

"Not so young, then. It's urgent."

"You're badmouthing, Lambert."

"I'm sorry. I was joking. I was just thinking about your first wife."

"But I'm four years older now. You seem to forget."

Anselme married Elisabeth Langlade at the end of the year, putting an end to three years of widowhood.

Elisabeth's father had introduced her to Anselme during a birthday party in her honor. Anselme had given her a sumptuous gift and then courted her discreetly before meeting with Eugène to set the terms of the marriage.

Unlike the first wedding, this one took place with great pomp and ceremony. The Langlade family wanted a celebration that matched its standing among the region's power brokers. That made Anselme uncomfortable. He worried that a gauche display could make him the laughing stock of Nîmes's high society. But once again, Lambert convinced him that he had made a good decision.

"This alliance will strengthen your position. And that is well worth a gilded ceremony."

Catherine was almost four years old. At her age, she wasn't aware that her father was remarrying. She didn't know what it meant. When Mrs. Combe explained that she would soon have a mother, the child jumped with joy and was more affectionate with Anselme.

"Your daughter has finally come around," the nurse said to Anselme, who was surprised by Catherine's reaction.

Late on the wedding night, as Elisabeth awaited her husband in their nuptial bed as he changed out of his tuxedo, Anselme made a request. "My dear, I would like to ask a favor of you. A big favor."

"Is this the right time for that, Anselme?" his bride asked. "Can't it wait until tomorrow?"

"I don't want there to be any misunderstanding between us about Catherine."

"Catherine? I don't understand."

"This child has never had a mother."

"I know that. You are a widower and her father. I accepted that when I married you."

"True enough. But I have more to ask of you."

Elisabeth seemed intrigued. "Speak, Anselme, if it's so important."

"I would like you to treat Catherine like your own daughter. With time, she will believe you are her true mother. At her age, the memories of her infancy will fade quickly. Later, the children we have together must believe that Catherine is their full-fledged sister and not their half sister."

Anselme saw the confusion in his bride's eyes. "Children from two different beds do not always get along," he said. "I don't want our children to reject their half sister. And I don't want Catherine to be tempted to go looking into who her real mother was. Do you understand? If she learned that her mother put an end to her days, she could be deeply upset."

Elisabeth agreed with her husband. "I understand,

Anselme. If this white lie makes Catherine's life happier, I will do as you say. Don't worry."

Thus, Anselme and Elisabeth began their long life together, putting the finishing touches on consolidating Rochefort Industries. For many, the marriage represented the perfect union of two wealthy families. Soon the birth of their first child polished their image as a happily married couple. Jean-Christophe was born one year after the wedding. Elodie arrived two years later. Elisabeth wanted that to be her last pregnancy, but seven years later, she unwittingly became pregnant with Sebastien, who was born premature after a difficult labor. Elisabeth was only thirty-five at the time, but for a number of years had felt her husband was distant and she suspected him of having affairs.

Anselme did, indeed, occasionally have flings. His business success made him as carefree and playful as he had been in his youth. Young women seemed to surround Anselme. And some told stories about him that stretched reality.

Elisabeth, however, was an irreproachable mother and virtuous wife. She refrained from criticizing her husband. Divorce was unheard-of in their social circles. Furthermore, she loved Anselme and had no proof of her suspicions. She expressed her resignation to one of her friends. "Few husbands remain loyal to their wives after several years of marriage. That's the way it is. Men need to have affairs from time to time. As long as the affairs are fleeting and don't disturb the marriage, there's no reason to separate. It all works out over time."

In reality, that wasn't exactly what Elisabeth thought. And she wanted to believe in her husband's love. For his part, Anselme strove to be pleasant with his wife and always managed to reassure her.

"You are the only one I love, my darling," he would tell her. After Jean-Christophe's birth, they had become more comfortable with each other in private. "Don't pay any attention to the gossips. People are jealous of our success."

Elisabeth tried to avoid betraying her fears. Didn't Anselme always show the same enthusiasm in bed? A man hiding a mistress wouldn't be that eager with his wife, especially after ten years of marriage.

When she got pregnant again three years after Sebastien was born, her worries were calmed a bit. But she was still unsure.

Anselme was thrilled. "A father of four! I am truly fulfilled."

"Of five!" Elisabeth corrected him. "You forget that before our children, you had Catherine."

"Yes, of course. Catherine."

Elisabeth had abided by Anselme's request on their wedding night and had raised Catherine as her own. The little girl was growing up without asking any questions. As Anselme had predicted, she forgot her first childhood memories. For her, Elisabeth was her mother, and Anselme was her father. And she rejoiced every time a new brother or sister came along.

Mrs. Combe continued working for the Rochefort family and had sworn never to reveal her master's lie. She, too, thought it preferable that Catherine be raised in ignorance of her past. Family harmony was well worth that little secret.

Mrs. Combe, however, was the first to notice that the child suffered from a lack of paternal affection. Catherine might have been convinced that Anselme and Elisabeth were her real parents—there was no reason for her to think differently—but she couldn't explain why her father was so distant. She was well-behaved, kind, and attentive to her brothers and sisters, even to the point of mothering them.

"Your daughter is lovely," everyone said when Anselme and Elisabeth had guests in their home.

The child was radiant and endearingly modest, quite like

her mother. Nobody found it odd that she didn't resemble Elisabeth, whose charm never equaled that of Eleanor Letellier but still attracted men's admiration, something that both flattered Anselme and piqued his jealousy.

By the time Catherine was a teenager, she felt completely rejected by Anselme, who showed her nothing but indifference. Try as she might, she never managed to touch his heart. Catherine couldn't help but notice that Anselme did not behave the same way with his other children.

"Father doesn't love me," she cried to Elisabeth one day.

"Why do you say that, my darling? You're talking nonsense. Your father loves all his children the same."

"No, I see that he doesn't love me. I don't know why, Mom. Is it because I'm a girl? Did he want his oldest child to be a boy?"

"You're misinterpreting things, dear. Your father makes no distinction among you."

Elisabeth strove to prove Catherine wrong, but deep inside, she knew the girl was right. Anselme had no fatherly feelings for the child she herself accepted as her own daughter. She suffered from having to lie to Catherine. The longer the lie was told, the more devastated the girl would be if she learned the truth.

Little by little, Catherine seemed to accept that she would never have Anselme's attention and affection. She focused on Elisabeth and her brothers and sisters, who returned all the love she gave them.

The Rochefort family gave the impression of being perfectly united, and nobody who knew them could imagine any internal strife.

At fifteen, Catherine was already attracting handsome young suitors. Her mother's personality was slowly rising to the surface, and she was longing to live her passions to the limit. Her father's continued lack of affection and attention, however, frustrated her and chipped away at any lingering admiration she still had for him.

She ended up trying to find the love she sorely missed in the embrace of a young man from a penniless family, whom she met at a society party given by her parents. She drank up his fancy words, stopped counting the glasses of Champagne he gave her, and forgot her sorrow in his arms.

They had been seeing each other for several months when Anselme decided to bring the relationship to an end. It was out of the question that his daughter be seen any longer with the son of a nearly bankrupt family.

But Catherine kept seeing him, rebelling ever more fiercely.

That was when tragedy struck. A rumor circulated that the girl had become seriously ill after being forced to leave her suitor. Anselme sent her to recover at La Bastide, in Lozère. Anselme gave laconic answers to those who asked how she was. His daughter was still weak, and the mountain air was good for her.

The day he announced Catherine's death, everyone understood that her illness was more serious, certainly, than a heartache. Some said she died of consumption. But no one dared to ask the unfortunate parents for more details.

The calamity that fell upon the Rochefort family attracted real and not-so-real friends. The major families in the region understood how to react when tragedy struck one of their own. Whether it was bankruptcy or some other misfortune, they knew how to keep their distance or move in at just the right time. Those who had disgraced their family names were wise to be especially cautious with their assets. The world of business was ruthless, and the loss of money could quickly follow the loss of reputation.

Part One

THE ALLIANCE

4

The Adoption

Tornac, near Anduze, 1905

The peaks of the Cévennes Mountains rose on the horizon against a porcelain sky. There wasn't a cloud to disturb the early-morning spectacle. The north wind had cleared the air, making it shinier than the purest Murano glass. The air was brisk, just the way Donatien Rouvière liked it when spring shoved aside winter's final hoarfrost. Calm reigned for miles around. Nature was awakening. Birds chirped in the new oak leaves. This was the time of day when nature overflowed with pleasures.

Donatien found himself a spot under a tree to contemplate the springtime show. He pulled out a loaf of brown bread his wife, Constance, had made before the sun had risen. He opened his pocketknife and cut two thick slices. He spread on a little lard, topped it with goat cheese and a little meat, and chewed each mouthful slowly, as if to take in every bit of flavor it had to offer—the smell of the wheat he grew, the aroma of ash from the oven in which his wife baked the bread, the whiff of salted meat he dried in the attic, out of reach of vermin, and the inimitable taste of Constance's freshly made goat cheese. For nothing in the world would he give up this magic moment before he began to work his land at the start of the day.

Yet on that morning, Donatien Rouvière was sad. Regret was keeping him from appreciating what normally made him ecstatic and gave him the strength to make it through a hard day's work. For several weeks now, since his fortieth birthday, he had been tormented by the thought that there was nobody to follow in his footsteps. He had married Constance Duchêne fifteen years earlier, and they had had three girls: Louise, born a year after their wedding, Julie four years later, and finally Aline, who had inaugurated the new century. That's when he had despaired. "I just make girls."

At the time, his comment seemed like a joke, especially because Constance—whom he had married out of love and not self-interest—seemed thrilled to be surrounded by girls. Girls are always closer to their mother, she thought. Wasn't she closer to her parents than her husband was to his? But she understood that not having a son weighed on her husband.

Over the years, Donatien learned to love his daughters as if they were sons. He was tough on them, inculcating in them the idea that they would be expected to work shoulder-to-shoulder with any husbands worthy of them. "That's the only way to guarantee your equality," he explained, as if to justify the labor he required of them when they were still young enough to deserve pampering.

Donatien Rouvière owned a fine piece of land in the town of Tornac, which rose over the ruins of a medieval castle that once belonged to the lords of Anduze. He had inherited the prosperous farm—La Fenouillère—from his father. The property spread along the right bank of the Gradon River. A hundred and twenty-five acres of vineyard, sown parcels, and prairies planted with mulberry and olive trees ensured the better part of his income. The neighboring hills held vast expanses of fallow land where he raised a herd of three hundred sheep, which he sent to summer from June to September in Lozère, on land that belonged to Anselme Rochefort, a rich manufacturer from Nîmes. The man was also his closest neighbor—his estate, the Clos du Tournel, adjoined La Fenouillère. The two men had known each other for a long time. Both had roots in Anduze stretching back several generations. Every time Anselme Rochefort spent time in Anduze, he would visit Donatien. Sometimes the two men would meet at La Bastide in Lozère after the sheep were moved in the summer transhumance.

The Rouvière farm was one of the most prosperous in the region. Large stone buildings rose around an inner courtyard where chickens, geese, and ducks could free roam. The buildings seemed to have been built to last forever. At least eight generations of Rouvières had lived on this farm, all of them Protestants as far back as Donatien knew.

Donatien had three farmhands. They worked under the orders of his main hand, Victor. At forty-five, Victor already looked like a doddering old man. Donatien's daughters, whose grandparents were no longer around, had made him their adopted grandfather.

Judging by Victor's gaunt body, one might have thought that La Fenouillère's main hand was malnourished and exploited by his employer or that some disease was eating away at him. Nothing could have been further from the truth. Donatien and Constance took good care of Victor and did whatever they could to make his life easier. Few people could work as well or as hard as Victor, and Donatien often said he couldn't bear the thought of losing the man.

But even the most capable farmhands could not compensate for not having a son, as far as Donatien was concerned.

Constance tried to reassure her husband when he fretted over the future of the farm. "The girls will marry one day," she said. "Our sons-in-law will be the sons we never had."

"Sons-in-law are nothing but late additions. They aren't real sons. Besides, they'll work for their fathers, like all farmers' sons, and they'll take our girls with them. We'll be left alone."

In the end, Constance interpreted Donatien's lamentations as criticism. She started feeling guilty about not having had boys. Then, little by little, the idea of adopting a son made its way into her thoughts.

On that fine spring morning, Donatien dwelled on his regrets over not having a son as he gazed at his acres of fine land giving off the strong smell of humus under the first rays of sunlight. *What good will have come of all my work—and the work of my ancestors—if La Fenouillère were to fall into the hands of a stranger, even if he were a son-in-law?* he asked himself.

He thought about Constance's proposal to adopt a boy. First, shape him into a real farmer and then, with time, if he proved his merit, make him a son, adopted, yes, but a full-fledged son. He would give the child everything: an education, know-how, and, one day, his land—without disinheriting his girls, of course. And why not his name? If he recognized him officially, the boy would have his name: Rouvière. His family line would not end.

But no Rouvière blood would flow in his veins. He would just be a late addition, like a son-in-law.

These contradictory thoughts bounced back and forth in Donatien's mind, and he couldn't focus on work. He had three days of weeding in the vineyards ahead of him. During that time, Victor had to care for the herds, watch over the late lambing, and prepare for the transhumance just a few weeks away. Constance had her hands full tending the silkworms and watching the girls. Besides, Donatien never asked her to help with the land, except when they were harvesting the grapes. Constance hired a servant to do the cooking and care for the children during those weeks, when seasonal workers also flowed in. That freed her up to help her husband and Victor bring in the grapes. Everyone had a role to play at La Fenouillère and could count on the others when they ran late or something happened. But Donatien asked for help only when he was forced to. It was a question of pride.

After finishing his bread and taking a swig of wine, he slowly closed his pocketknife and put it away. He wiped his mouth with his sleeve and said aloud, "It's decided. We'll do it."

He gathered his tools and hurried back to the farm, where Constance was making cheese in the back kitchen.

When she saw Donatien walking toward the house, his face set and his hoe over his shoulder, she thought something bad had happened. He wasn't expected until noon. "What's wrong, Donatien? Why aren't you in the vineyards? Does Victor need some help?"

"No, this is not about the vines or Victor, but about us."

"Us? I don't understand."

Constance stiffened with anxiety. The night before they had had their umpteenth discussion about the sons they hadn't had, the boy he was so missing. In a fraction of a second, her feminine intuition told her that he was going to announce what every woman feared.

"You're going to leave me. That's it, isn't it? You don't want me anymore. You've found someone else."

"What are you talking about? Stop talking nonsense."

"You want a woman who will give you a son. You're going to repudiate me."

Donatien put a hand on her shoulder to calm her. "You're the only one I love, Constance. How could you think for even a second that I would divorce you to have a son with another? Besides, nothing says I would succeed. Maybe I'm the one who's responsible for making girls. Yes, I want a son. But that's not how I'm going to have one. I'm accepting your proposition."

Constance exhaled. "You know it's just chance. We could try again. The next time we might have a boy. I'm only thirty. I could still have more children."

"No, you seem to forget what the doctor said after Aline was born. He said you shouldn't get pregnant again. You could die if you had another child."

Constance had not forgotten. But she was willing to risk her life to make her husband happy.

"What would I have left if you gave your life so that I could have a son? Do you think that would make me happy?"

"So . . ."

"So I thought it through. As you suggested a while ago, we'll adopt an orphan. A little boy we'll raise as though he were our own son."

Tears rolled down Constance's cheeks. She knew that she would never be able to give her husband another child. His decision was a gift.

"We'll have a son," she said, rushing into his arms. "A son who one day will take over for you. A son you will be proud of."

"Yes, we'll turn him into a good little Rouvière worthy of my ancestors. I have too much work to do here to go to the orphanage with you. I trust you to make the decision. I just ask one concession."

"What's that?"

"Ask for a boy who is six or seven years old, just old enough for me to talk to him and teach him. I don't want a child who was just born."

"Fine," Constance acquiesced, although she had already gotten attached to the idea of pampering a baby. "We'll save a few years that way."

At the crack of dawn three days later, Constance and her eldest, Louise, set off for Alès. Despite the early hour, the city's streets were bustling. Shopkeepers, laborers, and railwaymen were rushing to workplaces throughout the city. At eight, Constance and Louise boarded the train for Nîmes. On the Arles road, there was an orphanage run by Catholic nuns. Although the Rouvières belonged to the Reformed Church, Constance was on good terms with the priest in Tornac, and he confirmed that the Sisters of Charity were known for running an exemplary institution.

Outside the Nîmes train station, Constance waved down a carriage and asked to be driven to the exact address she had written down in a little notebook.

"Should I wait for you?" the driver asked when they arrived.

"I don't know how long it will take," Constance answered, not sure what to do.

"If it's to leave your kid to the good sisters, it won't take long," he said. Under his breath, he added, "Isn't that shameful! Making kids and abandoning them when you can't take care of them anymore."

The driver's words shocked Constance, who had overheard. "I don't need your services any longer, sir," she said curtly. "The child that I'm adopting can walk."

The nuns were coming out of their midday service and preparing to go to the refectory, where the children were impatiently waiting for lunch. Sister Angela was hurrying, as her flock was quick to let her know when hunger gnawed at their stomachs. Leaving the chapel last, she clapped to encourage the sisters to move along. The service had run late.

Just as she was about to enter the refectory herself, she heard a knock on the vestibule door.

"Oh dear," she said and sighed.

Sister Agnes was usually the nun sent to face unexpected visitors. The mother superior had given her this job several years earlier, when she became aware of the novice's anxieties. Since then, Sister Agnes had impressed the mother superior with her courage. On this day, however, Sister Angela decided to relieve Sister Agnes of that one particular duty. She had no desire to go to the refectory, where she could already tell that some of the children were running amok.

"You handle the mischief makers this time," she said. "I don't have the patience for it today. Remind them that any rule breaking will be severely punished. You can choose the punishment that will allow the lost souls to find their way back to the path of righteousness."

Sister Agnes obeyed and slipped away to reprimand her young delinquents. She knew they were just expressing a desire to live a freer life in this prison, where they lacked love more than anything else.

Sister Angela opened the grate and found Constance on the other side.

"What would you like, ma'am?" she asked curtly.

"It's personal, Sister."

"I'm mother superior of this convent," Sister Angela said. Seeing Louise next to her mother, she added, "We are no longer accepting boarders. We're full."

"That is not why I'm here, Mother. Quite the contrary."

Sister Angela closed the grate and opened the door. "Come in then and explain what it is that you want. But be quick."

Constance held Louise's hand and succinctly explained why she was there. Sister Angela relaxed and ended up smiling.

"So you want to adopt one of our little orphans. Your generosity is commendable, Mrs. Rouvière. I thank the Lord

Jesus Christ for having guided you to us. You will first need to handle some formalities. That will take about an hour, and it will give the lucky girl time to get used to the idea."

"My husband and I would like to adopt a little boy, Mother," Constance said. "We already have three girls."

"I understand. That is not a problem, although a girl would have been preferable. There is less demand for girls. Farmers tend to take boys to help in the fields. Immediate manpower. But of course, we give our adopting parents the freedom to choose."

"We would like a little boy who is six or seven years old, so . . ."

"You don't need to explain yourself, ma'am. That you've come here is enough. Just one thing: Are you religious?"

"Yes, Mother."

"Catholic?"

Constance stiffened. "I am Protestant, as is my husband. But we are religious and if the child is Catholic, we will allow him to go to church. We are tolerant."

"Hmm, Protestants. That's not what I want for our little ones."

"Mother, please."

"Why didn't you go to the Protestant orphanage?"

"I'm sure you are aware that there aren't many orphanages. And the priest in our village praised your institution."

"The priest? So you're on good terms with your village priest? That's strange for a Protestant."

"Mother, the Wars of Religion ended centuries ago."

"You are right, but in these times, the Antichrist seems to be everywhere. You understand that we need to be careful. The republic is after us Catholics. It wants to close our schools and keep us from teaching, and you Protestants are everywhere in the corridors of power."

"Mother, my husband and I have no interest in politics. Our only desire is to adopt a child and make him happy."

Sister Angela's face grew dark. She regretted having let Constance in. She was facing a perfect angel of deceit. And wasn't the child holding her hand a ploy to soften her up?

She stared at the visitor thoughtfully. Then she had an idea. While she was talking to Constance, Sister Agnes had taken the chief refectory troublemaker into her office. Sister Angela had seen them go in. This was not the first time he had caused problems. The boy, whom she had named herself after a stranger had dropped him off in the middle of a cold winter night, was surly and fought authority. Punishment had no effect. He showed no feelings, as if his heart were made of stone. Sister Agnes was the only one who could get him to obey—a little.

The boy, Vincent Janvier, already felt like an outcast in a world filled with obstacles. Unconsciously, he had put on a coat of armor to protect himself, as if he foresaw a future beyond the orphanage in which he would have only his fists to defend himself and make his way.

Sister Angela looked at Constance and said, "I'm going to entrust you with the future of our little Janvier. He is seven years old. We've had him since birth. He seems brave. He already knows what he wants, and I think that life in the countryside would be perfect for him."

"Can I see him?" Constance asked.

"I'll inform him. You will see him in an hour."

Sister Agnes prepared Vincent for what lay ahead. The child said nothing. His eyes, however, revealed the sadness he felt over being separated from the nun he loved deeply. Defensive and inarticulate when it concerned emotions, he had never told her how he felt. Sister Agnes talked to him with tenderness, explaining that the woman who had come for him wanted him to be happy. He would be the son she always wanted.

Vincent remained stoic. "Nobody loves me. Nobody will ever love me."

"I love you, Vincent," Sister Agnes said.

"That's not the same." The boy was scowling.

Sister Agnes led Vincent to the mother superior's office. Moved at seeing him, Constance stood up immediately. She didn't say anything. All dressed up, the child looked so handsome, she could barely hold back the tears. Louise stood still next to her, not sure how to act under such circumstances.

Sister Angela broke the silence. "Vincent, come forward," she said sweetly. "Let me introduce Mrs. Rouvière and her daughter, Louise. Say hello, my boy."

"Hello," Vincent said without looking up.

"Mrs. Rouvière and her husband are going to become your parents. Starting today, you will live with them. They have a large farm in the country, with animals. They have three daughters who will be like sisters. You can play with them and go to school."

"I don't like school."

"Pay him no mind, Mrs. Rouvière. Vincent is a little wild, but he has a good heart. You'll see. You'll get along well with him."

Constance was in heaven. Despite his frown, he looked like a sad angel. She suspected that he carried a lot of pain inside, but she didn't show the pity she was beginning to feel. She moved closer to him. "Hello, Vincent. I have come to take you far away from here and offer you, if you want it, the family you haven't yet had."

Sister Angela stiffened. "Vincent has had a happy childhood here," she said.

Constance paid no attention and continued. "You'll need a little time to get used to us, but I'm sure it will go well. My husband and I will love you like a son, as much as we love our own daughters. You have a family now. We are your family. Your real family."

The boy seemed intimidated. Constance and Sister Agnes asked him questions to soothe him. He answered in snippets. Little by little, like a stubborn animal letting himself be tamed, he looked up at Louise, twisted and turned, and became less hostile. His mistrust subsided, and he agreed to follow Constance and Louise to the door.

As he stepped out, he turned around and shot into Sister Agnes's arms, burying his face in the folds of her dark habit to hide his tears.

"Now, now, my boy," Sister Angela said. "No sentimentality. Go, and God be with you."

Vincent shot a threatening look at the mother superior, then slowly let go of Sister Agnes and followed Constance to his new life.

5

Adaptation

Life at La Fenouillère continued as usual. Summer settled in, offering long, infinitely mild evenings. The crickets replaced the cicadas when the stars rose in the sky. The hills gave off the aroma of scrubland blended with the pronounced smell of sweet grapes and wheat ready to burst. The stables, emptied of their pasturing occupants, gave off the warm, humid fragrance of freshly cut hay. The cleaned silos waited for the next harvest.

"You see, boy, when the wheat begins to sing in your hand, it's time to harvest," Donatien explained to Vincent.

Vincent had arrived three months earlier and had caused no problems for his adoptive family. He didn't talk much, and his reserve was sometimes disconcerting, but he hadn't had any run-ins with anyone, did everything he was told, and seemed to adapt to his new lifestyle. He addressed the girls by their first names, but always called Donatien "monsieur" and Constance "madame." They had asked him to use "Dad" and "Mom," as their own kids did, and although he had initially agreed, he couldn't seem to do it.

"It will come with time," Constance said when Donatien seemed concerned.

In truth, Vincent seemed more at ease with Victor than his adopted parents. Victor had taken the boy under his wing the day he arrived. The child followed him everywhere—out to the sheep, the vineyards, and the fields and into the equipment shed, where he liked to touch the tools and machines. He helped without making any fuss, completing even the most disagreeable tasks. Donatien let him be and worked with Victor to be closer to the boy. The boy was young but already valiant.

"Keep it up, and you'll become a good farmer," Donatien would say to encourage him. "But I also want you to have an education. In the fall, you'll go to the village school with Louise and Julie. You are seven and a half, and it's time you went to public school."

Vincent made a face at the word "school." It brought back bad memories. At the orphanage, Sister Bernadette would pace up and down the rows as she looked over the pupils' shoulders. When she found a mistake, she would point a ruler at the notebook. At the second mistake, she would strike the child's hand with the ruler and make him start over again. Vincent could still remember how her black habit smelled of incense and mothballs. He also couldn't forget the day he was unable to hold it in after recess and peed his pants, leaving an accusing puddle behind him. Pupils could not leave the room for any reason, so he hadn't asked to be excused. He was punished and humiliated in front of his schoolmates. He loathed school. And he thought he had escaped it by living with a family of farmers.

"I would rather work with Victor," Vincent answered. "I'll be of more use."

That day, Donatien thought it best to tell him gently, "First of all, boy, I would like you to call me Dad. And you are too young to work. In the Rouvière family, the children help during vacation, but their first obligation is to go to school and get instruction. I want you to grow up to be a good person, even if you are just a farmer like me."

"First, you're not my father!" Vincent shouted. "You're no better than the nuns at the orphanage." The child ran off as fast as he could.

Donatien wanted to follow, but Victor stopped him. "Let him go, boss. I'll take care of it. He won't go far."

But Vincent was agile and fast. He disappeared into the vineyards and quickly reached the neighboring woods. Victor knew the property inside out but came back empty-handed. "He disappeared," was all that he could say when he got back to the farmhouse a good hour later.

"He couldn't have gone far," Constance said, worried. "We have to go look for him. He can't spend the night outside."

Donatien, Victor, and the three other farmhands went over the land with a fine-tooth comb, from the house to the banks of the Gardon. The five of them took two leashed hunting dogs that were unbeatable at finding hare and boar.

At nightfall, they gave up. Vincent was nowhere to be found.

Constance fretted. "I hope nothing bad has happened to him. The little one doesn't know the danger out there."

"It had to happen one day," Donatien said. "Since he got here, I've had the feeling that he's been up to something. He's a wild one, and he's taken the first opportunity to run away."

"You're wrong, Donatien. He didn't plan to do this. He's impulsive and still on guard. With the life he's had until now, it's understandable. We need to find him at all costs, or else it'll be the gendarmes, and that won't be good for him. A judge would send him to a correctional facility."

"We'll go out again at dawn."

Donatien did not need to go out again to find the missing child. When the sun rose over the horizon, Perline, one of the house dogs, started barking and sniffing at the kitchen door.

Constance opened it and found Vincent, looking sheepish and defeated.

"My boy! What a fright you gave us," she said, taking him into her arms.

"I'm sorry, ma'am. I'm sorry."

"Oh, little fellow."

Donatien ran out from the bedroom, still buttoning his pants.

"Don't scold him!" Constance said. "He came back by himself. That's important."

Donatien rubbed his unshaven chin as he assessed the situation. "Sit down, boy," he grumbled. "The two of us have to talk."

In reality, Vincent hadn't gone far. He had hidden in a cave in the rocks that separated La Fenouillère from the Clos du Tournel, a chalky headland covered with shrubs, brambles, and sarsaparilla plants that ran right to the waters of the Gardon. The river had carved out cavities where foxes, badgers, and wildfowl sometimes took refuge. One of the caves, which was more hidden and darker than the others, had been a hiding place for Protestant insurgents. It still bore the name Cave of the Camisards, after the French Protestant insurrectionists who fought persecution after the Edict of Fontainebleau. More recently, vagabonds and outlaws used it. That was where Vincent had spent the night.

Donatien respected Constance's wish and did not lecture the boy. He explained that Vincent was home now, at La Fenouillère, where everyone wanted what was best for him. Donatien warned Vincent about the dangers he could encounter alone in nature if he didn't know what to expect. He spoke to him the way he would talk to a son. "In the fall . . ."

"I know," Vincent interrupted. "I'll go to school."

"No, that is not what I was going to say. In the fall, on Sunday mornings, I'll take you hunting."

"With Perline?"

"No, Perline is not a hunting dog. Her job is to guard the house with Patou when we are not here. To hunt, we'll use the two Brittany spaniels I have in the kennel."

"What do you hunt?" Vincent said, letting down his guard for the first time.

Donatien pretended not to notice. "Boar mostly. Sometimes hare and partridge. It depends."

"Boars are dangerous."

"You need to be careful. A wounded animal is unpredictable."

Vincent seemed to be letting Donatien in. Constance smiled, happy that her little one had come back in a better mood.

"So will you go with me to hunt boar?" Donatien said to end the conversation.

"There's no school on Sundays. I'll be able to go with you."

Donatien smiled. Vincent had made a concession.

The child wasn't finished. "Does the school teacher smack your hands if you make a mistake?"

Donatien looked surprised. "Hitting a child's hand! If he dares to touch even a hair on your head, he'll be hearing from me at the hunt the following Sunday. The first bullet won't be for a boar. No, just joking."

"Does he go hunting with you?"

"Of course. He's part of my team. And we hunt on my land. So you see, he'll behave himself."

"Will I see him on Sunday, too?"

"Does that bother you?"

"No."

"The teacher is a friend of mine, boy. You've got nothing to fear. He's an excellent schoolmaster."

"Then I'll be happy to go to his school."
"That's a fine idea, boy. I'm pleased."
Constance interrupted, suggesting that he go to his room. "You need some rest. You must be tired."
"Okay, Mom. I'm dying to sleep."

Vincent kept his promise and went to school in October. For the first day of school, Constance had gotten him new shoes, a gray school shirt, and a large brown leather book bag that was meant to last for his entire schooling. She also gave him a pretty wooden pencil box with two penholders, a white eraser, and a sharpened pencil.

"Your teacher will give you notebooks, books, and the rest of the supplies you need. During recess, you'll be able to see Louise and Julie on the playground, but I'm sure you'll make friends quickly," Constance told him.

"Isn't Aline going to school?"

"She's too young. She'll go next year. She'll take Louise's place. Louise will be moving on to the upper class."

The Rouvière sisters introduced Vincent to his new teacher.

"This is our brother, Vincent," Louise said. "Mom couldn't come with us, because we've got a sick sheep."

"You father told me that Vincent would be coming to school."

Rolande Porte, the boys' teacher and schoolmaster, looked over his new pupil and then warned him, "Boy, we work seriously here. You'll prepare to pass the first level of exams. The children obey and do their homework."

Vincent kept his eyes down.

"Look at me when I speak. Did you understand what I said, boy?"

"Yes, sir."

"Did you work hard where you were before?"

"Well..."

"I understand. We'll have to start over, undoubtedly."

"I know how to read and write, sir," Vincent said. "The sisters taught me. And I say my prayers morning and night."

"Read and write?"

"A little, sir."

"Good. As for the prayers, you are not in a Catholic school here."

"Luckily, sir."

"I see you've got a quick tongue for your age. Go on now. Join the others in front of the boys' door. And you girls, go on with your teacher."

Once in the classroom, Vincent took a desk in the last row, all by himself. He was intimidated and hadn't spoken to anyone. The other boys had known each other for a long time, because they all lived in the same village, and the older ones had been going to school together for a number of years. They hadn't paid any attention to him. From time to time, one of them turned and stared.

The teacher called Vincent to his desk. "Let me introduce Vincent, Mr. and Mrs. Rouvière's son," he said. "You already know his sisters, Louise and Julie."

Roland Porte had agreed to Constance and Donatien's request to introduce Vincent as their son. But the older boys, who were going on thirteen, immediately started winking at each other. Bertrand Laval, the blacksmith's youngest son, had the gall to say something. "But the Rouvières don't have a son. They just have three girls."

"Well, as of today, they have a son. His name is Vincent Janvier." The teacher immediately regretted how he had put it.

The class burst out laughing, and Laval spoke up again. "So, sir, that son of theirs grew up pretty fast, didn't he."

This brought on more laughter.

"And why isn't his name Vincent Rouvière if Mr. Rouvière is his father?"

"That's enough. Be quiet," the teacher shouted.

The boys quieted down. They knew when to stop joking.

Roland Porte asked a pupil in the first row to give his seat to the newcomer. The pupil relinquished his desk and shot a belligerent look at Vincent. "Don't pay any attention," Porte said. "This is their way of testing you. They're not mean."

Vincent found himself alone on the playground. All the other boys were avoiding him. Louise and Julie saw how sad he was and joined him.

"Are you okay?" Louise asked. "What's happening?"

"Yes, I'm okay," Vincent said. "But they made fun of me."

"Why?"

"Because they know I'm not really a Rouvière."

"It'll be better tomorrow. They won't say anything."

Louise was wrong.

The next day, a group of kids led by the blacksmith's son surrounded Vincent, pushed him, and shouted, "Little bastard! Little bastard."

"Are you really an orphan?"

"No mom, no dad! Guess what. The Rouvières took you out of the orphanage to be their servant."

"You're lying!" Vincent cried out, holding in his tears so his anger could take over. "They are my parents! I have a mom and a dad. You're just idiots."

The children continued to tease Vincent. Alone against all of them, the boy pushed up his sleeves and got ready to fight. Roland Porte saw what was happening and broke up the crowd with the help of his colleague, Miss Bernard.

"Stop bothering your classmate, right now. You will be punished."

After school that day, Vincent ran to his room without saying a word. Constance asked the girls what had happened, and they told her.

"I'll never be your son," Vincent shouted when Constance came in to console him. "It's not possible." He burst into tears.

As the months went by, Vincent adjusted to his new life as best he could. He was in a better mood when he could stay at the farm with Victor rather than go to school. As much as Roland Porte tried to discipline the other pupils, they continued to isolate Vincent, with the blacksmith's son leading the pack.

At the hunt on Sundays, Vincent ignored his teacher. And Porte didn't discuss his new pupil with the boy's father. When Donatien asked how things were going, the teacher wouldn't say much. "All is well, Donatien. Don't worry. But let's not talk about school. It's Sunday. It's the hunt. I'm not your son's teacher here."

Donation didn't insist but guessed that his friend was holding back the truth. And Vincent wasn't telling him anything either.

In reality, Vincent had quickly become the punching bag for Bertrand Laval's gang. Laval was twelve and already hefty, the opposite of Vincent, who was thin and handsome. The boy had dark skin and brown hair that curled at the nape of his neck. He's as bright-eyed as an angel, Miss Bernard thought as she watched him on the playground. His birth parents must have been extraordinarily beautiful. She speculated that he was Italian or Spanish.

Miss Bernard was sad that Vincent had not started out with the same opportunities as the other children. She knew what orphans endured, having been one herself. Sometimes she went up to him, ran her hand through his curls, and talked to him as if he were her own child. Vincent liked her but didn't dare stay long in her company, for fear of more teasing from his schoolmates.

One day, Bertrand Laval said, "You should go to the girls' class with Miss Bernard. With your long hair, you'll fit right in."

Vincent was at the end of his rope. He clenched his fists, locked his jaw, and threw himself at his nemesis. Because Laval weighed more, he was able to stay on his feet. He made faces at Vincent as the boy hit him. Seeing the confrontation, Roland Porte stepped in. Miss Bernard rushed to Vincent's defense, and the headmaster called the two boys into his office.

"My dad doesn't like orphans, especially dark-skinned ones like him," Bertrand Laval said. "I don't like 'em either. They aren't like the others. They're louts. They ain't got parents and are worse than gypsies."

The teacher knew the blacksmith was bigot. He was the village extremist, against Freemasons, Jews, atheists, foreigners, and socialists. He had openly taken a position against Alfred Dreyfus after he had read a newspaper article by Émile Zola claiming that the government was in the hands of the Jews, and the republic was being run by leftists determined to do it in.

The schoolmaster favored the new French Socialist Party formed by Jean Jaurès. He was not surprised to hear such things from the blacksmith's son. Like father, like son, he thought. If parents would just shut up around their kids, the children wouldn't repeat such idiocies.

"From now on, I forbid you to speak to the young Rouvière."

"His name's Janvier," Laval said.

"Enough! Keep being insolent, and I'll have to call your father in."

The boy scowled and said nothing.

From that day on, he left Vincent alone. And those in the class who hadn't dared to oppose Laval started to approach Vincent.

At a boar hunt during Christmas vacation, Roland Porte took Donatien aside. Vincent was off with Victor and the two Brittany spaniels and out of earshot. "I think your son has finally adapted. He's doing better at school. What about at home?"

"Oh, it's still hard sometimes. But little by little. At his age, there are lots of memories. It will take time to erase seven years of being an orphan."

6

Buffalo Bill

Nîmes, 1905

After Catherine's death, everyone in the Rochefort household did their best to hide their pain. They maintained their dignity and tried to conceal any signs of weakness in public. A captain of industry couldn't afford to let the smallest crack in family solidarity show, as it could be the telltale sign of deeper troubles. A strong, united family was good for business.

Elisabeth, however, was depressed, even if she tried not to show it. She avoided society for an entire year. She canceled and postponed the receptions she had enjoyed giving, both in Nîmes and at the Clos du Tournel. She stopped all her charity work. The rare friends she did meet with were surprised to see how distraught she was. She gave off a deep sense of remorse, as if she were responsible for Catherine's death.

No, Catherine was not her biological daughter. But Elisabeth had accepted her as such and had not distinguished between this daughter from her husband's previous marriage and her own children, who had always treated Catherine like their sister.

Now Anselme was becoming alarmed. His depressed wife was jeopardizing his vision of a strong family. One day, he clumsily criticized her. "I understand your sorrow, Elisabeth, but need I remind you that Catherine was not your daughter? Focus on our own children. They need your tenderness and love. Catherine's death shouldn't keep you from your duties as their mother."

"I knew you were harsh in business, Anselme, but I wanted to think better of you. I didn't want to acknowledge how detached you were from Catherine. Whatever that poor girl did, she never deserved so much scorn from her father. You dirty her memory."

"Catherine, Catherine. She's all you've had on your mind since she left us. Pull yourself together, Elisabeth. Your mourning won't bring her back."

"You're appalling, Anselme! Success has dried out your heart and turned it to stone."

Despite what Anselme said, Elisabeth had not distanced herself from her biological children. But her love for them could not diminish her pain over the loss of Catherine, who had shared bonds with her that seemed woven from a different kind of love—one that was full of complicity. It was almost as if the girl knew the terrible secret Elisabeth held. Neither of them ever cleared the air that thickened around their silences and understatements. But ironically, the privacy of their feelings, the things they never put into words, seemed to draw them closer. They seemed to vibrate on the same chord. They understood each other without speaking, with just a change in tone or a look. Anselme had never noticed their collusion, even after Catherine threw herself into the arms of the first man to show an interest in her.

"A penniless young man from a bankrupt family," Catherine had told Elisabeth. "I can already see the scowl on Father's face when he finds out."

"Don't expect me to tell him, my dear," Elisabeth said, laughing.

"You're not judging me, Mom?"

"Live your life, my angel. Don't worry about your lover's fortune. I didn't choose to marry your father, you know. I obeyed my parents."

"Do you regret it?"

"No. With time I learned to love him. Our children are the finest proof of that."

Elisabeth remembered that conversation, and she felt melancholy, even regret. Why hadn't she told Catherine the whole truth?

She chased away the bitterness, remembering that she still had four children. They were her most cherished possessions. Real treasures. Treasures that weren't tarnished by lies.

Jean-Christophe was now nearly twenty. The young man had very set ideas about how things should be and was the Rochefort child who most resembled his father. Anselme was proud of him. He was, after all, the eldest of his second marriage, and the future of the business was on his shoulders. Jean-Christophe was studying law in Montpellier, as his father had done at that age. He planned to pass the bar and dreamed of becoming a great attorney, although Anselme continued to remind him of his duty to the family business.

"First, I'll be a business attorney," Jean-Christophe had told his father. "Then I will be better equipped to outsmart the sharks. My knowledge of law and the justice system will serve our business interests."

Jean-Christophe was ambitious and charming. He had caught the attention of his parents' friends who had marriageable daughters. He had his father's height and long blond hair, and he involuntarily mimicked the elder man's gestures and intonations. He liked to flaunt his origins, and he did so with a certain cheeky humor. Strolling the streets in Nîmes, he casually shook hands and chatted with young women and their mothers alike. He was more wily and courteous with the businessmen he met with his father. He was winning over more and more fans. Some even thought he was destined for politics, considering all his charisma and presence.

"Your son will go far," friends told Anselme, boosting the father's pride.

In October, Anselme put Jean-Christophe to the test.

"You know that it is in our interest to strengthen our ties with the United States," he explained. "Several traders in Nîmes have been doing a prosperous business with that country, as we have. My father was already working with Levi Strauss when I joined the business. I want to build on what we've done so far and make our image stand out from all the rest."

"How would you like to do that, Father?"

"By appearing alongside a mythic American."

"I don't understand."

Rochefort wanted to link his company with the American dream. He was thinking that images of the rugged conquerors of the West would best symbolize the idea.

He saw his opportunity when he learned that the legendary Buffalo Bill would pass through the region. Colonel William Cody had started his third tour of Europe on April 2, 1905, with his Buffalo Bill's Wild West Show. On August 8, he had set up a huge camp in Avignon. He was scheduled to appear in Nîmes on October 27.

Jean-Christophe was doubtful. "What do you want me to do, Father? How can this cowboy running a circus show help us?"

"It's simple. Try to contact Mr. Cody. Well, Buffalo Bill. Everyone in the show wears denim pants. Even their tents are made from the fabric that we pioneered here in Nîmes. You can guess my intentions now, can't you? I want you to be seen publicly with him, Make us visible. I'll contact the reporters. Some good pictures and a few articles in the regional and national papers will get us more publicity than anything in the *Almanach de Gotha*. You could even invite Buffalo Bill to visit our factories. The fabric from his pants comes from our mills. Who knows?"

Jean-Christophe agreed immediately. The idea was clearly novel and forward-thinking.

First, they agreed that he would go to a show with his younger brother, Sebastien. As Elisabeth wasn't keen on rifle shooting and rodeos, she forbade her daughters from going.

"Dear me. Redskins in our good city of Nîmes!" Elizabeth said. "Now I've seen everything."

The Nîmes train station was exceptionally busy on the day of the show. The equipment and staff unloaded at seven in the morning. The show filled no fewer than three special trains and fifty wagons that together were nearly a mile long. They carried twelve hundred posts, four thousand poles, thirty thousand yards of rope, twenty-three thousand yards of tarp, and eight thousand seats, as well as eight hundred men, including a hundred or so Sioux Indians. It took less than two hours to set up camp outside the city. There were a hundred tepees and tents made of a fabric comparable to the serge manufactured by Rochefort, but rougher. Three enormous generators supplied electricity to this cosmopolitan traveling village. The show was to be held under a vast canopy measuring nearly a hundred and forty by forty-five yards.

Shows were planned for six and eight in the evening. Beforehand, people were invited to attend the sideshow.

Jean-Christophe went with his brother to the sideshow. Sebastien lingered in front of the different stands: Miss Octavia the snake charmer, the blue man Fred Walter, and sword-swallowing Professor Griffin. The giant, Aaron Moore, who was over eight feet tall, impressed him mightily, as did Princess Nouma-Hawa, who was just a foot and a half tall. But he was most fascinated by the Sioux Indians of the Lakota lands, with their traditional garb and war paint on their faces. It reminded him of the fabulous stories by James Fenimore Cooper and a novel by Gustave Aimard, *The Trappers of Arkansas*. He started dreaming about America.

"When I grow up, I'm going to the Indian lands to defend them against the whites."

"There you go again, always rooting for the underdog."

"The idea of the show actually distresses me. Mr. Cody helped to destroy the Indians, and now he's exhibiting them, as if they were circus animals."

"You seem to know a lot about it."

"I know about the supposed hero Buffalo Bill. But is his story as glorious as it's made out to be?"

"If you prefer not to go to the show, I'll find a way to meet Colonel Cody when it's all over."

"No, let's go. Out of curiosity."

Sebastien and Jean-Christophe had seats in a box below the grandstands, which could hold twenty-four thousand people. For nearly two hours, they watched the twenty-four sketches that made up the fast-paced show. Parades gave way to races, processions of horseback riders, mock Indian attacks on a pioneer house and the Deadwood stagecoach, a convoy of immigrants, and the Pony Express. Buffalo Bill himself was a big part of the show. The high point was a reconstruction of General Custer's final battle at Little Big Horn.

"It's all so grand," Jean-Christophe said. "Say what you like, but you have to hand it to those Americans."

Sebastien was more realistic. "Yes, but it's disappointing. I imagined America to be completely different."

"It's just a show."

"Sure, glorifying the conquest of the West and the massacre of the Indians."

Sebastien seemed upset. He saw America for what it was: a country of conquerors with a peculiar sense of entitlement. "The Americans criticize us because we have colonies, but their treatment of the Indians is hardly any better."

"You think too much for a kid your age."

"There's no set age to be interested in history and concerned about what's happening today."

After the show, Jean-Christophe led his brother backstage. He wanted to meet Colonel Cody, but the man was nowhere to be found. In fact, Buffalo Bill made it a habit to return to his apartment railcar—with a kitchen, a dining room, two bedrooms, and a bathroom—right after each curtain call. At that point, his workers would immediately start taking down the big top. Everything would be ready to head to the next city in an hour.

Jean-Christophe was about to go home empty-handed when the show manager approached him. "Colonel Cody was invited by the Marquis Folco de Baroncelli-Javon to attend an *abrivado* festival."

"Where would that be?"

The man hesitated. "What is it exactly that you want?"

"I'm a manufacturer. I want to talk business."

"In that case, they have a meeting early tomorrow in the Cailar."

As soon as they got home, Jean-Christophe spoke with his father, who told him to go.

"I know the Marquis de Baroncelli-Javon well. Folco is a friend. He won't refuse us."

"Who is he?" Jean-Christophe asked.

"An Italian-born noble living in Provence. He loves horses, as well as the region and its values. He lives for the herdsmen in the Camargue. He is also a bit of a poet and knows Frédéric Mistral well."

The next day, Anselme, Jean-Christophe, and Sebastien, along with two reporters from the *Petit Provençal*, went to the Cailar. The marquis did not give Anselme a warm welcome, as he hadn't been told that the group was coming. However, he did introduce Anselme to his guests.

"Let me introduce you to my friend Colonel Cody, and his traveling companions, Chief Iron Tail and Chief Solitary Bear. If you'd like, join us as we follow the *abrivado* riding festivities all the way to Gallargues. We're leaving now."

"Would you mind if these men from the *Petit Provençal* came along?" Anselme asked. "I'll explain why once we are on the way."

The marquis showed some reticence but agreed. The reporters were far from discreet. One kept scribbling notes, while the other took pictures. He always managed to frame the Rocheforts with Buffalo Bill and his cowboys. The marquis seemed irritated, but he didn't say anything.

When the bull run was over, the Indians, the cowboys, and the other guests were invited to dine with the marquis's friends, the herdsmen. They drank Champagne in honor of the races. They talked about the poet Mistral and the region. The atmosphere was friendly and warm.

Sebastien forgot his criticisms of the day before. The horses, the cowboys and the Camargue herdsmen, the Indians, and the fire that sent puffs of smoke into the blue sky all resonated with Sebastien. He had spent his childhood reading books about the Old West and watching the silent movies in Nîmes. The Indians and the local herdsmen fraternized, certainly finding some similarities in their way of life on the prairie. Sioux songs rang out, followed by cowboy banjos. The music transported the marquis's guests beyond the Appalachian Mountains to the Great Plains full of buffalo and wild mustangs.

Around half past noon, Baroncelli and his guests got back into their cars to head back to Nîmes. The Rocheforts and the two reporters followed, surrounded by twenty-five Camargue herdsmen on horseback, who raised swirls of dust as they herded the bulls.

Sebastien was jumping with a child's joy. He seemed inebriated by what was happening before his eyes.

"So, my son, are you happy?" Anselme asked.

"Amazed, Father. It's better than the movies."

"And you, dear reporters? Did you get some good shots?"

"We have what it takes to do an excellent story, Mr. Rochefort."

"Perfect. You'll give me the pictures so I can send them to other papers? Getting those pictures seen by as many people as possible is the best publicity for our products. I hope you got close-ups of the cowboy pants."

"From all sides, sir. Especially the ones Buffalo Bill wore."

"I can see the headline already: 'Buffalo Bill wears denim from the Rochefort Industries.'"

"That's a bit of a stretch, Father," Jean-Christophe said. "We don't know that the denim Buffalo Bill wore came from our workshops."

"You're wrong there. I said a few words to him in my bad English. He told me he wears only Levi's, and we supply them."

"We are not their only supplier, Father."

"That might be, but nobody is going to know. Business is business, my boy. All's fair, even small lies. In any case, I'm glad I was the first person to come up with the idea of using the Wild West hero to sell our fabric. You'll see, Jean-Christophe, workers will soon be clamoring for those denim pants. And it won't take long for workpants to become leisure pants."

"You're becoming visionary, Father."

"No, mark my words. One day couturiers will be working with denim. What Levi Strauss started fifty years ago with his canvas overall will revolutionize the clothing business."

A few days later, every regional newspaper and several national papers told the story in words and photographs of Buffalo Bill's stay in Provence. Praise-filled articles explained the history of the serge from Nîmes. Rochefort Industries was mentioned several times, so many times, in fact, that someone unfamiliar with the fabric might have thought that the Rocheforts were the only ones producing it.

7

The Heir

Nîmes, 1907

Anselme knew he could count on Jean-Christophe, but he was desperately trying to get Sebastien to listen to reason. The boy was already rebelling and hostile to the path that had been laid out for him.

Sebastien Rochefort was Jean-Christophe's exact opposite. He had no interest in following his brother's example. He was studying without much conviction at the local lycée. His teachers said he was smart and talented, but the young Rochefort had little motivation to do what was expected of him.

He didn't look like either his father or his mother. His face was not exactly homely but it wasn't especially appealing, either. He had more than the usual number of adolescent blemishes, which didn't seem to inhibit him. His eyes were close together, always attentive, revealing constant dissatisfaction. He liked sports but demonstrated no desire to go into business, as his father would have liked. Whenever he had the opportunity to escape school, he wandered off. He often opposed his father—and his older brother, whom he considered too dominated by their father.

"When I grow up, I'll do what I decide to do. I'm going to defend the underdog," he said.

Anselme despaired.

It had been two years since Colonel Cody and his Indians had been in Nîmes. That encounter had changed the boy, who was now thirteen. He dreamed of traveling the world and becoming a great reporter or writer. He was interested in the news and grabbed his father's newspaper as soon as he had finished it. Anselme let Sebastien dream but also criticized his lack of ambition and pragmatism. Sebastien's grades were a sore point.

"You bring shame to our family. Why don't you be like your brother?" Anselm would shout when he couldn't control his anger in any longer.

This would anger Sebastien in turn. He would run off and lock himself in his room.

Sebastien defied his father in other ways, as well. Despite his upper-class origins, the teenager had a penchant for defending the unfortunates of the world, and he openly sided with striking labor party workers. When the winemakers demonstrated on June 2, 1907, he sneaked out of the house to watch the procession go by. It was his way of supporting the oppressed of the region, as he called the rebellious farmers. That night, in front of his parents, he boasted about having been approached by the group's leader, Marcelin Albert. The next day, he skipped school to see what would follow the event that had shaken the town. This angered Anselme more than anything else the boy had done, and he forced Sebastien to go to the principal the next day to apologize.

"If this child continues to show so little interest in school, I'm going to send him to the Jesuits. They'll know how to handle him," Anselme grumbled.

Elizabeth, however, took the boy's side, finding that he had qualities Jean-Christophe lacked. Yes, he was stubborn, but he had character. He was generous, and he was a dreamer.

Sebastien didn't mind being punished, because he had witnessed a major historical moment in an uprising that had monopolized the front pages of the regional newspapers for several weeks.

While Jean-Christophe was fulfilling his father's ambitions, and Sebastien was testing him, Elodie was doing neither. She had withdrawn into a world of her own. She was the sibling who seemed the most profoundly affected by Catherine's death. And she had become almost morbidly sad. Elodie had been Catherine's confidant, despite their seven-year age difference. She adored her older sister. She would listen to her endlessly and respond with naïve comments, even though she was too young to understand everything Catherine was talking about. Elodie brightened her sister's life. And when Elodie was sad, Catherine would talk with her as though she were an adult, fully aware that she was innocent and pure. Elodie grew to resemble her big sister, melting into her aura and vicariously experiencing the same emotions and disappointments.

"Despite their age difference, they could have been twins," Elisabeth said, worried about the young girl's vulnerability.

Anselme paid no attention to the girl's feelings. As far as he was concerned, it was childish simpering. He was only concerned about his sons and their future.

Yet when his fourth child, Faustine, was born, he showed an interest that surprised those close to him. Catherine had died a few months earlier, and Elisabeth thought the death might be responsible for the change. Or perhaps he was softening up a bit as he neared fifty. She wasn't about to complain. Whatever the reason, Anselme proved to be an affectionate father to his youngest girl, finding more qualities in her than he had ever seen in his other children, including Jean-Christophe.

No matter what she did, Faustine found favor with her father, even when she was endlessly mischievous. She was a vivacious, joyful child who seemed to charm everyone, even the stiffest, most unfeeling adults. At the same time, she was sweet and kind. She never tried to dominate other children and managed to stand out without being ostentatious. She made her mother proud and gave Elisabeth a newfound youth.

After several years of mourning—Elisabeth's more than Anselme's—the Rochefort family started inviting guests to their sparkling mansion.

They had bought this mansion on the heels of Catherine's death. Anselme had said he wanted to turn a page and think only about the future of his other children. His real motivation was to prove to the world that he was one of the city's most prestigious and influential residents.

The sumptuous mansion in old Nîmes was an architectural jewel from the eighteenth century. The city was known throughout the region for these sumptuous residences. Anselme had been coveting this particular mansion for some time. He had finally managed to acquire it for a ridiculously small amount from an old Ancient Regime marquis whose family line had died out. The residence was on the Rue Dorée, the town's most aristocratic street. It had a majestic gate that opened onto a cobblestone courtyard. The home had a dozen rooms, all decorated in the finest Régence style. The second floor was accessible by way of a magnificent staircase with an ornate iron banister. In the cellar, there was a small apartment for the help. Unfortunately, the former owner had neglected the property for a long time, and it was in a pitiful state.

After several months of renovation, Anselme was proud to be living side by side with other illustrious families, some of whom still belonged to France's old nobility. Yes, socialists held the city hall, but those living in this neighborhood were the most right-wing conservatives of Nîmes.

Since the beginning of the century, socialists from the extreme left had governed Nîmes. Anselme was a moderate republican who was suspicious of those in power. He criticized them for belonging to the revolutionary movement and feeding popular discontent. Gaston Crouzet, who had been mayor since 1900, had participated alongside the winegrowers on June 2. Anselme worried that the unrest would spread, endangering the republic. Winegrowing farmers had won over the working classes, and even some priests had demonstrated along with them. Now workers in the factories were beginning to stir with socialist ideas and notions of unionizing. In the spring, they had supported the revolt led by Marcelin Albert, a café owner from Argeliers. Anselme was glad that his workers had stayed out of it. They were primarily women, and as far as Anselme knew, they didn't intend to unionize. However, at his attorney Lambert's suggestion, Anselme had given his entire workforce a raise to keep them happy.

That day, Jean-Christophe had his first run-in with his father. He accused the patriarch of being too soft. Young Rochefort's intention was to put Lambert in his place. "Father, if you want me to become your top man, please ask my opinion before going along with whatever Lambert suggests," he had said.

"I didn't think you would be opposed to the decision we made," Anselme said, sounding surprised.

"You're too indulgent and even weak when it comes to your workers. You need to be fair but firm. Don't give the impression of bending with the slightest breeze. We are from a race of oak trees, not reeds. And no matter what La Fontaine says, it is rare that a storm uproots century-old oak trees."

His son's peremptory tone and self-assurance surprised Anselme, but it rather pleased him. "So you'll be ready soon to be my right-hand man?" he asked.

"I'll be an attorney in a year, Father. Then I will take care of our mills. At that point, I would like you to get rid of Lambert. There isn't room for two business attorneys in the same company."

"But Lambert has served me for a long time. I owe him," Anselme said.

"It's him or me."

Despite his youth and inexperience, Jean-Christophe imposed his will on his father. Anselme swelled with pride at having such a devoted and business-minded son. That same night, he announced the news to Elisabeth.

"My dear, in less than a year, our eldest son will become my associate. I'll have the name of our business changed to Rochefort Industries, Father and Son."

Elisabeth was proud of her son. "Are you reassured now?" she asked her husband, full of tenderness. "I knew Jean-Christophe wouldn't let you down."

"If only we could hope as much for our other son," Anselme said. "I worry about Sebastien. His rebellious idealism concerns me. I'm afraid I'll lose him."

"Why do you always want to determine his future? Let him choose his own destiny."

"His life has been laid out for him. His brother understood that."

"Jean-Christophe is like you. Sebastien isn't. And what about our daughters?"

"The girls are not a problem. We just need to find them good matches before it's too late."

Elisabeth couldn't help but react. "So that we don't repeat our mistake with Catherine, right?"

Anselme's face darkened, as it did every time they discussed Catherine. He pushed his wife aside and grumbled.

"Stop talking about Catherine. She ruined the opportunities we gave her."

"You never loved her, Anselme. She suffered greatly from that. How often did she look for comfort in my arms? And I wasn't even her mother."

"That didn't change anything. She never knew." Anselme was annoyed. "How many times have I asked you not to talk about it anymore? Catherine is dead. It's a great misfortune that has affected us all. But now we have to think about the future of our other children. Catherine belongs to the past. So please stop bringing up these memories."

It did no good to press when Anselme felt backed against a wall.

This Elisabeth knew. He would act like some high lord to mark his dominion and cut the conversation short. Before taking her leave, she dared to add, "I won't let you make the same mistake with our children. Jean-Christophe chose the path you wanted him to take. I'm happy for him. I wish him success. But I'll do everything in my power to ensure that Sebastien and his sisters do whatever their hearts desire with their lives."

8

Summer Encounter

1908

Vincent had a happy life at La Fenouillère. It had been three years since Constance had taken him from the Sisters of Charity. The young orphan had managed to make a place for himself in his adopted family, and everyone in the town now considered him Donatien and Constance's son. But the ten-year-old child still seemed to keep his father at arm's length. And he seemed to fear him a bit.

Donatien complained about this to his wife. "I don't understand why he's afraid of me. Who knows, maybe his birth father beat him before he was abandoned. That might explain it. He wouldn't remember anything, because he was too young. But perhaps the trauma is still lodged in his memory. After all, we don't know anything about his background, about why his parents gave him up."

Constance insisted he was wrong, because Vincent had been abandoned at birth. But Donatien was convinced that

Vincent held a secret that only the sisters at the orphanage could shed any light on.

Vincent didn't show much enthusiasm at school, although his teacher insisted he had enormous abilities that he wasn't putting to good use. Once, during a boar hunt, he confided in Donatien. "I wouldn't be surprised if your son came from a good family. There's something in the way he expresses himself, in how he behaves. It's as if part of him is rising to the surface and trying to get out."

"What are you getting at, Roland? Most abandoned children come from poor families. Their mothers are girls made pregnant by boys who are too poor to feed any babies. Or they're unfortunates who fall for upper-class dandies who wind up using them and leaving."

"Maybe you're right, but in any case, your son does not resemble the other kids in his class. He really doesn't look like a farmer's kid either."

"And still, he's been getting his training at La Fenouillère for three years now. And no offense, but he'd rather be making himself useful in the vineyards and the stable than doing the homework you give him."

"Yes, I admit he could be better in school. But something is holding him back. I get the feeling that he doesn't want to surpass his classmates and show his real worth. The teasing has stopped."

"That's not what he says. Some kids still call him 'little bastard' on the playground. My daughters have heard it."

Truth be told, Vincent didn't like school. It reminded him of the orphanage and Sister Bernadette. He was attentive in school and applied himself to his studies, but he didn't hide his preference for farmwork. He helped Constance milk the goats, assisted Victor with the lambing, and knew how to wield a rake, a pitchfork, and a pruning knife, depending on the season. When he finished his homework, he slipped outside to make himself useful and never said no when Victor or one of the hands asked for help.

When Donatien asked Constance about his schoolwork, she would say, "Be happy. Didn't you always want a son to help you?"

"I didn't want a son who could just help me. I wanted a son who could do better than I did. There will be many changes in this century. I want La Fenouillère to become one of the finest farms in the region. The wine crisis affected us all and is far from over. Because of it, those of us who were enterprising are now better armed to deal with the well-to-do. Too often, they consider the land no more than a financial investment. They speculate with it, to the detriment of those who work it."

"Are you referring to our neighbor, Anselme Rochefort?"

"Not necessarily. I'm not aware that the Rocheforts speculate. They have inherited much of their real estate. We get along, and I'm grateful that they allow us to use their pastureland in summer."

As the owners of La Fenouillère, the Rouvière family had no reason to be envious of any neighboring farms. The mix of vineyards, crops, and pastures gave the family what it needed to envision a decent future, despite the rough times farmers had been facing in recent years. What was bothering Donatien was his certainty that in order to get through the coming decades, his farm would need an enterprising son who could manage it with the efficiency of a factory. That was why he had put all his hopes in Vincent and also why he was so distressed to see him drag his feet in school.

"I don't want Vincent to be like me," he told Constance. "If he wants to do better than survive, he'll need ambition. The era of hand-sowing and horse-drawn plows is over. In the future, farmers will have to juggle figures and think about what's happening in the world. Vincent will need the means to invest. For that, he'll have to be comfortable talking to bankers, and he'll have to team with others to lower production costs."

"You're talking like a businessman," Constance said. She wondered what had gotten into him.

"I just got back from a meeting with other farmers in the area. The cooperative movement is growing, and we're setting one up. Union representatives told us that if we don't get organized, we'll be on the road to ruin. Our vineyards are especially vulnerable."

"You're letting the fancy talkers influence you, Donatien. Be careful."

"Don't worry! I'm just worried about La Fenouillère's future."

Even though Donatien was considered a well-off farmer, he was a radical socialist at heart. He had criticized Interior Minister George Clemenceau's repressive policies against striking winegrowers and miners. In fact, Donatien's ancestors had always been on the side of the oppressed. They were Protestants right from the Reform, opposed the Dragonnades under King Louis XIV and Jacobins during the revolution. They were already for the republic during the First Empire, never ceasing to stand up and join the poor against the powerful. Donatien felt like a worthy descendent. The comfort they had acquired over the generations came from hard work, courage, and tenacity, but also from marriages with a few prosperous farming families.

"I'm not ashamed of what I own," he would say when he felt attacked by friends who teased him about the contradiction between his leftist ideas and what he owned. "I don't exploit anyone. I pay my workers well, and I defend the oppressed against the oppressor."

Nobody could contest that.

At his age, little Vincent was not aware of the problems his adoptive parents were facing. The bonds he had with his new family had become the surest way for him to ensure that he would never have to return to the orphanage. And at La Fenouillère, everyone considered him to be a full-fledged Rouvière. That included the three girls—Louise, Julie, and Aline—who had quickly accepted him as their brother.

Right away, Vincent had shown more affinity for the two younger girls than Louise. At seventeen, Louise was already a young lady. She seemed distant and even arrogant. She liked to remind Vincent that she was the eldest of the four and that La Fenouillère would be hers one day. Vincent interpreted this as jealousy more than meanness. In fact, she wasn't mean to him at all. Constance said she was just that way. It was a trait acquired from her paternal grandmother, who was a proud woman. In reality, Louise always defended her adopted brother against uncalled-for remarks in the schoolyard, just as her sisters did. She knew how to stick with Julie and Aline to preserve family unity.

When Vincent turned ten, Donatien promised to take him along for the transhumance. The child had only worked with the sheep on the farm. Vincent had helped Victor with lambing, weaning, and sheering, and he knew most of the diseases the animals got, but he knew nothing about a sheepherder's life in the summer pasture: the difficulties, dangers, traps, and moments of pure happiness.

With the first days of spring, he could think of nothing else from dawn to dusk. He was ready to leave and follow the flock on their journey, even though he knew it would be tiring and they wouldn't have many comforts in the highlands.

Donatien had warned him. "Up there, my boy, you'll have a simple straw mat instead of a bed. You'll have to sleep in a casket under the night sky."

"In a casket! Like a dead man?"

"No, in the summer pasture, we call the wooden bunks caskets. They protect you at night. The ones we use have wheels, so they're easy to move. Very modern, you see."

The child hung onto every word as Donatien explained the adventure they were about to embark on. Donatien often exaggerated the facts, adding bits and pieces until the stories sounded more like tall tales than actual experiences.

Vincent loved it. He already imagined himself dressed like a shepherd, crook in hand, carrying a backpack filled with food and everything else he needed. At night, he dreamed about living outdoors, having absolute freedom on the mountain, and being in charge of his own life.

"When I grow up, I'm going to be a shepherd," he said every time Donatien shared a story.

"Before you can be a shepherd, you'll be a *traspastre*."

"What's that?"

"An apprentice shepherd. In life, you need to learn the job before you can do it."

Constance would often interrupt with a smile. "Stop bedazzling the little one with your stories, would you?"

It gave her joy to see Vincent's face glow with happiness.

"He's going to end up thinking that going to pasture is paradise," she said. "He might be disappointed. You should tell him about the problems you face."

"What problems?" Vincent asked, eager to know everything.

"Tell him, Donatien. It's not always fun up there. There are accidents. Lightning can strike the flock. There are feral dogs. The heat can be crushing, as well as the solitude for four long months. And that's just a start. Why don't you tell him about that, Donatien?"

Donatien's face clouded over. He picked up his pipe, cleaned it, and filled it with tobacco. "Yes, you're right. But he's got time to learn about that."

At the beginning of June, Donatien told Roland Porte that Vincent would miss the last three weeks of school, which didn't make the teacher happy.

"In June, it's transhumance. In October, it's the grape harvest," Porte said. "There's always some reason for farmers' kids to miss school!"

"Don't get mad, Roland. It's just because Vincent turned ten this year. Next year, he'll finish the term, same as the other kids. And I promise he won't miss school for the grape harvest. He'll wait until after school to help in the vineyards."

"His schoolwork is going to suffer."

"He'll work twice as hard, won't you, Vincent?"

"I promise," the child said, already impatient to start up the mountain.

As in previous years, the move to the summer pasture began right after the Feast of Saint Menard, which was June 8. For four long months every year, Donatien, Victor, and another farmhand, named Léonce, would leave Constance, the girls, and the two other workers at La Fenouillère. Constance never went with him. Like sailors, the shepherds didn't want women accompanying them.

"It's men's business," Vincent kept saying to the three girls, who envied him for being able to go off with their father.

All of eight years old, Aline eyed Vincent with longing, certainly seeing him as older than he was. She admired him, and even before the flocks were rounded up, she was sad that he would be gone. For the occasion, all the animals had been decorated with multicolored pompoms, and they each wore a bell attached to a hand-painted collar. Donatien made it a point to decorate his livestock the day before their departure. That day was a celebration for everyone at La Fenouillère, as well as the neighbors who helped the Rouvières get the sheep ready.

Victor led the flock. Léonce took the right flank with the dogs, and Donatien and Vincent brought up the rear with the heavily loaded pack mule. They each carried packs filled with the days' provisions and a change of clothes. A cape and an umbrella completed their gear.

Donatien gave the signal to depart—a hoarse cry from

deep in his throat. The animals trembled and started along the trail in unison. Hundreds of bells chimed, filling the air with a melody that could be heard for miles around. The lead ewes wore deeper-toned bells, which set the pace, and the others added their higher-pitched sounds. All combined, it was a joyful din.

As usual, Constance and the girls accompanied the flock until the sheep and the men branched onto the trail that led to the Anduze highlands. They watched until the flock was no more than a thin white line snaking up the green hillside. Then they returned to the farm, sad but looking forward to seeing their shepherds return with a 1,001 stories.

Aline cried that year. It wasn't because her father was leaving, but because Vincent was going. He had unwittingly opened up her young heart.

The climb to the pasture would last six long days. They made their way through the bronze-tinted schist crests of the Cévennes mountains, as sharp as blades. Then the trail joined Mount Lozère and its prairies, dotted with blocks of quicksilver granite. In this season, the smell of broom filled the air. The plants decorated the mountain with their deep golden leaves. The blue sky seemed to open up to the animals, which moved instinctively, never drifting off the trail. At night, the men would meet up with old acquaintances who offered food and a roof to sleep under. They would recall memories from the previous year, discuss the latest news, and ask about the grazing lands. The next day, Donatien would take on a few extra animals for his hosts, so they, too, could graze in the lush high country.

Vincent demonstrated exceptional courage for his first transhumance. The steep climb wore out his legs, but he never complained, and he refused to let the pack mule carry his load. At the end of each day, he would gulp down a copious meal, collapse, and fall into a deep sleep until daybreak. In the early morning, the ringing of the bells and the bleating of the sheep would rouse him from his dreams. The heat of the animals and the smell of straw, wool, and manure kept him far from the nuns and the orphanage, where he still worried he would have to return one day.

The flock reached the vast spreads of the Margeride on the fifth day, after crossing the Goulet Mountains and Mount Lozère. The Mercoire Forest darkened the horizon. Suddenly, the sky was threatening. The shepherds urged the animals to quicken the pace and barely outran the thunderstorm.

"We will reach the Taillades before noon tomorrow," Donatien said.

"The Taillades?" Vincent asked.

"That's the land where we pasture. It belongs to Mister Rochefort."

"Who's that?"

"A manufacturer who lives in Nîmes. He rents the land to us for the summer. He has a farm with a country house a few hundred yards from the sheepfold. You'll have a chance to meet him. He usually comes to spend a few days with his wife and sometimes his kids during summer."

"Is he rich?"

"Oh, much richer than I will ever be. But you must have heard of him. He also owns the Clos du Tournel, which is next to La Fenouillère. We are neighbors."

"I didn't know the man was named Rochefort. I never saw him. But one day, I saw a little girl about my age in the distance. She was with a lady."

"That was probably his youngest daughter and his wife, Mrs. Rochefort. Since their eldest daughter died, she doesn't come back very often. You were lucky to meet them."

"I didn't meet them. I just saw them from a distance. I would never have dared to talk to them."

Donatien didn't know that Anselme Rochefort had gotten there before him this year, and just as Donatien had wanted his ten-year-old son to experience the move to the highlands for the first time, Anselme had wanted his nine-year-old daughter, Faustine, to see them arrive for the first time. The girl loved the idea of seeing the colorful, lively show, with all the decorated animals. She was also looking forward to the celebration that accompanied the arrival.

Every year, when Donatien arrived in the middle of the day, the neighbors would come to see the flocks arrive. And they would bring food for a lavish welcoming meal.

Little Faustine knew all about it, having heard the details from her brothers and sister, who had attended in previous years. It was her turn now.

When the flock arrived, and Faustine and Vincent's eyes met for the first time, they immediately understood they would share much more than this moment in their lives.

9

Negotiations

Donatien Rouvière and Anselme Rochefort spent time together at the start of every grazing season. It was just a few days, because the businessman didn't like to stay away from his mills for long. They generally spent more time together in the autumn, during the grape harvest, which was Elisabeth's favorite season. For a number of years, Anselme had given Donatien his vineyards in Tornac and Anduze to harvest, in exchange for half of what he collected.

The two men respected each other and always found common ground. Work, the future, and the current economic situation brought them closer together, while they disagreed on matters of politics and social unrest. They kept these differences to themselves, as they didn't want to harm their good relations. One would hide his preference for right-wing conservatism, while the other wouldn't give voice to his penchant for the radical left. Inside, Anselme Rochefort felt superior to his Anduze neighbor because of his wealth and business acumen, but Donatien, as a hardened man of the land, never felt inferior and treated Anselme as an equal.

When the men shook hands after the sheep were in the field, they couldn't resist showing off their children.

Donatien started. "Let me introduce Vincent, my son. He is ten years old. That is why I've brought him for his first transhumance. This year, he is beginning his shepherding apprenticeship. I don't believe you've met."

"I saw the boy on your land in Tornac, but I didn't know he was your son."

"Vincent has been with us for more than three years now. To tell the truth, he spends more time on the benches at school than on our land, although he really prefers the farming."

"I didn't know you had a son," Rochefort said.

"I have one now. He has my name. Later, he'll take over La Fenouillère."

Anselme hadn't heard that Rouvière had adopted a child. But he didn't think it would be polite to ask any questions. "It's true that we never talk about our families," he said. "We're both hardworking men and stick to practical matters when we talk. Isn't that so?"

"You're right. Our time is precious, and we don't have much of it to spend talking."

Shyly clinging to their respective fathers, Vincent and Faustine looked at each other.

"Come on, boy, shake Mr. Rochefort's hand," Donatien said.

The boy did as he was told, taking off his hat and greeting the man politely. Faustine didn't move.

"Do the same, Faustine," Rochefort ordered in turn. "Don't be shy."

The girl stepped forward and bowed. "Hello, sir," she said without looking up.

Vincent couldn't take his eyes off of Faustine's satin dress.

He had never seen a girl his age dressed so elegantly. She was like a living doll, so delicate, with golden curls dangling around her neck, lace ribbons on her collar and sleeves, and small shiny boots.

The two children didn't dare to greet each other and ducked back into the shadows of their fathers. The two men spoke for a few more minutes, and then Donatien excused himself.

"The flock awaits me," he said.

"We'll see each other later, Rouvière," Anselme said. "I want to discuss something important with you."

Donatien thought the landowner might want to revise their rental agreement. Surprised, he asked, "Nothing's changed between us, Rochefort, right?"

"Don't worry. It's not about the land, at least not directly."

Donatien didn't press but thought the man was being very mysterious.

That evening, he confided in Victor. "I fear that Rochefort might raise the rent for the pasture. If he's not reasonable, I'll find a better situation elsewhere. There are lots of meadows in Lozère."

"I have a cousin in Durfort who summers on the Causse Méjean, near Hure-la-Parade. You probably know him. It's Antoine Chabrol. He could help us."

"I know him well. He's got a large herd. If we need to, I'll go talk to him about grazing land for next year."

Donatien was wrong. Anselme Rochefort had no intention of changing his rental agreement.

His proposition was much more important.

Several days went by before Donatien met with Anselme Rochefort again. From time to time, he saw the man's wife, Elisabeth, walking with their daughter along the paths or across the meadows. Their two umbrellas shone like splashes of light on an emerald setting. On some days, they would spend hours contemplating the sheep. Little Faustine marveled at the lambs suckling their mother's milk and hated to see one of them lost, bleating to find its mother again.

Vincent wanted to see Little Lady Rochefort again—that's what he called her. He hung around outside, hoping to spot her. But he didn't dare go near her, as he feared she would send him away, despite the affinity he thought they shared when they met. *I'm way too clumsy for her to deign to talk to me*, he thought. *I'm just a farmer. She is a little lady from the city.*

When he was lucky enough to see her, he hid behind a rock or a knoll to avoid being discovered. He took her in, imagining extravagant stories about little princesses falling in love with shepherds. Sometimes he forgot to watch the sheep, and they wandered off. Fortunately, his dog, Patou, would help him bring the strays back to the fold.

As he watched the girl this way one late afternoon, she stumbled in a patch of marshy land. Seeing the bottom of her satin dress and her pretty varnished boots muddied, she cried inconsolably. Elisabeth tried to soothe her, telling her that the dress could be washed, and the boots could be cleaned. The scene moved the shepherd, who was sad to see his beautiful princess weeping. Then Vincent daydreamed for a long moment, forgetting about the sheep. When it was time to bring the livestock back to the sheepfold, Vincent looked around and discovered that his sheep were no longer there. He was alone in the middle of a huge pasture.

He panicked and set out looking for the animals and calling for Patou as loud as he could. But the dog had obeyed his sheepdog instinct and followed the flock. Vincent started running down to the sheepfold. At a split in the path, he turned the wrong way and found himself near a large house. Now he was completely lost. He approached the house, not knowing who lived there. His heart was beating fast. He didn't want to draw attention to himself, yet he hoped someone would come out and show him the way. He knew his father would be worried if he didn't get back soon. He hadn't made it all the way around the house when he heard a door open behind him.

"Where are you going like that, young man?"

Vincent turned around and recognized Anselme Rochefort. The man didn't give the boy time to answer. "Did your father send you? Perfect timing."

"Well, um, I mean, no, sir. It wasn't my father. It's me. I . . ."

"You've come to visit us."

"Well, um, not really, sir. It's just that, well, I got lost trying to go back to the sheepfold."

"Where are your sheep?"

Chagrined, Vincent tried to hide the truth. "I sent them on ahead of me with my dog," he said. "I was looking for a stray."

"And if I understand correctly, you didn't find it."

"Uh, no, sir. I got lost."

"I see. You're not that far from the fold. About half a mile."

At that moment, Faustine came to the door. Vincent saw her and immediately turned his attention to her. Anselme could tell the child wasn't listening anymore and turned to his daughter.

"I get the impression that Faustine interests you more than I do. Come closer," he said.

Anselme took a step toward Vincent, encouraging him to say hello to Faustine.

"You've already met. Don't be so shy. It looks like you're afraid of each other."

"Hello, Vincent." Faustine was the first to talk. "I saw you and your dog in the meadow earlier."

"I was watching my sheep."

"And he has lost one," Anselme interrupted. "That's why we got this unexpected visit. But now he's also lost. Faustine, show him the way back. If it gets too late, his father will worry."

Then he turned to Vincent and said, "Tell your father to come see me tomorrow, when he has a moment. I have something important to tell him."

Vincent was fiddling with his hat, finding it hard to hide how uncomfortable he felt in Faustine's presence.

Faustine wasn't as shy. "Come on. I'll show you the way. I know these paths by heart. I go for long walks with Mom every afternoon. I know where you live with your father and your two farmhands."

"Léonce and Victor?"

"I don't know their names, but I've met them."

Vincent said good-bye to Anselme Rochefort and followed Faustine, feeling a little more self-confident.

"That boy seems awfully awkward," the businessman said to Elisabeth when she asked whom he had been talking to.

"What boy?" she asked.

"The Rouvière son. The adopted one."

"Adopted, adopted. He's their son," she said.

"In any case, he seemed pretty out of it. When he saw Faustine, it was like he turned to stone."

"He must have been intimidated. He's a country boy. Our daughter must seem, well, sophisticated to him. When they know each other better, he'll feel more comfortable. It makes me happy that Faustine has a little farmer friend. It will open her mind and be good for her."

"I don't see how. Besides, who said they're friends? That's going a bit fast."

"Faustine lives in a very sheltered world, far from reality. Unlike her brothers, she's never even seen your factories."

"Thank God for that," Rochefort said. "We're not from the same world as our workers."

"Spending time with a young farmer could open her eyes. She'll learn that there are a lot of children her age who are working already and that children like her, who wear silk and polished shoes, are privileged. We need to teach her to have compassion for others."

"We've never really discussed these things before," Elisabeth. "I'm surprised."

"Showing Christian charity has always been important to me, Anselme. Our social status should not make us unmindful of the poverty most of our workers live in and the hardships that plague the world."

Rochefort had no desire to discuss philosophy with his wife. His thoughts were elsewhere. Just before coming to the Taillades, he had talked to his eldest son, Jean-Christophe, and had made it understood that the boy needed to think about marriage when he finished school and joined the family business.

That was what he wanted to discuss with Donatien Rouvière.

The two men met the following evening. The nights were often cold, even in the summer, and Elisabeth had the servant light a fire. She had made a little something for her husband's guest—an *île flottante*, prepared according to her own secret recipe.

"I don't usually eat sweets, but tonight, I'll make an exception," Donatien said. "Your dessert looks so delicious, I can't refuse."

"What would you say to a good cigar, my dear Rouvière?" Anselme asked, inviting him to take a seat near the fireplace.

"No offense, Rochefort, but I only smoke the pipe. May I?"

"As you like, Rouvière. Would you like a little Cognac?"

"With pleasure."

Having dispensed with the polite small talk, Rochefort dived in, not wanting to make his guest wonder any longer why he had been summoned.

"I enjoy our friendship, Rouvière, and have ever since we met. How long ago was that?"

"Oh, it's been forever. Your father and mine always got along well. Our families are two of the oldest in the area."

"Yes, it's like we grew up together as good neighbors. That builds bonds, doesn't it?"

"Land certainly unites families."

"I agree. I may be a captain of industry, but I still feel my farming roots deep down. And I have to admit, I sometimes envy you for being so loyal to your roots."

"What are you saying? I'm sure that your lifestyle is much more pleasant than mine. Living in a city mansion is not at all comparable to the life on our country farm. And let's not even mention the work."

"You are certainly right, however . . ."

Anselme Rochefort was hedging. Even though he had prepared for this talk, he didn't know quite how to approach the subject.

Donatien took matters in his own hands. "Why did you want to see me, Rochefort? Is it about our contract?"

"Not at all."

"The grape harvest arrangement then?"

"Not that, either. I have no problem with the way we've been working together. In fact, we could improve on it."

"I don't see how. Explain yourself."

Anselme started pacing the room, as was his habit whenever he had an important decision to make. He sidestepped the issue again. "You must know that my eldest son, Jean-Christophe, will soon be coming to manage my mills with me."

"No, I didn't know that."

"Starting in September, our factories will be called Rochefort and Son."

"I'm happy for you. I've always wanted a son to ensure the future of my operation, as well. I, too, needed a son for that. Nature didn't give me one, so I took another path, and now I do have that son, Vincent."

"I applaud you, my dear Rouvière. There is nothing worse for a man with property than not having a son to inherit from him. So Vincent will inherit La Fenouillère. Is that what you're saying? You will provide your daughters with another dowry?"

"I've considered the matter. All my children will be treated fairly."

Anselme had managed to steer the conversation where he wanted it to go. He continued. "But when girls marry, there is always a rupture in continuity. The girls carry off their family assets in the dowry they take to their husbands. It's hard on their parents."

"There's nothing we can do about that, alas. That is the way it's done."

Anselme saw that it was time to announce his proposal. "There is one way to avoid this: If the alliance between the two families unites the land, rather than splitting it."

"That's true. But such an alliance isn't in the immediate future for any of my daughters. They are still very young—even the eldest—and no opportunity has come up."

"You're wrong, Rouvière."

"I'm not following you."

"I'm getting there. My son Jean-Christophe will be twenty-three at the beginning of the year. He's no longer a young man. He has his law degree with honors, and in the fall, he'll be working with me. He is now an accomplished man."

"I have no doubt about that, but where are you going with this, Rochefort?"

"Your eldest daughter, Louise, is old enough to marry."

"She turned seventeen at the beginning of the year."

"That's what I'm saying. Well, let's get to the point: We could unite our two families by marrying our children."

"My daughter married to your son?" Donatien said, removing the pipe from his mouth.

"That's right. Would you have any objection to that?"

Donatien grabbed the glass of Cognac and emptied it in one gulp.

"Are you surprised by my proposition?" Anselme asked.

"A little. Actually, it astonishes me."

Elisabeth was keeping her distance. She slipped in to offer more dessert.

"Later, my dear, later," Rochefort said, turning back to Donatien. "Our discussion is too serious to be disturbed by your delicacies."

Elisabeth left without saying a word. But her look made it clear how affronted she felt. Donatien seemed sorry to see her being treated like a servant.

"Where were we?" Rochefort said. "I was saying that our children's marriage could strengthen and consolidate the interests of both our families. You would bring the real estate, the noble land, worked over centuries by rich farmers."

"Not that rich, Rochefort," Donatien noted.

"Don't be so modest, Rouvière. I would represent industry and business. It would be the perfect union of tradition and modernity. And even more important, the marriage would be good for our children. You and I would ensure the future of our families' heritage. Isn't that what you want too?"

Donatien was taken aback by his host's straightforward proposition. He had never envisioned anything of the sort. He had always imagined that his daughters would marry farmers, rich or poor. He had no preference, as long as the boys they chose were decent and made his daughters happy. Donatien seemed to hesitate. Rochefort noticed and attacked again, softening his approach.

"We could wait until your daughter turns eighteen. In the meantime, we could celebrate the engagement, and the young lovebirds could get to know each other."

"Precisely. What bothers me, Rochefort, is that our children don't love each other. They don't even know each other."

"They'll have their entire lives to learn to love each other.

Their similarities and their values are the things that count. And you and I, Rouvière, come from the same world. We hold the same things dear."

"My wife and I married for love."

"That's old-fashioned, Rouvière. I'll tell you the truth. I married out of self-interest—twice. That didn't keep love from uniting us later. Love, like wine, gets better over time. No, I'll say it again. Marrying for love is a thing of the past. Let the poor do that. For them, love is the only wealth that a marriage with no dowry can provide. Let's think bigger, further into the future. What do you say?"

Donatien continued to have his doubts. He imagined his daughter married to his wealthy neighbor's son. Certainly, it would ensure that she would never be in need of anything. At the same time, he had scruples about negotiating a marriage without even talking to her.

"How do you see this marriage bringing our families closer?" he asked.

"It's simple. As I said, you represent land, and I represent money. Your daughter's dowry would join the capital I'm giving my son in the form of shares in my business now and an inheritance later. Anduze and your land in Tornac adjoin each other. It would be a prosperous beginning for our children. Their children—our grandchildren, Rouvière—would one day benefit from this alliance of two fortunes. The combined fortune would remain in the same family bosom. Are you following me? Imagine how good it would feel to know that we've safeguarded everything we've worked so hard for."

The more Anselme talked, the more Donatien seemed convinced. He imagined more than keeping Louise's land within the Rouvière family's grasp, even if it meant accepting the inevitable name change. Louise would represent the wealthy Rochefort-Rouvière family. And his family name would not die out, as Vincent would carry it on. What fortune!

"You're not answering me. Silence gives consent."

"I'm . . . I'm thinking about Louise's dowry."

"You're not lacking in land, Rouvière. Your mulberry-tree groves are next to my vineyard. I'm ready to give my vineyards to Jean-Christophe, if you give your mulberry trees to Louise. I believe the two plots are comparable. You can keep harvesting my grapes—well, they would be your daughter's—and your silkworms would go to my mill. You see, Donatien—may I call you Donatien?—we have everything to gain, thanks to our children. Furthermore, you know that Jean-Christophe will take my place when I retire. That ensures a fine future for your daughter and our future grandchildren."

"Looking at it that way, I think I'm going to agree. But first, I'll have to convince my wife. And perhaps you'll have to do the same?"

"When it comes to business, Donatien, I'm the only one to decide. A word to the wise: stand your ground. Don't let your wife decide for you. And be persuasive with your daughter. Give her a glimpse of the life she will have once she's introduced to high society. I know few who would resist such an opportunity."

Donatien promised an answer before the grape harvest. He would talk to Constance in August, when he took part of the flock down a month before the summer pasture season ended. Then he would talk to Louise and do his best to convince her.

The two men shook hands, like horse traders striking a deal, and ended up embracing each other.

"This marriage will make us brothers-in-law in spirit," Rochefort said. "What a fine alliance it will be."

10

Planning

October 1908

Clusters of grapes just ready to burst were weighing down the vines. The plains were bustling all the way from the ramparts of the Cévennes Mountains, dominated by the Pic Saint-Loup and its twin, Mount Hortus. Under the watchful eyes of stewards, a hive of cutters was making its way through the rows of grapevines. The air was heavy with the aromas of must and alcohol. The harvesters rivaled each other in dexterity and speed. It was no time for rest. Woe to any slowpoke if a storm started to brew.

Indeed, the sky looked menacing. Heavy slate-colored clouds had risen from the south and loomed over the first hills.

"We'd better hurry, or we'll lose what's not harvested," Donatien told Victor.

"There's only a day's work left."

"The weather won't hold until tonight. We'll need to finish before noon."

"That gives us five hours. We need at least ten to finish."

"There's only one solution. I'm going to get my children from school. They can join the harvesters. On the way, I'll hire anyone from the village with time on his hands."

Donatien knew the headmaster would object, but he decided to do it anyway.

"No," the teacher said. "The kids have been back for only a week, and you already want to take them out. You promised me you wouldn't do this."

"I don't have a choice, Roland. I could lose the harvest, and missing a day won't kill my son and daughters. I'll owe you. I'll give you two legs from the first boar I kill when we hunt together."

Roland Porte smoothed his moustache, put on his sternest face, and said, "Okay. This time only. Don't come asking again, Donatien! Their education is important."

"Yes, yes, I know," his friend said. "I know what you have to say about school."

Without any delay, Donatien took his kids back to La Fenouillère. On the way, he hired a few elderly men who were still sprightly enough to lend a hand.

He hadn't reached the vineyards yet when he heard a horse galloping toward the farm.

"Who's that?" Vincent asked.

"I don't know. Go join Mom and Louise in the vineyards with Julie and Aline. Don't lose any time. I'll go see what the horseman wants."

Patou and Perline were barking and growling in the farm's courtyard. The rider was attempting to rein in his frightened horse, which was on the verge of bucking.

"Whoa, whoa," the man said to calm both his horse and the two guard dogs.

"Please excuse them," Donatien said. "Don't be afraid. They aren't mean." Then he recognized the man he was talking to.

"Oh, Jean-Christophe. I didn't realize it was you. I haven't seen you in some time."

"Indeed, Mr. Rouvière. The last time we saw each other, I was just a teenager. I believe it was when I graduated from lycée. We celebrated my success at Tournel. Since then, I haven't set foot in these far reaches of the Cévennes. To tell the truth, I've been very busy with my studies. And I must admit that I don't especially like the countryside."

"To what do I owe the honor of this visit?"

"My parents are at the Clos du Tournel. They arrived last night for the grape harvest. But I believe they have come a little late!"

"The grapes ripened early this year, so we moved up the harvest."

"My father asked me to come say hello. Of course, he'll be seeing you shortly."

"I am honored. But you're here at a bad time. The vines await me. The sky is threatening a storm, and we have to finish before it rains."

"I understand. When you farm, the land is the boss. You must do tend to its every need. Isn't that right?"

The young Rochefort had a proud bearing in his riding clothes and an undeniable presence. But he also had a certain haughtiness that made him hard to like. He resembled his father, Donatien thought, but there was an extra layer of arrogance.

"Come back at the end of the day with your parents," Donatien suggested.

"That is exactly why I am here, Mr. Rouvière: to ask for an evening of your hospitality to get to know you better. I won't bother you any longer. I'll see you tonight."

Jean-Christophe Rochefort pulled on the reins and spurred

his horse. The animal whinnied, reared, turned around, and galloped away, leaving a cloud of dust.

The teams finished the harvest in the middle of the afternoon. To Donatien's relief, the storm passed in the distance. At sunset, there was a fine light in the sky, a warm red that set the horizon ablaze.

According to tradition, on the last night of the harvest, everyone would gather around a full table, usually outside, and dine until late in the night to the sound of fifes, drums, and violins. Constance and her cousin Madeleine, who had lived at the farm since losing her husband five years earlier, had spent hours preparing the meal.

When the Rocheforts' carriage arrived at La Fenouillère, followed by Jean-Christophe on his chestnut, everyone stopped eating and drinking. Donatien asked them to continue and went to greet his guests.

"Good timing, Rochefort. We're celebrating the harvest tonight. You'll be joining us, right? With your wife and your son, of course. After all, it's your vineyard my men harvested."

Anselme was wearing a wide, satisfied smile. With his top hat, black suit, and perfectly trimmed mustache and goatee, he was the picture of an elegant gentleman. Elisabeth stood next to him, looking regal in her black dress but ill at ease.

Constance had known the Rouvières for a long time and had enjoyed many long conversations with Elisabeth during her walks around La Fenouillère. She walked over to Elisabeth and took her hand to welcome her. "Your other children didn't come? We would have loved having them."

"Sebastien and Faustine stayed at Tournel with the governess," Elisabeth answered. "And poor Elodie is too frail to make long trips. She tires easily. She's in Nîmes."

"It's nothing serious, I hope."

"I'd rather not talk about it. It will ruin my evening."

Constance did not insist. She knew that the Rochefort girl

had a wasting condition that the doctors called neurasthenia. It was considered an emotional disorder, and one of the symptoms was severe depression.

Donatien asked his newly arrived guests to sit down. He suggested that Elisabeth sit at Constance's right, and he introduced Louise to the Rochefort son. The latter was very civil and, to tell the truth, left a rather good impression. Donatien and Constance had not yet informed their daughter of their intentions. They had just suggested that their neighbors wanted to get to know her."

During the meal, the two young people were reserved, but Jean-Christophe's bearing, charisma, and friendly conversation put Louise at ease, and she allowed herself to relax.

Anselme, bloodhound that he was, observed the scene while conversing with his host. Elisabeth tried to put on a good face for Constance, who continued to try to make her feel comfortable.

"Our children seem to get along perfectly," Anselme ended up saying.

"You're right. Your son seems to have my daughter's attention."

"I would say that it is Louise's charm that has worked on my son. Your daughter is such a sweet beauty. Nobody could remain indifferent to her. She resembles her mother."

The compliment made Constance blush. She was not used to flattery. *That Rochefort is a smooth talker*, she thought. *As clever as an old fox.*

"How is it that you daughter Elodie is not married?" Donatien asked to change the subject and relieve his wife's discomfort.

"Elodie leads a very private life."

"How old is she now?"

"She's two years younger than Jean-Christophe. She'll soon be twenty-one."

Elisabeth frowned. The conversation was embarrassing

her. Anselme paid no mind and continued. "Elodie never got over her sister Catherine's death. The two of them were very close."

"It's been ten years, if I recall correctly," Donatien said.

"That's right. It was 1898."

"Donatien, you should serve our guest some more wine," Constance said, changing the conversation.

Donatien did as she suggested.

"Thank you," Elisabeth whispered.

"We women understand each other, isn't that so? What if we talk about why you are here today?" she said before turning to Louise. "My dear, would you be kind enough to show Mr. Jean-Christophe around the farm?"

"Please, Mrs. Rouvière, call me Jean-Christophe," the young man said.

"Fine, Jean-Christophe. Follow Louise. She'll show you around."

The two young people left the table.

And as the harvesters continued their festivities, Constance and Elisabeth and Donatien and Anselme built their castles in the air.

Considering the commotion at the table, Constance found it preferable to invite Elisabeth inside.

"It'll be quieter," she said. "We'll be able to talk."

Elisabeth didn't have to be asked twice. The festive atmosphere was getting on her nerves.

"Donatien told me about Mr. Rochefort's idea," Constance said. "I admit that I was a little surprised."

"My husband didn't consult me before making his decision. But after some thought, I found his choice to be rather judicious."

"So you would like our children to get married. But their social circles are not the same."

"I have no problem with that. Quite the contrary. Jean-

Christophe is a very talented boy with a lot of good sense, but he's too isolated in his ivory tower. Mind you, as his parents, we are responsible for that. So a young girl like Louise at his side could make him more pragmatic. People who come from the land have a greater sense of reality, don't they? If the two of them can get along, I'd be the first to rejoice. What do you think?"

"I have to admit that at first I was against the idea of this marriage. Not because of their different social circles and not because of—how should I say it?—the negotiations that we'll have to undertake, but simply because I didn't want to coax Louise into a marriage in which she had no input."

"If I understand what you're saying, she still doesn't know anything."

"We haven't told her everything. We just told her that Jean-Christophe wanted to meet her. We would like her to make her own decision."

"I understand perfectly. That seems fair. We did the same with our son. We simply suggested that it was time for him to think about marriage, and we would be very happy if he would agree to meet your daughter and get to know her better."

"How did he react?"

"He agreed right away. I have to admit that surprised me."

"Why is that?"

Elisabeth hesitated. Throughout his studies, her son had gotten more attention from the young ladies than his professors. Both in Montpellier and in Nîmes he had a reputation as a Don Juan. And were it not for Anselme's personal involvement, the courtesans he kept with the family money would have invaded their home.

She skirted the topic. "Jean-Christophe always swore that he would not be married before the age of thirty. It was a pledge that he made as a teen, and I didn't know if he would break it."

"Anselme barely knows our daughter."

"You're wrong about that. Anselme is very clever. He's watched your children grow up. He even told me that he chose your daughter for our son a long time ago. Louise was quite young when he perceived that she would make a perfect wife for our son."

Elisabeth didn't dare say the real reasons for her husband's choice: the acres of mulberry trees that Donatien had agreed to include in Louise's dowry.

"I will double my silkworm production with this marriage," he had told her. "I won't be dependent on anyone else for our silk. No more silkworm traders."

Anselme had not hidden this detail from his son. And it was easy to convince him of what they both had to gain from a union with the Rouvière family.

"Furthermore, when your future father-in-law dies, what he hasn't already given to his children will be divided, and you will inherit a third of his assets," he said.

"A fourth, Father. You're forgetting little Vincent."

"He's just an adopted child. You are an attorney. You will find some argument in favor of blood bonds and direct lineage. In the worst-case scenario, you'll break the will, if there is one. But we're not there yet. In the meantime, once you're married, make yourself indispensable to the Rouvière family, the one who helps in every decision. As their eldest daughter's husband, you should have no trouble imposing your will. And let any feelings you have for Louise grow over time. Between us, you are not forbidden from finding entertainment outside the marital bed. You do understand me, don't you? Marriage is not a prison and shouldn't keep you from living your life."

Jean-Christophe was easy to convince. He agreed to meet Louise and her parents and consider an alliance between the two families, as his father had cleverly arranged.

One question bothered Constance: Where would the

newlyweds live? Like all other mothers, she expected her children to leave when they married. She already envisioned herself alone at La Fenouillère after Aline was gone. She would be over fifty. Yes, Vincent would be there, or so she hoped. Wasn't that one of the reasons they had adopted him? But deep down, she had to admit that her daughters were her own flesh and blood, and their departure would leave a real hole in her life, a deeper void than the one Vincent would leave if he decided to follow a life path other than the one they had laid out for him.

She was ashamed of these thoughts. But she couldn't help herself. The blood she shared with her daughters spoke to her, reminding her that Vincent had not come from her own womb. *Donatien doesn't understand the way I do*, she sometimes thought. *He doesn't know what it is to bear and give birth to a child.*

For Elisabeth, where the couple would live was no issue. "Our children will live with us at the Cordeliers," she told Constance. "Our house in Nîmes is large enough for two families. There is an entire floor we still have to renovate. There's room for a fine apartment with a separate entrance. They'll be entirely independent. And they'll have the Clos de Tournel. We go there only once or twice a year. Your daughter will be able to visit you as often as her husband allows her to be away from him."

"You have thought of everything, Mrs. Rochefort."

"Call me Elisabeth, please. Let's drop the formalities. We'll be seeing a lot of each other, won't we? We should set an example for everyone else in our families."

Anselme and Donatien hadn't waited for their spouses to abandon the formalities. With the help of the wine, the two men, their collars open and their vests unbuttoned, were having a friendly conversation as everyone else at the table looked on. By the time the cheese was served—small goat rounds on a bed of grape leaves—Anselme and Donatien were no longer whispering about their intentions to marry off their children. The entire table knew and seemed pleased. One of the partygoers, who was more inebriated than the others, even dared to raise a toast in honor of the young couple.

"Here's to the future newlyweds!" he said, standing on his bench and encouraging his friends to do the same. "Long live Miss Louise and her happy fiancé."

Nobody moved. Everyone fell silent. Louise and Jean-Christophe had returned to the table. They looked at each other, embarrassed. They hadn't broached the subject of an engagement and certainly not a marriage. And although Louise was not all that young, naïve, and innocent, she was still surprised and uncomfortable. Jean-Christophe hadn't intended to ask for her hand until the negotiations had been finalized. In polite society, there were conventions to respect.

Donatien didn't know what to say. Constance was still talking with Elisabeth inside the house, so he turned to Anselme, looking perplexed.

Anselme, the shrewder of the two, said, "My friends, I would have wanted our wives to be here for this most important moment in the meal, but you know women, always talking about fabrics for dresses and such."

Everyone laughed, and the hubbub started again. Donatien called for silence.

Anselme continued. "It seems a speech is in order. I won't make one right now. But I'd like to take advantage of this opportunity, given to me by this gentleman—whom I don't know and who just raised his glass—to announce the engagement of Miss Louise and my son Jean-Christophe. They will be married in the spring."

Hurrahs rang out around the table, and everyone went back to eating and drinking.

Victor was sitting next to Cousin Madeleine. He whispered in her ear. "That Rochefort is a bit quick. Louise didn't even know."

"You're wrong there. Constance told her, but Louise was free to choose. Rochefort just pulled the rug out from under her."

"Now she's presented with the fait accompli."

11

Preparations

Once the engagement was officially announced, the marriage was scheduled for Saturday, April 10, 1909. Elisabeth Rochefort chose the date, which she thought would bring good luck, as it was the day before Easter and the celebration of the Resurrection, a perfect symbol of new life. They had six months to organize it. The Rochefort family worked out every detail and was not at all concerned about offending the Rouvière family. For that matter, the Rouvières seemed a little overwhelmed by how quickly it had all come to pass, as well as the magnificence that Anselme wanted to give this union.

For once, Anselme gave his wife carte blanche, on the pretext that weddings were more of a woman's affair than a man's. Signing the nuptial agreements was for the men. In this area, he was clear about the terms. Jean-Christophe had five years of law school, but Anselme had no intention of seeking his counsel before getting Donatien Rouvière to accept the final clauses of the contract that would forever bind the families.

Anselme deliberately divulged that the vineyards he was adding to the lot had been the subject of land speculation that had greatly increased their value. Some entrepreneurs from Montpellier had wanted to build an automobile facility and had contacted him to purchase some of the acreage. He had taken advantage of the situation and had insisted that they buy all of the land or none at all. Anselme told Donatien that even though the negotiations had fallen through, the land was now worth far more than it was when Jean-Christophe and Louise became engaged. So Donatien, who took Anselme at this word, felt obliged to increase his dowry. The two children were publically engaged. He couldn't back out.

The wedding would be celebrated in the country. As dictated by custom, the bride's family would host it. But Donatien and Constance did agree to have the reception at the Clos du Tournel and not at La Fenouillère. Anselme had encouraged Elisabeth to use all her tact to convince Constance that the Clos was the ideal wedding venue.

"If the weather is good, we'll set tables under the big elm tree in front of the house," Elisabeth told Constance. "If necessary, we can go inside. The dining room is big enough to hold seventy to eighty guests."

"If that's not a problem for you, I couldn't ask for more," Constance responded politely. She wasn't one to stand on principle.

The two women decided to meet two or three times to hash out the details of the ceremony and the meal.

The crucial question concerned the religious ceremony. Anselme Rochefort didn't care at all that Louise belonged to the Reformed Church—he abhorred going to Sunday Mass with his wife and preferred to hang out with his business buddies in Nîmes. However, Elisabeth did care. She was a practicing Catholic and couldn't imagine her son being married anywhere but in the Catholic Church. This was the first obstacle she wanted to overcome. She brought it up with Constance.

"Your family is Protestant, right? That shouldn't interfere with our plans. Would you have any objection to our children being married in our local church? You must understand that my beliefs would keep me from giving my blessing if my son married outside our religion."

Constance had expected this. Donatien had warned her.

"It will all go well with Rochefort, but his wife is very religious," Donatien told Constance. "She's involved in Catholic charitable work and always has a place set at the table for the bishop. Rochefort advised diplomacy. Tell her that we went to the Sisters of Charity orphanage to adopt Vincent. That will help you win her over."

Constance was religious, as well. But she was also pragmatic. When time was short, and there was too much to do on the farm, she sometimes missed church. Donatien and she strived to be good people, but they didn't obsess over religion. For that matter, they had agreed to let Vincent go to Mass, as he had in the orphanage. The child had gone for a number of months. But then he had asked to attend services with them at the Reformed Church, and they had agreed.

"My husband and I have thought this over," Constance said. "Yes, we would like our daughter to be married in our church, but if you agree to compromise, we are ready to meet your request."

"Believe me, it's not my demand, Constance. Jean-Christophe is following his own conscience."

"We accept a mixed marriage. Although it would be ideal if both our pastor and the priest could officiate, all we ask is that our pastor be there for the benediction.

Elisabeth was relieved. She would have preferred having her son married by the bishop himself in full pomp, but she could never for an instant imagine asking a high dignitary of the Roman Church to leave his cathedral in Nîmes for a little village church, in a Protestant region to boot.

"So be it," she said without a single regret.

After the infamous post-harvest festivities, Jean-Christophe started seeing Louise once a week at La Fenouillère, and he demonstrated extreme gallantry. He courted her gently, not pushing her or doing anything objectionable. He was courteous to her parents, which convinced them that he was the best choice for their daughter. Louise was on a cloud and waited impatiently every week for her beau to come whisper sweet nothings.

Everyone in the area thought the Rouvières had found an excellent match for Louise. And when they saw her galloping into the hills behind her fiancé on his chestnut, some gossips suggested that Donatien might have to move the wedding date up. But Louise was a serious young woman who didn't need to be told how to behave. When Jean-Christophe became overly insistent, she pushed him away gently, brushed his lips with her fingers, and whispered in a seductive tone that wasn't natural to her, "My love, wait just a little longer to savor me. The sharper your desire, the greater your pleasure will be. I'll be yours on our wedding night, when you slip my immaculate dress off of my shoulders."

When he responded with a contrite look, Louise laughed and teased him. "Don't take it badly. I want to, as well. But I don't want us to act impulsively and have regrets."

Jean-Christophe had a hard time resisting his desire to be more cavalier. In other circumstances, he would have overridden his companion's reticence, proving the man was in charge. He'd done it before, making love to inexperienced and frightened virgins. How many had complained afterward? They had all come running back, begging for more, once he had abandoned them, which he always did.

"I'll respect your wishes until you decide to be with me, my friend," he said every time his efforts failed.

This was how Louise's influence over her beau grew week by week.

Anselme's business was thriving and kept him occupied, as did supervising the renovation of the future newlyweds' apartment. He continued to let his wife prepare for the big day. In January, the mothers decided to see each other as soon as they could.

Elisabeth went to the Clos du Tournel for a couple of weeks with Elodie and Marie-Jeanne, her assistant. Sebastien and Faustine stayed in Nîmes with their father.

Elisabeth had no idea how a woman in the countryside could stand being a prisoner to so many domestic responsibilities. In Nîmes, she had very few domestic duties, but she still felt there was never enough time to take care of her charity work, her social obligations, and her meetings with the bishop, her confessor. She was raised in high society and knew little about the everyday life of someone who had to work for a living.

Constance did have a comfortable life, but she owed it to hard work, which left her little free time. However, she managed to free up a few afternoons to see her daughter's future mother-in-law, and she made it a point to be as gracious as a Nîmes woman of means.

Her cousin Madeleine objected. "I don't see why you're bending over backward for that highfalutin lady who put you in your place at the harvest feast," she said before Elisabeth arrived.

"You misunderstood. She didn't say anything rude."

"Didn't she say that people of the land didn't know how to make the most of life?"

"I don't recall her saying that."

"You have a short memory. Or you don't want to remember."

THE ROCHEFORTS

Constance hadn't noticed Elisabeth's remark. She knew that Anselme Rochefort's wife belonged to another world, but she didn't feel inferior to her, just as Donatien didn't feel inferior to Anselme.

"You should get over it, Madeleine. One day, women will have the same rights as men, and when that happens, all women will be equal. We might as well start now."

In fact, Elisabeth didn't feel superior. Her manner, bearing, and somewhat affected language were the fruits of her education. She was cultivated, but she never called attention to herself. She was quick-witted and perceptive and skilled at listening to others.

Her son's marriage to the daughter of a well-off farmer suited her perfectly. She had been sincere with Constance about Jean-Christophe. She was happy to see her family united with that of a girl who embodied simplicity, honesty, and attachment to her roots and genuine values. She liked Louise.

She hoped the alliance of the two families would bring happiness back to her family, which still bore the shadow of Catherine's death ten years earlier. She thought of Catherine as she greeted Louise. Catherine had been Louise's age when she died.

"Your daughter has so much charm, it wouldn't matter what she wore on her wedding day," she said to Constance when they began talking about the bride's dress.

Constance had already thought about it. She had always made her daughters' dresses. It was her favorite pastime during the long winter nights. Madeleine drew the patterns and cut the fabric, which was sent from a shopkeeper on the Ruse Saint-Vincent in Alès. Their fingers were as agile as a pianist's when it came to using scissors, thread, and needle, embroidering lace, attaching ribbons, and adding just the right ruffles.

"I would like your opinion about the fabric," Constance said. "I have to tell you that I love working with silk satin. It has luster, and it's very sturdy. If Louise is careful with the dress on her wedding day, she can wear it on other occasions. I hate to see a wedding dress worn only once."

Elisabeth's expression darkened. It hadn't occurred to her that Constance would want to make the dress herself.

"I thought that Louise could go to Nîmes for fittings with the couturier I always use. A wedding gown is unique. I don't mean to offend you, but a professional seamstress will know better than anyone else how to highlight your daughter's beauty. Let's leave our own sewing for everyday. A wedding is an exceptional event. Louise should be a princess. Let her have the pleasure of being dressed by an artist."

Constance didn't know how to answer. Madeleine was scowling but didn't dare say anything. Seeing her hesitation, Elisabeth thought she understood what was bothering them. "Of course, I'll help pay for the cost of the dress," she said. "It would give me great pleasure. Please, let me pamper Louise as I would pamper my own daughters."

Constance was aware that a dress by a fancy couturier would cost a small fortune. Money, however, was not the issue. She wanted to make Louise's wedding dress simply because she loved her daughter. But faced with Elisabeth's insistence, she agreed.

"I don't want us to disagree over a wedding dress," she said. "We'll go to Nîmes for the fittings. But there won't be any issue of money between us."

Madeleine excused herself and left the room. She was furious that Constance was being pushed around.

Louise was happier than anyone else when she learned that her future mother-in-law was putting her in the hands of her own couturier. Jean Paturel made clothes for all the high-society ladies, and his dresses hung in the most fashionable salons. He boasted of having the prefect's wife as a client, along with the spouses of other government officials. Some even said that Georges Clemenceau's wife used him.

"You will see, my child, Mr. Paturel will turn you into a princess like no other. The guests will have eyes only for you." Elisabeth had conquered Louise.

Her fourteen-year-old sister Julie, who was less romantic, kept advising her to be careful. Julie was much more down to earth. She thought the novels Louise loved had gone to her head.

"Life isn't a romance novel," she would say. "Right now, you're on a cloud. But if you're not careful, you'll take a hard fall."

Julie wasn't as pretty as her sisters, and her constant scowling didn't help. But she felt she had even more reason to scowl now that Jean-Christophe was showing up every week and her mother was preoccupied with the wedding.

"These people are bothering us," she complained to her sister Aline, who was her confidant. "They've invaded our farm."

"I don't agree. Mrs. Elisabeth is really nice. And she is so beautiful in her elegant dresses."

"Don't judge a book by its cover."

"What do you mean?"

"You can't trust appearances."

"In any case, Vincent gets along perfectly with Faustine."

"They don't even know each other."

"Yes they do. They met last summer in the mountains. And again when the Rocheforts came back to the Clos du Tournel at the end of the harvest."

"Why didn't you tell me about it?"

"It was a secret between him and me."

"A secret! What's so secret about that?"

"Vincent asked me not to say anything."

"So, silly, why are you telling me?"

"Because you asked me! It's your fault. You wormed it out of me."

Little Aline felt she had betrayed Vincent, the brother she had worshipped secretly since he had joined the family. She was mad at herself and swore she would never say anything else to Julie, who was just angry over the attention their older sister was getting.

When it came time to discuss the trousseau, Elisabeth let Constance decide what was needed. In matters of housekeeping, Constance didn't need lessons from anyone. She remembered everything that had been in her own trousseau.

"I made a list so I wouldn't forget anything," she said, handing Elisabeth a notebook in which she had carefully written down everything she intended to give her daughter.

It did have everything: four sets of linen-cotton sheets, four pillowcases, two thick wool blankets, a dozen towels and washcloths, two dozen table napkins and four linen tablecloths, and three dozen quality Cholet cotton handkerchiefs. Everything was embroidered with the married couple's initials. There were also two everyday dresses and two Sunday dresses, underskirts, camisoles, and aprons. Everything a young woman needed to start her married life.

"Did you think about dishes?" Elisabeth asked after reading the list.

"Not yet, I have to admit."

"Then please let me provide them. Limoges of course. We couldn't have anything else. I'll order them personally from our regular supplier. You have to be careful these days. A lot of small producers are offering poor-quality sets at cut-rate prices. You have to make sure each piece is stamped. That's the only way to make sure it's not fake. For glasses, I'm hesitating: Baccarat, Murano, or Bohême? What do you think?"

Constance didn't know anything about fine china. And she had never set a table with crystal. She expressed no shame at her ignorance. "I don't know the difference. You'll make a better choice in that area."

"I'll think it over. The cutlery will have to be silver. What about Christofle?"

Elisabeth guessed that Constance was lost and added, "It's a very old producer of copperware and silverware. They supplied King Louis-Philippe and Napoléon III."

"I'll have to trust you on that, Elisabeth."

"Don't be embarrassed, Constance. I understand. You must be wondering what's in store for your daughter."

"No, you're wrong. That's not at all what I'm thinking. It's more that here in the countryside, we're used to eating on earthenware plates, and our cutlery isn't silver."

Elisabeth smiled and touched Constance's hand. "It's all trivial convention. Louise will have to maintain her station. So we might as well make it easier for her, right? But don't worry. I'm sure she'll stay loyal to her roots. The elegant manners she'll be quick to adopt will never distance her from you, her real family. Louise has a pure heart. I knew that the very first time I saw her."

"I'm not at all worried about that."

"So let's forget the frills and flounces and just be glad that our children are happy. That is the whole point of this union, isn't it?"

Something shifted inside Constance. She didn't see any reason to remain guarded. Elisabeth had tried to put her at ease. Despite her upper-class airs, she could be likable and reassuring, going right to the heart. There was no reason to butt heads. *After all, isn't my attachment to this wedding connected to my sorrow over the impending loss of my daughter?* she asked herself.

"What if we talked about the wedding meal later?" Elisabeth suggested.

"Yes, I would prefer that. I don't think we have to talk about it today."

"So during my next visit, we can meet at the Clos du Tournel and discuss the meal and our guest list."

"I'd enjoy seeing you there. But now let's taste a pastry that Louise made especially for you. I'll call her. She can't be far."

In fact, Louise was in the adjacent room, listening to the entire conversation. She carried in a silver platter—the only one she could find in the kitchen. On top of it was a chestnut cream cake she was very proud of.

Elisabeth took a bit, and tears glistened in her eyes. "My darling child, you are a gem. How lucky my Jean-Christophe is to have you as his betrothed."

"As if his parents hadn't shoved them together," Madeleine mumbled as she cleaned up in the kitchen.

12

Fine Tuning

Anselme Rochefort's cotton mill was a state-of-the-art factory producing fabric made of the highest-quality cotton. Nîmes had long been known for its serge, and Anselme enhanced that reputation by investing considerable money in his equipment, including his looms. Anselme was well aware that his denim was for work clothes, and his profit margins were slim. His production efficiencies kept the cost of his fabric competitive and his market position strong. He didn't hesitate to take out the loans needed to keep his facilities as efficient as possible, and his banker at the Société Générale approved all the credit lines he asked for, considering the overall worth of his assets.

While Anselme's cotton mill continued to operate at capacity, his silk mill was also doing quite well. Despite the lingering effects of pebrine disease and competition from the Far East, his facility was turning out a quality product that even attracted international buyers. The silk thread was prepared, spun, and reeled entirely on site.

"The future is in export," Anselme kept telling Jean-Christophe. To continue expanding the business, Anselme needed his son. But the young man was dragging his heels. He was working at the largest corporate law firm in Nîmes. Jean-Christophe still had something to learn about corporate law, and he thought that staying at the firm a while longer would ultimately benefit Rochefort and Son when it was time to join his father.

"You will have to go to the United States to strengthen our relationships with our partners there," Anselme insisted. "I've done a lot of thinking since we met Colonel Cody four years ago. As you know, Levi Strauss died in 1902, and his nephews have continued his work. In fact, they've made the company even stronger—this despite the San Francisco earthquake and fire in 1906."

"They rebuilt at 250 Valencia Street, right?" Jean-Christophe interjected, proud to show his father that he was up to date on information related to their business.

"That's right. I see you know as much as I do. So you must know that they've done well with their Levi's 501 jeans. But they're facing stiffer competition these days, and other producers are imitating them. We can leverage that to our advantage."

"Who's capable of undermining the Levi Strauss Company? I thought they were the strongest in the market."

"Two other companies have made a name for themselves across the Atlantic: the Henry Lee Mercantile Company and the Hudson Overall Company, founded by the Neustacter brothers."

"What do you have in mind?"

"There aren't that many of us in Nîmes making denim. Yet it is very popular in the United States, thanks largely to Levi Strauss, which started importing serge from Nîmes more than fifty years ago. And demand is growing. Cowboys and gold miners aren't the only ones wearing denim these days. Workers throughout the country are beginning to wear denim. Meanwhile, industrialization in the United States is speeding up. Overalls, pants, and other heavy-duty clothes represent a huge market with a promising future. Believe me, the United States will soon surge ahead of the old industrial nations of Europe. And we need to be the ones supplying the nation with the fabric for the clothes its workers will wear."

"Let's hope that a war doesn't interfere with our plans."

"What are you talking about?"

"A war, Father! I fear it's going to happen soon. Germany is getting puffed up and could try to lay claim to even more of our lands."

"I don't want to shock you, son, but war has never been an enemy of business. And our cotton serge is an excellent fabric for soldiers' uniforms."

"You're so calculating, Father. Even cynical."

"Are you complaining? You stand to come into a fortune, you know."

"You're the one who wants me involved in your business."

"True enough. A father's greatest desire is to have something to pass down and at least one son to give it to. When I think about that poor bugger Rouvière, who had to adopt an orphan . . ."

"Do you feel bad for him?"

"Not at all."

"You don't seem to like him that much. There's always contempt in your voice when you talk about him."

"Between us, he's just a peasant. He'll never evolve. When I asked him to increase Louise's dowry, considering the real value of the vineyards I'm turning over, he said I was trying to take advantage of him and giving up any more land would hurt his other daughters. We almost argued over it."

"I didn't know that."

"I don't have to tell you everything, Jean-Christophe."

"Have you worked it all out?"

"Yes, I finally convinced him, and, between us again—don't tell your mother, who has a lot of regard for the Rouvières—I pulled one over on him."

"What do you mean, Father? I'm curious."

"I can tell you now. To persuade Rouvière, I told him that developers were interested in buying the vineyards, which greatly appreciated their value. But as it turns out, nobody is interested in buying the land at this point, and it's worth what it's always been worth."

"So what did he add to the dowry?"

"A nice parcel of grapevines, which we can add to our vineyards. Right now, we need to diversify and reinvest some of the mill's profits in winegrowing. The 1907 economic crisis was like a purge. The future belongs to large estate owners. The cooperative movement that the crisis sparked isn't going anywhere. The little winegrowers will disappear, one after another. I have no problem with that."

Father and son loved talking about their business prospects. They cared little about the fate of the lower classes, whether they were small farmers who worked the land or laborers who turned out fabric.

"Let's go back to what I'm most preoccupied with. I'll ask the question again: Would you agree to go to the United States? A bit after your wedding, of course. I don't want to take you away from your bride too soon. And you don't want to give the impression of picking up and abandoning her."

Jean-Christophe feigned hesitation. He was as calculating as his father, and he wouldn't concede without making it known that his acceptance had a price. "You'll owe me," he said to himself.

"A lengthy absence will sadden my wife, for sure. But she will have to get used to it. I have no intention of playing the housebound husband. My position allows me to—how should I say it—take some liberties, isn't that so?"

"Your mother never said anything about my absences. It'll be up to you to get your future wife onboard with that."

"Of course. I'll leave for the United States after our honeymoon."

"You could wait a little longer. What about July?"

Constance and Louise went to Nîmes at the beginning of March. Anselme provided his best silk for the wedding gown. He let the women handle the rest.

The first fitting with Jean Paturel thrilled Louise. A host of cutters and seamstresses surrounded her. They turned her one way and then the other, making her arch her back to highlight her tiny waist. They also fitted her with an undergarment few other women were wearing: a brassiere.

"Mademoiselle, be happy that we won't make you wear a corset, like our mothers did," one of the seamstresses told her.

At the back of the fitting rooms, Elisabeth and Constance discussed the final details of the clothes the two families would wear.

"Do you think the men should wear redingotes?" Elisabeth asked.

"Redingotes? My husband has never worn one before, and he's never put on a top hat," Constance said.

"Anselme is very old school. But I'll manage to convince him to dress, well, more stylishly. First, I'll get him to shave his goatee. A moustache alone gives a better impression, don't you think? I noticed your husband doesn't have one."

"When he shaves, it all goes. He doesn't like to waste time pampering. I like him just the way he is."

"So our men will be dressed nicely for the ceremony: fitted black jackets, white shirts, bowties, and derbies. Of course, the boys will be dressed the same. What do you think?"

Constance didn't dare contradict Elisabeth, who continued. "These days, a derby is more becoming than an opera hat, which I think is out of style. Bowlers are the rage in England. All the lords are wearing them. They're a sign of respectability."

"I can't even imagine Donatien in a top hat," Constance said. She sighed. Clearly, these high-society women have too much time on their hands, she thought.

Occasionally, Louise let out a sharp cry. "Ouch!"

"Oops, I pricked you with the needle. Pardon me, young lady. It won't happen again. We've finished the basting."

Jean Paturel had not yet come out to greet Elisabeth, a long-time customer. This surprised Constance.

"He'll be here for the next fitting," Elisabeth explained. "His workers use his drawings to assemble the basic piece, and he makes the final adjustments, based on Louise's shape."

Two additional fittings were needed to put the final touches on the dress. Jean Paturel was present for the second fitting, and like a magician, he transformed the simple composition of silk, lace, and tulle into a work of art.

Elisabeth couldn't find enough praise for the designer, while Constance, as ill at ease as ever in this world, just stared at her daughter. She could barely recognize the young women, all done up like a princess.

"Jean, do you have a little time now for my dress?" Elisabeth asked the designer.

"Of course, darling. All of my seamstresses will be at your service."

"I'll send you my girls, Elodie and Faustine, as well. They'll need matching dresses. Constance, what do you intend to do for the big day? And your girls?"

Embarrassed, Constance glanced at Louise, who came to her aid immediately. "Of course Mom doesn't have Mr. Paturel's know-how, but she's a very good seamstress. She and my cousin Madeleine make very beautiful dresses."

"Yes, I had forgotten," Elisabeth said.

"If you'd like, madame, I could send you the patterns for

some beautiful dresses I offer my customers," the couturier responded. "I would be very happy to see my creations made by somebody other than me."

"I wouldn't dare, sir!"

"Now, now, Constance," Elisabeth said. "Don't be so uptight. Mr. Paturel offered you his patterns, so accept them. I'm sure the dresses you make from them will be masterpieces."

Louise sighed. She knew her parents would never overspend on dress clothes. She even felt uncomfortable being the center of so much solicitude. She was beginning to wonder if it was such a good idea to join this family, which belonged to an entirely different world.

Mid-March, three weeks before the wedding, the women met again at the Clos du Tournel to finalize the details.

Sebastien and Faustine accompanied Constance this time. Elodie remained in Nîmes, silent as ever. Rochefort made a quick trip to meet with Donatien and give him the nuptial agreement his notary had drawn up. The two men had worked out their differences and agreed on the key items. Above all, Donatien Rouvière wanted his daughter to be happy. What he gave in the dowry was, for him, just an advance on her inheritance. He hoped that one of his grandchildren from the marriage would show an interest in farming, so he had faith that the land would somehow remain in the family, even though it would be shared.

"Rochefort, you do realize how painful it is for a farmer to split up his land," he said. "A farmer strives to make his estate bigger during his lifetime and hopes to hand it down undivided."

"That was the way it was once," Anselme said. "But today, big families have to give substantial dowries to their daughters."

"I don't disagree, and I don't regret giving Louise all those acres. She appreciates the value of her dowry. And your son will know how to keep the land fruitful. He may not be a farmer, but he will take on someone to care for the land. It needs to be worked. There is nothing worse than letting good land lie fallow."

Anselme saw the vines and mulberry trees as additions to his own assets, even if they were part of the dowry. He couldn't imagine Jean-Christophe acting without his consent. Anselme believed his business would be his own as long as he lived, and even when he retired, Jean-Christophe would follow his directives. That was the price Jean-Christophe paid to be his heir. Jean-Christophe understood, as Sebastien had never understood. His younger son was cut from different cloth.

For two consecutive weekends, Faustine and Sebastien had time to become better acquainted with their brother's future in-laws.

Faustine had already met the Rouvière family and bonded with Vincent, whom she had watched from a distance. He was a little awkward when he was outside his element and much more at ease when he was working with the vines and the animals. But Faustine found him very approachable.

"You never stop working," Faustine said. "In the mountains, you were always running after your sheep. Here, you're a farmer. When do you take time to have a little fun?"

"Fun is for little kids. All the boys my age work. I'm lucky my parents even send me to school."

"Do you have time to do your homework?"

"I do it as soon as I get home. I have to be organized. On a farm, helping your parents is more important than school."

"You're wrong. School is more important than anything else if you want to be educated and intelligent."

"You don't have to go to school to be intelligent."

"I've been going to middle school since September. I'm in sixth grade. What about you?"

This confused Vincent, who didn't know the difference

between primary school and middle school. "I'm in my last year. No, I mean next year is my last year."

"That can't be."

"I mean this year I'll finish the first school, and next year I'll go to, well, middle school, I guess, and that's when I'll prepare my first-level exams."

"Oh, I understand."

Faustine didn't correct Vincent. She had her mother's grace and gentleness, which made her a real princess at eleven. She knew she was beautiful but didn't play on it to get what she wanted. She was quick and intelligent and elegantly attired whenever Vincent saw her.

"If you do well, you could keep going to school after you passed your first-level exams," she said. "Then you could do what my big brother did and go through the end of secondary school."

"What's that?"

"It's a diploma that allows you to get into university."

"Why would I want to do that if I intend to farm, like my dad?"

Faustine didn't know that Vincent was adopted. These days, he never told anyone that he had come from an orphanage.

But one day, Faustine blundered. She told him that he didn't look like anyone else in his family. They had light hair and blue eyes. He had long brown hair, brown eyes, and dark skin.

"I'm a black sheep," he said, poking fun at himself. "Except nobody ever excluded me."

Faustine laughed.

From that day on, the two children shared an understanding that grew every time they saw each other.

Sebastien Rochefort was as taciturn as Faustine was expansive. Elisabeth thought Sebastien was a lot like Elodie and worried that the tiniest thing could put him into a tailspin leading to depression. The fifteen-year-old spent his time daydreaming of faraway places and reading. Jules Verne, Herman Melville, James Fenimore Cooper, and Mark Twain were prominent on his bookshelves, alongside scientific works about expeditions and aviation exploits. His immersion in a fantasy life exasperated his father, who didn't know what to do with him. When the boy did deign to be with his father, he was rebellious and quarrelsome.

"I fear nothing good will become of him," Anselme would say when the boy had angered him yet another time.

Elisabeth was more patient and knew how to handle her son. She wouldn't argue with him, even when he said things that tore her up inside.

"As soon as I can, I'm leaving to live my dream," he had told her just before they departed for Anduze. "I don't care about Dad's factories. I'll gladly give my inheritance to Jean-Christophe. For that matter, I'm against inheritance. It's theft. And family is a prison—a lifetime sentence. Good-bye freedom, good-bye love and adventure. Jean-Christophe is nothing more than a serf. He agreed to marry the Rouvière girl with one goal in mind, making Dad happy. He's just pretending to love Louise. I'm sure of that."

"How can you say such awful things?" Elisabeth asked.

"It's the truth. Father arranged the whole thing with Louise's father. I heard the conversation he had with Jean-Christophe."

"So you're eavesdropping now."

"I didn't need to be sneaky. They were so thrilled with their scheme, they were nearly shouting."

"Sebastien, you're going too far. Fortunately your dad can't hear you. I won't tell him, because if I did, he wouldn't wait until next fall to send you off to the Jesuits."

Elisabeth had said too much. Sebastien didn't know that his father was planning to send him to boarding school in

Avignon. It didn't surprise him. He answered calmly. "If he wants, he can send me in the spring, after my brother's wedding. I'll be out of your hair sooner."

"Sebastien, I won't allow you to talk like that."

"Nobody loves me in this house. Nobody understands me."

"You're wrong there, son. I love you as much as I love your sisters and your brother. A mother doesn't differentiate between her children. Come on, say you're sorry, and we can make up. I've already forgiven you."

Sebastien was clearly sad as he took a step toward his mother. But he resisted the urge to go to her, and Elisabeth didn't insist. She had tears in her eyes.

"Mother . . . "

"Don't say anything, son. I know what you want to tell me. A mother doesn't need to hear her child's words to understand."

"I want to go to Anduze with you and Faustine. May I?"

"I think it would be a good idea for you to get away from your father for a few days. So this conversation has served a purpose."

Sebastien accompanied his mother and sister to Anduze for the final wedding planning. And one day, while he was walking in the vineyards, he met a wild girl with the exotic name of Esmeralda. She would do nothing to bring him back to the family fold.

13

The Big Day

April 1909

More than eighty guests were expected on the wedding day. They were coming from as far away as Lozère, where the Rouvières had family, and Montpellier and Lyon, where the Rocheforts had acquaintances and relatives. People from the countryside—large and small farmers who were friends of Donatien and Constance—and the city—manufacturers, shopkeepers, and elected officials—started arriving early in the morning. Rochefort had invited the prefect, who could not attend but sent his chief of staff in his stead. The bishop of Nîmes could not bless the couple in the Tornac church, but he had sent the parish priest a sermon for the nuptial Mass.

The mayor of Nîmes, Jules Pieyre, did show up for the civil ceremony in the tiny Tornac city hall. That surprised Donatien. He didn't think the socialist would be among Rochefort's friends. When the mayor's car stopped in front of the town hall, Anselme proudly walked over to greet him. Clearly, if the two men had any disagreements, they weren't coming between them on this day.

"Sir, it is a great honor to have you," Anselme said, holding out his hand.

"Please excuse me, my dear Rochefort, for not being able to attend the religious ceremony. Other duties call. But I'm pleased to attend the civil ceremony and want you to know how much I appreciate your contribution to the economic well-being of our community."

Victor, who had joined the winemaker demonstrations in 1907, couldn't help saying something to Cousin Madeleine. "That Rochefort eats out of everyone's hand, doesn't he. Everyone knows he's a right-wing conservative, and there he goes inviting a left-wing mayor to his son's wedding."

"Does that surprise you? Donatien should be the one who's surprised, but ever since Rochefort pulled the wool over his eyes, he's been too subjugated by the man. We should be worried for Louise."

"You don't seem to think much of this marriage."

"It's a marriage without passion. It won't last long."

"What do we know? The two seem to love each other."

"If the son is as calculating as his father, I'm sure Louise will soon be unhappy."

"You're a bird of ill omen. You're going to bring them bad luck if you keep on like that."

The little church in Tornac was stuffed, as Rouvière's neighbors came in droves. The marriage between a farm girl—even a well-off one—and a rich Nîmes businessman didn't happen every day.

The guests waited outside the church at the end of the ceremony. Under a torrent of rice, the newlyweds stepped into a carriage decorated with roses, carnations, and olive branches. Their parents climbed into a second carriage, and

Rochefort himself took the reins. There was a spacious sedan for the children from both families.

Some of Anselme's guests from Nîmes had come by car. The vehicles, lined up in an impromptu caravan, backfired in unison, to the great amusement of the village children who had turned out for the event. It was the first time that so many gasoline-fueled cars had passed through the town. There were a De Dion-Bouton, a Delage, a Lion-Peugeot, and several Renaults, all gleaming with chrome and copper. A 1906 eight-horsepower DFP caught the most attention. It belonged to Elisabeth's brother, André Langlade, who ran the civil engineering company their father had founded. Vincent couldn't resist taking a closer look. André Langlade wasn't smiling behind the wheel. He was worried that a bystander would damage the bright green paint job.

In all his naïveté, Vincent cried out, "She's a beauty, sir."

The businessman relaxed, pleased with the compliment, and asked, "Are you with the wedding party, young man? I believe I saw you in the church with the bride's family."

"She's my sister, sir."

"Well, climb aboard."

Surprised, Vincent looked over his shoulder to make sure the man wasn't talking to anyone else. Behind him, Faustine smiled and said, "Go on. He's my uncle."

"You come too, Faustine. There's room in the back," André Langlade said.

The two children scrambled into the back seat. They were dressed like their elders. In fact, they looked like young newlyweds as they proudly sat behind the driver. Faustine's aunt smiled.

"How charming the two of you look. You make a fine little couple. Is Faustine your partner?"

"Partner?"

"Yes, Auntie, Vincent is my partner," Faustine answered.

Distracted by all the details that needed her attention,

Constance had forgotten to tell her son that the boys would be given partners. She and Elisabeth had paired him with Faustine.

After the traditional photo shoot on the grounds, Anselme wanted to immortalize the festive table that had been set up under the hundred-year-old elm tree. He asked the guests to take their seats, which had been carefully assigned by Elisabeth to keep couples together and everyone else close to friends or family members. The Rouvières found themselves together at one end of the table, while the more numerous Rocheforts and their relatives occupied two-thirds of the space.

The poor photographer didn't know how to orient his bellows. The camera was always missing someone. He finally managed to bring everyone together. Then he ducked his head under the black cloth and looked through his lens. When the scene was in focus, he slipped in a final photographic plate, stepped away from the camera, called the group to order, and took the picture.

"Good," he shouted. "You're free."

"It's about time," Anselme said. He was ready to pour the Champagne.

The bride's father raised his glass and invited the guests to enjoy the festivities.

"Let the party begin," he said, happily.

The dishes started coming out. Constance and Elisabeth had agreed on the menu. After the apple pastries, pears and foie gras, salmon with fresh herbs, and shrimp in a sorrel sauce, the servers—all in red and gold ceremonial dress—came out with the fish: turbot in sauce, grilled bass, and Sétois-style angler fish. Then came the game: venison, hare, and deer, both roasted and stewed. There was something for everyone. Roasted meats followed: filet mignon, tournedos, and leg of lamb. The ladies preferred the salads and vegetables. Constance wanted them to come from her own garden, but it was too early for some vegetables, and Elisabeth insisted on having them delivered from Nîmes.

At about five in the afternoon, when the guests were still enjoying the cheese platters, the wedding cake was brought out. It was four and a half feet high and three feet in diameter. It had ten layers in various flavors. At the top, there was a newlywed couple of sculpted olive wood. Cupids with spread wings surrounded the bride and groom.

With the wine and spirits flowing, the men had unbuttoned their collars and jackets. Some were talking loudly, while others were nodding off in their chairs. Some had slipped away to nap under the trees.

Anselme had moved closer to Donatien. The two fathers-in-law weren't hiding their joy on this blessed day. Their wives were already talking about baby clothes.

"Pink for a girl, right?" Elisabeth said. "And blue for a boy, of course."

"Pink and blue," Constance said. "How predictable."

"Yes, but other colors would be in bad taste."

Once again, Constance decided there was no point in disagreeing. She did make it clear, though, that she and Madeleine intended to make at least some of the clothes. "Both of us knit. So we'll make wool hats, slippers, and little undershirts. Of course, we'll buy the other clothes."

Elisabeth nodded, not bothering to contradict the plans. She didn't want to mar the happiness she and Constance were sharing in the prospect of being grandmothers.

The Rouvière and Rochefort children were still at the table. Vincent and Faustine had spent the whole meal talking, but Sebastien hadn't said a word to his partner, Julie. The Rouvière girl was talking to the boy to her right, Antonin Porte, the teacher's son.

At dusk, the servants lit torches on the lawn and along the drive. They lent a touch of magic to the balmy evening.

Musicians set up their instruments on the steps of the house and started playing a Viennese waltz. The guests stood up and gathered around the newlyweds. After the couple had waltzed, Constance and Anselme and Elisabeth and Donatien joined in. Then the other guests started dancing, as the elderly watched from the veranda.

The party was at its height, but Sebastien was bored to death. He stood up and slipped away from the crowd. Nobody noticed. The young Rochefort had just spotted Esmeralda crouching behind a bush.

Sebastien was attracted to this girl, who lived in an old shepherd's hut with a mother who called herself a witch. Esmeralda said her father was an Italian sailor who had met her mother when she was only fifteen. Esmeralda's grandparents had kicked their daughter out when she became pregnant. She had wandered from place to place before finally settling in Anduze. Now mother and daughter lived by plundering, gathering, and poaching. To others, it seemed like a hardscrabble life. To Sebastien, it seemed wild and free.

Esmeralda didn't have any friends, but she didn't harbor any rancor about that. Everyone knew this girl with black hair down to her waist, a torn but colorful dress, and bare feet was the witch's daughter. No one paid attention to her. If someone did, she instinctively understood how to avoid confrontation. When she saw Sebastien, however, Esmeralda didn't try to slip away. He intrigued her.

Slowly, the two young people got to know each other. Sebastien had no preconceived ideas, and Esmeralda let go of her initial fears. She was bursting with happiness at the idea of being treated like anyone else. He was thrilled to meet a girl who lived outside the established order. She represented freedom, travel, and faraway countries. That was what he saw in her laughing eyes, what he felt when he breathed her intoxicating aroma.

The night of the reception, the music and hubbub had

attracted Esmeralda, who dared to approach in the hope of seeing her new—and only—friend. She didn't need to do anything to get his attention. He immediately recognized her scent. He caught the silvery shine of her eyes in the bushes and the warmth of her coppery skin illuminated by the flames of the torches. He rose from the table with a mix of determination and discretion and went off to join Esmeralda, whose heart was already pounding with joy.

Without looking back, the two teenagers left the party, the noise, and the torchlight and walked into the darkness of the woods, with only the moon as their witness.

At around eleven that night, the newlyweds disappeared. They were spending their wedding night in a suite at the luxurious Hôtel du Prieuré, not far from Nîmes. Anselme had insisted that the couple spend a few days there before their honeymoon in Venice.

"All expenses on me, of course," he had said.

By staying in the luxury suite, the couple would be able to avoid the traditional garlic soup and olive oil when they awoke on the first day of their marriage. They would also avoid the customary teasing.

"Such customs are vulgar. I hope you agree, Constance," Elisabeth had said the day before the ceremony.

The Rouvières did not want their daughter to be embarrassed by any teasing. And the soup wasn't all that important. So once again, they went along with the Rocheforts.

At about midnight, when all the guests had left, the two families found themselves in front of the Clos du Tournel. The Rouvières were getting ready to return to La Fenouillère, when Elodie Rochefort, breaking her customary silence, called attention to Sebastien's absence.

Everyone stopped talking and looked at each other,

incredulous. Amid the festivities, nobody had missed the young Rochefort.

Elisabeth was the first to react. "Where could he have gone?"

"I saw him get up from the table," Julie Rouvière said. "I thought he was going . . . Well, you know."

Anselme was blunt. "You thought he was going to take a piss."

"Well, yes. But I didn't see him come back."

"You should have said something sooner."

"But it was a party. I was having fun with Antonin, Aline, and Vincent. I thought he was probably with some other people."

Constance tried to reassure Elisabeth, while Anselme scowled. "That rascal has done it again. The day his brother gets married, he has to draw the attention to himself."

"What can we do now?" Donatien said. "It's the middle of the night." Anselme was pacing. "Let's go inside. The party is over."

The servants were putting out the torches and taking the remains of the meal back to the kitchen. In the background, Vincent and Faustine were the only ones who didn't seem worried. That was because the two of them had seen Sebastien leave with Esmeralda. They didn't intend to tell their parents. The two children were too young to fully comprehend the complicity they shared or their affinity for each other. They just knew they liked being together.

"I like your brother," Vincent said not long after Sebastien had gone off. "I didn't talk to him much tonight, but I know he's different from the others."

"My brother refuses everything my father wants to impose on him. He's determined to be free and live the way he wants. He's a dreamer."

"I'd like to get to know him better."

When the young Rochefort had left the table to join Esmeralda, he had winked at Vincent and put a finger up to his lips. Vincent had given Faustine a questioning look, and the girl's smile had said, *I didn't see anything.*

"Don't worry," she told her brother. "We won't say anything."

Anselme was like a caged lion. "If he's not back by dawn, we'll scour the area. I want to find him before the police do. The shame he would bring us if they brought him back like a thief. The brat will get what's coming to him. I'm sending him to the Jesuits next week. At least there, he won't be able to misbehave behind our backs. They'll straighten him out."

"Let's not spoil our happiness just yet," Elisabeth said. "I'm sure Sebastien is not very far off. He probably wanted to get away from the noise, and maybe he fell asleep in one of the huts in the vineyards. You know he's a little wild. The night cold will bring him back before dawn."

Elisabeth was trying to calm her husband, but she herself didn't believe what she was telling him. She was worried, as well, because she knew her son was capable of almost anything.

The men didn't need to scour the hills. At about three in the morning, Sebastien came back on his own, surprised to find that the party was over. He had attended several wedding other celebrations with his family, and they had all ended at dawn. He didn't think he'd be missed.

His father was waiting for him when he tiptoed into the house. Anselme gave him no time to explain. "Go to your room. We'll discuss this in the morning."

At eight in the morning, Donatien and Constance stopped by for news. They found the Rocheforts reassured, but Anselme was far from happy.

"Everything is fine. Sebastien came home on his own,"

Anselme said, inviting the Rouvières and their relatives to join them for leftovers at noon.

"Yesterday was the union of the newlyweds," he said, taking Donatien by the shoulders. "Today, it's the alliance of our two families that we are going to celebrate.

Part Two

ILLUSIONS

14

A New Start

Nîmes, summer 1909

Anselme Rochefort was delighted. Everything seemed to be going well. His alliance with the Rouvière family had strengthened and enhanced his position in the silk business. In fact, the mulberry trees that Louise had brought into the marriage had allowed him to double his silkworm production. Freeing himself from his outside suppliers gave him a major advantage over his competitors. He told his biggest customers that he would soon be supplying higher-quality products at a lower price.

He told his sales representatives to stress that all of his silk was from the Cevennes. "Emphasize that our silkworms are carefully selected and come exclusively from our own farms. It's a guarantee of quality. My competitors are importing more and more cocoons from Turkey and the Middle East. I want to play the made-in-France card."

And he had not forgotten about his denim. "The new

decade, a new beginning," he told Jean-Christophe. "We'll work on growing our denim exports across the Atlantic. I plan to hand the American side of our business over to you. You'll have carte blanche."

Jean-Christophe had finally agreed to give up his job as a lawyer to focus entirely on his father's business. He was aware that he was the only son who would do so in the near future—or in the long-term future. Sebastien hadn't shown any signs of wanting to join the business. And the older he got, the more hostile to the idea he appeared to be.

"In business, the sharks greedily feast on the backs of the workers," Sebastien liked to say to shock those around him. "I'll never be one of those sharks."

"You renounce your background, yet you have no problem living in luxury," Jean-Christophe said to him one day.

"What else can I do at my age? As soon as I can, I'll live my own life."

"So you would reject your family?"

"I didn't say that. I'm not rejecting my family. I just want to live my life as I choose. That's what Father did."

"You are wrong there. Father took over the family business because his father asked him to. He considered it his duty."

"I don't have the same sense of duty."

Jean-Christophe knew he would never get his brother to change his mind. He was too determined, and their father's decision to send him to school with the Jesuits just intensified his anger.

"Father thinks I'm a renegade. He'll end up banishing me from his house."

"You're both stubborn, but you are his son, and you should make an effort."

"He is my father. He could try to understand me."

When Jean-Christophe left for the United States in July, Anselme had already enrolled Sebastien in the Jesuit school in Avignon. Lycée Saint Joseph, founded in 1850, had a fine reputation. Anselme thought the school would give his son needed boundaries, and the distance from the family would be beneficial. In boarding school, Sebastien wouldn't be influenced by pernicious ideas from the outside world. And the strict Christian education would get him back on the right track.

During summer vacation, he asked his staff manager, Norbert Lesage, to find Sebastien a job in one of the factories. "He's always standing up for the workers. He'll be able to find out what their lives are really like."

"Do you want him to work on the machines, sir?"

"Absolutely, as an apprentice. That will teach him about life, which is what he wants."

Sebastien didn't rebel. He started his summer job without flinching, as though it were an experience that might be useful to him later, in the life he intended to lead.

Lesage assigned him first to cotton winding, where workers prepared the weft and warp threads for the looms. He got his first taste of the working world, where laborers toiled in noise, smells, and an oppressive lack of privacy under the watchful eye of a caustic foreman who was ready to reprimand and demand more. Punishment came at the first weakness. Pity the person who slowed down, showed up late, or was caught chatting. Under these conditions, the day seemed endless, ten hours with no rest other than thirty minutes for lunch. Breaks were rare and short. At the end of the day, the workers were too exhausted to even talk among themselves. They left the factory when the shrill siren rang out and went home without even changing.

This quickly confirmed Sebastien's opinion of working conditions. Despite the passage of laws that shortened the workday and gave laborers some time off, conditions remained deplorable. And Sebastien didn't even know how paltry the wages were.

During his second month, Sebastien was sent to the actual weaving facility. The atmosphere was much the same, although the machines were different, and there were more male workers. The Jacquard looms made a loud clacking that he became used to after a few days. Even then, however, it was necessary to shout to be heard above the noise. A number of apprentices, who were all younger than he was, helped the beamers prepare the warp for weaving, a long and meticulous job that required a lot of know-how. Others took care of the shuttles, which they filled with spools of thread. Most worked barefoot, their shirts unbuttoned and their sleeves and pant legs rolled up, because the summer heat was suffocating. They would climb onto the machines to reach what they needed, often risking their safety.

"That's dangerous," Sebastien yelled when he saw a boy climbing atop a machine the first time.

"That's for sure," the foreman in charge of the apprentices said. "When you do it, follow the instructions you're given. It's easy to have an accident. You're the boss's son. It'll be on me if something happens."

Amédée Duruy didn't know why he had been made responsible for Sebastien. Nor did he understand why Sebastien was working in this place. Perhaps Anselme Rochefort wanted his son to become familiar with the manufacturing processes. "But your older brother, Mr. Jean-Christophe, never worked in the factories, and that's not keeping him from helping your dad. Did you ask to come here?"

Sebastien hesitated, smiled, and decided on a straightforward response.

"I totally disagree with my father about everything. I'm not at all interested in his factories."

"So why are you here, if I may ask?"

"My father hopes to bend me to his will. But nothing in the world will get me to live my brother's life."

"What do you mean?"

"He gave up everything: his career and his love life. He stopped being a lawyer after many years of study. And he agreed to a marriage that our father arranged from top to bottom. She's a farm girl, and that speaks in her favor, really. But I can't condone what our father did and what my brother agreed to."

"Don't tell me any more, boy. Your family stories are none of my business. You father is my boss, and I respect him. I don't want him to think I tried to wheedle information out of you."

"You're afraid of him, aren't you? Just like the others. That's no way to improve your conditions. You will always be exploited."

"That's a funny way for the boss's son to talk."

The foreman thought Sebastien was a tad rebellious, but he was starting to like him. *He has character*, the man thought as he took him to his new work station.

"I'll put you in Albert's hands. He's our best weaver. With him, you will learn all about producing serge. You see those large rolls of fabric at the back of the facility? They are ready for shipping."

He turned to the weaver and said, "Albert, this is Sebastien Rochefort. He's the boss's second son. His father sent him here to do an apprenticeship. Show him the job. He'll be with us until the end of September."

Intimidated, Albert Laporte brushed a lock of hair off his forehead, wiped his hands on his apron, and said, "Um, hello, young man. I'll do what I can to be worthy of the task and helpful to you." He was already fretting that his boss would come down on him if he made even the smallest mistake with the boy.

"You don't have to be so formal with me. I'm not my father's son here. I'm just an apprentice."

"I'm good at my job, but I'm not used to talking to people of your rank," the worker said, as if apologizing in advance. "I'm used to training apprentices from my own class."

"You don't have to be afraid of me. I will never be your boss, and you might as well know that right away. I won't be reporting back to my father. What we talk about stays between us."

The worker, still feeling uncomfortable, decided to show him around the facility before giving him his first task.

"Weaving has several very precise phases, and the most important one is winding, which you've already learned. Then comes warping, which consists of preparing the warps on the loom and threading the heddles and sleying the reed. Let me show you."

Sebastien was all ears. He had no intention of joining his father at the factory, but he was very interested in what the workers did.

"What are warp threads?" he asked.

"They are the base of the fabric, parallel threads that run lengthwise. They are prepared on the loom, which is what's right in front of you. The beamer has the longest and most delicate job, and he is responsible for the quality of the fabric. The warp threads need to be the same tightness and precisely parallel. That's why this work is so meticulous."

Sebastien took it all in. As he listed to the master weaver, he watched the others work. They were taking no notice of him. They had probably been told that the boss's son would be working with them and they should be cautious around him. Sebastien made a mental note to tell them he was on their side.

For his part, Albert Laporte was beginning to relax a bit and becoming more comfortable in his role as teacher. "To make cloth, you need to crisscross the rows of thread. You know what the first threads are?"

"Yes, the warp threads."

"I see you learn fast. The second are the weft. Look at this loom. The threads running across the width—the ones crossing the warp threads—are the weft threads. To cross the warp, you lift every other thread. This creates what we call the shed. The shed is the space between the upper and the lower warp threads. Then you run the fly shuttle that holds the weft thread through the shed. Are you following me?"

Sebastien didn't dare tell him that it was all too complicated. He just said that such expertise deserved better pay. Albert Laporte didn't respond to that but seemed surprised.

"Did you know that these looms are Jacquard looms? They're named after their inventor, Joseph Marie Jacquard from Lyon."

"Um, yes, I do know. My father always boasts that his Jacquard looms are more modern than what his competitors have."

In any case, since he put electricity in the workshops, our yield is greater, and our working conditions are better. It was really hard with the steam machines."

"Don't you think it still is?"

"True enough. Just between us, it's much more pleasant in one of the front offices."

"The noise is aggravating."

"The noise is bothersome. That's true. And after a while, it affects your hearing. The guys in Lyon call the Jacquard looms *bistanclaque-pan*."

"What a weird name!"

"It's a combination of the four sounds you hear when the loom's working. Listen. It goes 'bis' when the warp threads are opened up to make room for the shuttle, 'tan' when the sley is pushed, 'claque' when the shuttle goes through and hits the edge, and then 'pan,' to finish, when the sley hits the final warp."

"It's an onomatopoeia," Sebastien said.

Albert stared at him, then said, "An uno . . . Well, sure, you must be right. One last thing: Your father makes mostly a kind of serge called denim. You must know what that is, right?"

"Not exactly," Sebastien said. "I know the name, but to

tell the truth, I don't know exactly how it's different from any other fabric."

"Serge is a twill—or diagonal—weave. Here, let me show you a piece of cloth."

Sebastien followed the man to the back of the workshop. On the way, people greeted him with deference.

"Do they know who I am?"

"Word gets around quickly. But after I talk to them, they'll treat you like you belong here."

"I would prefer it that way. Is it this blue fabric over here?" Sebastien asked, pointing at a roll of denim.

"Exactly. This denim is Rochefort Industries' special fabric. But I'm sure you know that."

"All too well! That's why my brother went to the United States."

"This cotton fabric has a white warp and a blue weft. On one side, you see the blue weft, and on the other, you see the white warp. It's used to make work pants and not so long ago to make—"

"Yes, that I know," Sebastien interrupted. "Sails for ships and tarps for wagons."

"Exactly, boy. But that fabric was rougher and less supple. Weavers here in Nîmes improved on the quality. That's what people say. And as a result, the fabric was adopted by the clothing industry."

"Thanks to Levi Strauss in the United States. I know that, too."

Albert was becoming acquainted with his apprentice. He wound up giving him a simple warping task.

"You need to start at the beginning. I'll show you how."

And together, they went to work.

Sebastien seemed to forget that his father had sent him to the factory to mend his ways. Deep down, he wanted one thing: to bear witness someday to what he had experienced working alongside these people. He swore that he would defend workers such as these when he was able to make his own life for himself.

So Jean-Christophe left Louise with his mother, barely three months after they were married.

 Before leaving, he had taken her to Venice, as his father had pompously told her father. The bride had spent her honeymoon in heaven. Jean-Christophe proved to be as gallant and kind as he was eager. On their first night, they frolicked until dawn and then they spent four idyllic weeks in the Italian city. Between gondola rides, candlelight dinners overlooking Saint Mark's Square, romantic escapades to the Laguna Islands, and sunsets over the Grand Canal, Louise couldn't fathom that her dream would end. At her side, Jean-Christophe found that his wife's beauty heightened his desire, and he hid his calculating self-interest so well, he got caught up in his own game. He nearly forgot his promise to go to the United States, and would have gladly stayed on, playing a temporarily faithful Casanova to his bride.

But when they returned to Nîmes in mid-May, he told Louise that he had to go to the United States for business.

She was thrilled. "Another trip! You didn't tell me," she said, impatient to know more.

"It's a business trip, not a lovers' trip. I'm going alone this time. I'm so sorry."

"You're leaving me already!"

"Not immediately. In July. Before I go, we'll have time to finish the apartment my father prepared for us on the second floor. The contractors will be done at the beginning of June. I won't leave until you are completely settled in with our furniture."

Louise's expression darkened. The thought of being left behind saddened her. "You knew you would be leaving even before we got married, didn't you?"

Jean-Christophe didn't hesitate before answering. "Yes, my father asked me to go. It was planned."

"Why didn't you tell me?"

"I didn't want to ruin our honeymoon, darling."

With her husband gone, Louise filled her time putting the finishing touches on the apartment. Elisabeth introduced her to the city's best decorator, who helped her choose the wall hangings and curtains, the tapestries to decorate the walls, the rugs to cover the wood floors, and even a few paintings by some well-known regional artists, which were sure to impress guests at the receptions they would have in the future.

"But it will all cost a fortune," Louise said, unaccustomed to such sumptuous spending.

"Don't worry about that, my dear. I just want you to be happy. I want you to feel at home here, the same way you felt at home at La Fenouillère," Elisabeth said to reassure her.

"At my parent's farm, I was not used to living in such luxury."

"That is true, child. But I hope that won't keep you from feeling comfortable in this apartment now that it belongs to you and your husband. You became a Rochefort the moment you were married. You need to get used to living in comfort. It reflects your husband's position in society. And his position is yours by the very fact that you are Jean-Christophe's wife."

As kind as she was, Elisabeth was always grandiloquent when she talked to her daughter-in-law. Elisabeth's advice and recommendations concerning her elevated station in life never seemed to end. Soon, the bride felt the constraints inherent in her new position weighing her down.

Alone in her room at night, Louise would sit on the edge of her large four-poster bed with its finely embroidered cover. Her life felt superficial, far removed the real life she had led before meeting Jean-Christophe. His absence only exacerbated her feelings of frustration. She spent her days with her mother-in-law, focused on fashion, charity work, and society receptions. *If Daddy saw me living this way, what would he think?* she asked herself. *Would he regret urging me to marry Jean-Christophe?*

As the weeks passed, Louise grew sullen. The gloominess showed in her eyes. Her lack of enthusiasm began to worry Elisabeth, who thought she was depressed over Jean-Christophe's absence. To compensate, she started taking her daughter-in-law wherever she went. She had no idea that the more she sweetened the world around Louise, the greater the bride's disenchantment became.

Louise ate with her in-laws. Anselme didn't seem to notice his daughter-in-law's morose mood. "Our business is booming in America," he announced one night, two months after Jean-Christophe's departure. "Jean-Christophe sent a telegram saying he got some big contracts with Levi's and Henry Lee. We're a year out on our orders."

Surprised, Louise dared to interrupt. "You've heard from Jean-Christophe?"

"Of course. He sends me a telegram every week to keep me up to date. Modern communications are wonderful. It takes two weeks for a letter to arrive from the United States."

"So I should have received at least three or four letters by now," Louise said, mortified.

Elisabeth was shocked. "Do you mean Jean-Christophe hasn't written to you, child?"

"Not even once, Mother."

"His letters must have gotten lost. There's no other explanation."

At the other end of the table, Sebastien was squirming in his chair, dying to give his opinion. "Jean-Christophe has other fish to fry," he ended up saying.

"What do you mean?" Anselme lashed out.

"Oh, nothing."

"So shut up if you have nothing to say. Besides, nobody asked your opinion."

A cold silence fell on the table.

Anselme spoke again. "I don't want to disappoint you, my dear daughter-in-law, but since Jean-Christophe is doing such excellent work in San Francisco, I asked him to prolong his stay for another three months to open branches of our company in California and New York. They will make it easier for us to do business with the Americans."

"Another three months!" Louise couldn't hold her tears back. "You make these decisions as if Jean-Christophe were still single. But he's a married man now."

"My dear, you'll have to get used to the idea that you and your husband will not be spending all your time together the way your parents do. They work the land. The Rocheforts are entrepreneurs, not farmers. Now you know. Your role is to respect your husband and honor him with your presence when it's useful to him."

"Anselme, please," Elisabeth said, clearly embarrassed by this turn in the conversation.

Elodie and Faustine were silent, but their eyes showed sympathy for their sister-in-law. Elodie was as white as a sheet and asked to be excused.

"Go on, my dear," Elisabeth told Elodie before turning to her husband. "Once again, you've upset the girl with your tone. You know how fragile she is."

"Stop treating her like a child," Anselme said. "You forget that she is twenty-two."

"Our quarreling is too much for her. She can't handle it."

Faustine stood up and walked over to Louise to console her.

"I like you, Louise," she whispered in her sister-in-law's ear. "Vincent did nothing but praise you during the wedding reception. My brother is very busy, but as soon as he can, he'll write to you."

"Stop, Faustine," Anselme said, his face turning red. "Go sit down. Don't meddle in adult business."

Faustine looked contrite and did as she was told.

"Nobody can say anything in this house," Sebastien said, looking straight into his father's eyes.

"That's enough," Anselme shouted, slamming his fist on the table. "Children, go to your rooms. As for you, Louise, I would like you to keep your feelings to yourself from now on, and don't go on in front of everyone else. Maintain your composure."

Louise wiped her eyes, pushed her chair back, and, without a word, went to her apartment.

That night, she understood that her honeymoon in Venice had been a dream, and a much less romantic life lay ahead of her.

15

Uncertainty

Tornac/Anduze, fall 1909

Nobody had been hired to do the jobs Louise had handled at La Fenouillère. It was time for Julie to leave school and take over those responsibilities. But Julie, who was now fourteen, balked at the idea of quitting school to work full time with her parents. As he had with Louise, Donatien had allowed Julie to stay in school two extra years. He didn't think it was necessary to educate his girls any more than that. The principal had protested. He was always disappointed to lose a good student. But in the countryside, the habit of putting children to work was still deeply rooted, even among those with means. And most of the time, the boys stayed longer than the girls.

"My girls stay in school until they're fourteen," Donatien said. "They know enough to get by in life and do what they're destined to do. Look at Louise. She married well and lives like a lady. Going to school any longer wouldn't have done her any good."

Roland Porte argued with all his heart. He thought Julie would make an excellent teacher. As far as he was concerned, teaching was a noble goal for a farm girl.

"One achieves true happiness and self-esteem by working toward worthy goals, such as getting an education and finding a decent profession," he had told Donatien. "An alliance with a wealthy family does not ensure a satisfying and enriching life."

He got nowhere with Donatien. But from that day on, Donatien felt bad. Was his friend the teacher criticizing him for having married off his daughter to an upper-class family? He didn't want to argue, so he said nothing. At the hunt the following Sunday, the two men barely spoke to each other.

Unlike Julie, who had been forced to quit school, Vincent couldn't wait to get back home when classes were over. Once his homework was done, he rushed out to relieve Julie. It was the end of the grape harvest. The poor girl, who was picking from morning till night for the first time, couldn't hide her fatigue when the last basket of grapes was taken to the cellar.

Her back was stooped, and her neck was stiff. Her fingers hurt from cutting grapes for eight hours. She didn't hide her disappointment when, not long after she got back to the house, her mother called her to help prepare the evening meal for the workers.

Julie had hoped to escape her lot as a farm girl. She had dreamed of continuing her studies so that she could take the entrance examination for the teachers school. Both Miss Bernard and Roland Porte had encouraged her. She was embittered over her father's refusal to consider the idea.

Donation scolded her over her lack of motivation during the harvest. "Julie, I'd like you to show more enthusiasm. The head cutter in your group complained about you. You're always the last to finish your row. You slow down the whole team."

"Why don't you ask Louise to come help us?" she answered, a dark look in her eyes.

Louise had come back to spend a few days at La Fenouillère while waiting for her husband to return. Neither Constance nor Donatien had dared to ask her to help in the vineyards. The elegant dresses she wore made her unrecognizable to those who were more used to seeing her in work clothes.

"Louise is a city lady now," Donatien responded. "We're not going to ask her to mix with harvesters and dirty her hands. Besides, she doesn't have the right clothes."

"If that's all that's keeping her from giving us a hand, Mom still has her old clothes."

"That's enough, Julie," Constance said. "You're being rude to your father and envious of your sister. That's not good behavior or a pretty sight."

Vincent helped Julie set the table and then slipped away to talk to Louise in her room.

Early the next morning, Louise, in her old farm clothes, arrived in the kitchen, ready to start picking grapes.

"What are you doing here?" Constance asked.

"I'm going to harvest with you. I still know how to pick grapes, you know."

Standing at the stove, cousin Madeleine smiled. The night before, she had seen Vincent go talk to Louise and had heard what he said. He's a good boy, she thought. He's got a good heart.

With her husband gone and nothing meaningful to do, Louise missed her family and the life outdoors she was used to. She had no interest in her mother-in-law's artificial society activities.

"I feel like it's all pomp," she told her mother. "I just . . . I just feel like . . ."

"You feel like you're not yourself anymore," Madeleine blurted out.

"Yes, the life there feels so false. I don't do anything interesting with my days. But more than that, the atmosphere is uncomfortable. Mealtimes are deadly, especially since Sebastien left for Avignon. Elodie walls herself up in her room and doesn't come to most meals. Faustine isn't allowed to talk because she's too young. I can't wait until Jean-Christophe comes back to free me."

Constance didn't know what to say to her daughter. She was beginning to feel guilty over pushing her into Rochefort's arms at Donatien's urging.

"I knew it," Madeleine said. "I said as much to Victor."

"What did you say?" Constance asked.

"No, nothing. Forget it."

"Go on, explain yourself. Tell me."

Madeleine hesitated to say anything in front of Louise. "I just said that I didn't see anything good coming from this marriage."

"But I love Jean-Christophe!" Louise protested. "And he loves me. Everything will be fine again as soon as he gets back. Don't worry, Mom. I was wrong to say anything."

Louise didn't express her unhappiness again for the rest of her stay. But Constance knew that a crack had already appeared in the fine family structure that they had supposedly built with the Rocheforts.

From the end of September until the end of December, Sebastien had lived away from his family for the first time in his short life. Unlike Louise, he didn't feel especially bad about that. Boarding school freed him from his father's oppressive authority. And the Jesuits didn't keep him from dreaming about the life he wanted to lead. Locked up in this closed world, he felt free to envision his life.

Like his apprenticeship in the factory, this banishment to the boarding school wasn't a hardship. It was an adventure that would serve him well one day. He considered it an experience that would toughen him up. As time went on, Sebastien became stronger and better prepared to face the obstacles that his adult life would hold for him.

Sebastien wasn't among the best students, but he did quite well, nonetheless, except in mathematics, a subject he considered too abstract and removed from reality. He didn't put much effort into it. Nor was he wasn't interested in major thinkers, such as Plato, Descartes, Rousseau, and Saint-Simon. They were too old-fashioned and out of touch, he said with conviction. The works of Saint Augustine were part of the curriculum, and it bored Sebastien so much, he had a schoolmate, Alexandre Legendre, write his essays for him. He paid him from the small allowance that his mother sent without her husband's knowledge.

He preferred literature and history. And on the sly, he found an upper-class student who was responsible for the library and could slip him books by Proudhon, Marx, and Louis Blanc, along with novels by Emile Zola, which he thought were more representative of the struggles of the working class. The books were kept under lock and key, as the Jesuits considered them too subversive for the young minds they were conditioning. That made Sebastien enjoy them even more.

When he arrived at Lycée Saint Joseph, he was quick to make friends with Alexandre Legendre, whose family had sent him to the Jesuits before leaving for Tahiti.

"We'll get settled in, and we'll send for you," they had told him. Two years had passed since then. Six or so letters, each of which arrived two months after it was sent, were all he had to show for his wait. And there was no spending money in any of the envelopes. Sebastien's arrival was a breath of fresh air in a suffocating life.

Together, they built castles in the sky and imagined their great escape. With Sebastien, everything seem possible to Alexandre. The horizon wasn't so dark anymore. It was filled with the light of a faraway island, where he saw himself showing up one day to surprise his parents.

"All we have to do is get to Marseille," Sebastien said one night after lights out. "We'll catch a cargo ship headed for the Pacific. Or maybe we'll take off for America. Once we get there, it will be easy to go farther. Nobody will find us."

"Do you think it's really possible?"

"At our age, we could get hired on as ship's boys."

"When could we leave?"

"In the spring. Between now and then, I'll weasel some money out of my mother. It'll be warmer, so we'll be able to sleep outside on the way to Marseille. And we'll have time to prepare: to get clothes, food, maps, and a compass—everything we'll need to survive. Then we'll just wait."

Sebastien was losing his sense of reality and was dragging his friend into his dreams of freedom. He already saw himself conquering the world and fighting poverty and everyone exploiting humanity. He had ambitions of becoming a great reporter.

"I'll be like Zola. I'll write exposés!"

"You'll be prosecuted."

"So what? When you defend a fair cause, the truth will ultimately triumph. I will write books, too, to educate people and open their eyes."

"Why don't you go into politics?"

"Politicians are too far removed from everyday life. They don't really know the working class. I want to stand beside those who suffer and be their spokesman. I'll do so by writing."

"Will your father let you do whatever you want?"

"If I ask him, no. That is why we need to get out of here, Alex. You want to find you parents, and I want to find my freedom."

When the holiday season arrived, the Rochefort family descended on the Clos du Tournel—in two brand-new four-cylinder Ford Model Ts. Anselme had bought the splendid cars to celebrate Jean-Christophe's glorious return at the end of November. He insisted on driving through Anduze rather than around it. Anselme was behind the wheel of the first car, proud as a peacock. Jean-Christophe was no less arrogant behind the wheel of the second vehicle. Louise sat at his right and felt uncomfortable parading through town as its residents gathered on the sidewalks to stare at the display of wealth. She was afraid they would see someone she knew.

"You're not saying anything, my dear!" Jean-Christophe sounded surprised. "You haven't said a word since we left. What's the matter? Aren't you happy to spend the holidays in Anduze? You'll be seeing your parents. You should rejoice."

In the backseat, Sebastien, who was home for his one-week Christmas vacation, and Faustine didn't seem to be enjoying the family's arrival either. Sebastien spoke for Louise. "We could have been more discreet. Father keeps honking so everyone will notice us."

"What's wrong with that? We're happy to be here. We want to share our joy with others. Isn't that right, Louise?"

The bride said nothing. The speed, the noise, and the gas fumes had made her sick all the way from Nîmes. And even though the top was up, and she was wrapped in a warm blanket, she was frozen stiff.

"I can't wait to get there," she finally said. "It's freezing in this car. And I'm not feeling very well."

"Don't tell me you're already pregnant," Jean-Christophe said, paying no attention to Faustine and Sebastien.

"Jean-Christophe! Please!" she said.

Jean-Christophe had lost the fine and elegant manners that had won Louise over during their courtship and had seduced her in Venice. He had become aggressive, haughty, and even disdainful. She didn't find him eager to please her anymore, or gallant, or thoughtful. He had changed in America. And the change had made him less likeable.

For the past month, she had been hoping to find in her husband the man she had met a year before, at the end of the grape harvest. But instead, she had met with repeated disappointment.

Whenever Faustine could escape from her parents' watch, she went looking for Vincent. She knew he would be somewhere on the land at La Fenouillère, not far from the acreage her father leased to a farmer named Auguste Mazel. Mazel took care of the vineyards and the mulberry trees given to Louise and Jean-Christophe on their wedding. He also looked after the Clos du Tournel when the family was gone. He would open the windows regularly to air out the house and prepare the fireplaces when Anselme announced that his family was coming. Donatien said that Anselme exploited the poor Mazel. But he was childless widower and never rebelled. He had originally been taken on as a sharecropper, and he never found the courage to ask for more, despite his ever increasing responsibilities.

Seeing the little Rochefort girl running toward him filled Mazel's heart with joy. She was a ray of sunlight in his gray life.

"Hello, pretty one," he would say every time he saw her. "You've grown so much. You're a real young lady now."

Faustine liked the old man. He was fifty-five and seemed to be in the twilight of his life already. Her whole life, she had treated him like the cherished country grandfather she never had. She enjoyed his company and his stories, especially the terrifying fairy tales kept alive by the old-timers.

Today, however, she wasn't rushing toward him. She didn't even seem to notice him as she ran across the fields. Where was she headed so fast? He called after her, but his voice didn't carry far enough. Faustine disappeared on the other side of the vineyard, like a butterfly spreading its wings in the bright sunlight.

"She must have someone important to meet to ignore me like that," he said aloud.

Faustine was heading toward the stone shepherd's hut, where she had started meeting Vincent when they wanted to be alone. For them, hiding from their parents in this secret place was a game that made them accomplices in a part of their lives that belonged only to them. All they did was talk, share stories, and fantasize. Sometimes Vincent lit a fire against the stone wall. He used vine shoots and dry kindling and would grill chestnuts he'd slipped out of the house. He'd also offer his friend a little grape must, a sweet juice from the first days of the harvest.

She waited, sure that he would come. Vincent knew that the Rocheforts had arrived at the Clos du Tournel. So he would join her when his work was finished, before nighttime blanketed the hills.

It didn't take him long. Saying he needed to bring the sheep in from the hills on the other side of the estate, he had left Victor to work on the hedges and had headed straight to the hut where Faustine was waiting. When she saw him at the other end of the vineyard, she ran toward him, dirtying her leather boots and the bottom of her dress. They fell into each other's arms, glowing with happiness. Then they walked hand in hand to the lair of their nascent love.

They were still only children. Their feelings were as pure and untainted as an azure sky following a triumphant dawn. Their gestures were naïve. But what they felt together didn't need to be expressed. They understood each other without saying a thing. They read in each other's eyes the words that neither dared to speak. It was their way of loving. They were not yet prisoners of their bodies, and simply being together was enough.

Faustine slipped away from her parents every day to meet Vincent. A joyful expectancy blossomed inside the two of them, the beginnings of great happiness, the kind that made pure-hearted children passionate beings.

And while Faustine took flight with Vincent, Sebastien just as discreetly met with the one who represented freedom to him: Esmeralda.

16

Problem Children

1910

Elodie was the Rochefort child who worried Elisabeth the most.

The young woman *would* soon be twenty-three but was so thin and pale, she looked like a waiflike adolescent who refused to grow up. Her tiny appetite concerned Elisabeth, who didn't know exactly which saint to pray to. Saint Clement, a patron saint for sick children? Saint Bartholomew the Apostle, for nervous diseases? Perhaps even Saint Jude, the patron saint for desperate causes? Elisabeth was not blind. She was aware that her daughter would slip away and throw up in secret.

The family doctor, Dr. Blanchard, had made the diagnosis. "Your daughter has anorexia, Mrs. Rochefort. It is a very serious illness. According to Dr. Charles Lasègue, it's in the mind."

"Do you mean to say that my daughter is—"

"No, let me stop you there, Mrs. Rochefort. Your daughter is not crazy. Anorexia is not a mental illness per se. But we need to look for the cause in the person's mind. The lack of appetite is the consequence of a trouble that goes deeper and is nestled in an individual's thoughts. Unfortunately, medicine still has a lot of progress to make in this area."

Elisabeth felt that the root of her daughter's problem was Catherine's death. But she didn't understand why Elodie was still so troubled. "Catherine's death was a great shock for Elodie," she told the doctor. "But she was just eleven at the time, and it's been twelve years now. She should have gotten over it."

"I've been caring for your family for a long time, Mrs. Rochefort. It seems obvious to me that your daughter's state of health has gotten worse since she entered puberty. It's as though she has never wanted to grow up."

"Would you say that her sister's death stopped her development?"

"Yes, I would say that. But even more important, Elodie herself wants to stop that development. Your daughter never accepted her sister's death. Her unconscious mind is using every means possible to stay where it was when her sister was alive."

"That borders on madness."

"That's not what I'm saying, Mrs. Rochefort."

"You're scaring me, doctor."

Elisabeth was overwhelmed. She had always refused to see her daughter as seriously ill. But Elodie had fainted and stayed unconscious for more than an hour. Elisabeth feared she had fallen into a coma. Dr. Blanchard had dropped everything and rushed to the Rocheforts' home. When he arrived, Elodie slowly returned to consciousness, as white as a shroud, with vomit on her lips. Her eyes were empty, her cheeks were gaunt, and she was shivering.

"What does Mr. Rochefort think?" the doctor asked quietly.

"Oh, my husband! He's totally focused on business and only pays attention to our eldest son, Jean-Christophe. He always thought Elodie's behavior was nothing but meaningless simpering. I wouldn't dare to tell you what bothers him the most, doctor."

"You're not obliged to."

"What does it matter now?"

Elisabeth led Dr. Blanchard to the other side of the room, so that her daughter, who was lying on the bed with her eyes wide open, couldn't hear.

"What bothers my husband the most is that he could not find an acceptable husband for her. Elodie's at the age when most girls are thinking about marriage. But considering her state, nobody would be interested in her. And marriage isn't even on her mind. As for me, I'm her mother, and I would oppose any attempts my husband might make in that area. As long as she is ill, marriage is out of the question."

Although Elisabeth thought Elodie was out of earshot, the word "marriage" startled the girl. "Mom, whose marriage are you talking about?"

"I was talking about your brother's wedding, my darling," Elisabeth said, hurrying to her daughter's side. "Did you hear what the doctor and I were saying?"

"No, I think I fell asleep. But why is Dr. Blanchard here?"

"It's nothing, my darling. You fainted. The doctor will make you better. But first you need to eat to get strong again. You must do that for us."

Never in twelve years had Elisabeth and Anselme Rochefort suspected that their daughter blamed them for the death of the one she considered her sister. But deep inside, Elodie Rochefort was convinced that her parents were hiding a dark family secret related to Catherine.

When spring arrived, Sebastien and Alexandre put their escape plan into action. They first needed to figure out how to slip away. During the day, it was impossible, as they'd be caught by the teachers and tutors. So they waited until the lights went out and the monitor was asleep before sneaking out of the dormitory. When Sebastien heard snoring, he called Alexandre, and the two slipped through the hallways like ghosts. They quickly encountered a number of locked doors—classrooms and offices—and had to go back to look for another way out. They went through every floor, exploring all the hallways that were off-limit to students, and searched in the kitchens and pantry, the storage rooms, and the maintenance workshop. They even went to the infirmary, the chapel, and the sacristy. They were unable to find an exit that wasn't locked.

Discouraged after five futile attempts, Alexandre said, "There is only one way to get away from here. We have to jump the wall."

"Don't even think about it. It's too high. We would need a ladder and strong rope. We don't have either," Sebastien said. He thought for a few minutes, and another idea came to him. He pointed to a small basement window. All around the main buildings, the basements had small barred windows to the outside. "We haven't visited the cellars yet," he whispered.

"But there are bars everywhere," Alexandre said. "We'll never be able to slip through."

Sebastien thought for a while. "Maybe they aren't all barricaded. Anyway, it's our last chance to get out. Come with me."

The boys waited long into the night, until the school clock rang three. The dormitory was dark and calm. The mewing of stray cats was all that broke the grave-like silence. Of the two, Alexandre was the less foolhardy. He never took the initiative, and afraid of being left behind in the dark, he always followed Sebastien's footsteps. They found a door at the end of a more or less abandoned hallway, not far from the music room.

"I often wondered where this hallway went," Sebastien said quietly. "I've never actually seen anyone use it."

The door was locked but didn't seem to give much resistance. Sebastien pushed his friend aside, took a deep breath, and banged his shoulder against the door. It gave way to a black hole.

Sebastien was excited. "It's a staircase. I think we found it."

They started down. Each kept one hand on the wall while using the other to sweep a lamp back and forth to light the steps.

"It smells like mold," Alexandre said.

"Of course. These steps lead to a cellar. We were right."

They discovered a whole network of dark galleries, each corresponding with a different building. They found a hodgepodge of abandoned school desks, chairs, benches, blackboards, and cupboards, along with boxes full of registration forms, accountant's balance sheets, and ancient notebooks filled to the last line. There were even old stage props from some ancient play. Dust and spiderwebs covered everything, even the rusty pipes.

"Now I smell coal," Alexandre said. "I know that smell. I lived in Saint-Etienne before. The furnace must not be far."

They soon came to a vast room filled with coal.

"If they store it here, it must come in somewhere," Sebastien said. "Either there is a door to the outside or it gets poured in through a window. If so, there wouldn't be bars on it. Let's look."

The minutes were flying by. The boys had thought of everything except a watch.

"I found it. Here," Alexandre said.

They stood in front of a large window covered with a grate. It didn't take long for Sebastien to open it. He gave a quick look outside and cried out. "This time, Alex, we're on the right track. Come on. We need to stake the place out."

"Do you think it's smart to go out now? I'm sure it's getting close to sunrise."

"We won't stay out long, just long enough to see where we are."

The two teens pulled themselves out of the cellar, and once they were outside, they took a deep breath.

"It smells like freedom," Sebastien said.

"I can already get a whiff of the sea," Alexandre said.

On their way back, they paid careful attention. They needed to take the same route the next time, and in the dark, all the cellars looked the same. Once they were under the kitchens—which they didn't know—they noticed wooden boxes without any dust lined up along a wall.

Sebastien walked over to the crates to get a closer look. "Well look at that, Alex. Champagne and red and white wine. The headmaster's reserve. It can't be for Mass."

"I guess the Jesuits don't deny themselves, do they? And to think that all we get in the cafeteria is water!"

"What if we opened one up?"

"We don't have a corkscrew."

"So what? We'll take the Champagne. We need to celebrate."

Sebastien took out a bottle of Dom Pérignon, grabbed a metal shaft off the floor, and sabered the bottle. The wine shot out of the bottle, splashing the two friends, who were giddy.

"To our success," Sebastien said.

"To freedom," Alexandre added, no longer thinking about the time.

Excited and then quickly drunk, the two boys soon abandoned any precautions against being discovered. They opened a second bottle, leaving broken glass and puddles of wine as evidence of their theft.

The sound of the clock striking six brought them around like an ice-cold shower.

"We need to get back," Sebastien said. "It's time to get up. They're going to see that we're not there."

When they got to the dormitory, they didn't have the opportunity to slip into their beds and conceal their night foray. A welcoming committee was waiting for them on the other side of the door: the dormitory monitor, still in his pajamas, the general superintendent, and the assistant principal, who was already holding the punishment register.

"Where were you?" the assistant principal asked coldly. "What were you doing outside the dormitory, dressed and all?"

The two boys mumbled inaudible explanations.

"Sirs," the assistant principle said, slicking back his hair. "I'll have to notify your parents immediately. Well, at least yours, Mr. Rochefort. I'll summon your father immediately. As for you, Mr. Legendre, you forget that your parents placed you under our responsibility. Your punishment will be severe and serve as an example. Now go join your schoolmates. You'll see me again this morning with the headmaster."

Their nighttime expedition had been a resounding failure. But Sebastien wasn't discouraged. "We'll try again, Alexandre," he whispered. "And next time, we'll escape."

Anselme Rochefort flew into a rage when he got the call from the school. That very morning he went to Avignon, met with the headmaster, and asked to see his son. Sebastien knew his father's anger would equal the gravity of his misdeed, and he was ready for anything, including being placed in a detention home with delinquents.

He had to wait a long time in front of the office, accompanied by a monitor, who seemed to feel sorry for him. "You should say you're sorry. Cry a little. That will soften up your father. Swear to all the saints that you won't do it again."

"You obviously don't know my father. He doesn't like me. We've been warring for years."

"Now, now, it can't be that bad. You just pulled a prank.

We've seen worse. Last year, one of the boarders slipped into the courtyard in the middle of the night and painted graffiti all over the wall. You should have seen the headmaster's face when the gendarmes arrived and told him. In comparison, you didn't do anything. You just went out for a walk and then came back."

"It won't be the last time."

Sebastien had decided that he would face his punishment gallantly and use his innate stubbornness to defend himself against his father's reprimands.

More than two hours passed. Sebastien began to wonder what his father and the headmaster were up to. It would soon be lunch. He could hear the other students going into the cafeteria.

"What are they doing?" he asked the monitor.

Just then, the door opened.

"Mr. Campillon, bring Mr. Rochefort in," the headmaster said.

"Come on," he whispered into Sebastien's ear. "Don't forget what I said." He put his hands on the boy's shoulders and led him into the room.

Anselme Rochefort was standing behind the headmaster's desk, looking more serious than ever. The headmaster asked the monitor to leave. Campillon excused himself and went to sit in the hallway. He didn't think he'd have to sit very close to hear the shouting and slapping that would soon commence. But he heard none of that.

Anselme was as still and as cold as ice when he announced his final sentence. "You disappoint me, Sebastien. You are a dishonor to the name I gave you. I told the headmaster that I don't want you to get away with anything. Starting today, you'll no longer be allowed to go on the chaperoned outings on Thursdays and Sundays. You'll be here while your schoolmates go out and have fun. You'll stay, and study, and work. You'll remain at the school on Easter break, and all summer, as well. The headmaster will find maintenance work for you to do. You will leave the school and return to Nîmes only after you graduate."

Sebastien didn't flinch. While his father pronounced his sentence, he held his head high and looked him straight in the eye, careful not to let the slightest sadness show.

"So you have nothing to say for yourself?" Anselme said.

The headmaster interceded. "I am sure that your son sincerely regrets what he did. This punishment will do him good. Give him time to realize that all misdeeds are punished. But we must not forget that repentance leads to forgiveness."

"I know my son, sir. He's more stubborn than an ass."

"Mr. Rochefort, if I may, I do not think that is a judicious comparison. Sebastien is a good student, except in mathematics, and even there he has made progress."

Anselme passed his son on his way out without looking at him or saying good-bye. Sebastien, still standing at attention in front of the headmaster, heard the office door close behind him. A single tear rolled down his cheek.

"You love your father, don't you, my boy?" the headmaster asked. "And you don't dare show him. He loves you, too. I'm sure of it. You are his son. But mountains of misunderstanding stand between you. You are both too proud to give a little. You'll need to break down your certainties and your arrogance. They hurt you more than they protect you."

Sebastien returned to the cafeteria with the monitor. He found Alexandre, who had been the first in the headmaster's office.

"So? How did it go?" Alex asked.

"Poorly. My father doesn't want to see me again. I can't go home for two years, not until I graduate."

"So now that makes two of us."

"Don't worry, Alex. We'll be on the road before the end of the term."

17

The Storm

The atmosphere in the Rochefort household was becoming even gloomier. Since learning of Sebastien's misdeed, Anselme was looking depressed and found nothing to his liking. Icy silence reigned over family meals. Even Jean-Christophe seemed to have gone down a peg or two in his father's esteem. The only conversations he could have with his father were about business, and those were gloomy, as well. Revenues had taken a turn for the worse, and they were facing the prospect of letting people go.

The silk industry was going through a rough patch, with harsh competition from the Middle East and Asia. And the United States was producing more of its own cotton fabrics, something that Jean-Christophe had not picked up on during his trip. Cone Mills, a North Carolina company that had been producing denim since 1895, had become a Levi Strauss supplier. This had caught Jean-Christophe and Anselme by surprise. Cones was elbowing into Rochefort Industries' market share, and orders were not coming in as fast as Jean-

Christopher had predicted. Further clouding the business horizon was the impending development of synthetic fibers. A Frenchman, Hilaire de Chardonnet, was already spinning an artificial silk, and Anselme feared that mass production wasn't far off.

Anselme also feared that his employees would soon be making demands. The socialist leader Jean Jaurès had visited Nîmes in February in a prelude to the 1910 French Section of the Workers International conference. He had riled up people with his speeches about workers' rights to pensions. Meanwhile, workplace reforms had been put in place across the country. As a result, factory owners anticipated a major leap in payroll expenses.

"These left-wing politicians are going to bankrupt us," Anselme complained. "Jean Jaurès is a public agitator!"

Jean-Christophe shared his father's political views and was even more conservative.

"This country needs to be run with an iron fist," he said during one of their evening conversations. "The working class needs to be brought in line. They used to be happy to have jobs. Now they want to make more money and work less. They've already gotten their days off every week. Soon they'll expect vacation time. There's no chance that I'd agree to that!"

Louise bristled every time her husband spoke. She didn't dare take part in the conversation. It wasn't a woman's place to get involved in politics. In the world she lived in now, her place was in society, where her job was maintaining their social status, as Jean-Christophe reminded her at every opportunity. But Louise didn't agree with his positions, which, in her view, undermined the welfare of the people who worked for him.

Jean-Christophe went on. "Who's in charge of this country, anyway? And Nîmes is no better. Our mayor comes straight from the working classes."

"Could we talk about something else?" Elisabeth asked.

"It's like you don't even see us, and if this goes on, we'll eat at another table."

Surprised, Jean-Christophe stopped talking.

Elisabeth continued. "Louise has some good news to announce, but I'm not sure you're interested."

"My dear, what could be more important than our business?" Anselme said. "You women have all the benefits without any of the responsibilities. We men must make all the decisions."

"Well, perhaps you should share in some of that decision making," Louise let out.

"Excuse me?" Anselme said, staring at her.

"I said that maybe you should give us some responsibility, instead of relegating us to the role of being your mere accessories at society receptions."

"Louise!" Jean-Christophe said, putting down his fork. "How dare you talk to Father in that tone?"

"She's right!" Faustine's voice rose up. She was breaking yet another dinner rule.

The volume of the conversation rose. Elodie took advantage of the uproar and left without excusing herself. She returned to her room after a quick run to the bathroom.

"Who would believe it?" Anselme said. "Protest reigns even in my own home. Now the children are rising up. Faustine, go to your room. You'll stay there until I say you can leave. As for you, Louise, I never knew you to be so—"

"Impertinent and ungrateful, Father? That's it, isn't it? I owe you everything, so it's my duty to shut up! Nobody in this household dares to raise a voice when you talk. You crush everyone with your arrogance. Even Jean-Christophe, your rightful heir, shrinks before you and your demands. I married a loyal dog that spends its days licking its master's feet."

"That's enough, woman! Jean-Christophe, rein in your wife. She's going mad and doesn't know what she's saying."

"Come, child," Elisabeth intervened. "What we have to

announce can wait. This is not the right moment." She shot her husband a castigating look.

Reacting to his wife's glare, Anselme calmed down. He took on a syrupy tone. "What is this important thing, then, that you have to tell us?"

Elisabeth took her daughter-in-law by the hand and pulled her in front of Anselme. "Go on, my dear. It's not good timing, but it will make them treat you with more consideration."

Louise hesitated. Her father-in-law turned her to stone. He was staring at her as if he were waiting for bad news. She took a deep breath and said, "You're going to be a grandfather, Mr. Rochefort."

Surprised, Anselme cleared his throat, looked away, and then stood up and walked over to the window.

"Why didn't you say something?" Jean-Christophe said, offended that he hadn't been the first to know.

"Here, everything goes to your father first. I saved it for him. You, my dear, will be a father in seven months. I hope that makes you happy and doesn't interfere with your plans."

Anselme was speechless and struggled to sound more conciliatory. "Why did you hide it from us for so long?" he finally said with a slight quiver in his voice.

"Louise wanted to be sure," Elisabeth said. "And she was looking forward to telling you tonight. But as usual, you men were only interested in your business."

"I'm sorry, my dear." Jean-Christophe tried to repair the harm. "Our worries distract us from what is most important."

Louise left the next day to tell her family the good news. Jean-Christophe drove her to Tornac and left her there to spend a couple of weeks with her parents.

"You should stay away from Nîmes for a while," he said. "I'll come see you every weekend and stay until Sunday night."

Constance and Donatien were overjoyed at the idea of becoming grandparents. Julie, Aline, and Vincent pressed

Louise to know what names she had thought about, whether she wanted a girl or a boy, and who the godparents would be.

Constance, however, knew her daughter was hiding her feelings. She saw the sadness in her daughter's eyes. One evening, when everyone else had gone to bed, Constance lingered in her daughter's room and asked her directly, "What's wrong, my darling? What's making you so sad? I see the pain. Are you worried about having a child? There's nothing to fear. Everything will be all right."

"That's not it, Mom."

"What is it then?"

Louise poured out her feelings, not hiding how disappointed she was with her husband and the hard time she was having with his parents.

"So you don't feel the same way about Jean-Christophe. Not so long ago, you said you were very much in love with him."

"I still love him. I love him as much as ever. But I have the impression that he doesn't love me the same way he did before. He doesn't pay any attention to me. He comes home late, saying he had a lot of work at the factory. He never tells me what he does. And I can't go on living in his parents' house. It's too much. I'm suffocating."

"Now, now, dear. You'll get over it. The baby will change your life and your husband's. It will bring the two of you closer."

But Constance couldn't find any good arguments to reassure her daughter. Deep down, she now thought her cousin Madeleine was right to be concerned about this marriage. That night, she opened up to Donatien, who had stayed awake, wondering what was so important that she needed to talk with her daughter when it was well past bedtime.

"Louise is unhappy. Jean-Christophe is not a good husband."

"Come on, what makes you say that?"

Constance told Donatien what Louise had poured out to her. "Do you remember how you convinced me that this wedding was an opportunity? That aligning ourselves with an important family would raise our children above their station? Well, if you ask me, you were wrong. We are a respectable landowning family. Louise didn't need that kind of marriage or a gilded name. We sacrificed our daughter for the sake of bettering our social standing. And look what's come of it."

"You're exaggerating, Constance. Louise fell in love with Rochefort. You're forgetting that."

"But weren't we the ones who pushed her into his arms?"

"We didn't do anything wrong, Constance. It will all work out, I'm sure. Everyone knows that passionate love doesn't last long. Louise is too idealistic. Having a child will make her more realistic, and that will bring her closer to her husband."

Donatien didn't suspect that Jean-Christophe had returned to his capricious ways. The marriage had satisfied him for a while, as Louise had met his expectations and had never let him down in that respect. But his long stay in the United States had not been conducive to fidelity. Far from his bride, he felt no guilt about bedding pretty Americans or Mexicans, usually barmaids lured during a drunken evening with other businessmen like himself.

His father hadn't needed to beg him to stay on for those additional three months. Life in San Francisco and New York seemed very far from his existence in Nîmes. He had even entertained the idea of never returning to France, where everything felt so small and the people so narrow-minded and unambitious. From a distance, his father's factories looked like nothing more than an inheritance destined to stagnate and decline. America, on the other hand, was a vast horizon open to a promising future. It was full of challenges and opportunities. He almost understood his brother Sebastien, who yearned for space and freedom.

"In France, it's the ice age, compared with what you're doing here," he admitted to his new friends. "Our work methods are archaic, and our machines are out of date. We are prisoners of social laws that give workers advantages to the detriment of their bosses. We are at the mercy of strikes, labor unions, and revolutionary parties. The word 'liberty' has no meaning."

He felt no scruples about abandoning his wife. Perhaps he would ask her to join him in America. She could always refuse, and he would be free to start his new life. Louise didn't count for much in his future plans. After all, Mother never counted for much in Father's career, he thought. The younger Rochefort didn't know that his father owed his fortune to his two wives.

Despite these stirrings, Jean-Christophe never had the courage to tell his father that he wanted to stay in the United States. He knew he would lose his inheritance. So he returned to France and put on a good front.

Jean-Christophe's return to France, however, didn't put an end to his extramarital escapades. In fact, they multiplied. He frequented the city's posh brothels, where he met with his business ties, and discretion was guaranteed. The madams always found him the most refined, cultivated, and attractive girls. Not a week went by without a visit to one of the region's temples of lust. Sometimes the merrymaking took place in a château just outside Nîmes. Orgies worthy of the Romans took place under sparkling crystal and gold chandeliers. The more Jean-Christophe grew to enjoy his debauchery, the more his feelings for Louise dissipated.

Sebastien hadn't given up on his plan. He had just decided to postpone carrying it out. Alexandre and he had agreed to wait until October. They were being watched more closely than ever, so it was best to keep their noses down and pretend to fall back in line. Sebastien studied harder, read more of his favorite writers, and made progress in mathematics. His grades improved, leading the headmaster to believe that the young Rochefort was on the road to redemption.

When informed of these changes, Anselme refused to change his position. He was more determined than ever and sent the school a long letter explaining that the punishment should be applied to its full extent. He was not about to let up. Sebastien would remain at the lycée during the entire summer, working alongside the maintenance men. "It's for his own good. Don't let him get away with anything," Anselme had insisted.

Anselme forbade all family visits. "The rebel needs to understand where his duty lies," he said when Elisabeth brought up the possibility of going to Avignon.

Faustine suffered the most from this shunning of Sebastien. She missed him and thought her father was being entirely too harsh. "It's unfair that he's stuck there through every vacation," she confided to Louise, with whom she was sharing more and more. "Father is going too far."

Louise was feeling awkward. She wanted to help her little sister-in-law, but she didn't want to get involved in a family quarrel that didn't concern her directly. Nevertheless, she promised Faustine that she would talk it over with her husband to see if he would intercede.

"I know that Jean-Christophe isn't happy about Sebastien's punishment either," she said.

Jean-Christophe refused to confront his father but agreed to pay his brother a secret visit. "Make sure you don't say anything," he told Louise. "Father will explode if he finds out I've gone to see Sebastien."

Sebastien was overjoyed to see his brother. And his feelings of rejection soon seeped through his veneer of resignation. "Father doesn't love me anymore, right? He doesn't want to see me again."

"You're wrong, little brother. Father loves you as much as

his other children. I'm sure that he suffers more than anyone else from this separation."

"He doesn't show it."

"And do you?"

Jean-Christophe felt a little responsible for this brother. Because of their nearly ten-year age difference, they had never had the same friends or played together. But as Sebastien grew older, Jean-Christophe became a caring older brother, a role that was all the more important because their father was gone much of the time. So despite their different personalities, the two brothers had strong fraternal feelings. Jean-Christophe considered himself his younger brother's teacher, and Sebastien looked to his older brother for what his father did not give him.

"Will you come back and see me?" Sebastien asked when Jean-Christophe was getting ready to leave.

"If you promise to stop your foolishness."

Sebastien was still determined to escape. But he forced out a lie. "Okay."

"So I'll come back. But it must remain secret. The headmaster has agreed and promised not to say a word."

Jean-Christophe, however, quickly became preoccupied and put off seeing his brother.

It was nearly the end of summer. Faustine had gone to Bastide with her mother and older sister. Five months pregnant, Louise had gone with them, and she was thrilled to see her father and Vincent, who had brought the animals up to pasture, as they did every other summer.

Sebastien stared at the main entrance on his way to the maintenance facility every day, hoping to see it open and his brother come through. Eventually, he realized that Jean-Christophe was not coming. This intensified his feelings of abandonment and rejection and made him more determined than ever to escape. "Your brother must be very busy. He'll come as soon as he has some free time," people would say. Or "maybe your father found out, and he's keeping your brother from coming again." Or "maybe the headmaster didn't keep his word."

In reality, with Louise away, Jean-Christophe had become infatuated with the pretty Dolores, one of his mother's servants. The man who had sworn to his friends that he would frequent prostitutes but never take a mistress was having an affair right under the Rochefort roof.

Dolores had started working for Elisabeth not long after Jean-Christophe had returned from America. The twenty-year-old from Spain immediately attracted the Don Juan's attention and did nothing to discourage it. Jean-Christophe kept his distance at first. But left alone in August—his father had joined his mother at La Bastide—he couldn't resist the temptation to seduce the beauty. The mansion was free for their frolicking. Other than the butler and a cook, there was nobody to witness their misbehavior.

His wife was preparing for the birth of their child, and his brother was languishing in his school-prison. But Jean-Christophe Rochefort was far removed from his duties. He was weaving a love story with a beautiful and hot-blooded Iberian.

18

Anselme's Wrath

Summer melded into fall. October still offered fine sunlit days. The mountains were bathed in warm colors, and sweet, subtle aromas wafted from the overripe soil.

Louise was at La Fenouillère for the beginning of the grape harvest. As she anxiously awaited the big day, she convinced Jean-Christophe that Tornac would be the best place for her to give birth. She would feel more at ease there, with her own mother and Madeleine.

Elisabeth had been a little offended, but she swallowed her pride and acknowledged that a woman needed her mother more than her mother-in-law when she was having a baby. Anselme, however, didn't see it that way. Swearing to all the saints on the calendar that his grandson would be born in Nîmes, he flew into a rage without for a moment thinking that she might give birth to a girl.

"A Rochefort must be born in the Rochefort house," he shouted when he learned of Louise's decision.

Elisabeth managed to settle him down a bit, but Anselme

was still indignant. "I wonder if I didn't make a mistake choosing that Rouvière girl," he said. "With her righteous game, she's good at hiding her true self. She's as rebellious and stubborn as Sebastien."

When Louise walked in the vineyards, her father's harvesters all turned to smile. The boys stared at her belly. The girls imagined the suffering in store for her. The long-married women gave her warm, reassuring looks.

"Miss, look how round your belly is. It'll be a boy," one of the women said. "You're carrying it low. It won't be long now."

"A month," Louise said.

"I doubt you'll have to wait that long."

Long walks in the countryside made Louise feel calmer about the birth of the baby. Sometimes Aline went with her. The bonds between the two sisters had grown with each of Louise's visits. At ten, the youngest Rouvière was already very maternal and had a lot of insight for her age. Aline doubted that Louise was really happy, and she did everything she could to distract her sister from her worries. Aline talked about Vincent and was very clear: She was infatuated with her adopted brother.

"So you're in love!" Louise teased Aline. "Don't forget that Vincent is your brother."

"Vincent is adopted and not my birth brother. I plan to marry him!"

"Does he know this?"

Aline blushed and looked away. "It's my secret," she said, taking Louise's hand. "You won't say anything, will you? Especially not to Vincent?"

"Mum's the word, dear. It will be our secret."

When she was with her sister, Louise forgot her troubles. Her joie de vivre returned, and she became the young woman everyone remembered. In fact, having the entire family around her gave her the support she had come in search of.

When Jean-Christophe arrived, her face would lose its glow. Louise shut down. Everyone saw what was happening, but nobody broached the subject of the obvious rift.

Louise gave birth three weeks ahead of schedule.

Aline was alone with Louise when her water broke. Everyone else was in the vineyards. Louise felt intense contractions in her back and belly. Bent over in pain, Louise couldn't breathe or even talk. Aline panicked and starting screaming with all her heart.

"I'll go get help," she finally managed to say.

"No," Louise said, barely getting the words out. "Don't leave me alone. Go heat some water and bring over the bag that's on the chest of drawers in my room."

Aline did as she was told, not understanding what her older sister was doing.

"It's happening too fast," Louise said, panting. "The baby's coming now."

"Hold on, Louise! I'll go get Mom."

"No, it will be too late. Do what I say."

Shaking with fear, the little girl obeyed. Louise lay down on the bed and gave Aline instructions. "Get a clean blanket. The scissors are in the bag. Take them out. You may need to pull the baby out while I'm pushing. I'll tell you. After he's out, I'll cut the cord. Quickly wrap the baby in the blanket." The contractions were getting closer and closer. Louise knew the baby's head was ready to crown.

Aline listened carefully and didn't flinch.

After two or three more contractions, Louise let out a high-pitched scream that echoed all the way to the vineyards. Nobody but Aline heard. But Constance felt a wrench in her heart.

"Louise!" she said, dropping her bucket.

"What's wrong?" Madeleine asked from the next row.

"It's Louise!"

Madeleine straightened. "I don't see anyone. Nobody is coming."

"Louise is having her baby. I have to go."

Constance left the harvesters and ran to the house.

When she got to the kitchen, she heard Aline singing a lullaby. She ran to Louise's room. The young woman lay on her bed, unconscious and covered in blood. Aline was rocking the swaddled baby.

"Sh, Louise went to sleep. Look, Mom, it's a boy. I took care of him all by myself."

Madeleine arrived, and the two women began to take care of the mother and baby. They sent Aline to get the village doctor. Louise had regained consciousness by the time he got to La Fenouillère. He examined her and the newborn and expressed surprise at how well Aline had done. "Without you, Aline, that baby would have been in danger. Your sister can be proud of you."

Louise was weak and stayed in her room for several days. Her life was not in danger, but she had lost a lot of blood, and the doctor said she needed to regain her strength.

When Jean-Christophe arrived on Friday night, he briefly asked how she was before launching into the significance of the newborn boy. "A son. I was sure of it, Louise. The Rochefort lineage will continue. His name will be Anselme Jean Louis. He'll bear the names of his grandfather, father, and mother."

Louise sat up and found the strength to say, "That is out of the question, Jean-Christophe. He'll be called Pierre—like the apostle—and nothing else."

Jean-Christophe looked at his mother-in-law, doubtful.

"She made that decision herself, son," Constance said. "And I don't think anything will get her to change her mind."

Anselme didn't show any joy at becoming a grandfather. Jean-Christophe's news just seemed to enrage him. His son not only intended to give the child an entirely unexpected name, but also planned to move his wife and baby out of their fine apartment in the family mansion.

Jean-Christophe, softened up a bit by the birth of a son, had acquiesced to his wife's demand. Louise had talked to him openly, hiding none of her sadness at a time when she should have been feeling nothing but joy. Jean-Christophe, usually so arrogant, had let himself be convinced that a move into a home of their own would be for the best. Actually, he thought it would work in his favor. He also wanted some space between his father and himself.

He had no intentions of giving up Dolores. The beautiful Spaniard made Jean-Christophe forget his responsibilities and respectability. She had gotten under his skin, and he had become nearly ridiculous in his efforts to continue to enjoy her favors.

"After I move, I'll rent a little place near the train station, and we can meet there," Jean-Christophe promised her. "We won't be bothered by nosy people."

Dolores, however, wasn't quite as eager to continue their affair. When she saw Louise return with his child, she distanced herself from him, saying it was not appropriate to continue their relationship. Despite his pleadings, she closed her door to him, if not her heart.

"You have a child now, and I can't go on like before," she said. "Children are sacred. We're not allowed to hurt them."

"You should have thought of that sooner, beauty, instead of teasing me," Jean-Christophe answered, full of disdain.

Dolores slapped him and refused to give him the opportunity to say any more. "You're horrible," she shouted. "I don't want to see you again. Get out of here."

The fight festered and brought their relationship to an end.

Jean-Christophe settled down temporarily. He lost his taste for late nights in the brothels that he had frequented just a few months earlier. He arrived home earlier. But his mood was darker, and he did not give his wife and son much attention.

In their new home—a magnificent house surrounded by shady grounds—Louise continued to worry about her husband's behavior. She took refuge in loving her son. Holding him in her arms, she could forget her sorrow.

At the Cordeliers, Elisabeth had to accommodate her husband's moods. Incensed by Jean-Christophe's behavior, Anselme complained about him day in and day out. He also carped about the economy and accused the labor unions and left-wing parties of trying to kill off French business. At the end of October, the railway workers went on strike, paralyzing the flow of goods. It didn't take long for supplies to run dry, and Anselme had to cut back production.

"All those strikers are leftists. They're giving no thought to what this is doing to our economy."

As it was probable that he would not be able to honor his orders if the strike continued, he told his workers that layoffs were likely. This immediately created discontent.

"Let's not act rashly," Jean-Christophe suggested. "The government will have to do something. They won't let this go on. The railways are of national importance, particularly now, with Germany to consider."

"I don't trust that Aristide Briand, even if he did refuse to give civil servants the right to strike."

Actually, Briand had reacted quickly and had tried to break the strike by drafting railway workers into military service. His authoritarian move had immediately provoked disturbances throughout France. In Paris, demonstrations had degenerated into street fighting. In the end, the workers drafted into military service were reassigned to their jobs on the railway, which completely canceled the effects of the strike. Rail traffic returned to normal, without any concession to the workers. And Anselme avoided a strike by his own workers, which he had feared.

"I told you the government wouldn't just stand around with its arms crossed," Jean-Christophe said.

"I didn't think a former socialist could act so decisively," Anselme said.

"Apparently he said he was willing to do anything that was necessary to maintain control of the railway. Briand is not the dangerous one. Jean Jaurès is. He and his friends are the real enemies of business."

Politics were the only topic the Rochefort father and son could agree on these days. As with Sebastien, Anselme was too proud to make a move toward reconciliation with Jean-Christophe, whom he reproached for wanting to be independent. He had not gone to see Jean-Christophe, Louise, and their son in their new home, and he never asked about his daughter-in-law or grandson. Cold anger showed in his eyes every time Jean-Christophe mentioned them.

"We are going to baptize Pierre soon," he told his father not long after the railway strike, when he thought Anselme might be more receptive. Anselme pretended that he hadn't heard.

"Will you be coming to the ceremony and the meal, Father?" Jean-Christophe asked.

"Baptized? Where? You are Catholic, and Louise is Protestant."

"I'm like you, Father. Religion is not my cup of tea. I leave that to the women. I agreed to a Protestant baptism to make Louise happy. She is more religious than I am. I managed to convince Mother, although it wasn't easy."

"So you gave in! Again. And what about the meal?"
"We'll have it at our house."
"Of course!"
"Can we count on your presence? Everyone will be there. The entire Rouvière family . . ."

Anselme hesitated.

Jean-Christophe continued. "There's just the question of Sebastien."

"Sebastien?" Anselme shouted. "Until I say otherwise, he is restricted to his school. Under no circumstances is he leaving."

"But Father, it's for Pierre's baptism. We could make an exception."

Anselme was in a rage again. *Clearly, everyone is against me,* he thought. He threw his just-lit cigar out the window.

"I'll come to my grandson's baptism," he said, coughing up the smoke he had just inhaled. "But I don't want to see your brother! Is that understood? It's nonnegotiable."

Sebastien had resigned himself to never seeing his brother again. But then Jean-Christophe had visited him, not once but twice—in September and in October, right before and right after school was back in session. Jean-Christophe had implied that their father was coming around, and so Sebastien had second thoughts about carrying out his escape plan. But when he learned in early November that his father had no intentions of letting him attend his nephew's baptism, Sebastien's determination returned stronger than ever.

"My father still hasn't forgiven me," he told Alexandre. "We should get out of here right away, before it gets too cold."

The two schoolmates had saved up some money by doing papers and homework for other school kids. And Sebastien had money that Jean-Christophe had slipped to him during his visits. They had clothes to change into from their uniforms. Finally, they had enough food to get through the first days.

The night before they ran away, Sebastien approached his friend, opened the top of his bag, and whispered, "Look at this, Alex!"

Alex's eyes widened. "A bottle of Champagne! How did you do that? Did you go back to the cellar?"

"Just once, to make sure we could still get through."

"You should have told me. I would have gone with you."

"I didn't want you to take any extra risks."

In secret, the two boys reveled in this latest theft.

Around one in the morning, when everyone else in the dormitory was asleep, they returned to the cellar, took the same route they had used several months earlier, and easily made it to freedom.

Once outside, they headed to the banks of the Rhône River. A thick layer of clouds weighed down the sky, and a deep silence covered the streets of the city. They hurried past the massive palace, which seemed foreboding in the darkness. When they reached the waterway, the clouds opened. Silvery moonlight reflected off the water, highlighting the Saint Bénézet Bridge and, on the opposite bank, the Saint André Fort, with its crenellated King Philip IV tower. Fall rains had raised the water level. The river was muddy and loud, full of eddies and dangerous for navigators.

Sebastien had an idea. "If we find a barge heading down to the delta, we'll be safer from the gendarmes. They won't come looking for us on the river, and we'll get there quicker."

Alexandre was more pragmatic but hadn't considered all the possibilities. "Why not take the train?" he said. "That would be the quickest way. We have enough money for tickets."

"The train? Don't even think about it. As soon as our descriptions got out, the authorities would be all over the train stations. The gendarmes would verify every passenger getting off the train. We'd be picked up even before getting to Marseille. No, the river is safer. That is, if we find the right boatman."

As dawn poked over the horizon, they went to the first pier at the edge of the city. They saw several barges along the embankment. They approached one, where an older man and an apprentice were getting ready to cast off.

"Sir, you wouldn't need some help, would you?" Sebastien asked.

The man stopped what he was doing. "Help, eh? You young fellows looking for work?"

"Yes, sir. To help our parents."

"I don't have enough to pay one man, let alone two."

"Shelter and food will be enough. We won't ask for anything else."

The boatman thought for a while, then said, "I could use some help in Beaucaire. I'll have a big load to get on board. Then I'm going down to Arles to unload. I'll load up with beams there and take the canal to Port-de-Bouc."

"Port-de-Bouc. That's near the sea. That's perfect. We could help you all the way down, and then we'll leave you to join our uncle in Marseille. We don't need to be paid, sir."

"If you're headed to Marseille, that's where I'm going. But you'll get there quicker by train."

"We have no money, sir."

Once again, the man seemed to be thinking.

"He's wary of us," Alexandre whispered. "We should take off."

"What do you think, Jeannette?" the man asked his helper. The apprentice wasn't a boy, as Sebastien and Alexandre had thought. The girl saw the surprise on their faces and smiled. Sebastien and Alexandre saw kindness in her eyes.

"They look honest, Grandpa. They could help us, and we could use a hand."

"Since my granddaughter seems to accept you, I agree. Come on board."

The two boys jumped at the chance, happy to escape discovery by the gendarmes, who most certainly had already been informed by the headmaster.

"You see, Alex. We're on a boat. We're off to a good start."

Five days later, they were making their way along the La Joliette pier in Marseille. The docks were bustling. Dockers, merchants, fishmongers, and onlookers hurried here and there, and the two runaways felt like they were in the heart of an anthill. Tramways brushed dangerously close to trucks being unloaded. Horse-drawn wagons carried wine to traders' warehouse. Farmer's carriages, upper-class coaches, and shiny cars fought for space on the street. On the docks, sacks of grain rose alongside crates of tropical fruits, containers of fabric, crockery, and hardware from the Far East and North Africa. Steamships were anchored alongside magnificent three-masters, the final vestiges of a bygone time. On deck, watch officers in their immaculate white uniforms looked out disdainfully.

Sebastien and Alexandre were a little lost in all the hubbub, and they hesitated to approach any of the ships. They asked a few people to direct them toward the vessels headed to the Atlantic or the Pacific. Finally, an old seafarer pointed to an enormous steamer.

"We're heading to America, and we pull up anchor at dawn tomorrow," a man onboard shouted down to them. "If you're here at six, I'll take you on as ship's boys."

The two teens leaped with joy and spent the night impatiently waiting for the sun to rise. They were shivering, not so much from the cold, but from the excitement of seeing their dream come true. Sebastien took out his bottle of Champagne to celebrate.

"Now's the time to drink it. Let's toast everything that's

awaiting us," he said. "Back at school, they must be wondering what's happened to us. They have no idea that we're about to climb aboard that ship."

When they showed up early in the morning, two gendarmes grabbed their collars.

"Are you Sebastien Rochefort and Alexandre Legendre? We were told you ran away. Please follow us."

The sailor from the night before watched from the railing as they were hauled away like thieves.

That same night, they were back at the boarding school, contrite and shattered, having failed when they had come so close to their goal. Anselme Rochefort stood rigid in the headmaster's office. Afraid not only for his brother, but also for his father, Jean-Christophe had made the trip with him.

Anselm had passed out when he learned that his son was missing from school. Jean-Christophe watched helplessly as his red-faced father clenched his jaw and fists and fell to the floor. Elisabeth called the doctor, who at first thought Anselme had suffered a stroke. But then the doctor diagnosed the problem as a weak heart.

"Don't get so worked up, Mr. Rochefort," the doctor said. "You need to stop smoking cigars. Your lungs are engorged, and your heart is winded. It's beating irregularly. That's not a good sign. You need to go to the hospital for more tests."

"That is out of the question," Anselm shouted, out of breath. "As soon as they find my worthless son, I'll go take care of him. He must stop dishonoring my name."

Jean-Christophe refused to let Anselme take the wheel of the car when they finally got the news that Sebastien was back at school. He drove Anselm to Avignon, and the entire way, he tried desperately to calm his father. It was futile.

"He was brought back to the school by gendarmes, like a murderer! Can you imagine?" Anselme raged on, staring at the road but seeing only the shame splattered all over him. "What are we going to do with him?"

"Please, Father, let me handle it. I can take care of it."

"I don't see how!"

"I'll tell you later."

19

Trials

1912

Vincent celebrated his fourteenth birthday at the beginning of the year and was impatiently waiting for school to end so he could work full time on his adopted parents' farm. Like Louise and Julie, he was expected to take two additional years of study after passing his first-level exams.

Donatien was proud of his children's success. He had even let his friend, the headmaster, persuade him to allow his youngest get her higher diploma. Aline was good in school. She was always reading and much more eager to do her schoolwork than help her mother with household tasks. The girl wanted to become a teacher, which pleased her own teacher, Miss Bernard. She would only lift her nose from her notebooks for Vincent, the big brother who had her heart.

At La Fenouillère, everyone agreed that adopting Vincent Janvier seven years earlier had brought nothing but happiness. The teen was growing up and not causing any problems.

He was perfectly integrated. The servants and farmhands had immediately considered him the same as a birth son. Even the villagers accepted him as such. Vincent was respected at school, too. If a schoolmate lapsed and called him Janvier, he pretended not to hear and only answered to Rouvière. He finally put those who still saw him as a bastard in their place when he received the best grades in the class on his first-level exams.

While Aline had eyes only for Vincent, he was increasingly drawn to Faustine Rochefort. And his feelings were reciprocated. When she came to the Clos du Tournel with her mother, Elodie, Louise, and the baby, the two teenagers spent as much time together as possible. Their friendship had become real love. But because they were too young and still too clumsy to express what they felt for each other, they used simple everyday words, tender gestures, fleeting glances, and long moments of silence to convey their affection. Sometimes those things were far more expressive than the most eloquent words.

They were the happiest in the mountains when they met for the summer. Faustine would accompany Vincent everywhere the flock led him. She would go home with her shoes full of manure and her dress splattered with mud and grass. Elisabeth was pleased to see her child happy. Anselme, however, didn't understand the girl's fascination with the rustic lifestyle.

"I wonder if seeing that young Janvier is good for her," he told Elisabeth.

"Why do you call him Janvier, dear? He's a Rouvière. You know that." "Yes, but his real name is Janvier. That's what's written on his birth certificate. Donatien told me."

"He's Donatien's son. You shouldn't make any distinctions, not in front of Faustine, nor in front of Louise."

"I'm sorry, but for me, he is not and will never be the same as a birth son. He's just the bastard son of unknown parents."

"You're a monster sometimes, Anselme."

"I just tell the truth. And I have to say that I'm not keen on this growing friendship between our daughter and that boy. It's clearer and clearer that the bonds between those two are . . . Well, how can I say it?"

"Growing!"

"I don't like it, and I intend to put an end to it."

"Anselm, even your children's feelings aren't safe from your intrusion."

Anselme seemed determined to get his family under control, but this was only making the situation worse. There was constant vexation over Sebastien. The young man was finishing his third year with the Jesuits and had gone home only once. The previous summer, he had stayed with Jean-Christophe, who had promised to take full responsibility for his brother. With Elodie, Anselme showed the same lack of understanding. He denied that she had any real problems. He was suspicious of Jean-Christophe, despite all the loyalty he had shown. And now Faustine was annoying him by getting caught up with an orphan boy, whom her father considered a good-for-nothing farmworker.

The more Anselme tried to impose his will, the more his children and wife distanced themselves. And the more bitter he grew. At work, he scolded his staff for no reason, gave even his most qualified workers a rough time, and ranted at his salesmen. He got angry with suppliers who were delivering late and customers who weren't paying on time. The economy, political conditions in France, and the international situation all seemed to be working against him.

Elisabeth would try to keep him calm, but Anselme was locked in an emotional fortress. This undermined not only his family and work relations, but also his health. His habit of smoking one cigar after another led to another heart attack.

A few days later, he suffered a stroke that left him paralyzed on his right side.

He was rushed to the hospital, where Jean-Christophe made sure he was tended by the best doctors from Montpellier. They could do nothing to reverse what had happened. "He'll be confined to a wheelchair," the neurologist, Dr. Souche, told them. "Fortunately, the paralysis didn't touch his face. He can breathe and speak normally. And his vital functions aren't affected."

The news that Anselme would remain paralyzed distressed Elisabeth, who had always loved her husband despite his heavy-handedness. Surrounded by her four children, she maintained her dignity and composure. But she felt terribly alone and overwhelmed by the responsibilities she would now have to assume.

"You will need a lot of patience, Mrs. Rochefort," the doctor told her. The neurologist knew Elisabeth was already preoccupied with Elodie's illness, and so he urged her to hire someone to help with Anselme's care. "Don't try to do everything yourself."

Sebastien had been called to his father's bedside. He took his mother in his arms and whispered, "Don't worry, Mom. The Rochefort family is strong. Nothing can beat us."

Sebastien was finishing high school in Nîmes. In September, he had taken up residence with Jean-Christophe and Louise in their new house. Anselme had finally given in. Jean-Christophe had convinced him that Sebastien was only trying to get his father's attention by running away.

"Father, I promise to look after him and make him behave. I'll let him know that he'll be back at the boarding school for good if he does anything wrong."

Persuading Anselme hadn't been easy. Anselme seriously doubted that Sebastien would straighten out. "Rebellion is in his blood," he said. "He'll start up again at the first opportunity. How will you keep an eye on him? At least the boarding school had monitors and school guards."

"Not so many of them, considering how easily he got away."

"Hmm. So how are you going to keep him in line?"

"I don't know yet. First, I need to talk to him, to build trust, to show him we love him. For him, too much authority is like harassment, and it pushes him to act the way he does."

"I treated him the same way I treated you, Jean-Christophe. He doesn't want to understand where his duty lies."

"That is precisely where you are making a mistake, Father."

"Are you saying I'm wrong to expect him to fulfill his obligations to his father? I've wanted only what's best for him."

"No, but you need to listen to what he has to say before you impose your will."

"So what do you want to tell him for me?"

"That you love him, Father. That's what he needs to know."

"How could he think otherwise?"

A few days later, Jean-Christophe went to Avignon and met with his brother. "Would you agree to come live with me, Louise, and Pierre?" Jean-Christophe asked. "Father approves."

"Father agreed to let me out of this prison. So he has given up on me."

"It's just the opposite. He wants to give you another chance."

"So why didn't he come to tell me himself?"

"You know him. He has his pride."

Suspicious, Sebastien hesitated for quite some time. He wondered what was hidden in this proposition.

"I suppose I need to give something in exchange."

"Nothing, other than a promise to stop acting like a wild boy. You'll finish your last year of school in Nîmes. I'll sign you up for the boys' school there. Father agrees. You'll go to classes just as you do now, and you'll come home every evening. You see, Father and I trust you."

"And after that?"

"After what?"

"When I've graduated? Will I be able to continue my studies and study what I want?"

"Father and I discussed it. I think I convinced him that you're not made for managing our plants."

"That's convenient for you."

"If you want to know the truth, yes, it is. That way, we won't have any fights over the business."

"Then if father gives me a free choice, I'll do Sciences Po and journalism school."

"That's very ambitious of you. You have big dreams."

"Most important, it will allow me to travel."

"The itch is back. If you want my opinion, I would refrain from bringing this up with Father right now. And keep it from Mother, as well. It would make her sad."

So it was decided that Sebastien would return to Nîmes. Anselme found Sebastien a summer job at a regional newspaper run by a friend, the Marquis de Baroncelli's brother. Sebastien was thrilled and was quick to forget the dark hours during the two seemingly endless years he had spent with the Jesuits in Avignon. In August, he learned that his friend Alexandre Legendre had left for Tahiti with his parents, who had finally come to get him.

Sebastien started his new life. With Jean-Christophe and Louise, he quieted down. He liked his sister-in-law and his nephew, Pierre, and he was unaware of any problems between Louise and Jean-Christophe.

The new trials faced by the Rochefort family brought everyone together, and Anselme became the focus of attention.

After spending several weeks in the hospital, he returned home to begin his long convalescence.

"No more tobacco or alcohol for you, Mr. Rochefort!" his specialist from Montpellier told him. "And don't get angry."

"You're burying me already. What kind of life are you sentencing me to?"

"Mr. Rochefort, you are sixty-two, and you should seriously consider stepping back and letting your son assume more responsibility."

"So you're telling me to retire."

"You need to rest and take care of yourself."

"My right side is paralyzed, Doctor, but I'm left-handed. And this wheelchair is not going to keep me from getting around and going to my factories."

"You have to think about your heart too. You have already had two small heart attacks. A third could be fatal."

Anselme didn't let any facts interfere with what he wanted to do—or not do. The thought of relying entirely on his son to run the business was unbearable. He would only promise to go rest at his country home in Anduze for a few weeks.

"But I don't want to see anyone, other than you, Elisabeth, of course," he said when he got home. "Tell the children I need quiet. And you'll send away any friends who come to find out how I am. I don't want their pity. Some will be happy to find out that I'm disabled. They would be all too thrilled to spread the word that I'm a cripple. When I'm feeling better, I'll come back to Nîmes and host a reception to show that old Rochefort is as hale and hearty as ever, even in a wheelchair."

Elisabeth didn't insist. Trying to reason with him would have put him in a bad mood and endangered his life again.

"I'll order Dolores to prepare our bags. We'll leave for the Clos du Tournel tomorrow morning. Jean-Christophe has offered to drive us."

"That won't be necessary. My chauffeur will do. Besides,

I'll need him when we are there. Tell him to get ready to come with us."

Elisabeth did what her husband wanted, but she was extremely worried about Elodie, who still refused to eat and had sunk into a deeper depression since her father's stroke. At twenty-five, she was incapable of managing her own life. She was lost without Elisabeth and couldn't bear having her mother gone for more than a couple of hours. She didn't actually converse with her mother. She just answered her questions with a few words. She stubbornly refused to mix with friends her mother invited to the house. She would see only her brothers, her sister, and Louise and Pierre. The baby boy was the one person who managed to bring a smile to her emaciated face.

"Seeing this child would have made Catherine so happy," she would say when she held the baby.

Elisabeth never said anything when Elodie mentioned her dead sister. She avoided feeding the memory. But sometimes she wondered if telling Elodie the truth about Catherine could possibly shake her out of her malaise.

"It's too late to bring it up now," Anselme said, still opposed. "And why would it matter to her that Catherine was my birth daughter and not yours? Catherine was still her sister. Well, almost."

Worried about leaving Elodie in Nîmes, Elisabeth asked Louise to look after her. Louise agreed immediately.

"The house is big, and Pierre's presence will distract her."

"I knew I could count on you, my dear."

"What about Faustine? You can't leave her alone."

"Faustine's not a little girl anymore. She's fourteen and can amuse herself. And the help will look after her."

"If you want, she can stay with us. Jean-Christophe will allow it. She's his sister."

"I can't ask you to do that, not in your state."

This surprised Louise.

"I noticed a good two weeks ago. You're pregnant again, aren't you?"

"Does it show that much?"

"I can tell by how you hold yourself, and it's in your face. How far along are you, if I may ask?"

"It'll be eight weeks soon."

"Does Jean-Christophe know?"

"Not yet."

"Why are you waiting to tell him?"

Louise's expression darkened, but she chose her words carefully. "I'm going to tell him, Mother. But I want to wait until his father gets back to Nîmes and is feeling better."

Anselme and Elisabeth quietly departed for the Clos du Tournel. Rochefort had delegated everything to Jean-Christophe and had spread the news in the factories that he would be back as soon as his health permitted.

Although her mother's absence was temporary, Elodie couldn't bear the separation. She felt like a stranger in her brother's house. Even little Pierre couldn't get Elodie to smile.

"If she continues to eat so little, she'll end up getting really sick," Louise said.

Jean-Christophe was busy with his work and didn't pay any more attention to his sister's suffering than his father. Furthermore, he had taken up his bad habits again. He was frequenting the brothels and was a regular at the reputed Villa Diane in the Trois-Ponts neighborhood.

Louise had her suspicions. On several occasions, she had smelled a heady perfume on Jean-Christophe. She chose not to say anything and instead lavished attention on Elodie and Sebastien, as well as her own child. Meanwhile, the pregnancy was beginning to slow her down.

Jean-Christophe didn't seem to notice. He was as blind and egotistical as his father.

When Louise told him what should have been exciting news, all he had to say was, "Already? Couldn't you have waited? This was not a good time to get pregnant."

Louise clenched her fists and left the room, slamming the door behind her.

Sebastien wanted to say something, but Jean-Christophe cut him off. "Don't get involved. It's none of your business."

Elodie wasn't impermeable to what was happening around her. On the contrary, she was highly sensitive to the slighted vocal intonation, the tiniest gesture, and any fleeting look. She couldn't bear being witness to quarrels, lies, and suspicions. They pushed her deeper and deeper into despair.

One morning when nobody but the help was home, she slipped out with nothing but a coat and shawl. She wandered across the city without paying attention to where she was going. She walked for hours, her eyes empty and her face expressionless. Nobody paid any attention to her. When night fell, she realized she was walking along a railway line. A locomotive's shrill whistle caused her to jump. The train whizzed past just a few feet away. Pulled out of her lethargy by this brush with death, she looked for shelter. Even though she was shivering, she was tired and just wanted to sleep.

As soon as Louise got home, she sent someone to the factory to tell Jean-Christophe. Enraged at being bothered in the middle of negotiations with an Italian trader, he rebuffed the servant his wife had sent.

"Tell her to take care of it herself. My sister couldn't have gone far. Tell her to call the police if she needs to."

When evening fell, and Elodie still hadn't come back, Sebastien offered to go look for her.

"That would be like looking for a needle in a haystack," Jean-Christophe said, furious because he had been forced to cancel a date at the Villa Diane.

The two brothers spent all night looking for Elodie. It was

futile. At dawn, they went to the police station to report her disappearance.

"You say she's sick, do you?" the officer said.

"She's crazy," Jean-Christophe let out.

"No, she isn't, sir," Sebastien intervened. "Elodie is depressed and anorexic, which means she certainly hasn't eaten anything since she left. She must be very weak. She'll die of starvation if no one finds her."

"What a damned nuisance," Jean-Christophe said.

"Calm down, Mr. Rochefort. I'll send a squad out to look for your sister. Go home now. I'll let you know as soon as I have some news."

Nobody found Elodie. Against Louise and Sebastien's wishes, Jean-Christophe called Elisabeth. She dropped everything and hurried back, leaving Anselme with Dolores and his chauffeur, Henry.

For four days, Elisabeth made the rounds of places where she thought her daughter could have gone, including the cemetery where Catherine lay in the family tomb. Sebastien went with her.

"What would she be doing in the Rochefort tomb?" he asked.

Elisabeth hid her thoughts. "Something tells me she could be there."

It had not occurred to the police to go to that final place of rest, which held the Rochefort family secrets. Elisabeth's heart started pounding when she arrived in front of the small mausoleum. The monument looked like a chapel, rising up nearly anonymously in a green square surrounded by century-old cypress trees. On the pediment, a shiny epitaph with gold letters chiseled in the stone indicated who lay there: The Rochefort Family. Seven first names, including Catherine's, along with the dates of the birth and death of each, followed.

Elisabeth pushed open the tomb's wrought-iron door.

It took a few seconds for her eyes to adjust to the darkness. Then she saw a form lying on the floor, next to a large marble sarcophagus.

"Elodie," she cried out.

Sebastien hurried inside to help his sister. He felt for her pulse. "She's alive!"

They took Elodie home in Dr. Blanchard's coach. She had wandered through the city for more than two days without eating or drinking. Then she had gone to the Catholic cemetery. In her troubled mind, Catherine was waiting for her there, having invited her on a fine voyage to a place where the shadows of the mind no longer existed and where everyone got along marvelously. She had heard Catherine call, "Come with me. Join me. You'll see, where I am, your troubles will be gone. You'll know eternal happiness, and you'll finally know the truth."

Elodie had listened to the voice. She had entered the Rochefort tomb and had laid down at the foot of the sarcophagus. She had let herself be carried away in Catherine's arms. Three more days had passed.

"Her condition is very serious, Mrs. Rochefort," the family doctor told Elisabeth. "I won't hide the truth from you. We need to hospitalize your daughter and get some nutrition and fluids into her right away. Otherwise, she'll die within two days. She is completely dehydrated and anemic. Her blood pressure is very low, as well."

So Elodie was taken to the hospital, just as her father had been rushed there a few weeks earlier. And just as they had saved her father's life, the doctors saved Elodie's. Two days later, when she came back from her long journey through the depths, she immediately asked, "Where is Catherine?"

Elisabeth didn't know what to say. Sebastien came to her rescue. "Catherine is fine. You don't need to worry about her.

She would want you to get healthy. And we're here to help you do that."

Elodie began her convalescence. She had lost all her strength and couldn't stand or walk without help. She had to learn to accept herself and reality. Catherine was gone and would not come back. When Elodie returned home, she understood that no one could come back from the place where she had wanted to flee.

She looked to Elisabeth, her eyes filled with tears, and asked, "Mother, will you help me to live?"

20

The Lull

Summer 1912

Anselme spent the entire summer at the Clos du Tournel. Far from his daily worries, he ended up appreciating the calm of his estate. Elisabeth returned with Elodie, whom she wouldn't leave in Nîmes, even with Louise.

Anselme enjoyed long drives with his wife through the Cévennes Mountains. Nearly every day, his chauffeur, Henry, took him into the highlands, where the brisk air made him feel good. He had Henry push his wheelchair up to a certain crest so that he could admire the view. Planted terraces carpeted the hillsides. He did his best to make out a tiny spot in the distance, nearly lost in a chestnut grove, where his ancestors had built their first home. They had been Huguenots until their conversion to Catholicism not long after the revocation of the Edict of Nantes.

He also had Henry drive him along the former royal cliff road and often told him to go all the way to Florac, where the cold water of the Tarn River cascaded into the heart of the little town. He would go into rapture in front of the Causse Méjean cliffs and refuse to return home before dusk. He wanted to linger in cafés where well-off tourists enjoyed regional dishes. He forgot about his disability and his wheelchair and was pleasant with everyone who approached him.

Elisabeth rejoiced in the change. His disability was making him more human, she thought with compassion.

He did, however, still fume when he couldn't do things that required two hands, such as cutting his meat at dinner, getting dressed and undressed, and moving from his bed to his wheelchair. He refused to ask for help and tried to figure things out on his own. Finally, he'd grumble, give up, and call for assistance. Elisabeth preferred to send Dolores, whose happy disposition helped to keep him calm.

Although he was easier to get along with, he was still entirely self-absorbed. Elodie's hospitalization and convalesce didn't seem to affect him in the least. He was focused entirely on himself and convinced that one day he would rise out of his damned wheelchair.

"I'll walk alone soon, even if it's with canes. I will walk, for God's sake!" he would rage when, despite his best efforts, his right side remained motionless in his chair.

Elisabeth now had to split her time between two patients. But she kept her chin up. Faith was her solace. She never missed Sunday Mass in the small Anduze church, and every night she asked God to heal her husband and daughter. When Anselme and Elodie were napping, she would visit Constance, whose friendship gave her strength. Although very different, the two women understood each other.

"We're going to be grandmothers again," Constance said when she saw Elisabeth. "Louise told us the good news. Let's hope it's a girl this time."

Elisabeth found the warmth and friendliness in the Rouvière household that were missing in her own. She had often thought about confiding in Constance, whose simple hospitality touched her deeply. She would have loved telling her how the tension between Louise and her son, her husband's lack of interest in his grandson, and her suspicions of Jean-Christophe's infidelity were eating away at her. But what good would it do? Constance was better off not knowing, she thought.

Anselme allowed Faustine and Sebastien to spend August and September at the Clos du Tournel. Faustine pouted about not being able to go to La Bastide to see Vincent, as she had ever other summer, but Sebastien seemed to appreciate his time in Anduze.

Sebastien had graduated with honors at the end of June and immediately asked his brother to register him at the Ecole privée de sciences politiques, known as Sciences Po. Anselme was not opposed to this and thought that sending his son to Paris would actually lessen his own responsibilities. He did, however, give Jean-Christophe a warning. "Tell him that I agree to this only if he works seriously. If he does, I'll pay for his studies, his food, and his lodging. If he doesn't, I'll cut him off. That's a promise."

So Sebastien thought he would spend his few months of free time doing nothing. "I want to enjoy some leisure time before going back to work," he told Louise when she asked about his plans. Peace seemed to have settled between father and son, much to Elisabeth's relief.

Elisabeth, however, was still concerned about Elodie's health. Despite her efforts, the young woman had not overcome her anxiety or developed an appetite. Anselme had agreed to let a psychiatrist come to the Clos du Tournel so that she could undergo therapy. Twice a week, Elodie spent hours locked up with the doctor, listening to his advice, and working on herself, digging deep inside her troubled mind to bring the causes of her torment to the surface. The progress proved to be slow but real. The psychiatrist was the first to say so and reassure Elisabeth.

"Your daughter is very determined. She really wants to get better. I'm confident, but she will need extensive therapy. With your permission, I would like to continue working with her when you return to Nîmes."

It didn't take long for Sebastien to get bored with his life at the Clos du Tournel. After a few weeks, the leisure time he had been looking forward to began to weigh on him. He roamed La Fenouillère every day in hopes of finding Esmeralda, the young gypsy he had not seen since his father had confined him, first to Nîmes and then to Avignon. He discreetly asked Donatien's farmhands and others if they knew where she was. No one had seen her in a very long time.

"Both mother and daughter left," an elderly woman in a neighboring hamlet finally told him. "I knew them well. They never hurt anyone. People didn't like them very much, though, so they didn't stay."

"Do you know where they went?"

"They didn't have any friends or family here. They must have gone back to the gypsies."

"Where? In Camargue?"

"Maybe. Who knows."

Sebastien didn't learn anything else. *I probably wasn't that far from her when I ran away*, he thought. La Camargue was close to the place where he and Alexandre had gotten off the barge at the end of the Port-de-Bouc canal. He thought a lot about that young woman, who had opened his heart and taught him that one should always follow the path to freedom.

Dispirited and a bit lonely, Sebastien lingered on the outskirts of the Rouvière farmstead one night. He heard voices.

The Rouvière family was outside, enjoying the warm evening. Forgetting that his parents were waiting for him for dinner, he stole closer to the house.

"What are you doing?" It was a female voice. Startled, Sebastien turned toward the voice and found Julie Rouvière. "Oh, it's just you," she said.

"I was out for a walk and heard people talking," he said, justifying himself.

"So you thought you'd come close and listen."

Caught, Sebastien didn't know what to say, so he changed the subject. "It's been ages since we've seen each other."

"Yes, at least two years."

"You've grown a lot."

"I'm seventeen now."

"You're a young woman. You are . . . "

"A young woman," Julie repeated.

"Yes, that's it."

Julie seemed as embarrassed as Sebastien. She looked away and smoothed her farm dress. "I didn't change after work. Don't pay attention to how I'm dressed. It's awful."

"No, not at all," Sebastien said. "I think you are very pretty. You've changed so much. Um, no, that's not what I meant to say. You were pretty before, but . . . "

"But what?"

"Now you are not quite the same."

"You also have changed."

The two teens seemed to be getting acquainted for the first time. They walked into the vineyard and lingered there. And as they talked, their shyness slowly dissipated.

After promising to see each other again, they began meeting every evening, at the end of Julie's workday. With Donatien and Vincent gone with the sheep, there was a lot to do to at La Fenouillère.

"Sometimes I've had enough of this life," she complained

one evening. "Since Louise married your brother, I have to do everything. She was so lucky to escape farm life."

"Doesn't Aline help?"

"My little sister decided to become a teacher. She's going to continue her studies, so I'll be the only one working the farm."

"With Vincent."

"Yes. Fortunately, he'll be here. He helps my father a lot. And *he* likes it."

Julie seemed bitter. She wasn't jealous of her sisters. Rather, at seventeen, she felt imprisoned. She saw herself working at La Fenouillère until she married and then spending the rest of her days as a farmwife. This was not what she wanted.

"You need the courage to rebel," Sebastien said, taking her gently by the shoulders. "That is what I did, and now my parents listen to me."

As the days went by, Julie opened up. She had found an ally in Sebastien, who soothed the pain she held in her heart. She had been feeling not just confined, but also isolated. Aline was always preoccupied with her studies, and Vincent, at fourteen, had already fallen in love. Her brother had not been able to keep his feelings for Faustine a secret from her.

For his part, Sebastien forgot about Esmeralda. Julie made him feel good. Slowly, the two teens became irresistibly attracted to each other. They walked side by side in the vineyards and hills. Sometimes they spent time beside the river. Sebastien would go for a swim at the end of the day, when the water was still warm. Julie didn't know how to swim, so she would just soak her feet.

Although they let their hands brush when they walked, neither dared to make the first move. Julie waited for Sebastien to say something. Sebastien hesitated, unsure of himself. One night, however, he led her farther into the grapevines. It was a beautiful evening, with a silver moon lighting the sky. It seemed like the crickets were chirping just for them.

Sebastien invited Julie into a field hut. A layer of fresh hay covered the floor. The two of them undressed, daring to look at each other. And then they let their bodies express what they were feeling.

At the end of September, Anselme decided to go back to Nîmes.

"My convalescence is over," he said in a tone that left no room for discussion.

"Don't you want to wait until the grape harvest is over?" Elisabeth asked, surprised. "The harvest meal will take place in a few days. Constance invited us. You haven't had an opportunity to see Donatien and Constance since you got here."

Anselme balked. He didn't like the idea of being observed in his wheelchair by so many people. But Elisabeth insisted.

"Please, Anselme. Do it at least for Elodie. She's getting better. I'm sure the festive atmosphere will be good for her. And it will be an opportunity to visit with your friend, Donatien. He's been busy with the grape harvest since he got back from the mountains. You'll finally be able to spend some time with him."

"Donation is not my friend, dear. He is just my son's father-in-law."

Anselme finally let himself be persuaded to go, but he made it clear that they would all return to Nîmes the following day. "Sebastien has to get ready for Paris. I found him a good boardinghouse for students not far from his school. The woman who runs it doesn't tolerate any pranks. She takes in the sons of fine families like ours."

A few days later, they found themselves celebrating the end of the grape harvest at La Fenouillère. Constance had cautioned Donatien to treat Anselme as if nothing had happened and not express any sympathy, as it would rub him the wrong way.

"I'm happy that we are all gathered together," Donatien

said. "We're just missing Louise and your son. And our grandson."

Louise had come to spend a few weeks with her parents, but the summer heat had gotten to her, and she had decided to return to Nîmes at the end of August. This pregnancy was proving to be harder on her than the first, and she wanted to be closer to her doctor.

Faustine and Vincent were thrilled to see each other and didn't try to hide it. As soon as they could, they slipped away, not at all concerned about what their parents would think. They headed to the vineyards to be alone and spill out their hearts. Anselme didn't say anything but swore he would take his daughter to task that very night. She also had a thing or two to learn about family duty. "And that Janvier!" Anselme said to himself. "He has some nerve thinking he could have anything to do with a young girl from a family like ours! He has clearly forgotten that he is just an orphan."

Sebastien and Julie didn't feel comfortable leaving the celebration because their parents knew nothing about their relationship. But they did find a quiet corner in the courtyard, where they could talk.

"When will we see each other again?" Julie asked, sad that the end of his vacation meant that her ordinary life would resume.

"I'm leaving for Paris in two days," Sebastien said.

"For Paris! You didn't tell me."

Sebastien liked Julie. His affection for her had been sincere, and he had not wanted to take advantage of her. But for him, it was little more than a summer interlude, something to ward off the boredom. He didn't feel any true or deep love for her, and he was not about to alter any of his plans. Furthermore, he never imagined that Julie would take their relationship seriously. So he was surprised by her reaction and didn't know exactly how to tell her that there was no future for them.

"I'm going to school," he explained. "I'm going to study political science. Later, I want to be a reporter."

"But will you be coming back?"

"Um, yes, of course, for summer vacation. The rest of the year I'll be busy with my studies. And Paris is far away."

Julie's face darkened, which moved Sebastien. He took her face in his hands and wiped away her tears.

"What we've had is good. Don't cry. I will write to you."

21

Embezzlement

In October, Louise gave birth to magnificent twins: a boy and a girl, who were promptly named Thibaud and Alix. She was overjoyed, but Jean-Christophe didn't show any feelings. He had been in Lyon on business when she gave birth, and when he learned the news upon his return, he expressed only scornful surprise.

"Twins! Well, those country girls are prolific, aren't they! The house won't be quiet anytime soon."

Any lingering love between Louise and Jean-Christophe seemed to have burned out. Louise tried to make the best of it but had trouble hiding her deepening sadness. Jean-Christophe didn't seem concerned in the slightest. This worried his mother, who reproached him for neglecting Louise.

"Father is the one who wanted this alliance. I agreed because it was good for his business. Don't ask me to love her too!"

"You seem to forget that you've had three children with her. That counts for quite a bit, doesn't it?"

"I never wanted them."

"You should have been more careful, then. Now you're a father three times over, and you have to assume your responsibilities."

"I didn't make them alone. When Louise wants something, Mother, she has a way of getting it. I can assure you of this. But if she thinks she's going to get me to have more affection for her by making babies, she's wrong."

"You're horrible, son. Your father is no easy man, but at least he has always respected me."

She felt sorry for Louise, who had never deserved such treatment.

Fatigued after his return from the Clos, Anselme had followed his doctor's advice and put off any return to work. He continued to let Jean-Christophe handle everything, and his son had seized the opportunity. He moved into a large office and ordered it remodeled according to his own taste. He put his own people in key positions and drew up a list of supervisors whom he planned to replace.

"Men, from now on, you will deal with me and me alone," he told his managers. "My father has given me full authority to run the company. No one will second-guess or question my decisions."

Jean-Christophe also got back in touch with the attorneys for whom he had worked. He had maintained excellent relations with them, especially Mr. Bosson, who had been in his class. The man was skilled, and once hired by the law firm, he had quickly become the right-hand man of the head litigator, Mr. Francesci. Both Bosson and Francesci were known for their lack of scruples. Jean-Christophe asked Bosson to meet him one evening at the Corne d'Or inn on the road to Avignon. It was a place where they wouldn't be seen by anyone from Rochefort Industries.

The Corne d'Or inn was a former postal relay stop that

was popular with ladies' men and adulterous lovers. The owner and staff knew how to keep the names of those who frequented the establishment a secret and were quick to clear up any problems with the law. A few months earlier, a jealous husband had followed his wife and her lover to the inn and had shot the adulterous couple at close range. The wife died on the spot, and her lover was seriously injured. The investigating magistrate declared the inn an affront to public decency and ordered it closed. But the inn remained open anyway. The innkeeper held that much sway with the local big shots.

Jean-Christophe was a regular. He frequently dined there with a companion. After a dinner by candlelight—always at the same table—he would lead his mistress for the night to his preferred room. Its brown and lavender wall covering heightened his desire. He never stayed later than four in the morning, as he wanted to be home before dawn. Once home, he would sleep in the guest room next to the bedroom he shared with Louise. In the morning, he would tell Louise that he had eaten with a business client, and even though he had gotten home before midnight, he had slept in the next room because he didn't want to wake her up. Louise knew better. She never went to sleep before hearing him come in, so she knew he was lying. But she chose not to say anything and clung to her hope that he would change one day.

Gilles Bosson was surprised by the choice of meeting place but understood that his former classmate had something special to ask and wanted to keep their conversation absolutely private.

"So I'd like to get rid of our silk mills," Jean-Christophe said.

"Has your father agreed to this?"

"That is not a problem. That is, if you help me."

"Explain what you want. It's legal, isn't it?"

Jean-Christophe seemed annoyed. He took the time to take out a cigarette and offer one to his friend.
"No, thank you. I don't smoke."
"Wise decision."
"It's to make my wife happy."
"Holy smoke! Are you still in love, after... How long have you been married?"
"Five years."
"Your love is strong."
"Are you trying to say that you no longer love your wife?"
"I never said anything of the sort. But between us, it's not the way it was in the beginning. For me, love is a passing fancy. But let's get back to business."

An attractive waitress came to take their order. She brushed past Jean-Christophe in a suggestive manner.

"We'll take the chef's special," he said, tapping her lightly on the behind. "And don't come back to bother us, beautiful. The man and I have serious things to discuss."

"Yes, sir. Tonight, the chef's special is..."

"Sh, I want it to be a surprise."

Turning back to his guest, he lowered his voice and said, "Our silk business has been on the ropes for some time now. Natural silk is not fashionable anymore. And what we produce in France is not competitive with what's made overseas. At this point, we need to act decisively. I've considered the options, and I've seen two. On one hand, I could fire half of our workforce. This would cause general discontent, possibly a strike. And it would make our business fodder for the left-wing press, which would certainly not miss an opportunity to drag our name through the mud. On the other hand, I could sell the business before it's too late. That's what I plan to do. I've reorganized our management staff, and I've gotten the accountant on my side."

"What do you want from me? I don't understand how I could be of use to you."

"I have a couple of problems. First, I have to convince my father that it is time to sell. He has been very committed to the silk business, and even though our situation is serious, I need to make it look even worse to persuade him. My accountant has come up with a fake financial statement with negative budget projections, based on doctored data. In his present state, I don't think my father will examine the figures too closely."

"Has his mind been going?"

"No, not that I know of. It's just that he tires quickly. But make no mistake, he's stubborn enough to hang onto the notion that he'll return to work. He's just waiting for the day."

"And if that happens, you won't be in charge anymore."

"Exactly. The old goat can talk all he wants about making me a full partner, but in reality he still considers me nothing more than an assistant in charge of foreign markets."

"You said you have a couple of problems."

"Yes, I need to make the business look worse than it is to convince my father to sell. But to get the best price, I need to make the business look better than it is. As I told you, our revenues have been dropping for some time. The business is worth far less today than it was years ago."

"I'm beginning to see what you want from me," Bosson said.

"I would give you everything—all the accounts, both the real ones and the others."

"The doctored ones."

"If you will."

"So you want me to falsify the data and pump up the revenue to attract a buyer and get a good price."

"You got it. You'll be in charge of preparing the papers, including the taxes, so that we can find a good buyer. There are lots of small businesses in the region that want to expand."

Gilles Bosson took a cigarette from Jean-Christophe's case, which he'd left on the table.

"So now you're smoking."

"Starting now."

"Does that mean you're on?"

"I need to think about it. You know, if your little sleight of hand is discovered, you could be brought up on charges. And if I handle the paperwork, I'll be risking a lot. I could be disbarred."

"I'm aware of that. But you also stand to gain quite a bit. I'll give you eight percent of the sale price and more if you find a buyer who's willing to pay top dollar."

"Can I have some time to think?"

Jean-Christophe smiled and slowly inhaled his cigarette.

"You know things now, Gilles. You do understand what I mean, don't you?"

"You mean I know it is already too late to refuse?"

"You got it."

The tone of the discussion had suddenly changed. In the face of his friend's hesitation, Jean-Christophe appeared to be holding something over the man.

"And if I refuse?"

"You'll have to consider the consequences. You forget that I once worked for the firm, and I know certain things that could get you and your mentor Francesci into hot water if word ever got out. You don't want that to happen, do you?"

"Why don't you handle this matter on your own? You know the ropes as well as I do."

"In this kind of transaction, I can't act as the company's attorney. And even if I could, my father wouldn't trust me. You know him. But if the papers are presented by an attorney from the Francesci firm, he'll accept them with his eyes closed. That I know for sure. He won't be suspicious. The buyer will also be more confident."

Gilles Bosson promised to give his answer in forty-eight hours, the time needed to take a good look at Jean-Christophe's books.

"If everything looks okay, I'll handle this," he said.

"But there is one condition," Jean-Christophe said.

"Which is?"

"Before the sale is finalized, you deposit half the amount in a Swiss account that I've opened. The rest will go through legal channels when the transaction is closed."

"Are you already planning on a big sale?"

"I didn't say that, but I'm careful. If things turn bad, I want all contingencies covered."

The attorney called Jean-Christophe the following evening to say he would handle the sale.

Busy raising her three children and unaware of her husband's scheming, Louise was spending more and more time at La Fenouillère. It was the only place where she could feel comfortable and accepted. Jean-Christophe didn't complain about her frequent absences. He was happy to be free to engage in all the hanky-panky that he wanted. Elisabeth, who surmised his indiscretions, talked to him about his duties as a father—which were even more important than his duties as a husband as far as she was concerned. But she only managed to get vague promises out of him. She grew tired of pleading with him and ended up telling her husband.

"Anselme, our son is debauched and is bringing shame to our family."

Anselme scowled. "What's gotten into you now, Elisabeth?"

"I'm telling you, Jean-Christophe is dirtying your name with his brazen behavior."

"Explain yourself."

Elizabeth told him what she had learned and what she had suspected for several months.

"I've known about that for a long time, my dear," was Anselme's answer.

"And you've never spoken to him about it? How can you tolerate such behavior?"

"Jean-Christophe is a man. He needs his freedom. Louise is suffocating him."

"So you're saying that you have no problem with his behavior."

"I don't want to get involved in his private life. I'm only interested in his work. And in that area, I trust him entirely. He's doing a fine job. He has, for that matter, just convinced me that it is time to sell our silk business. One of his lawyer friends from the Francesci firm is handling the papers for the transaction."

Elisabeth was surprised by her husband's easy acceptance of Jean-Christophe's greater role in the company. Perhaps Anselme had realized that it was time to step back. She decided to drop the matter of her son's behavior and focus on the family's next trip to Anduze.

"Will you be coming with us? We will celebrate Christmas and New Year's with the Rouvières. Elodie is coming, of course, as is Dolores, who will help with the twins."

"Do I have a choice?" Anselme muttered. "If everyone is jumping ship, I'm not going to stay here all by myself. My heart couldn't take it."

They all gathered at the Clos du Tournel for the end-of-year festivities. Elisabeth had decided that they should stay for two weeks, and Anselme didn't oppose her. Since suffering his stroke, he was happy to let his wife make some of the decisions. He was, in fact, feeling very tired.

Jean-Christophe stayed in Nîmes at first, using the excuse that he had the details of the sale to attend to. So Louise went without him and chose to stay with the children at La Fenouillère until her husband arrived.

The Rouvière household was festive. Constance was

thrilled to be spending the holidays with her grandchildren. She wanted to invite the Rochefort family for Christmas Eve and counted on Louise to convince Elisabeth and Anselme.

"Will Jean-Christophe be here?" she asked.

"He promised to spend Christmas and New Year's with us. He'll join us when he can get away."

Vincent was thrilled at the prospect of being with Faustine again. But when the first few days passed, and he failed to catch any sight of her taking her usual walks, he grew worried. Louise thought it best to tell him.

"Her father has forbidden her to go on walks with you. I'm so sorry, Vincent. I know how much you care about each other. I talked to my mother-in-law. She wouldn't give me any more information. I think your friendship doesn't please them very much. Or at least not my father-in-law."

"But why? We're not doing anything bad. Is it because I'm an orphan? I'm not good enough for them. I'm sure if I were your real brother, they'd accept me."

The boy slammed the door on his way out and ran toward the Clos du Tournel. "I'll give that Anselme Rochefort my two cents," he vowed to himself.

The days went by. It started snowing in the mountains, and soon the hills and plains were covered with a thick cottony coat. Life outside seemed to stand still. The streets in the neighboring village were deserted. The only sounds came from the houses and the church, which were filled with joyful activity. In the church, the priest, surrounded by altar boys, was busy preparing the manger scene. The choir was rehearsing Christmas carols. A wood-burning stove stuffed with oak logs hummed in the central aisle, giving off a fine aroma and so much warmth, the church doors had to be swung open.

Vincent didn't have the opportunity to see Anselme Rochefort, who remained closed up inside the Clos. He wandered around the Rochefort home for several days, hoping that Faustine would come outside. His cheeks turned pink, and his fingers grew numb as he waited hour after hour. When he returned to La Fenouillère, he wouldn't say anything. Donatien thought he had been out with the farmhands and wasn't worried. But when he learned from his help that Vincent hadn't been with them, he asked for an explanation. Vincent confessed.

Donatien gave him a warning. "If you go on like this, I'll have trouble with Anselme Rochefort. Is that what you want?"

"Faustine and I have loved each other for a long time. You know that."

"You love each other, sure enough. But you are a little young, don't you think?"

"Those two children have loved each other since they first met in the highlands," Constance said. "That's the way it is. There's nothing we can do about it."

"So you knew?"

"They aren't doing anything bad. Let them love each other."

Donation mussed Vincent's hair. "Promise me that you won't do anything stupid. Okay, boy? If Rochefort catches you, don't count on me to defend you. You'll have to work that out alone."

"I promise, Dad. But don't worry. He won't surprise me."

Louise then invited her mother-in-law and the two girls to have coffee at La Fenouillère. Anselme thought Vincent was working with Donatien, so he stayed at the Clos with Dolorès, who had become indispensable to him. While the women chatted and marveled over the twins, Faustine and Vincent sneaked off and fell into each other's arms.

Julie, meanwhile, was missing Sebastien. True, he had told her that he wouldn't be back before summer, but deep down, she had hoped he would show up for Christmas. She did not doubt what she felt for him, but she was afraid she had made a mistake. Three months had gone by since his departure, and she hadn't received a single letter. Hadn't he promised to write?

Julie felt even worse because she couldn't talk to anyone about the looming crisis in her life. It was what every young woman feared after an impulsive carnal encounter. Since that night with Sebastien, she hadn't had her period. She had barely paid attention the first time she missed her period, but she started worrying when she missed the second. The nausea of the past few weeks had just exacerbated her fears. She couldn't tell anyone, not even her mother, who was so understanding about Vincent and Faustine. She didn't dare say anything to Louise, who did everything so conventionally: a fine wedding, children, and a dream life, or so she thought. She considered writing to Sebastien. But he hadn't given her an address. All she remembered was the name of his school in Paris.

Julie was distraught and desperately alone. As everyone else prepared to celebrate Christmas, she felt cursed and abandoned, a victim of fate.

22

Confessions

1913

With Sebastien gone, Louise felt very alone in her mansion. She was never really alone, as she had the children and a houseful of domestics hired by Jean-Christophe. But the children were young, and the domestics were reserved. Even though she felt closer to them than her in-laws, who were always bragging about their social status, establishing any kind of friendship with the help would have been unseemly.

Jean-Christophe, who had managed to pull the wool over his father's eyes, did bring people into the home. He liked to entertain Rochefort's major customers and business allies there. With his father's approval, Jean-Christophe had transformed the company into a limited partnership. Prospective partners courted him, convinced that investing in the business was a shrewd move. With the capital they promised to bring into the company and the earnings from the sale of the silk operations, Jean-Christophe intended to expand his denim production and diversify into other types of serge and cotton cloth. He would double the number of looms in his factory.

"My goal, sirs, is to crush our competitors in the region and rival the master textile producers in Roubaix-Tourcoing," he would tell his business associates.

As Jean-Christophe's power grew, his father's continued to decline. Anselme still wanted those around him to believe he intended to return to work, but that appeared less probable as the days passed. And with each passing day, Anselme became even more irascible, never finding anything to his liking and scolding everyone who took care of him—both relatives and domestics. He grumbled about everything that went on in his good city of Nîmes, which he said had fallen into the hands of miscreants and dangerous revolutionaries. He thought the country was on the road to ruin, governed by a clique of incompetent politicians.

"If my father were still alive, he'd miss the empire for sure. Both Napoleons, even the little one, knew how to get people to obey."

Jean-Christophe would remind his father of his influence. "Father, the Second Empire is history. Today, real power is not in the hands of politicians, but in ours. We are not their playthings. We businessmen and industrial leaders and our elite families are the ones who wield the power."

Certainly, Jean-Christophe wasn't telling him everything, but as far as Anselme was concerned, his son's sentiments made him a worthy descendent. He was proud of his first born.

Louise got it into her head that Vincent should come live with her in Nîmes. His faltering romance with Faustine saddened her. She had woven the tale: two teenagers—one fifteen, the other fourteen—madly in love since meeting at the age of ten. She was from an elite family. He was an orphan taken in by an honest, well-to-do farm family. Her people were opposed and kept the pair apart. It was a clash of love and duty. Which would win out? Louise thought love could triumph. All the two young lovers needed was a good fairy.

Louise was also motivated by self-interest. She needed more love in her somber world. Yes, her children did give that to her in abundance. Their innocent smiles filled her heart. But it wasn't enough. She needed older family members with whom she could talk and share freely without feeling that she didn't belong.

At the end of February, she returned to La Fenouillère and told her parents what she wanted.

Donatien was surprised. "Take Vincent in? But I don't see what he would do in Nîmes. I'm teaching him here, and later he'll manage the farm. I never hid my intentions."

"Dad, I don't want to take Vincent away from the future you've planned for him. It's the opposite. I've thought about that."

Constance was listening attentively. She didn't understand what Louise was getting at either.

Louise continued. "Vincent did well in school."

"He got the best grades in his class."

"He could continue his schooling with the end goal of doing a better job of managing La Fenouillère. In his hands the farm could become truly modern, and Vincent could become an extraordinary farmer."

"Louise, you're making me feel bad."

"I'm sorry, Dad. I didn't mean to do that."

"Go on. I'm listening."

Louise explained her idea, without mentioning that she needed someone to talk to and without admitting that she wanted to make it easier for Vincent and Faustine to see each other.

"Have you talked to Vincent about this?" Donatien asked. "Vincent was eager to quit school and come work full time on the farm."

"I haven't said anything yet. I wanted to talk to you first."

"I'm afraid his reaction may disappoint you."

"Does that mean that I can ask him and that you would agree?"

"Okay, okay, let me think about it."

Constance smiled.

Now Louise just needed to convince Vincent. The idea caught him by surprise. At first he wasn't thrilled about the notion of going back to school, but when Louise made it clear that he would be close to Faustine, he was onboard.

"Would I be free to go out?" he asked, excited about this new prospect.

"If you promise to be reasonable."

"How long will I have to go to school?"

"I don't know. You decide. If you do well, you could make up for the time you lost and go to the lycée. You'll start by finishing middle school."

Vincent wasn't all that bothered by the idea of going back to school. What really troubled him was leaving the farm, with the vineyards and animals. He would miss silkworm season and the grape harvest. He wouldn't be spending so much of his time outside. And he wouldn't be with Donatien and the farmhands.

"Victor will miss me," he said.

"I know. But he'll understand that you'll be working for your future."

"Do you really think I have a future with Faustine?"

Louise didn't answer. She changed the subject. "You need to know how to appreciate the present. So what do you think? Dad is waiting for your answer."

"I agree, on the condition that I'm not a burden to you. But, by the way, does your husband agree?"

"Jean-Christophe took care of his brother for more than a

year. So he can't object to me taking care of you. You are my brother, aren't you?"

"As far as the Rocheforts are concerned, I am just an orphan adopted by the Rouvières."

When Louise presented Jean-Christophe with her arguments, he agreed, with some reticence, to open their home to Vincent and allow his wife to take the teenager's future in her hands. So Vincent moved to Nîmes in March. Louise had registered him in a private school near the center of town, where he would complete the third term of the year.

"The principal warned me that you will have to repeat those classes in October, as one term won't be enough to make up what you've missed. You could double up and work through the summer. If you did that, you could take a test in the fall and go on to the next year."

"I'll do my best, Louise. You can count on me."

A new life was starting for Vincent, a life that brought him back to his beginnings, although he didn't realize it. He had pushed the bitter and sad memories of his dark hours at the Sisters of Charity orphanage to the recesses of his mind. For him, life had really begun when he arrived in La Fenouillère one fine spring day. After the gray-walled orphanage and the monastic austerity of the dormitory, the classrooms, and the cafeteria, the Rouvière farm seemed like a haven of happiness, with its hillsides covered with oak trees and vineyards. For him, it was a real and finite paradise, unlike the hazy one the sisters alluded to in their catechism lessons.

During Vincent's seven years at the orphanage near Nîmes, Sister Agnes had occasionally taken him on excursions. They had gone to see the cathedral and the amphitheater. Taking in its high circular tiers around a dusty arena, he had imagined gladiators fighting and poor Christian martyrs being devoured by lions. He remembered the strange fortified palace constructed inside the Roman building during the Middle Ages. All these images were now blurry in Vincent's mind.

"Will you take me to visit the old monuments?" he asked Louise the day he arrived. "I remember the arena, but not very well."

"I'll give you a tour of the city. You'll see. Nîmes is beautiful. We'll visit it on the tramway. Then we'll go to the theater."

"And to the movies?"

"If you want."

Vincent was thrilled. "You know, Louise, I wanted to tell you . . . " He hesitated, clearly embarrassed.

"Yes? What is it?"

"Well, at the beginning, when I first got to La Fenouillère, I had the wrong opinion about you."

"Is that so?"

"I thought you were, well, how can I say it—a little full of yourself and haughty because you were the oldest and seemed to be letting me know that you were first in line to inherit La Fenouillère. I was wrong. I'm sorry to have had such thoughts."

"Maybe you weren't entirely wrong. Teenagers sometimes say things they don't really mean to make an impression on others. We sometimes get our sense of self-worth at the expense of others. I don't hold it against you. I'm sure I deserved it."

"You were always a real sister to me. And I'll never forget what you are doing for me today."

Julie managed to hide her state without too much difficulty. Five months pregnant, she was not showing much, and she was wearing baggy clothes to disguise the little that she was showing. Cousin Madeleine, however, had picked up on something different in Julie's behavior. She had seen her throwing up. Madeleine suspected something but didn't say anything to Constance, as she didn't want to worry her. She suspected that Julie might have the same illness that Elodie Rochefort suffered from. But Madeleine soon realized that it wasn't anorexia that they needed to be concerned about.

Julie was filled with dark thoughts. *I'll never be able to tell anyone*, she thought endlessly. And the more she thought, the more she tried to deny reality. In front of the mirror in her room, she would press in her belly to get rid of the growing bump—the irrefutable proof of the sin she had committed on one fateful night.

Now Constance was concerned about her behavior, as well. The girl was unusually pale. Her eyes were dull, and she had no energy. Constance decided to break the wall of silence that Julie had built.

"What's wrong, Julie? I've been watching you lately. You're hiding something. You can talk to me. I'm your mother."

"It's nothing, really."

"You're lying."

Julie refused to answer.

Madeleine had seen Julie and Constance go off together and guessed that her cousin was trying to pry open Julie's secret. "I know you're worried about Julie," Madeleine said to Constance afterward, when they were alone in the kitchen. "Did she tell you anything?"

"She's hiding something, but she won't tell me what it is."

"Have you noticed that she's throwing up a lot? I didn't say anything, because I didn't want to scare you. But it's been going on for a while."

"No, I haven't noticed," Constance said, surprised. "You don't think that she's . . ." Constance couldn't finish the sentence. The idea seemed too ridiculous.

"I think she could be," Madeleine said.

"That's impossible. Come on. Julie hasn't been seeing anyone. We would have known about it."

"If you want my advice, you need to have a serious talk with her."

"I just did. She says everything is fine."

"You need to clear the air and be quick about it."

Constance took Madeleine's advice. That night, she walked into her daughter's room without knocking. She found Julie standing naked in front of the mirror. Embarrassed, Julie put on her nightgown without saying a word.

"Daughter, we need to talk," Constance said. "Madeleine and I think you are pregnant. Tell me we're wrong."

Julie didn't say anything.

"Say something. Don't just stand there. Are you pregnant?"

The poor girl started sobbing. The tears Julie could no longer hold back gave Constance the answer she had feared.

"So that's it. Why, Julie? Why?" Angry and heartbroken, Constance started crying, as well.

Julie finally spoke. "I'm sorry, Mom. I'm so sorry. I didn't think that . . ."

"You didn't think. But you're not a little girl anymore. You're seventeen. You knew what you were doing."

"Forgive me, Mother. What can I do now? I'm lost!"

Constance calmed herself. "How long has it been?"

"Five months."

"Five months! That's impossible. You must be wrong. We would have noticed. It would show more than it does."

"I'm sure, Mother. It's been five months. There was only one time."

"Tell me who did this to you!"

"I can't. Don't make me."

"We'll end up finding out, Julie. You should tell us now."

"What will Dad say?"

"You should have thought of that before. So who was it? If it's one of our servants, don't try to protect him. He'll have to repair the damage he's done, or else he'll be fired immediately."

"It's not someone from La Fenouillère."

"Who was it then? Have you been going into town? I trusted you! Tell me, Julie, or else I'll call your father right now, and you'll explain to him."

"It's Sebastien."

"Who?"

"Sebastien Rochefort!"

Julie was sobbing uncontrollably.

Taken aback, Constance grabbed a chair. "Sebastien Rochefort!"

"I love him, Mom. I'm in love with him. I have the right. He's the only one who ever noticed me. He seemed so nice and so sincere."

"My darling, that's no reason to do what you did."

"We didn't think. It just happened."

"I suppose your Sebastien doesn't know anything about this."

"I haven't heard from him since he left for Paris."

"Of course. My dear, it is too late to cry and be sorry. What's done is done. Now you have to accept it. First you need to tell your father."

"No. Not Dad."

"Do you think you'll really be able to hide the truth from him for long?"

Julie finally came around.

"We'll talk to him when we've calmed down," Constance said. "Tomorrow morning, okay? Try to relax now. Tomorrow is another day. We have time to decide what to do."

23

Confrontation

Donatien was not a man who easily lost his temper. When Constance told him what had happened to Julie, his first thought was to go see Anselme Rochefort and find a fair solution to the sticky problem his son had created by abusing of his daughter's naïveté. Distraught, Julie had no intentions of going with him. She was too afraid of Anselme, having seen him reprimand both Sebastien and Faustine. Constance thought they should wait for Rochefort's next visit to the Clos du Tournel.

"Julie has already shilly-shallied too long," Donatien said. "If they don't come soon, it will be too late to hide her state. We should tell them quickly, so they can inform Sebastien, and we can arrange the marriage right away. I don't want my daughter to be married with a big belly. What will people say? We'll be ridiculed."

"Then this needs to be taken care of in the coming month. After that, it will be too late. She'll show," Constance said.

Julie didn't say a thing. She was too ashamed to say what she knew in her heart and her head. She had changed since confessing her sin. She wasn't relieved, but she was wiser. She knew that her feelings for the father of her child had been built on sand. *I got carried away*, she thought. Her interlude with Sebastien was no more than a passing fancy, a stray moment, a flash that blinded her. She had deluded herself.

"Sebastien will never agree to marry me," she mumbled, interrupting her parents' conversation.

"I would like to see that," Donatien said. "When you make a mistake, it's your duty to make amends. Besides, he's not the one who decides. He's still a minor. His father and I will decide. If need be, I'll go to Nîmes."

Donatien was sure of himself. *After all*, he thought, *our two families are already united. I'm sure Rochefort will be reasonable.*

Rather than call Anselme on the phone, Donatien decided to take the train to Nîmes to see him in person. Constance went along. Julie remained at La Fenouillère.

The Rouvières arrived at Louise's house after letting her know they were coming. They hadn't told her why. Louise was surprised, because her parents had never before visited her in Nîmes. When the taxi dropped them off in front of the house, Louise ran out to meet them.

"I hope nothing's wrong," she said, rushing into her mother's arms.

"No, don't worry, my dear."

"It's nothing serious, but it's something that needs attention," Donatien said.

"Well, come in. We can talk inside."

Tended by their nurse, Louise's children were upstairs. Jean-Christophe was at work. Vincent was at school. The servants were busy with their tasks, and the house was calm.

"So what brings you?" Louise asked.

Donatien asked Constance to talk first. She got right to the point.

Louise was stunned. "I never thought that would happen

to Julie. And five months went by without anybody noticing? I can't believe it. I'll have to keep a sharper eye."

"What do you mean, Louise?" Constance asked.

"Oh, nothing. I was thinking about Vincent and Faustine."

"Are they seeing each other here in Nîmes?" Donatien asked, surprised.

"Occasionally. Vincent walks Faustine home after school when their schedules permit."

"Do the Rocheforts know?"

"No, I don't think so, or else I would have heard about it."

"Those two need to be careful. If there is the slightest problem, you have to let me know," Donatien said. "I'll bring Vincent back to La Fenouillère immediately."

They decided that Louise would go that evening to tell the Rocheforts that her parents were in town and had asked to see them. She refrained from telling her husband, preferring to let Anselme and Elisabeth know first. Louise didn't want to talk to Jean-Christophe anyway. He barely acknowledged Donatien and Constance when he came home, and when he did, he was rude.

"So, you've come for some fresh city air!" he said. "What a change from the smell of manure."

Donatien and Constance had just spent a happy afternoon playing with their three grandchildren. As Constance took in her son-in-law's comment, Donatien watched the joy drain from her face. Although he had always been slow to anger, Donatien wanted to rebuke him. But Louise put a hand on his shoulder to keep him from saying anything.

"My parents want to see your mother and father. That is why they came."

Jean-Christophe didn't respond and went into his office, saying he had work to do.

Two days later, the two families met in the Rochefort mansion, Les Cordeliers, on the Rue Dorée. As they crossed the old city with its narrow alleys, Constance kept saying to her daughter, "How can you live in such a closed-up world? I feel like I'm suffocating. I miss the open spaces."

"That's why I asked Jean-Christophe to live on the outskirts of the city," Louise said. "It's easier to breathe there. The streets and avenues are wider. There are trees. It's closer to the countryside."

"I don't envy you, my dear. Now I know why you like to come back to La Fenouillère."

Louise wanted to confess the more important reasons she often sought refuge in her childhood home. But she refrained, as she had no desire to upset her parents before their meeting with the Rocheforts.

"To what do we owe this pleasure?" Elisabeth asked, welcoming Constance and Donatien with open arms. "How delightful it is to have you in Nîmes."

Uneasy in this ostentatious mansion, the Rouvières sat down. Anselme was in his wheelchair, a wool blanket covering his legs, a cigar in his mouth.

"My dear, you could put out your cigar in front of our guests," Elisabeth said. She turned to Constance and Donatien. "The doctor forbade smoking, but he only hears what he wants to hear."

Anselme did as he was told.

"Before anything else, let's have some tea. What do you say? We can discuss the purpose of your visit afterward," Elisabeth said.

In truth, neither Donatien nor Constance knew how to present what they had come to announce. The discussion wandered a bit, focusing for some time on the grandchildren, a subject everyone seemed to agree on. Elisabeth invited Constance to tour the house.

"Cordeliers is an aristocratic house," Elisabeth said. "We renovated it, but its walls are still full of history. There is a portrait gallery along the stairwell of all those who have lived here for the past several centuries. We didn't touch it. Come, my dear, I'll show you. Let's let the men talk. They'll be better off without us."

Constance gave Donatien a look. Donatien understood it to mean that he should take advantage of their absence to broach the reason for their visit. Donatien cleared his throat.

"We've become friends, haven't we, Anselme? The marriage of our children tore down the barriers that could have continued to separate us when I farmed your land."

Anselme's expression darkened. He wondered what the man was going to ask. He jumped in. "Do you want to revise our summer pasture contract? It's a generous contract, you know. Or maybe you want to give me more land in Anduze."

"This is not about what already unites us, Anselme, but about what will unite us even more in a short while."

"I don't understand."

"I'll get right to the point, Anselme. The business is serious and needs to be addressed without delay. Here it is: My daughter Julie is pregnant."

"But . . . Well, that's an awkward situation to be in. How old is she?"

"She will be eighteen at the end of the year. But that is not the problem."

"She's old enough to marry. I don't mean to offend you, but I don't see what this has to do with me. Do you know who the father is?"

Donatien hesitated and then spit it out. "The father is your son, Anselme."

Anselme started coughing. "Damned cigar. I can't live without them, you know. So my son is what?"

"You son Sebastien is the father of the child my daughter Julie is carrying," Donatien said.

"You're imagining things, dear man. Sebastien is in Paris and has been for five months. How do you think he got your daughter pregnant? It's not possible. Unless you believe the holy ghost had something to do with it."

"I assure you that Sebastien got my daughter pregnant. It was during the grape harvest, just before he left for Paris."

Anselme reddened with anger, and he made an effort to hoist himself out of the wheelchair, using his good arm. He slumped back, helpless. "I don't believe you. You're lying. My son and your daughter? It's impossible."

"Alas, it's the truth."

"What are you looking for, Rouvière? A father for your bastard grandchild? And you thought I'd fall for that! You must have thought we were already united by one marriage, so it would be easy to get me to agree to another. Your daughter's the one who got pregnant. Don't count on me to hand over my son to give that bastard child a father. I'm no pigeon. I got what I wanted when Jean-Christophe married."

In his anger, Anselme didn't realize that he was giving himself away.

"You got what you wanted? What do you mean?" Donatien said.

"Nothing. That's not the issue here."

The men were raising their voices. Alarmed, the two women ran back to the room.

"Anselme, what is going on?" Elisabeth asked.

Donatien looked at Constance. "Constance, we have nothing more to do here. Let's leave this house immediately."

"Donatien, please," Elisabeth said, upset that the two men were angry. "There must be some misunderstanding. Tell me what's going on."

"My husband had something serious to tell you," Constance said as diplomatically as possible. "I believe your husband took the news poorly."

"What news? What's this all about? Talk to me, Anselme. Don't stay walled up in your anger."

Donatien spoke calmly. "Mrs. Rochefort, this is about our daughter Julie and your son Sebastien."

"It's a lie," Anselme said.

"Please, let Mr. Rouvière speak."

"Julie is five months pregnant. Your son Sebastien is the father of the child she is carrying. She told us. There is no doubt."

Elisabeth let the information sink in. Then she asked, "Does Sebastien know?"

"No, not yet," Constance said.

"What do you plan to do?"

"We came to talk to you about that."

"They will not get married," Anselme shouted. "One marriage was enough to bring our two families together. Your daughter is nothing but a tramp. She seduced our son. Let her figure things out."

"Anselme, please," Elisabeth said. "Don't add your ridicule to our friends' distress. Our children sinned together. We are their parents, and we need to support the only honest solution there is in these cases."

"Never!"

"It must happen."

"In that case, I'll disinherit Sebastien. He won't get anything. Nothing. Do you hear me? Nor will your daughter." Cemented in his anger toward his son, Anselme stood his ground. *My rebellious son will be the end of me*, he thought. *But I haven't had the last word yet.*

Unable to travel, Anselme asked Jean-Christophe to go to Paris and resolve the problem. Jean-Christophe jumped at the opportunity to spend a few days in Paris without his wife. But he also wanted to take care of his brother. Although Jean-Christophe's nature was haughty and even surly, he had genuine brotherly feelings for Sebastien. He felt responsible for his younger brother's destiny and did not want to see him totally cut off from his family because he had a stubborn temperament like his father's.

Jean-Christophe took the first train for Paris and arrived on a freezing-cold night. March was coming to an end, but winter was still very present. Jean-Christophe hailed a taxi outside the Gare de Lyon train station and asked to be driven to the Duleu Boarding House in the fifth arrondissement, which was in the heart of the Latin Quarter. Considering the late hour, the landlady refused to open the door. Jean-Christophe had to negotiate, prove his identity, and remind the woman that his father, Anselme Rochefort, had gone through a member of parliament to register Sebastien in her honorable student home. Tired of arguing, the landlady called Sebastien to verify what the visitor was saying.

When he saw Jean-Christophe through the crack in the door, he asked her to let him in. "What are you doing in Paris? And why are you here? I hope you don't have any bad news. Let's go to my room so we can talk."

"Mr. Rochefort, you know that visits are forbidden at this time of night," the landlady said.

"Mrs. Duleu, he's my brother!"

"Rules are rules. But just this once, I'll look the other way."

"My father will appreciate that, ma'am," Jean-Christophe said.

"You're in from the provinces, right?"

"Exactly, from Nîmes."

"And I suppose you don't know where you are going to sleep tonight."

"That is also true, ma'am. I didn't think to reserve a hotel room."

With her head down and her double chin resting on her chest, Mother Duleu, as the boarders called her, was thinking. The students who stayed in the boardinghouse ran straight past her severe looks when they went by her room but made fun of her behind her back. She was committed to running an upright boardinghouse for young people from well-off families. Germaine Duleu had no equal when it came to keeping the riffraff out and making sure none of her boarders brought home company for the night."

"Because he's your brother, I will allow Sebastien to put you up for the night. But only for one night! And just to help you out."

Jean-Christophe thanked her profusely and went to Sebastien's room.

"It's not very big," Sebastien said. "There's just a little bed and a couch. I'll sleep on the couch. You must be tired after such a long trip."

Jean-Christophe didn't want to put off the news he had for his brother. "Father sent me," he said as soon as he got to the room.

Sebastien made a face. "So I thought. What is so important that I need to be told in person and not in a letter?"

"What I have to tell you simply couldn't be said in a letter. And since father can't travel, I agreed to come here myself."

"Okay, I'm listening."

"You made a mistake, Sebastien. Well, let's say you were careless, because at your age, what you did was really quite normal. I won't be the one to throw the first stone. I did the same and even earlier, not to boast or anything. But you weren't careful."

"Dear God, what are you talking about?"

"Julie Rouvière, Sebastien. You slept with her. But sleeping with her is not the issue."

"You haven't come to tell me that she is . . . "

"Pregnant. Yes, brother. In four months, you will be a family man."

"But that can't be! Tell me it's a joke."

"Alas, no. Would I have made such a long trip for a joke? And I'm not finished. Her parents want you to do the right thing."

"What do you mean?"

"They want you to marry their daughter as quickly as possible, before it becomes too visible."

"Did Father agree?"

"Father went into a rage. You know how he is. First against Rouvière and then against you. But Mother ended up convincing him that marrying is the only solution."

"But my studies . . . "

"You should have thought of that before. Between us, you acted like a real virgin. Maybe that was the case, eh?"

"That's none of your business."

Sebastien was completely beside himself. He had never imagined marrying Julie Rouvière. He had let himself go in her arms on that harvest night, but he had never promised anything or led her to believe they had a future together. In fact, he had quickly forgotten her and hadn't even sent her a letter.

"Father wants you to fix your mistake," Jean-Christophe said. "He says he plans to disinherit you, because he cannot stand the idea of a second alliance with my in-laws. I have to agree with him on that point. But I oppose his decision to disinherit you. Father doesn't have the right to disinherit one of his children, under any circumstance."

"Did you take my side?"

"Do you doubt me? Have you forgotten that I took you into my house for a year to get you out of that Jesuit prison where Father had you locked up?"

"I haven't forgotten anything. And although I don't approve of everything you do, I will be eternally grateful for that."

Sebastien had a hard time accepting his situation. And he couldn't bring himself to agree to a marriage. "I don't want to marry Julie," he confessed. "It's impossible."

"You'll have to, I'm afraid, or you will stain your own honor."

"It's impossible, I'm telling you."

"And why is that? You are not obligated to love the one you marry. And marriage is not a prison, if you understand what I mean."

"I don't want to be like you. You have nothing but disdain for those around you. You don't respect anything or anyone."

"Look who's talking, little brother."

"I don't want to marry Julie Rouvière. I love another woman, sincerely and deeply."

"So that's it! And who is this woman?"

"She's a student in my class. Her name is Pauline Andrieu. She comes from a modest family."

"Knowing you, I'm not surprised."

"And that's not all. She's pregnant too. The child's mine. I intend to recognize it."

Jean-Christophe couldn't believe his ears. He even had his brother repeat himself. "You're going to have a child with another girl."

"Yes, that's right."

"And do you want to marry her?"

"For now we are not thinking about getting married. We just want to live together, raise our child, and finish our studies."

"What do you know? That's a fine plan. You're very touching. You have very modern ideas. And what will you live off of?"

"That is not the problem. In any case, I knew Father would cut me off as soon as I told him."

Shocked to the core, Jean-Christophe dropped the whole matter. He had to admit that his brother had more audacity than all the Rocheforts combined. He didn't sleep a wink that night. He didn't know how he would break the news to his parents. He could only imagine his father's anger and his mother's confusion. As for Julie Rouvière and her parents, he didn't give them a second thought.

24

Uncertainty

The Rouvières stayed in Nîmes for a few days, the time it took Jean-Christophe to make his trip to Paris.

To distract them, Louise showed them around the old city. Donatien had been in Nîmes just once, during his military service. The only time Constance had been in the area was when she had gone to the orphanage to get Vincent. Donatien had given his son-in-law four days to get back to him.

Elisabeth wanted to be pleasant, so she offered to go along everywhere Louise took her parents. Together, they visited the arena, the Maison Carrée, the Jardins de la Fontaine, and the Tour Magne, where Constance went into rapture over the panoramic view of the hills where the city had nestled since the time of Augustus.

"Would you like to see our factories? Anselme would be happy to give you a tour," Elisabeth asked the evening of the third day.

"Do you think that is a good idea?" Louise asked, sounding doubtful. "Perhaps Father-in-law doesn't want visitors in the factories."

"There is nothing secret about the business. And the Rouvières are not visitors. The Rouvières are family."

Donatien was curious and agreed right away. "I'd like to see how the silk from our cocoons is spun. I've never had the opportunity to see that."

"So we should do that while we still have time. We won't have the mill much longer. Jean-Christophe persuaded his father to sell. There are already several prospective buyers."

Donatien was shocked. "So the mulberry trees I put in Louise's dowry won't be in the family anymore," he said to himself. "What will Rochefort do with that fine land? He didn't bother to tell me."

Anselme agreed to his wife's suggestion without hesitation, as he was proud to show Jean-Christophe's in-laws the full extent of his wealth. His family was a great industrial force in the region, and he thought the Rouvières could use a reminder.

Anselme arranged to meet the Rouvières the next day at the front entrance. Saying that she had a hard time breathing in the factory, Elisabeth chose to stay home. The chauffeur, Henry, had driven Anselme to the facility and gotten him into his chair.

The Rouvières had never been in a factory. In Alès they had been near the Tamaris foundries and the couple of silk mills in town, but they had never gone inside, where they workers labored in a world that was foreign to them. They were people of the land, and for them—as it was for many in their station—industrial work meant darkness, poverty, and slavery. In fact, in the countryside, a father would often threaten to send a son to the factories—or even the mines—when he wanted to rein in the child. Donatien believed that factory workers were justified in their struggle for better working conditions.

Surmising where Donatien stood, Anselme strived to show

him everything he was doing for his workers. "You will see how attached to modern production methods I am," he said at the start of the tour. "It's to improve the lot of my workers, of course. I had electric lighting installed everywhere. That way, my spinners can work until seven in the evening in the winter without damaging their eyesight. This has greatly improved their work and their yield. The comfort of our workers is my primary concern."

But the noise was deafening. The spinners and apprentices, bent over eighty basins in four rows, looked spent. Their hands were swollen from the boiling water. And their faces were wan and closed as they unwound the silk from the cocoons.

Oblivious to Donatien and Constance's reaction, Anselme went on. "Recently, we added twenty-four six-sided basins with electric motors. They replaced the old steam machines. Electricity is cleaner and quieter. Soon, all the workstations will be equipped, as we've done in our weaving factory, where we'll go next."

"I thought you were selling," Donatien said.

"That's right. We are going to focus on cotton. There isn't much future in silk, except for luxury items. Jean-Christophe and I agree that large-scale production of lower-cost consumer goods is a better bet for the future. That is why I'm expanding our serge production. The working class will grow considerably in the coming decades. They will need working clothes, and who knows, maybe those clothes will be worn for more than work."

Donatien thought it was strange that Rochefort was investing in a mill that he was getting ready to sell. "Clearly, I don't understand what industry is all about, and I've got no interest in speculation," he said to himself.

The humidity and temperature, along with the acrid smell of the heated silk cocoons, was making Constance nauseous. But she kept it to herself. She pitied the poor workers, so focused on their basins and their mechanical reels. They looked pale, tired, and sad. One was pregnant and clearly about to give birth. Constance was moved and said, "Dear God, that poor woman would be better off resting at home and ensuring a safe delivery for her baby."

"Our spinners are strong women," Anselme said, his voice full of haughty pride. "There's no need to pity them. If you do, they will keep asking for more. Managing a business is no picnic, you know. You have to be a firm leader. Authority is a key quality."

The Rouvières exchanged a stunned look but didn't say anything.

Anselme guided them toward the weaving factory at the other end of the central courtyard, which was surrounded by sheds, warehouses, repair shops, storerooms, and offices.

"The Rocheforts have been here for three generations," Anselme said, sweeping his arm across the manufacturing vista. "When I retire and leave the business, Jean-Christophe will continue the work started by my grandfather." "Sebastien won't be involved?" Constance asked. "You have two sons."

Anselme's expression darkened. "Let's not talk about that. The subject saddens me more than you could possibly know. Sebastien is, as we say in well-off families, a renegade. He has no respect for anything and refuses to listen to reason. He does only what he wants. But I'm sure he will beg for my forgiveness one day. He will humble himself and take the walk to Canossa, like all rebellious sons who need their fathers. I'm standing firm and waiting for him. But let's continue our tour."

Anselme's chauffeur stopped pushing the wheelchair. "What's gotten into you, Henry?" Anselme grumbled. "I didn't ask you to stop."

"I'm sorry, sir. I thought I saw Mr. Jean-Christophe go into his office."

"Could he be back? He didn't tell us he would be arriving today."

"Do you want me to take you to him?"

Anselme hesitated. What was Jean-Christophe going to tell him?

"Call Lesage for me. He'll finish the tour with Mr. and Mrs. Rouvière while I go see my son."

"We could cut it short," Donatien suggested.

"I don't want you to have to do that. It's not every day that you're in Nîmes."

The personnel manager accompanied the Rouvières to the cotton-weaving workshops. He gave a detailed explanation of the Jacquard looms and the various weaves.

"Weaving techniques improved tremendously with the invention of the Jacquard loom at the beginning of the last century. But today a worker can produce a lot more than his predecessors. Steam power and then electricity made it possible to greatly automate weaving."

He had to shout to be heard above the din. Still, Constance had trouble hearing. As they walked by, the workers—many of them young—stared at them. Constance felt embarrassed in this role of curious onlooker as they slaved away. Looking affable, Norbert Lesage stopped near a loom.

"Let me introduce our best worker," he said, putting his hand on the young woman's shoulder. "She produces nearly twice as much fabric as the others. She has golden fingers."

The worker seemed uncomfortable with Lesage. Donatien immediately understood that the manager expected more of her than producing fabric. Donatien saw distress in the weaver's eyes, and he felt disgust for Lesage. The young woman started coughing. She took a handkerchief from her smock. It was covered with blood.

"That woman is sick!" Constance said. "She shouldn't be working. And with that draft here, she's just going to get worse. She needs medical attention." "Ma'am, we're not running a charity," Lesage said. "We give work to decent people, and that's a commendable thing."

Constance was trembling with anger. Donatien took her hand to keep her from saying any more. There was no point.

"It's time for us to go," he said. "We will go say good-bye to Mr. Rochefort."

Lesage led them to the offices, where Anselme was in a deep discussion with his son.

"Hello, Jean-Christophe," Donatien said. "What news do you bring from Paris?"

"Sebastien asked for time to think. He was, well, how should I say it—very shocked by the news."

"That doesn't surprise me, but if you take advantage of a naïve young girl, you also need to take responsibility."

"My son will do what's right," Anselme said. "Or else I'll banish him from my household forever. No one will ever say that any of my children brought dishonor to the Rochefort name."

The Rouvières returned to La Fenouillère the next day without any definitive answer.

Weeks passed. In 1913, spring had trouble pushing aside the final chill of winter. It seemed that political events were making the skies even grayer, adding to Anselme's general dissatisfaction.

"France is in a bad way, I'm telling you," he grumbled.

Finally, he decided to do something about his own situation, even if he could do nothing about the country's politics. He went back to work, much to his son's despair.

"I can tell from your mood that your health is improving, and your sense of humor is coming back, as well," Elisabeth said.

"Humor is the best way to fight adversity, my dear. When things are going badly, it helps to taunt those in power. But with all the incompetents running this country, I'm afraid we are headed for a disaster."

In addition to his family worries, Anselme had business problems. Despite Jean-Christophe's schemes with his friend

Bosson, there still was no buyer for the silk mill, and the losses had risen since the beginning of the year.

"If we don't remedy things quickly, it will be a disaster," the accountant, Robert Mazaudier, had told Jean-Christophe. "Your father has decided to check the books. Soon, we won't be able to hide the truth from him."

The uncertainty of the times seemed to be slowing investment. Some thought that Germany was maneuvering toward a war. The Reich government, feeling threatened on both its eastern and its western fronts, had increased the size of the German army for two consecutive years. Now it appeared ready to mobilize more than 850 thousand men. The French army didn't even have five hundred thousand men.

Jean-Christophe, who had once believed that a war would be good for business, was beginning to think the opposite.

"Who wants a silk mill with war in the air?" he worried. "The troops need good cotton uniforms, not silk shirts and lace. If things continue the way they're going, we'll be stuck with the mill indefinitely. Meanwhile, why are we waiting to clothe the men who will be fighting? Germany is making sure its fighting men have what they need. The day the war breaks out—and it will break out, I'm sure of that—I fear our army won't be ready. In the rush, we won't be able to meet the demands. I'm telling you, we need strong-fisted men leading our country, not this soft center that is governing us now and especially not the socialist rabble in the parliament."

As always, the two Rocheforts got along when it came to politics. Were it not for their internal struggle—one to take back the reins and the other to keep them in his grasp—they would have been in near perfect harmony. But their bloated pride and smugness kept them from working as a unified father-and-son team.

Although Anselme was constantly in a foul mood, he had a renewed commitment to getting better. With fierce, if opinionated, determination, he spent several hours a day with a Chinese physical therapist Jean-Christophe had recommended. Master Chang, as he was called, had promised to return mobility to Anselme's paralyzed limbs. When Dr. Blanchard learned from Elisabeth that Anselme was seeing a master in Chinese medicine, he issued a warning. "You shouldn't trust your health to those charlatans who promise to heal you without knowing the real causes of your ailment. They could do more harm than good."

But Rochefort kept his own counsel and continued his work with the master. And eventually everyone—even his doctor—had to admit that by sheer strength of willpower, he was making real progress. He would never be healed, but he was regaining the use of his right arm. He could now grab an object with his right hand and push the wheels of his wheelchair.

"You see," he said to Elisabeth. "I don't need anyone to push me like a baby. Soon I'll be standing on my two feet and walking."

Elisabeth was thrilled to see her husband's progress. Despite his flaws, he was exceptional in many ways.

Only Jean-Christophe was unhappy. He even regretted recommending Master Chang. He had thought the master would keep his father busy and distracted from the business. He envisioned himself free to do as he pleased. He never thought the treatments would have such a dramatic effect on his father. Hadn't Dr. Blanchard and the neurologist, Dr. Souche, assured him that the paralysis was irreversible? But now Anselme was feeling better and better—so much better, in fact, that he had returned to work. And Jean-Christophe was back where he started. He was his father's underling.

"I'm not ready to retire," Anselme said the day he came into the plant without the help of his chauffeur. The entire administrative staff and all of his workers were amazed to see him wheeling himself around.

"The boss is back. He's almost all better," the spinners and weavers whispered to each other. They all feared him much more than they feared his son, whom they regarded as a wily buck with little real authority.

In Paris, Sebastien Rochefort had given his situation a great deal of thought. He was not indifferent to the consequences of his encounter with Julie. He had talked with the woman he loved, Pauline Andrieu. He did not lie to her, and he didn't try to blame Julie or find excuses.

"I am the only guilty party," he had told Pauline. "I did not consider the possible repercussions of my actions. Neither did Julie. That night, I believe that we loved each other. But for me, it lasted just one night. Now I don't know what to do. Whatever I do, I leave a fatherless child."

Pauline did not hold it against Sebastien that the revelation had significantly altered their love affair. She did not react angrily. Instead, she said she would let him go. She could not imagine building her happiness on someone else's misfortune.

"We could never be happy together, knowing that this young woman was in such despair," Pauline said. "You should marry her. She captured your heart first, even if it was only for one night."

His heart aching, Sebastien listened to Pauline and loved her even more for her sacrifice. "I will do the right thing, since that is what you ask of me," he said in tears. "But know that you are the one I love."

At the end of April, Sebastien wrote a long letter to his parents, telling them that he had come to terms with his conscience. He omitted no detail of the conversation he had had with Pauline. He told his parents that Pauline and he had broken off all contact. Finally, he asked them to transmit his marriage proposal to Julie's parents.

When Anselme had finished reading the letter, he turned to Elisabeth. "Sebastien has decided to marry Julie," he said in an icy tone. "He is saving his honor and ours, as well. But I will not debase myself by telling the Rouvières myself."

"Then I will do it for you," Elisabeth said, relieved. "I don't have your misplaced pride. I intend to go to the Clos du Tournel with Louise and our grandchildren next Saturday. Why don't you come to the Clos with us."

"I have too much work to do," Anselme said. "I'll be at the factory with Jean-Christophe. We need to be available in case we get any offers for the silk mill."

As planned, Elisabeth left on Saturday with her two daughters, Louise, Vincent, and her grandchildren. She was happy to be delivering the news that the Rouvières had been awaiting for a good month.

The next day, she went with Louise to La Fenouillère. When they arrived, the farm was strangely silent, and both Elisabeth and Louise had a bad feeling. There was a car in the courtyard, and the door on the driver's side was wide open. They overheard bits of conversation. "Such misfortune . . . be comforted . . . brave."

"It's the doctor's car," Louise said. "I know it. Something happened to my father."

She ran to the top of the front steps. Elisabeth was right behind her.

"Mom," she cried out. "Is it Dad?"

Constance was crying in the kitchen as she talked with the doctor. Surprised to see her daughter, she sobbed harder. "Oh, my darling."

"Talk to me, Mother. What happened?"

"It's Julie. She lost her child."

"But she's alive," the doctor said. "She's in no danger."

Part Three

THE STORM

25

Waiting

Summer 1913

Vincent was happy in Nîmes. In Louise's home, he quickly set aside the ups and downs of life at La Fenouillère. His days passed at a well-established regular pace. Up early every morning, he took the tramway to the school, where he was working toward his agronomics degree. He was not particularly keen on his theory classes, even though he was quite capable of absorbing and processing the information. But he loved the practical classes. Having been well trained by Donatien, he showed more know-how than the majority of his schoolmates. His professors sometimes had the impression that they didn't have much to teach him—with the exception of how to prune olive trees, an area in which he admitted ignorance. Unfortunately, he had missed two much theory. At the end of June, he agreed to repeat his first year, starting in September.

"You are young," Louise told him. "In three years, you'll only be eighteen. Then you'll be able to take over for Dad, and he'll be ready to give you more responsibility. He's almost sixty."

"Unless he won't let go, like Anselme Rochefort."

"Dad is not like my father-in-law. He does what he says he'll do. Believe me, you'll come back from you stint in the army, and he'll hand over La Fenouillère, as he promised."

"Yes, military service. Unless we go to war before that. That's what some people are saying. England, Germany, Russia, and even France are arming to the teeth, as if war's a certainty."

"You sound like Sebastien. By the way, we'll be seeing him soon. He's coming back to Nîmes for summer vacation."

"Yes, I know."

"Is that so? Who told you?"

"Faustine."

Vincent saw the Rochefort girl nearly every day. When he got out of school, he would pick her up outside hers—she went to a private school downtown—and walk with her a good part of the way home. The narrow streets of old Nîmes and its shady hidden squares were accomplices to their encounters, witnesses to their teenage love. Vincent dared to walk hand in hand with Faustine. But she was always afraid of meeting one of her mother's friends or one of her father's business acquaintances. She didn't want to have to explain herself to her parents.

Since Vincent had moved to Nîmes, the Rocheforts had never once asked Faustine if she ever saw him. It was true that Elisabeth had not forbidden her daughter from seeing the young Rouvière, and she was aware of the feelings they had for each other. She chose to look the other way, however, convinced that their infatuation would die out naturally when Faustine became aware of what the future held for a young woman with her education and social status.

Anselme was too preoccupied with his health and his business to be interested in anyone his daughter was or was not seeing. As far as he was concerned, she was still a child. He didn't need to be concerned about finding a match for her for three or four more years.

Louise had been careful not to tell Jean-Christophe about Vincent and Faustine. She was just afraid that Vincent would inadvertently mention Faustine at dinner one night. But Jean-Christophe was just like his father and not at all interested in others. Sebastien was the only one he paid attention to.

Vincent and Faustine were almost caught one Thursday afternoon. They had planned to meet in the Jardins de la Fontaine, near the ruins of the small Temple to Diana. Faustine often took advantage of her mother's outings. Elisabeth would go out with just Elodie, leaving Faustine behind to study. Once Elisabeth and Elodie had left, Faustine would slip out the back door, unseen by the servants, who assumed she was in her room. On this day, the young lovers would have a good three hours.

They liked to meet in the gardens, where they could be away from prying eyes. The Jardins de la Fontaine's Nemausus spring, with its silvery water, fed basins that a military engineer had built in the eighteenth century. Surrounded by the waterways, the pool, and the double staircase—the only remains of the ancient Roman baths—Faustine felt transported back in time. She sometimes recited Ovid and Virgil in Latin. Vincent was impressed with Faustine's erudition, but he wasn't intimidated. Their love for each other erased any differences.

On that Thursday, Vincent wanted to climb the winding path up Mont Cavalier. At the top, the Tour Magne dominated the city, offering a magnificent view of the Mont Ventoux, the Alpilles, the Vistre River, and the Garrigues plateaus. Faustine asked Vincent to go up first, as she had a feeling that they might get caught.

Vincent laughed. "What are you worried about here?" he said. "Your parents would never take a path this winding and steep. Besides, isn't your mother out shopping, and isn't your father at work?"

Faustine insisted, giving him a ten-minute head start.

When he got to the top, not far from the tower, he recognized a familiar car parked on the Rue Stéphane-Mallarmé. It was Jean-Christophe's. Vincent hesitated and then approached the car, his heart beating fast. He felt the hood. The engine was still warm.

Vincent backed away and retraced his steps, fearing he would run into his brother-in-law just as Faustine was arriving at the top of the hill. Then he spotted Jean-Christophe. He was with a woman in a frilly dress, and she was hanging on his arm.

"Hurry up, my dear," he said, leering at her.

Vincent stopped short. His eyes caught those of his brother-in-law, who was pushing his companion in front of him with a heavy hand on her bottom. *Faustine, please don't show up now*, Vincent said to himself.

The two men stared at each other for a few seconds and then looked away as though they had seen nothing.

Jean-Christophe dove into his car. Vincent ran to the path, ready to keep Faustine from going any farther. Winded from her hike, Faustine joined Vincent just as Jean-Christophe was racing off in the car.

"Perfect timing," he said.

"How's that?" Faustine said.

"Any sooner and you would have been spotted by your brother."

"My brother! Jean-Christophe?"

"With a woman."

"With a woman? Here? Are you sure?"

"As sure as I'm standing in front of you. Don't say anything to Louise, please. It would hurt her too much. But I know what I saw. Your brother is cheating on my sister."

"I don't believe it."

"With the wrong kind of woman. I'm sure of that. Fortunately, you arrived after he took off. He couldn't have seen you."

"What will you say when you see him tonight?"

"He's the one who'll be uncomfortable, not me. If he asks what I was doing up here in the middle of the afternoon, I'll tell him I was taking a walk, that I was visiting the Tour Magne. But I won't ask him anything."

That day, Faustine and Vincent understood that they were not safe from the wrong kind of encounter. But rather than give up their meetings, they were twice as careful, which strengthened their bond.

In July, Elisabeth and her daughters arrived at the Clos du Tournel for the summer. Louise had decided to split her time between her in-laws' home and La Fenouillère.

As usual, Anselme and Jean-Christophe stayed in Nîmes during the workweek. They still had no buyer for the silk mill, and they were beginning to worry.

"It's too expensive. We need to lower the price," Gilles Bosson said to Jean-Christophe.

"That's impossible. Father still believes the revenues are good. He would never agree to lower the price."

"We'll just have to hope the economy improves."

"In the meantime, I'm operating at a loss."

"Let some of your workers go, and find raw materials that aren't as expensive."

"Almost all of our silk cocoons come from our own trees, and we get them at cost."

"Then convert to artificial silk, which is catching on. You could do with artificial silk what you've done with cotton: produce it for mass-market clothing."

"My father would never agree to that either. Rochefort silk has always been known for its quality. It is our most prestigious line. He'll get a good price for the mill or he'll keep it. But he'll never tarnish the brand."

"Your father is too proud and not pragmatic enough."

"After what happened to him, I thought he'd retire and give me control of the company, but he just won't let go."

No doubt about it: Anselme was a force to be reckoned with. No, he was not the most pleasant man, but he had refused to let adversity get the better of him. And indeed, he was at the helm of the company.

"It's decided. I'm not selling the silk operation," he told Elisabeth before she left for the Clos du Tournel. "I'm going to modernize it and make it more productive. We'll lower our costs while maintaining our quality. And I'll hire a sales representative to court the country's top designers."

Jean-Christophe was outraged. "Don't you trust me?"

"I didn't say anything of the sort. I'm just not ready to let the silk operation go. It was my grandfather's, and I want to put it on track again. You're already handling our business in the United States, which is quite a lot to manage. I don't want you to take on too much."

Jean-Christophe had the feeling that his father distrusted him. He wondered if Anselme had discovered what he had hidden from him. "Have you checked the mill's books?" he carefully asked Anselme. "The accountant must have told you that profits are down. Nothing alarming. But selling is still the best option, particularly now. I thought you agreed."

"Mr. Mazaudier showed me the books, Jean-Christophe, and as you said, there was nothing alarming in them. Since there's no buyer on the horizon, I see no reason to sell."

Jean-Christophe was relieved that the accountant had succeeded in keeping the truth from Anselme. But his plan was falling apart. And if Anselme carried out his pledge to pour even more money into the silk mill, the entire company's position would soon be weakened.

That wasn't Jean-Christophe's only headache. His personal finances were suffering, as well. He had been frequenting clandestine gambling houses for some time. And he was losing far more money than he was winning. His debts were reaching dangerous levels.

Sebastien decided to pay his family a surprise visit in mid-July. He had hesitated, because he knew he could not ignore Julie's presence at La Fenouillère. Furthermore, he didn't like the idea of leaving Pauline alone in Paris.

But Julie had moved on. After her miscarriage, she told her parents that she would not accept Sebastien's marriage proposal. Donatien and Constance were saddened by the whole affair yet felt relieved by her decision. They gave her a few days in case she changed her mind and then informed the Rocheforts, via Louise. Anselme was satisfied with the outcome and immediately acted as if nothing had happened.

"The whole matter is closed," he said, full of self-importance.

Julie gave Louise a long letter for Sebastien in which she expressed her regrets and sorrow for their lost child. She didn't hold his stalling against him and thanked him for agreeing to marry her. But she also admitted that she didn't want a marriage without real love.

Released from his promise, Sebastien answered her, saying he also was sorry. In simple heartfelt words, he wished her happiness.

Sebastien had decided to go directly to the Clos du Tournel without spending any time in Nîmes. He was trying to avoid the inevitable confrontation with his father. At the Nîmes train station, he dived into a train for Alès and then took a taxi to Anduze. Elisabeth was thrilled to see her younger son, who had changed significantly since his move to Paris. He had grown a beard. His wavy hair fell below his temples, and his clothes were wrinkled. Despite the heat, he had a red silk scarf tied around his neck.

"Dear God," Elisabeth exclaimed. "You're not the same boy. You're a man now."

"A real Parisian student," Elodie added.

Brother and sister hugged.

"You've changed too, sis. You're looking well."

"I'm working on it, but it's not always easy."

"Your sister is making a real effort," Elisabeth said. "She's doing much better."

"Is Faustine here?"

Elisabeth hesitated. "She must be out wandering at La Fenouillère."

"With Vincent?"

"So you know?"

"No offense, but I've known for a long time. So is it serious between them?"

"Serious? They are still very young. It will pass. In any case, don't say a word to your father or brother when they get here."

That summer, Vincent told Donatien that he would be more useful at the farm than in the mountain pasture. He asked if he could stay at La Fenouillère, rather than go with Donatien to the Taillades in La Bastide.

Constance knew Vincent's real reason was Faustine. He wanted to be close to her. "I don't need another problem with the Rocheforts," Constance warned him. "I'm counting on you to be careful."

"Don't worry, Mom. Faustine and I are in no hurry. We really love each other. Faustine will be my wife one day. I know that. So we can wait."

Vincent undertook his work on the farm. Victor, the head farmhand, was happy to spend time with his young protégé again and treated him a little bit like his own son. Together, they returned to the fields and vineyards, inseparable, as before.

Alongside Victor, Vincent found the kind of satisfaction that he had left behind when he went to Nîmes—the satisfaction of working outside from dawn to dusk, breathing fresh country air, sweating under the sun, and getting a job done. "I feel like I've been gone for ages," Vincent said. "I can't believe it's been only four months."

"You'll be a gentleman when you've finished your studies," Victor said. "You won't deign to get your hands dirty, and for sure, you won't be shoveling any manure."

"That would surprise me, Victor. At school I'm a farmer too, although it isn't quite the same. I have practical classes, and I work in the dirt."

"Why didn't you go up to the Taillades? Your father would have liked having you with him."

"I know, but I'll see him when he gets back at the end of August. We'll do the grape harvest together."

"I know why you stayed, boy. I found out a long time ago."

"So why did you ask?"

"That little Rochefort girl . . . Well, she's a good girl. Don't hurt her. She really loves you, believe me. You can count on me if you need me. I won't tell anyone."

"Thank you, Victor. You really are my best friend."

Over the years, the old farmhand and the boy had woven an indestructible bond. Victor had never told him that he also had lost his parents when he was very young, and at the age of six, he had been placed with a farm family. That, however, was where the similarities ended, because Victor's life had been filled with hardship. He was abused and considered the lowest of the farmhands. His entire childhood and adolescence were unhappy. At sixteen, he rebelled and ran away. He was caught by the gendarmes, who returned him to the farm. From that point on, the family wouldn't let him get away with anything.

His only escape was military service. When he returned to civilian life, he worked from farm to farm until the blessed day when he met the Rouvière family in Tornac.

When Sebastien saw his father arrive at the end of the week, he was surprised and pleased at how much better Anselme was doing. But rather than express what he felt, he gave Anselme a cold and distant hug.

"Hello, Father. I hope that you are feeling better. Mother told me you took over the factories again."

Anselme showed no emotion, although deep down he couldn't help but think that with his strong personality, Sebastien had the makings of a better business leader than Jean-Christophe, whom he considered capricious, spineless, and venal. As usual, he reminded Sebastien of his obligations. "I want you to know that I will not tolerate any lack in your filial duties. I allowed you to go study in Paris, and you may continue doing that as long as you don't discredit the family honor. I remind you that you are a Rochefort, whether you like it or not. That will give you connections later. But it also gives you certain obligations and duties."

"Father—"

"Don't interrupt me. What happened with the Rouvière girl must not happen again. I'm counting on you to finish your studies. If you are serious, I'll be able to open some doors for you, and later I hope you will choose a wife from a family with a name as worthy as yours."

"A well-to-do family."

"That's right."

Sebastien had a hard time controlling himself. He had promised his mother that she wouldn't argue with Anselme. So he let him finish and asked permission to leave.

Jean-Christophe, who had arrived with their father, joined Sebastien in his room. "So you didn't tell Dad, did you? You didn't tell him about Pauline and the child you are expecting. Of course not. He's not going to take the news well."

"Yes. I know that. I'm sure he will cut me off. I won't be his son anymore."

"That doesn't seem to traumatize you."

"Father needs to understand that I alone decide what I do with my life. But I'd like to know what you think."

"I'm not as idealistic as you are. I didn't really want to marry Louise, but I did it because that was what Father wanted."

"Because it was good for his business, which is yours, as well."

"Yes, you are right."

"And you don't feel that you need to be faithful."

"What do you mean?"

"Faustine told me all about it, how Vincent saw you in Nîmes with some woman."

Stunned, Jean-Christophe didn't say anything. Then he whispered, "Whatever you do, don't say a word. You know that Louise doesn't suspect anything. It's not serious anyway. Remember what I told you when you thought you might have to spend your life with Julie Rouvière: Marriage is not a prison."

"On that score, we think alike, and then again, we don't. Marriage is really an institution more than anything else. One doesn't need to be confined by marriage. We agree on this. But I believe that you can be committed to someone without being married, and you break your marital commitment by straying. That's where we differ."

The two brothers had different values, but as always, Jean-Christophe promised to help Sebastien when Anselme flew into a rage, as he was sure to do when he learned the news.

26

Apprehension

1914

A new year had begun. Already, it seemed full of apprehension, both in business and in politics. More than ever, Anselme was following the news, as it appeared increasingly likely that war would break out. Meanwhile, the economy remained troubled.

In 1913, the majority moderate and radical members of parliament had passed legislation raising compulsory military service to three years. This had heightened the specter of war. Nearly as worrisome, an income tax loomed. The minister of finance supported the idea, but those in parliament were opposed. Until he could get the tax approved, the finance minister was raising existing taxes, adding to investor anxieties and general unhappiness.

"They will end up adopting the income tax," Anselme grumbled. "That will be their roundabout way of financing their military expenditures. The politicians are ruled by the generals."

Jean-Christophe tried to soothe his father. "Calm down, Father. The more disorder and discontent the politicians sow, the more favorable the climate will be for new leaders. Chaos must come first. Then we will finally be able to put people in place who are committed to defending our interests."

This didn't change Anselme's gloomy outlook. "The voters will end up putting a majority of left-wingers in parliament. We might as well get ready for a social republic. There will be no lack of Reds."

"That's why we should have sold the silk operation," Jean-Christophe said. "We could have put the money from the sale in a safe place abroad until the danger passed. If the left wing comes into power, as you say it will, there's nothing to keep them from seizing our assets."

Jean-Christophe was exaggerating to frighten his father into reversing his decision, but Anselme didn't trust his son.

"They may impose social legislation that is favorable to workers, but what you just said, son, is stupid. I don't think the socialists have any intention of displacing the leaders of industry and trade."

"You're wrong there. Some of them say that the state should own the means of production. Just ask Sebastien. He's familiar with their line of reasoning."

"Sebastien? Are you telling me that he's leaning to the left? That's all I need."

Jean-Christophe realized he had said too much, so he tried to play it down. "My brother is a passionate young man. Don't forget that he's studying political science, which covers the full spectrum."

Anselme looked doubtful. "Hmm, it seems suspicious to me. I shouldn't have agreed to let him go to that school. He'll end up corrupting his mind completely."

Far from his family, Sebastien led a life that was the complete opposite of the one he had led in Nîmes. He loved his classes and his teachers. He was friends with a number of students in his classes and spent evenings with them in the Latin Quarter, where they envisioned an entirely different world, one where the poor weren't exploited and outcasts had a place. Theirs was a world where weapons were laid down and people lived in peace and harmony.

Sebastien did lean to the left, despite his social class. His fellow students, most of whom came from less favorable situations, sometimes took issue with his origins. But he defended himself well and pointed out that none of them belonged to the actual working class. He told them that he had always taken up the workers' cause.

"Don't preach to me. No students in this illustrious school belong to the poorest classes. We are all bourgeois, like it or not. We'll be judged by our actions, not our words or our social backgrounds. We cannot choose where we come from, but we can decide what we become. And as far as I'm concerned, I know exactly where I'm going."

At the age of twenty, Sebastien believed the world was his, and his future lay wide open in front of him. He had no intention of veering from his objectives.

Sometimes his companion, Pauline, worried.

In September, she had given birth to their child, a boy they had named Ruben. Sebastien was thrilled. "He's a child of love and a child of peace," he said the first time he held the infant. Sebastien knew his father wouldn't see it that way, and so he didn't tell his parents.

"You'll have to tell your father one day," Pauline said. "We can't live in lies and hide forever."

"But we can't tell him now. My father would cut me off, and we're living on what he sends. We have no income."

Sebastien also wished he could share the happy news. Jean-Christophe was the only one who knew, but they hadn't been in touch since the baby's birth.

Sebastien's dreams were what worried Pauline the most.

When he opened his heart, telling her about his hopes and plans for the future, she got the impression that she wasn't part of them. She had never asked him to marry her. Living as an unmarried couple, even with a child, didn't bother her. On this, Pauline was as open-minded as Sebastien, and their view was rare at the time. But Pauline was afraid that Sebastien would one day choose a path that she couldn't take with him.

He always tried to reassure her. "We have the same ideas and the same ambitions. We want to become reporters. We love each other. What could separate us?"

"Our child!"

"Ruben? I don't understand."

"A child needs his mother during his first years. Have you thought about that? You dream of traveling the world and being a great reporter. I could never follow you, Sebastien. I need to find a stable job at a daily paper that would agree to hire a journalist with a child. And I don't need to remind you that women are still striving to make a place for themselves in the newsroom. I don't know what kind of reporting job I'll be able to find. I fear that your dreams and our reality aren't compatible."

It hadn't occurred to Sebastien that Ruben would interfere with his plans. "Right now we are in school," he said. "There's no sense in worrying about all of this before we need to. I'm sure that we'll be able to overcome any obstacles that we encounter."

This, however, wasn't what Sebastien was really thinking.

He, too, had begun to worry about the looming war. He had started mixing with the young socialists who sided with Jean Jaurès and were fighting for peace. He had not missed the first issue of the antimilitary paper *Le Bonnet rouge*.

In March and April of that fateful year, the major European powers accelerated the arms race. Russia, the Austro-Hungarian Empire, Germany, and England seemed ready to go to war. The scramble for alliances intensified as rivalries between Serbia and Austria-Hungary and Albania and Greece escalated. French voters responded to the situation by sending left-wing legislators to parliament in the May elections, which strengthened the Jean Jaurès socialists.

There was no end to Rochefort's ranting. "Now the Reds are in power. The moderates took so many unpopular measures, they ushered in the left wing."

Jean-Christophe wasn't trying to soothe his father anymore. His predictions had been off. No iron-fisted leaders had come to the rescue. And his personal life wasn't going so well either. His hopes of selling the silk mill had been dashed, and his finances were in serious shape. Unable to pay his gambling debts, he was getting serious threats from his creditors, some of whom had mob connections in Marseille. His mood was gloomy.

Louise had started to ask questions. But she suspected that the trouble was linked to his love life, not his finances. She couldn't tolerate the lies and ambiguity of her situation anymore. She wanted to know if Jean-Christophe intended to leave her. But before she spoke to Jean-Christophe, she needed to talk with her brother.

"Jean-Christophe doesn't love me anymore," she told Vincent. "I'm sure he's cheating on me, and it's nothing new. Tonight, I'm going to tell him that I'm leaving for La Fenouillère with the children, and I'm not coming back. I want to preempt him."

Vincent didn't hide what he had known for a year. "I didn't tell you, because I didn't think I should be the one to do it. I've known about Jean-Christophe's escapades for a long time now. I ran into him with another woman last year."

"You should have told me. But I understand. I've had my doubts for longer than that. I thought our relationship would get better after the twins were born. When we are alone, Jean-Christophe can be very attentive."

"That's not the impression his gives everyone else."

Louise didn't want to admit the whole truth. Until now, she had excused her husband for everything—his lack of respect in public, his rude comments, and his late nights. She had pushed aside her suspicious, telling herself that she had no proof. And when that didn't work, she held onto the hope that he would change and once again become the charming man who had taken her to Venice. But now she knew that she was the only one making an effort. She was tired and discouraged.

"Don't make any final decision tonight," Vincent advised. "Threaten him. Push his back up against the wall. That will make him think. Maybe all isn't lost."

She took Vincent's advice.

That evening, she waited for Jean-Christophe in the sitting room instead of going to bed at the usual time. When her husband returned at around eleven, he was surprised to see her waiting near the fireplace. She didn't give him the opportunity to say anything. "We need to talk," she said.

Jean-Christophe apologized, as if it were unusual for him to come home late. He poured himself a glass of Cognac and sat down near Louise, looking affable but worried.

"So, my dear, what is it that couldn't wait until tomorrow morning? I've had a rough day. I'm in no mood for talking."

"I'll get straight to the point. I want you to know that I'm not happy with you. The children are the only reason I'm still here. Were it not for them, I would have been gone a long time ago."

"Now, now, Louise! What's gotten into you all of the sudden?"

"Be quiet, and let me talk for once."

Like most other bullies, Jean-Christophe was able to lord his power over others only when he met no resistance. He had never been able to impose his will on his father, even on the occasions when he was right. Louise had always backed down, which hurt her pride and made Jean-Christophe feel all the more arrogant. But she was not going to be dominated on this night.

"I've suspected for a long time that you have been cheating on me," she continued without losing her composure. "I have never said anything, and I've always let you do what you like. I thought that our children were not suffering because of their father's escapades, so I swallowed my pride for their sake. But for months now, your mood has been even worse. You don't speak to me. You don't look at your children. You ignore us totally and seem to be falling deeper into a bottomless chasm. I don't know who you are anymore, Jean-Christophe."

"I'm having big problems at work, Louise. You should understand that!"

"The nature of your problems doesn't matter. You have a wife and three children who should not have to put up with your moods, your mistakes, and your scheming."

"What scheming?"

"Don't be such a hypocrite, please. This conversation has gone on too long already, so I'll say what I have to say. If you don't change your attitude, I'm leaving. I'll go live at La Fenouillère with the children."

Jean-Christophe slumped in his chair, stupefied by a wife who dared to spell out the plain truths in his own house.

A few hours earlier, he had received a strong-armed warning from a stranger who had quite aggressively made it clear that if he didn't pay off his gambling debt in forty-eight hours he would have reason to fear.

Clearly, it was a day of threats.

Louise decided to give Jean-Christophe more time to change his attitude. In June, while she was getting ready for her summer stay at La Fenouillère with the children and Vincent, she heard glass shatter in the sitting room. She let her chambermaid continue to pack the bags and hastened downstairs. Léonie, the cook, had already gotten there.

"Goodness. What happened?" she said.

The picture window overlooking the garden was broken. Glass covered the freshly waxed wood floor. In the middle lay a rock wrapped in a piece of paper.

Stunned, Léonie started sweeping up the bits of glass. "Who could have done this?" she asked.

"Did you see anyone, Léonie?"

"No, ma'am. I was in the kitchen."

"Bring me that rock. Look, it's wrapped in paper."

Léonie did as she was told. Louise unwrapped the rock and smoothed out the paper to see the message that was written on it. She paled as she read it out loud. "'This is the last warning. The next time, your house will go up in flames.' Someone's threatening us. But why?"

"Who would possibly want to threaten you, ma'am?"

Louise quickly surmised that it had something to do with the business. "In that area, you always have more enemies than friends."

"We need to tell the police, ma'am."

"My husband will do it when he gets back."

"Will you still be making your trip?"

Louise hesitated before answering. The threat looked serious. It would be best to stay away for a while, she thought.

"Yes, I think it's best that we make the trip. We'll leave as soon as my brother gets back from school."

"Should I tell sir?"

"I'll do it." Louise called her husband at the factory and told him to come home right away. He arrived quickly.

"What's the meaning of this?" Louise asked, showing him the threatening letter.

The blood drained from Jean-Christophe's face. He was cornered.

"I demand an explanation! Do you realize that you are putting your children in danger, not to mention Vincent, the servants, and me? I don't know what you're up to, but you have to put an end to it."

"I had promised to sell the silk mill to a customer from Marseille," Jean-Christophe said, making up a lie. "He was upset when we changed our minds and took the mill off the market. He thinks we found another buyer who was willing to pay a higher price."

"That's no reason to threaten us like this. He's behaving like a thug."

"You're right. I wasn't careful enough. The man didn't seem to be on the straight and narrow. This threat confirms my original doubts about him."

Louise suspected that her husband was hiding the truth. She almost asked why his father had not been threatened, but she restrained herself and pretended to believe Jean-Christophe's rather hasty explanation.

"I'm taking the children to La Fenouillère," she said. "We were planning to go on vacation anyway. Vincent will be with us, as well. He's finished with his classes. We'll stay as long as it takes to resolve this issue. I have no desire to be burned to a crisp."

A few days later, as Europe faced imminent war, three men in dark clothes emerged from the shadows as Jean-Christophe arrived home from the factory.

It was late. The night was dark, moonless, and as quiet as a grave. The only sounds were a few crickets in the grass.

The men waited until their prey had gotten out of his car. And then they pounced.

Jean-Christophe barely had time to see what was happening. He turned in the direction of the men, getting only a glimpse of bludgeons coming down on him.

He wanted to defend himself, to protect his head and face.

He fought and tried to call for help, but he couldn't articulate anything. It was as though his body was being pounded into the ground.

He felt a sharp blade slash his arm and leg.

A punch to his face half knocked him out. A red veil covered his puffy eyes. He could no longer open them.

He collapsed and curled into a fetal position to preserve what was left of him. His whole being was nothing but pain.

A kick to the abdomen shook his whole body. A dull sound rose from his entrails. It must be the end, he thought. Then he felt a strange deliverance, even though they were still beating him. His mind slowly drifted out of his body. He lost consciousness.

The men with the bludgeons stopped.

"That's enough. If he doesn't get it now, he'll end up in the morgue."

At La Fenouillère, Louise was sure that she no longer felt any real love for her husband. Still, she was worried about him.

Vincent, meanwhile, was thinking about the event splashed across the newspapers he bought for Donatien: the assassination in Sarajevo of Archduke Franz Ferdinand of Austria.

27

Threats

In June of 1914, many people in France still didn't believe that war was on the horizon. Some measure of domestic peace had returned, even though the government couldn't be considered stable. The working class was making more money and was less inclined to pursue additional demands. Major industries were doing well. The colonial empire seemed to be strong. Furthermore, many were convinced that the French army was unparalleled. But at the same time, the country's demographics were stagnating. At about forty million, the country's population hadn't risen significantly for decades. Some feared that meant insufficient resources if the nation did have to face its rivals one day.

Donatien was one of the people who had serious concerns. Unlike those who were more optimistic, he sensed that war was imminent. He had already sent his sheep up to pasture with a neighbor who had gone to the highlands with him every other summer. Donatien had decided to stay home.

"War is looming," he said. "I'll be more useful here."

"How pessimistic of you," Constance said.

"I know how to read," he said. He handed the paper to Vincent. "Here, boy, read this to your mother."

Vincent read the article about the repercussions of the archduke's assassination. Gavrilo Princip, the nineteen-year-old Serbian student charged in the slaying, had told police that he was avenging Austrian oppression in Bosnia.

"I don't see how this affects us," Louise said. Far from the turbulent international scene, the Rouvière women were among those who didn't believe a war was looming.

"Women don't understand a thing about politics," Donatien teased. "I'm going to start the harvest early. We can bring in the wheat and rye now. We won't have as much hay as usual. We'll start cutting it tomorrow."

"Even if a war does break out, what are you so worried about?" Constance said. "At your age, you won't get sent off to the military, and neither will Victor or Vincent."

"No, but the help will. Most of them are the right age to be drafted."

"Why would France go to war over the assassination of an Austrian archduke?"

"Alliances," Vincent explained. "France, England, and Russia are bound by the Triple Entente. Germany, the Austro-Hungarian Empire, and Italy are the Triple Alliance. And Russia is backing the Serbs in the Balkans against the Austro-Hungarian Empire. If the Serbs and the Austrians take up arms against each other, their respective allies will be dragged into the conflict."

"It's all too complicated for me," Madeleine said.

"Let's change the subject," Constance said. "It's summer. The weather is fine. Let's enjoy being together."

"My mother-in-law will be here tomorrow," Louise said.

"With Faustine?" Vincent asked immediately.

"Yes, with the two girls, as usual."

"And what about your husband? Will he be coming?"

Louise's face darkened. "He promised he would. With his father."

Louise still didn't know what had happened to Jean-Christophe.

The night of the beating, he had spent hours lying in front of his home. It wasn't until one in the morning that two police officers found him unconscious, covered in his own blood. An ambulance rushed him to the hospital, where the doctors determined that he would recover. The police, meanwhile, had called Anselme, who hurried to the hospital.

"What happened?" Anselme asked one of the officers.

"We found your son in front of his house," the officer said. "He was in a sorry state."

Anselme approached the bed where his son lay, bandaged from head to foot, unable to speak. He asked the doctor about the injuries.

"He has multiple contusions, two broken ribs, and a fractured nose. We had to suture his forehead. His shoulder is dislocated, and his tibia is broken," the doctor said. "Fortunately, there was no damage to his abdomen or lungs. With this kind of beating, we always worry about a broken rib puncturing a lung. But that doesn't appear to have happened to your son. We also worry about the spleen."

"Who did this?" Anselme asked the police officer.

"At this point, we don't know. We need information from your son," the officer said. "When he is able to talk again, he'll have to come to the police station to file a report and press charges. We'll need to clear this up quickly. In the meantime, Mr. Rochefort, the inspector would like to ask you a few questions."

"Me?" Anselme asked, surprised.

"Yes, you are his father, right? Perhaps you could help us find the people who did this."

"I'll stop at the police station this afternoon," Anselme said. "My chauffeur will drive me."

Anselme was not much help, as he had no idea why thugs had set upon his son.

"It's probably some random act," he told the police inspector. "Our city is no longer safe. Crime is on the rise."

"We are doing everything we can to ensure the safety of our residents," the inspector said. "Unfortunately, we are understaffed. We'll need to take a closer look at your son's life. Perhaps he had enemies he didn't know about."

"Enemies? What are you saying, Inspector? Of course people envy us, but people who would actually harm us? I can't imagine that."

Jean-Christophe spent a week in the hospital. He refused to see anyone but his father. Then, after giving the police a vague story, he went to the Clos du Tournel to recover. There, Louise, his mother, and his sisters awaited him impatiently.

In Paris, Sebastien read Elisabeth's letter. She wanted Sebastien to visit Jean-Christophe in Anduze as soon as possible. Jean-Christophe needed to talk to him, and in his state—he was still bedridden—he couldn't converse on the phone.

"I think he has something to ask you," Elisabeth wrote. "He won't talk to anyone but you. Not even Louise. And especially not his father. I don't know what he's hiding, but it must have something to do with the attack."

Sebastien was following the news closely. National and international developments were speeding up. In the previous few weeks, parliament had authorized borrowing eight hundred million francs for weapons. Military officials had updated uniforms for combat soldiers, and the Socialist Party—which he now belonged to—was calling for an antiwar strike.

Although he understood his mother's urgency, he was reluctant to leave. "Something's about to happen," he told

Pauline. "If I'm in Anduze when there's a call for troops, I'll have to go to Nîmes, where I'm registered. I won't have time to come back to Paris to say good-bye."

"Why not take me with you? It could an opportunity to introduce me to your family."

"With Ruben?"

"Why not?"

"I don't think this is the right time. My brother is in serious trouble. My father is up in arms. If he sees me arrive with you and Ruben, he'll be furious. Can you envision me saying, 'Father, this is Pauline, my life companion. She's a socialist, like me. And this is your grandson, Ruben, a love child.' He would kick us out before the introductions were even over."

"Is your father as horrible as that?"

"Worse. He is ferocious."

Sebastien took Pauline in his arms and smiled mischievously before kissing her tenderly. "I'm exaggerating. Let's just say he's a little stubborn, and we don't agree on anything."

"It is thanks to him that we can survive with Ruben. Without his money, I don't know what would become of us."

"He doesn't know about you or Ruben, fortunately. Otherwise he would have cut us off a long time ago."

Sebastien was about to ask her to go anyway. But Pauline decided to leave well enough alone. "Go to Anduze," she said. "Don't say anything to your father. Take care of your brother."

"And if war breaks out?"

"It won't."

Sebastien was relieved and promised Pauline that he would come back as soon as possible and lay the groundwork for her to be accepted by his family—including his father.

"My brother will help soften up my father. He helped me before, and he'll do it again if I ask him. I'm sure of that."

He left Paris on July 23, the day Austria-Hungary gave Serbia an ultimatum: Serbia was ordered to root out all terrorist groups within its borders and accept an international investigation of the archduke's assassination. Serbia refused to accept both terms. War broke out between the two countries five days later. Russia mobilized against Austria-Hungary and then declared war.

Anselme was still in Nîmes when Sebastien left for the Clos du Tournel. With the breakout of fighting to the east, he wanted to stay close to his business. He also wanted to shed some light on the sordid matter Jean-Christophe was mixed up in. He was convinced that one or more people had a score to settle with his son.

The police inspector was not overly enthusiastic about investigating the crime. He said assaults were frequent, unfortunately, and police investigations usually got nowhere. Anselme turned to a private detective named Charles Brossard. The man had no problem using underhanded methods. He specialized in solving murders and assaults, especially those connected to organized crime. Brossard didn't take domestic cases, as snooping on adulterous husbands and wives didn't interest him. So when Anselme met with him, he hesitated to take the case.

"This sounds like a jealous husband getting vengeance," he said.

Brossard knew Jean-Christophe Rochefort's reputation. They had attended law school together in Montpellier, and Jean-Christophe was already a Don Juan.

"It's more serious than simple jealousy!" Anselme said. "Jean-Christophe was left for dead. This might have something to do with our business. They might be after me, and Jean-Christophe could be a warning. I need to know."

Anselme persuaded Brossard to take the case and start his investigation without delay. Brossard promised to get back to him two weeks later.

A few days after his meeting with the detective, Anselme got a letter from the Ministry of Defense. Considering the state of things in Europe, he was alarmed at the sight of the official envelope. He tried to pull himself together. At his age and in his condition, not much more could happen to him. But what about his factories?

Irène Formont, his secretary, hadn't dared to open the envelope. "Sir, would you like me to read you the letter?" she asked.

"I'll do it myself. Open it and give it to me."

Anselme perused the letter, and a grin spread across his face as he read.

"Finally, some good news," he said. "My son was right."

"May I ask, sir, about the happy news?"

"The Ministry of Defense is ordering an enormous shipment of blue-gray fabric for the soldiers' new uniforms. Jean-Christophe told me war would be good for business."

"But we are not at war, sir," the secretary said, surprised.

"No, but believe me, it will come soon. And our revenues are going to explode."

"What about all those men who will be killed if war breaks out?" Irène said. "Your own sons could be called up to fight. Mr. Jean-Christophe has children. If something bad happens to him, he'll leave three orphans and a widow."

Anselme's joy at the news had offended his secretary, and he realized a little late how unseemly his reaction had been. However, he continued. "Unfortunately, politicians make these decisions. We don't. And I'm not going to be sad that we got an order from the Ministry of Defense. It's a real stroke of luck for the company. I'm going to tell my son. The news will make him feel better. He needs it. Please put a call through to him."

At the Clos du Tournel, Jean-Christophe was slowly recovering. Dr. Blanchard said he would be able to stand in a month's time and get around on crutches.

"In three months, this will all be a bad memory," the doctor said.

Far from being relieved, Jean-Christophe was worried to death. He doubted that those on his tail would leave him alone if he didn't pay off his debt. If only they had sold the mill!

He wanted to get in touch with his friend Gilles Bosson. He was the only one who could get him out of his mess. But it was impossible to meet him in his present state. He was hoping Sebastien would contact the attorney.

Jean-Christophe called Sebastien into his room the day after his brother arrived. Sebastien was planning to talk with him anyway, as he wanted Jean-Christophe to tell their parents about Pauline.

"I helped you quite a bit a few years ago," Jean-Christophe said, getting into his own dilemma first.

"I haven't forgotten. You are close to Father, and I truly appreciate your support, especially because we see things so differently. I have another matter that I would like to discuss with you."

"This time, I'm the one who needs your help," Jean-Christophe said.

Sebastien put off his request. "If I can be useful, I'm happy to help. What do you need?"

Jean-Christophe didn't know how to tell his sorry story.

"Here it is. I know who attacked me. Well, at least those who ordered the attack. As you can see from what they've done to me, they're bad people. And they're not about to stop."

"What do they want?"

"Money."

"That's blackmail. Does Father know?"

"No, you're the only person I've told."

"Why are they blackmailing you?"

"I told you, for money."

"You need to tell the police."

"No, I can't! These people will go after Louise and the children."

"What can I do, then?" Sebastien asked.

"I want you to go to Nîmes and meet an attorney, Gilles Bosson. He's a friend. Give him this letter." Jean-Christophe handed his brother a sealed envelope. "Tell him I'm in a fix, and I'm counting on him to get me out of it. Most important, don't tell anyone. Nobody, especially not Father, should know that I sent you to see Bosson. If the police find out, I'm dead."

"It's that serious?" Sebastien said.

"I can't tell you anymore. Find some excuse to go to Nîmes. You can say you're going to see Father. It would be an opportunity to tell him about Pauline and your child. The baby's about six months old now, right?"

"Nine months. I was counting on you to help me tell Father. But that can wait. Don't worry. I'll find a better time to tell him."

They were finishing their conversation when the telephone rang. Sebastien picked up the phone and brought it to his ear.

"Please hold. Mr. Rochefort is on the line," the operator said.

Sebastien gave the phone to Jean-Christophe.

"Hello, Jean-Christophe. I have excellent news. The Ministry of Defense has just placed a huge order with us. We're going to work for the government! Hello, are you there?"

"Yes, yes, Father. I'm happy . . . Well, I'm happy about the news."

"So why are you in a bad mood, son?"

"It looks like we are going to war, and you understand what that means as well as I do."

"What did Father want?" Sebastien asked after Jean-Christophe hung up.

"To announce that our company will supply serge for the army's new uniforms. They've placed a huge order."

"So we're going to war."

"I believe we are."

Of all of them, Vincent was the most carefree. He did, of course, know about the fighting to the east. But he didn't share Donatien's pessimism, and he didn't realize just how perilously close to chaos the continent was veering.

His thoughts were on the harvest and the fields. Summer was blazing, and heady fragrances were wafting off the earth. He was in love, and each day, his sweet dreams would meld into the rich colors of dawn. In the evening, when his day was over, he would find Faustine in the vineyards and go off with her, taking paths where nobody would bother them.

At sixteen, Faustine was simply beautiful. She glowed with a joie de vivre that lightened everyone's heart. Although she was innocent, she was aware of the looks she drew from the young and not-so-young farmhands. She understood that she was desirable, even if she didn't know just how much the other men envied Vincent. With her skin browned and her hair bleached by the sun, she was a princess. And her prince was Vincent. Her heart belonged to him, and for her, their lives were forever intertwined.

When Vincent worried about Anselme's reaction when he learned the truth—and that was inevitable—she would take his face in her hands and say, "All of the Rocheforts have strong personalities. If my father tries to get between us, I'll stand up to him, like my brother Sebastien."

"You're talking about two very different relationships."

"And that will work to our advantage. Father and Sebastien have always clashed head-on. I'm the baby in the family. Father looks the other way with me. I'm sure he'll end up accepting you if I can manage to convince him of the sincerity and depth of our love."

"I'm not so sure. But we've got our whole life in front of us."

Every night, Vincent would walk with Faustine part of the way to the Clos du Tournel. Vincent didn't go too far, as he didn't want them to be seen together on the road. Eventually, however, they were spotted. And it was by Anselme himself, who was arriving from Nîmes with his chauffeur.

Upon sighting them, Anselme told Henry to stop and back up.

There was nothing Vincent and Faustine could do.

"Faustine!" Anselme said. "What are you doing on the side of the road at this late hour? Does your mother know you are out? It's past nine. You should be at home."

Anselme didn't even look at Vincent, who tried to find excuses for Faustine. "It's not her fault, Mr. Rochefort. I'm the guilty one. I was talking too much and didn't pay attention to the time. I didn't want Faustine walking by herself—you can never be too careful—so I'm accompanying her home."

Anselme looked Vincent up and down and motioned to his daughter to climb into the car. "It looks like Faustine took some liberties in my absence. We'll talk this all over at home. Let's go, Henry. As for you, young man, I don't want to see you hanging around my daughter anymore."

Dispirited and vexed, Vincent returned to La Fenouillère. Anselme's words had knocked the wind out of him. "He'll shut her away and forbid her from going out alone," he said to himself. "We won't be able to see each other until school starts again."

So he decided to take matters into his own hands. He turned around and started heading toward the Clos du Tournel.

"I'll talk to him," he said out loud to build his courage. "I'll calmly explain that his daughter and I love each other, and nothing can keep us apart."

He marched down the road lined with plane trees and

passed through the stone archway that marked the drive to the Rochefort home. "Private property. Do not enter" was engraved in the stone at the top of the arch. Fifty yards later, a large building rose up. It was the eighteenth-century country mansion that had belonged to the Rochefort family for several generations. The only other time Vincent had been there was for Louise's wedding to Jean-Christophe. Since then, he had been careful to keep his distance.

Anselme's car was parked at the front steps. Vincent hesitated. A church bell tolled in the distance. He counted the strikes: ten. It's late, he thought. Too late. I'll come back.

Then he saw a window on the first floor open. Sebastien poked his head through.

"Vincent! What are you doing here?" He didn't give the boy time to answer. "They've assassinated Jaurès. Jean Jaurès is dead. Pauline just called to tell me."

"Who?" Vincent asked, both surprised and afraid to be overheard by Anselme.

"Don't stay there. Come in. We're at war, I'm sure. Jaurès was assassinated."

Vincent didn't wait for a servant to open the door. He ran down the dark drive as fast as his legs could carry him. When he arrived at La Fenouillère, all out of breath, he shouted, "Jaurès is dead. They assassinated him. It's war."

28

Mobilization

The war appeared to be just hours away. Germany had plans to take France swiftly—before Russia had the opportunity to fully mobilize. Germany's intentions were made clear by the ultimatums it issued to both France and Russia. The French people could no longer ignore the imminent danger, even if they didn't fully comprehend the real issues involved.

The French government called for general mobilization on Saturday, August 1. The news spread by word of mouth before the newspapers could publish it. Some farmers clung to the notion that the government was just being careful. Others, however, knew war was coming, and hardships lay ahead. What would happen to the harvests if the men had to go off to war?

At La Fenouillère, Constance was happily chatting with Elisabeth. Surrounded by their daughters and grandchildren, they hadn't yet heard the news.

Faustine had managed to escape her mother's vigilant eyes and was looking for Vincent in the vineyards. Accompanied by Victor and three farmhands, he was spraying the vines with copper sulfate. When he saw the love of his life arrive, Vincent stopped and hesitated. Victor asked him to keep working. But when he saw the Rochefort girl impatiently waiting, he said, "Oh, I understand now. Go on, boy, and don't get caught. I'll look the other way."

The two teens disappeared together.

Sebastien, who hadn't heard about the mobilization either, was like a lion in a cage. He felt trapped by the promise he had made to Jean-Christophe, and, as he had feared, he was stuck in Anduze. It was the weekend, and he had to wait until Monday to go see Gilles Bosson in Nîmes.

"There is no use going on a Saturday or Sunday," Jean-Christophe had explained. "He won't be at his office. He'll be at his country house, and I don't know where it is."

He had finally called Pauline to tell her he would be back in Paris as soon as he saw his brother's attorney. He was hoping to do that quickly. "Once in Nîmes, I'll take the first train for Paris," he said.

He had told Jean-Christophe that he would have the attorney call him or come to see him.

Sebastien collapsed in frustration when, on Sunday, August 2, he learned of the general mobilization. Anselme had gotten the news from his chauffeur and had promptly delivered it to Sebastian. Now he feared that he would never get back to Paris.

"It's too late!" he said. "I'm stuck."

"Maybe not," Jean-Christophe said to reassure him. "Things should calm down in the coming days. Mobilization doesn't always mean war."

Not far from the village, Vincent and Faustine were walking together when the church bells began tolling in unison with those in the neighboring villages.

"That's unusual. It sounds like a warning," Faustine said.

When they heard drums, they started walking toward the sound, not caring about being seen together. A crowd was gathering in the square.

"What's going on?" Faustine asked, more curious than worried.

"I don't know," Vincent said. "Let's find out."

The square was bustling, as if it were market day. Men, women, and children elbowed their way toward Ernest Poujolat, the rural policeman who was calling them to attention with his drum.

Word spread before he could even read the official announcement, which he had posted on the front of the city hall. "There's a general mobilization," the men and women shouted to each other. "We're at war."

Cries of protest rang out. People armed with pitchforks, pruning knives, and sickles raised them above their heads. The poor policeman did his best to calm them down, but nobody listened. Angry, he beat his drum again and shouted, "By decree of the president of the republic, France has ordered the mobilization of the army and the marine and has requisitioned the animals, vehicles, and tack needed by these forces. All French men eligible for military service must comply with the mobilization. Anyone who does not will be punished to the full extent of the law."

Faustine and Vincent held each other.

"Is there going to be war?" Faustine asked.

"I'm afraid so. There's been the threat of one for a long time."

They didn't linger.

When Faustine joined the women at La Fenouillère, she announced the news. "War is coming. There's a general mobilization."

"Now, now, my dear," Elisabeth said. "Settle down. Why are you interrupting our nice visit with such a horrible rumor?"

"Because it's not a rumor, Mom. The police posted the official announcement at the Tornac City Hall. I saw it with Vincent."

"Vincent!" Constance said. "I thought he was with Victor in the vineyards."

Elisabeth went quiet, not wanting to embarrass her daughter. Louise came to her rescue.

"I told Vincent to go keep Faustine company as soon as he saw her."

"It's true that he's become your little protégé ever since he started school in Nîmes," Constance said, trying to sound like she was teasing.

"They aren't doing anything wrong, Mom," Louise said.

Constance shot Elisabeth a questioning glance. Faustine's mother was wearing a pleasant smile, but Constance had the feeling that a measure of anxiety was hidden behind her expression.

"Oh, these children," Constance said. "At some point, youth passes, doesn't it?"

The next day, Monday, August 3, Germany declared war on France, after first attacking Luxembourg and Belgium.

"It's all over," Donatien said sadly.

"I'm afraid it's just beginning," Vincent said.

"I went into town to hear what people were saying. Everyone thinks it will be a short war, maybe a month long. The soldiers will be home for Christmas."

"You don't agree, Dad. I can tell."

"No, I think we're in for a long period of hardship. We'll be shorthanded. Most of our workers will be heading for the barracks soon. And in September, only the women will be left for the grape harvest."

"I'll stay here, rather than go back to school," Vincent said.
"No, my boy. You must finish what you started."

At the Clos du Tournel, Sebastien didn't know what to do. Should he leave for Nîmes and try to rush back to Pauline in Paris? Or should he stay in Nîmes and wait for his orders?

"Everyone's orders should be arriving any time now," Anselme said. "We'll lose all our male employees. I have to go to Nîmes immediately. Jean-Christophe, in your state there is no immediate risk that you'll have to serve. You'll get at least a temporary medical deferment. As for you, Sebastien, I recommend that you wait in Nîmes. I'll go see the prefect. I should manage to get both of you out of your military obligations."

"Father, that is out of the question," Sebastien said. "I must do my duty, like all other self-respecting French citizens."

"Don't be an idiot, Sebastien. This is no time for patriotic swagger. You are my son. We have our differences, but I don't want you going off and getting killed. You are incredibly lucky to be part of a well-respected family, so take advantage of it. I have connections, and I won't be opposed."

"Father, I thank you for your kindness. But I'll repeat myself. I will not be the recipient of any favorable treatment."

"Have you thought about Pauline and your child?" Jean-Christophe said, thinking it was a propitious time to bring up the matter of his brother's family. Sebastien was speechless. He looked at Jean-Christophe and then at his father, who looked dumbstruck.

"Pauline? Your child?" Anselme said.

"It's time to tell Father," Jean-Christophe said.

Sebastien calmly replied, "We both have important things to tell you, Father."

After the revelations, Sebastien went to Nîmes with his parents and his sister Elodie. He met with Gilles Bosson that evening and gave him Jean-Christophe's letter. Then he prepared for his inevitable departure for the military. He waited for his orders to arrive in the mail.

Anselme didn't have the heart to punish his rebellious son again. His imminent departure for the war was enough to worry about. As expected, Anselme managed to get a temporary deferment for Jean-Christophe. He had also tried to keep Sebastien away from the front, despite his younger son's wishes. That was when he was told about Sebastien's militant activism alongside the socialists. France's counterespionage authorities had an extensive file on Sebastien and weren't about to keep him off the front.

Anselme lost his temper. "I did what I could to avoid the worst for you. Since you want to do your duty, you will serve like all the other able-bodied men. I won't hide that I totally disapprove of your attitude. Clearly, you and I are not cut from the same cloth. I can only hope that in combat you will prove worthy of the Rochefort name. As for Pauline and her child, we have no intentions of bringing her into our household. After the war, you will have two options: Either you forget that girl and return to the family fold, or you continue to live like a renegade, excluded from your parents and siblings."

Sebastien had not expected anything else from his father. He was neither surprised nor saddened. What pained him was not having the chance to say good-bye to Pauline and Ruben in Paris. He called Pauline from Nîmes and sent a long letter promising to see them on his first leave. He, too, was convinced that the war would be short.

Jean-Christophe was hoping for a permanent deferment, and his father swore that he would keep pressuring his connections. After Sebastien's revelation, Jean-Christophe was forced to talk with his father. But he didn't tell the whole truth. He just admitted meeting some bad people. He said he had trusted them and had promised to sell them the mill. The decision to take the mill off the market had angered the men, and they had resorted to extortion.

"Because I refused to give them any money, they carried out their threat to hurt me," he lied.

Anselme believed him. "You ran into some thugs who wanted to get their hands on our assets. You were right not to warn the police. I asked a private detective to look into this. We'll soon know more."

The blood drained from Jean-Christophe's face. "A private detective? What do you plan to do with the information?"

"I don't know. But I want to find out who is threatening your safety and our company's well-being."

Caught in his own trap, Jean-Christophe didn't dare say any more. He knew his father would have another heart attack if he learned that the assault was the result of his gambling debts.

Sebastien joined his regiment a few days later. He was stoic with his father but couldn't hide his feelings when he hugged his mother and Elodie.

"Be careful, and come back soon," a tearful Elodie told him.

"I promise. Don't worry. We'll celebrate Christmas together."

"Will you bring your companion and your child?"

Elisabeth reprimanded her. "Elodie! Now is not the time." Then she turned to her son and said, "Don't take unnecessary risks. Remember that you are a family man now."

"I'll do my duty, Mother. But I know that I'm not alone now."

The good-byes finished, Anselme ordered his chauffeur to drive his son to the train station. "What a stubborn mule," he said as they drove away. "That boy is a real Rochefort!"

The city's streets were bustling. The train station was full of departing soldiers and their weeping fathers, mothers, and wives. Although some were still clinging to an optimistic scenario, many others were sure that these soldiers would be spending Christmas under the gray skies of Flanders or Lorraine.

Faustine had stayed in Anduze with Louise. Elisabeth had promised to return as soon as Sebastien had left. The girl remained carefree, despite the outbreak of war. Although the sons and husbands of Anduze were marching off, the countryside was as peaceful as ever. Yes, she would worry about Sebastien, even though she couldn't comprehend the dangers he would be facing. But she was distracted by love. Every morning, she had only one desire: to hurry outside and find Vincent.

Vincent wasn't really troubled either, despite the loss of the young farmhands who had been called into the service and the additional work it meant for him. The biggest change was not having any free time for Faustine. Without the farmhands, Vincent, Donatien, Victor, and the women were doubling their efforts, just as the wives, grandparents, and children on all the neighboring farms were working harder than ever. Faustine, who was already beginning to miss Vincent, didn't see why she couldn't help out, as well.

"Don't even think about it," Vincent said when she told him what she wanted to do. "Your mother wouldn't like that idea at all. Farmwork is not for a girl like you. It would be even worse if your father found out."

Vincent's words had no effect on Faustine. When Elisabeth returned to the Clos du Tournel with Elodie, Faustine made an announcement. "Rather than stand around and do nothing like a rich kid when there is so much work to do, I'm going to help out on the farm."

"You want to work in the fields?" Elisabeth said. "What an amusing idea."

"Yes, Mother, with Vincent and the women at La Fenouillère. Constance and her daughters didn't hesitate to replace the workers when they were mobilized. Louise suggested that I watch her children so that she could go work with them. I said no. I told her I wanted to take her place in the fields so that she could stay with her children."

Elodie chimed in. "Faustine is right. We should make ourselves useful. The men have been mobilized, and the women need help. I'm going to pitch in too."

"Now, now, Elodie, you're not strong enough to do farmwork. Your health isn't good enough."

"They can find something for me to do."

Elisabeth felt a little embarrassed in the face of her daughters' determination, Even though she did charity work, she hadn't given a second thought to the farmers who suddenly found themselves so shorthanded.

"Fine," she said. "If that's how you feel, I'll join you. Let's go offer our services to the Rouvières."

News from the front was discouraging during the first several weeks of the war. At headquarters in Vitry, Marshal Joseph Joffre was inundated with reports of defeat and retreat as German troops kept advancing.

Although Joffe was convinced that the enemy would never dare to invade neutral Belgium and attack France from the north, he was proved wrong. Still, French troops met with some initial success in Alsace. Sebastien was in the first army, which took Sarrebourg. General Paul Pau was optimistic. But the French victory was short-lived. Progress came to a grinding halt when the sixth and seventh German armies under Kronprinz Rupprecht and Josias von Heeringen counterattacked. The French troops were forced to withdraw. Sarrebourg was abandoned three days after it was taken. Nancy was threatened. More grim news followed.

At his factories, Anselme felt overwhelmed for the first time in his business career. Many of his workers were now fighting men. He had been forced to hire more women and older men, none of whom had sufficient training. As a result, productivity was down. At the same time, not all of his machines were running at full speed. And he still had to fill the army orders as quickly as possible so that the eight hundred thousand soldiers would have their new uniforms.

His worries multiplied when his private detective, Charles Brossard, gave him the results of his investigation, which had been delayed because of the start of the war. "My assistant was mobilized, as were most of my informants, so it took longer than planned," Brossard said. "And I wasn't able to go to all the places I wanted to."

"What are your conclusions?" Anselme asked, impatient.

"Conclusion is not the right word. It would be better to talk in terms of leads. To be frank, I was not able to follow all the leads to their end point."

"Why not?"

"The investigation became very complicated."

"Be clear."

"I've had extensive experience investigating cases involving organized crime, but your son is involved with a very diverse network that is too dangerous for even me. I don't have the means to infiltrate it without taking big risks."

"My son is involved with a dangerous network? What are you talking about?"

"The mob, Mr. Rochefort."

"You're crazy, Brossard. My son? The mob? That's insane."

"Your son fell victim to the Marseille mob. He has significant gambling debts. His creditors want their money. Do you understand?"

"Gambling debts? My son doesn't go to casinos. I would know."

"Not casinos. Clandestine game rooms."

Rochefort was stunned.

"How big is his debt?"

"I don't know. When I found out what I was dealing with, I dropped the investigation. It's too big. These people won't stop at anything. I don't want to end up with a bullet in my head."

"What do we do now?" Anselme asked, distraught.

"As far as I'm concerned, Mr. Rochefort, my job is done. You wanted to know who attacked your son. Now you know. The rest is up to you. If you want to take these people on, that's your choice, but I think you're better off handing this over to the police."

It had all become crystal clear. *Now I understand why Jean-Christophe was so adamant about selling the mill*, Anselme thought. *He was desperate for the money.*

At the beginning of September, Jean-Christophe returned to Nîmes with Louise and the children. His health had improved more rapidly than Dr. Blanchard had foreseen. The next day, he went back to work, where he found his father waiting for him. Anselme demanded an explanation.

Faced with the facts, Jean-Christophe couldn't deny the obvious any longer. "I confess, Father. I gambled, and I lost a lot. I didn't know who I was dealing with. If I had known it was the mob, I would have stopped immediately."

"You were putty in their hands. What an idiot you were. They wanted to take our mill."

"I couldn't help myself. I was winning in the beginning. I got caught up in it. The more I gambled, the more I wanted to. Then I started to lose. It was a spiral. So what do we do now?"

"Nothing. I won't be intimidated. You can't attack a family like ours. I also know people, and not just in politics. If you had to depend exclusively on members of parliament, prefects, state secretaries, and ministers, the world would be a much sorrier place than it already is. Thank God there are people in the shadows who are much more powerful than those men of straw who allow themselves to be manipulated."

"Who are you talking about?"

Anselme looked stone-faced. "That's none of your business. What's important is that I, Anselme Rochefort, know how to get in touch with them."

"Can we end these threats that are dogging me?"

"Dogging us, thanks to your stupidity. Yes, we'll do that. Because the people I'm thinking of wield clout even in the murky circles you found yourself in."

Jean-Christophe didn't know how to thank his father. One question, however, kept nagging him. "If your contacts are so powerful, Father, why couldn't you keep Sebastien from going to the front?"

"My son, your brother betrayed his own people. That's all I can say."

The Battle of the Marne in mid-September boosted the country's self-confidence. Thanks to Marshal Joffre's tenacity, the allied retreat was stopped, and a counterattack began. Two million men fought for six days along a 186-mile front. Finally, the German troops pulled back. A few weeks later, in October, the Germans marched into Flanders, only to be pushed to Yser in Belgium.

But in Paris, Pauline was worried. She hadn't received any news from Sebastien in several weeks. And in Tornac, the grape harvest was a near disaster, as there weren't enough pickers. The Rouvière family stood united in the face of difficulties and hoped the fresh victories on the front were a presage of peace. "Yes, they were right to think the war would be over by Christmas," Donatien said to himself.

Vincent returned to school in Nîmes and saw Faustine nearly every day. The two lovebirds were far removed from the ravages of war and the torments of families that had lost loved ones.

That was when, against all expectations, Jean-Christophe received his orders to join his regiment in Toul on the eastern front. His appointment with the army doctor had confirmed that he had completely recovered.

29

Explanations

1915

By the time Jean-Christophe joined his unit, the war had taken yet another turn. While just weeks earlier there was hope for an early end to the fighting, that now looked highly improbable. Soldiers on both sides were digging trenches to stabilize their positions. The fighting was bogged down. The only major fluctuations were in the East.

At the Rochefort mansion, the atmosphere was gloomy. Anselme was continually disagreeable. He had failed to get Jean-Christophe a permanent deferment, and now his shadowy associates didn't seem to be as reliable as he had thought. Anselme was upset.

"I don't understand," he told Jean-Christophe before he left for the army. "They're not delivering what I was promised."

"Your shadow contacts don't seem to be any more dependable than the politicians you see in broad daylight," Jean-Christophe said.

"Shut up, Jean-Christophe. You don't know these people. If you knew who they were and what they represent, you wouldn't say things like that. Besides, not everyone can enter that world. It's a very closed circle that encompasses many groups. You need an introduction to belong. It is all very clandestine."

"How intriguing. That doesn't change the fact that they didn't keep their promises."

Anselme didn't know why his intervention had failed. Jean-Christophe still had a death threat hanging over his head, and in the end, the only way to keep him safe was to have him mobilized. *What irony*, Anselme thought.

Jean-Christophe was commissioned as a reserve second lieutenant. It was the same rank that Anselme had held in the military.

Once Jean-Christophe was in the army, Anselme decided to close the silk mill. It wasn't making anything close to a profit.

"You just poured all that money into it," Elisabeth said, worried that her husband was behaving too rashly.

"Sometimes you need to cut off a hand to save an arm," Anselme said. "I'll sell off the equipment. I'll have no trouble finding buyers. With the money that brings in, I'll be able to purchase more looms and train more workers for the serge operation. My new weaving workshops will be operating at maximum capacity in a year, and I will be able to fill the defense orders more quickly. My friend the prefect assured me that the war won't be ending anytime soon, and more soldiers will be going to the front. They'll need the fabric from our plant."

"You're always speculating on other people's misfortune," Elisabeth said. She was outraged that her husband felt so cavalier about everything the country was going through.

"I don't speculate, dear. I foresee. And someone has to supply the fabric for the uniforms. If it doesn't come from my factory, it will come from a competitor."

"Are you sure you'll be getting more orders?"

"Of course I'm not the only one supplying the fabric, but I have enough leverage in the ministry of defense to make sure we get major orders in the future."

"Yes, let's brag about your friends."

"Our sons put themselves in indefensible positions. Thanks to my friends, they've avoided the worst. I managed to keep Sebastien out of the disciplinary regiment, where he would have gone because of his political activities. And Jean-Christophe was sent to the back lines. For now, he's not fighting. Believe me, he's safer where he is than in Nîmes."

"You're making me laugh. You have a grandiose notion of your own importance. Or you've lost your mind."

"I know what I'm saying, Elisabeth. Don't ask me to tell you more."

Elisabeth knew that Anselme had always wanted to be seen as a powerful man with connections. Some of his bragging was probably no more than fabrication, but still, there was much that he kept to himself. Early on, she had decided that it was best not to pry, not because she was afraid to learn the truth, but because she really didn't want to know.

"Nevertheless, I would like you to talk with me before making any irrevocable decisions about your business," Elisabeth said. "Do not forget that my family helped you financially when we were married. And what you inherited from your first wife, Eleanor, would have gone to Catherine if the poor girl had lived. You have a moral obligation to the children and me because of what my family and Eleanor's family did for you."

Anselme was not expecting Elisabeth to bring up this old story. "That was more than thirty years ago," he said.

"That doesn't change anything, Anselme! You still owe us, considering how you have benefited from what Eleanor and I brought to your marriages. And because of that, our children and I should be privy to what affects the family's fortune."

"I never thought otherwise, my dear."

"I just wanted to make sure. I don't pay much attention to your business. I trust you in that area, but that doesn't mean I have absolutely no interest in what you are doing."

Anselme wondered why his wife had found reason to remind him so directly about the origins of his fortune. She had never brought up the subject of his moral obligations and responsibilities before. She didn't understand anything about business. Why this sudden warning and this strange suspicion? Had she found out the real reason Jean-Christophe had been assaulted? Could she possibly suspect that he, Anselme Rochefort, had been involved in such a sordid affair?

The war was lasting longer than many had thought, and now it was spreading. Italy was on the verge of joining the conflict, along with Turkey and Bulgaria. The theater of operations extended from the United Kingdom to Switzerland on the Western Front and from the Baltic Sea to the Black Sea on the Eastern Front. Ten months after the beginning of the war, no one was predicting who would win or how long the fighting would last.

After many forays on the front lines, Sebastien had managed to repress any feelings of hatred toward his enemies despite the many atrocities he had witnessed. Sebastien knew the men in the trenches on the other side of the barbed wire were very much like him. He heard them talking, whistling, and even humming to overcome their boredom and fear.

"In truth, we are all the victims of the powerful, who are driven by their thirst for domination. They're canon mongers determined to get rich by selling increasingly sophisticated weapons," he told his more embittered comrades, who were focused on killing every last German. "We must take back Alsace and Lorraine, but our fighting should stop there."

Sebastien got his first leave in May of 1915. When he

returned to Paris on a fine sunny morning, he had the strange feeling of entering another world. The city seemed far removed from the war, although the fighting was just a hundred miles from the Eiffel Tower and the Champs-Élysées. There were just a few other soldiers on the streets. The boulevards were full of cars and wagons pulled by horses too old to be requisitioned. The metros were busy at rush hour. Only shop windows betrayed the daily troubles, as shortages were starting to be felt.

Pauline was still in school, more because she needed to forget her worries than because she was committed to her studies. Anselme wasn't sending money anymore. She could only count on herself. She did housework for rich families at night, while the building concierge watched Ruben. She was fond of the boy and wanted to help his mother, so she didn't ask for much money.

Sebastien hadn't told Pauline that he was coming. When he arrived at their place, unshaven, his hair a mess, and his uniform dirty, she barely recognized him. They fell into each other's arms. That night, they abandoned themselves in sweet lovemaking.

"I've got ten days' leave," Sebastien said the next morning. "I must go see my family. I'm taking you and Ruben."

"You're introducing us to your parents?"

"You could put it that way. You probably know that my father will not welcome you with open arms. That's why we will stay at my brother's house."

They took the first train to Nîmes the next day and arrived at Jean-Christophe's house late at night.

Sebastien didn't know that his brother had been called up. Elisabeth had thought it best not to tell him because she didn't want to add to his worries. Elisabeth knew her two sons were very close, even though they were complete opposites. *A sense of blood fidelity,* she thought. *They got that from my side of the family, not their father's.*

So Sebastien was surprised to find just Louise and the children. Louise immediately called her mother-in-law, careful not to announce the presence of Pauline and Ruben.

"He looks so much like you," she said, taking the child in her arms. "But he has his mother's eyes and smile."

Pauline didn't seem at ease in Louise's elegant home. The luxurious furniture, the servants, the carriage, and Jean-Christophe's car represented far more opulence than she was used to.

"Don't be intimidated," Louise said. "This is all for the sake of appearance. It took me some time to get used to it too. I come from a farming family that values work above everything else."

"I told you," Sebastien said. "My sister-in-law is a down-to-earth woman. We get along very well."

At that moment, Elisabeth arrived with Elodie. She cried at the sight of her son in uniform.

"It's been so long. You're so thin. You seem so . . . "

"I've toughened up, Mom. That's all."

Holding Ruben, Pauline stood in the background. Elisabeth looked the way she had imagined. She was a fine lady. But now that the woman was a reality and not someone Pauline was just envisioning, she was decidedly uncomfortable. Elisabeth's station in life was far above her own. She understood how different Sebastien's life had been from her own.

Elodie was the first to go to her brother's companion.

"You must be Pauline," she said, opening her arms. "And this is little Ruben. Sebastien, you could introduce us."

Looking stiff, Elisabeth approached the young woman. "Sebastien has not told us much about you, miss . . . or ma'am, I should say."

"Call me Pauline, ma'am."

"And this is your grandson, Mother," Sebastien said.

Elisabeth had no intention of being hostile or disdainful. But her upbringing got the better of her. She couldn't think of her son's companion as her daughter-in-law. Nor could she consider their child her grandson.

"I'll have to get used to the idea," she said a bit curtly.

"Mother, he's so cute," Elodie said. "And Pauline seems so nice. You made a good choice, Sebastien. I'm happy for you."

"Do you intend to . . . " Elisabeth had almost said the word "marry," but she diplomatically avoided it. "Do you intend to sort out your situation?"

Caught off guard, Pauline shot Sebastien a questioning look.

He answered without any hesitation. "No, Mother. We are fine living the way we are for now."

Elisabeth did not press.

Louise showed Pauline around the house and introduced her to her own children, who were playing with their nurse in a nearby room.

"I don't think it's a good time to introduce Pauline and Ruben to Father. Am I right?" Sebastien asked his mother once they were alone.

"You know well enough what kind of reaction he'll have. Even if you were married, I doubt that he'd accept her."

"In that case, if he wants to see me, he'll come here, to Louise's house. I won't go to the Cordeliers without Pauline and Ruben."

"You're being stubborn again, Sebastien. When will you understand that you have to be diplomatic with your father? Do you remember when you were with the Jesuits in Avignon? Jean-Christophe managed to convince him to let you out."

"He didn't let me go back home, though. Since then, I've always been excluded."

"You are the one who chose to cut yourself off from the family."

"No, Mother. Father banished me."

Anselme did not go out of his way to see his son. He wanted to, but his pride kept him from changing his mind in front of everyone. He refused to budge, despite pleas from Elodie and Faustine.

During his stay with Louise, Sebastien set aside the horrors he had seen at the front and did his best not to dwell on the duties that awaited him at the end of his leave.

He had long discussions with Vincent and got to know him better. Vincent was mature for his seventeen years, although he had no idea how serious the world situation was and how much suffering the soldiers and French citizens in combat zones had been forced to endure.

Sebastien had no desire to educate Vincent in that regard. He didn't like to talk about the terrible moments he had spent in the trenches, which had affected him profoundly. It was unseemly, and he didn't want to spoil his brother-in-law's dreams and illusions. He did talk about his vision of the world, his ideas on human relationships, and his sense of duty. He even expounded on the bourgeois education he had received and rejected.

"Why do you think I'm not getting married?" he said one night while Louise and Pauline were taking care of the children.

"Maybe because you are not sure about your feelings for Pauline."

"Absolutely not! For me, marriage is an institution that serves bourgeois society. It is designed to imprison man. It's no more than a societal straightjacket."

"I don't understand."

"Marriage, family, consumerism, education, work . . . it's all based on established patterns that deprive individuals of their freedom for the benefit of the ruling class. The ruling class conditions people to respond to its own interests. I'll go further: Even patriotism, which is exalted so that the people of the developed nations are united behind their respective banners, is nothing more than a pretext. It's used to get people to accept wars that nobody really understands or even wants. Powerful men make money from the blood we shed on the battlefields and gain even more power. They pull our strings. We are puppets in their hands."

"If you keep spreading ideas like that among your comrades in arms, you could be noticed and get into trouble."

"Oh, I'm not crazy. I'm careful about what I say. I don't want to antagonize my fellow soldiers. I need them beside me when we're fighting. I want to stay alive so I can bear witness. When the war is over, I intend to write about it and my ideas. I plan to raise awareness, to shake up people who are still in the yoke."

"I can understand why your father doesn't approve of your positions."

"We disagree about everything. That is true."

"But he's your father, all the same."

"Yes, he's my father. I respect him."

Vincent told Faustine about his conversations with Sebastien. She cautioned him. "Sebastien is a rebel and a great idealist. I like him. He is my brother. But don't let yourself be influenced by his ideas. He is hostile to the society in which we live and to the education we received. He denigrates the wealth my father is so proud of. But if he continues, he could turn into a bitter man, always negative and even intolerant. He imagines the best of worlds. He wants to impose it, to make others accept it for their own good. That is dangerous. You cannot make others happy by forcing something on them."

Unlike Sebastien, Vincent was not passionate about the world. His love for Faustine was enough for his happiness. In his teenage eyes, nothing was more important than the moments of bliss stolen from the uncertain times.

Sebastien approved of his relationship with Faustine, because it went against Anselme's wishes and tarnished the family image.

"Oh, the great Rochefort family," Sebastien said. "What's become of it? One son is a hooligan up to his knees in shady business. Another is a rebel who has betrayed the family and joined the commies. One daughter is vulnerable and secretive and at nearly thirty still hasn't found a husband. And the younger daughter, the most level-headed of them all, is in love with a boy who came straight from the orphanage. Yes, it's a fine family!"

Faustine had warned Vincent. But in the end, there was no need. Sebastien had no desire to change anything about Vincent.

"Each of us needs to decide on the life he wants to lead," Sebastien said the day before he returned to the front. "Life could have been much easier for me if I had taken full advantage of the privileges accorded to me by my social status and family. But I take responsibility for my decisions, and I'll go where my convictions lead me. I hope that you get what you want with Faustine. My father is not an insurmountable obstacle. Do not give up on what gives your life meaning. Fight for it."

The hostilities had intensified in Artois, near Vimy and Notre-Dame-de-Lorette. Sebastien's unit was waiting for him. He said good-bye to Pauline and Ruben in Paris and returned to the trenches.

Meanwhile, Jean-Christophe, who had spent long months in the rear lines, thanks to his father's intervention, was shocked to find himself fighting on the front. German artillery was shelling his regiment not far from Reims.

30

Persistence

1916

Anselme carried out his decision. He sold the equipment in his silk mill to a small company in Saint-Jean-du-Gard that was prospering. The basins and reeling machines were quickly taken apart and transported to the Cévennes. Once the workshops were empty, Anselme set up a line of state-of-the-art looms. He hired thirty workers, who underwent training for nearly two months. Then he placed them under Amédée Duruy, a foreman who was too old to be called up. Finally, he appointed ten or so young workers to ordinary tasks, such as cleaning the machines.

And so, at the beginning of 1916, his new weaving facility produced its first rolls of serge, which were destined for the army, as was the better part of his other output.

Far from Nîmes and the factory, Jean-Christophe grumbled in the trenches. His father kept him abreast of business developments—always much after the fact because of the slow mail delivery. Having tried in vain to profit from the sale of the silk mill, Jean-Christophe was quite unhappy that Anselme had poured what he had made from selling the equipment back into the plant.

"It's too risky," he had written when Anselme informed him of his plans. "The factory won't be producing as much fabric for military uniforms after the war's over, and if we can't find customers elsewhere, your investment will be for naught."

But Anselme hadn't really asked for his opinion. He didn't respond to his concerns.

Anselme was clearly energized. Running his company with no direct input from Jean-Christophe, he woke up with a fighting spirit every morning. Certainly, his handicap limited him at work. He couldn't get by without Henry, who was always in the background, ready to comply as soon as his master wanted to go someplace. But Anselme was making a superhuman effort to use his half-paralyzed body, and sometimes he amazed even himself with the things that he could do. He was convinced that he would soon walk again without anyone's help.

At the factory one day, he managed to pull himself out of his wheelchair and sit down on the sofa in his office. Using two canes, he then drew himself up. He stood for a long time without wavering. After a few weeks of tirelessly repeating this exercise, which required all of his energy, he took a little step under the watchful—and dumbfounded—gaze of his chauffeur, who was ready to intervene if his master fell.

As the weeks passed, Anselme started moving about in his office, first taking a few steps and then several more. He kept this miracle secret. He didn't want to reveal his achievements to those around him until he felt totally capable of walking in his own home. It was a matter of pride and arrogance.

"A Rochefort never gives up in the face of adversity," he boasted to Henry.

There was more to Anselme's drive to recover than the sheer satisfaction of using his body again. At sixty-six, he no longer hoped to spend years as the head of his business. But he was flummoxed. Who could take over after him? With his shenanigans, Jean-Christophe had disappointed him greatly. Sebastian had the makings of a leader. Unfortunately, he was irresponsible and hostile to both the business and the family. "He's a real Rochefort: hardened, proud, willful, and combative," Anselme said to himself. "What a waste of brains and character." Until he could solve his dilemma, he was determined to run his company, and that meant he had to be strong. The will to recover his full range of movement intensified.

By midyear, he thought he was ready to show his family that nothing was impossible. He ordered Henry to drive him to the Cordeliers and leave him alone in front of the imposing oak door. Leaning on his canes, he rang the bell the same way any visitor would. He waited for someone to open the door. Impatient, he rang several more times. When the governess, Marie-Jeanne, finally arrived and started turning the bronze doorknob, Anselme didn't give her time to finish. Using his cane, he swung the door open himself. "It's about time!" he shouted.

"It's you, sir!" Marie-Jeanne said, looking surprised.

"That's right. What are you doing looking at me like that? Go tell Mrs. Rochefort that I'm here, and I'd like to see her in the small sitting room."

"I'm on my way, sir."

The servant was so astonished to see her master standing up, she would have cried out "It's a miracle" if she hadn't known it would bring on more reproaches. She gave him another look to make sure she wasn't seeing things and rushed off to get Elisabeth, who was in the rose garden.

"Ma'am, ma'am, it's Mr. Rochefort."

"Calm down, Marie-Jeanne. I gather Mr. Rochefort has returned earlier than usual, but that's no reason to get excited."

"It's just that, well, he's waiting for you in the little sitting room."

"What's gotten into you, Marie-Jeanne? Pull yourself together. Go tell him I'm on my way. I just need to cut a few roses for my bouquet."

The servant calmed down and obeyed without explaining herself.

When Elisabeth entered the room, bouquet in hand, Anselme was sitting in a wing chair in front of the picture window.

"I was watching you gather roses," he said calmly. "Sometimes I envy you for being able to give so much attention to your favorite pastimes."

"You know, my dear, I have a hard time imagining you with enough patience to take care of flowers."

"You're right about that. My impetuous nature keeps me from slowing down and enjoying the little things in life."

"Did you come home early to discuss philosophy with me?"

"No, not at all, my dear. Not at all."

Elisabeth turned around and pulled the rope to ring for service. Marie-Jeanne came immediately.

"You called, ma'am?"

"Bring us some tea, please, Marie-Jeanne. And some cakes. For once, Mr. Rochefort has honored me at teatime. What's bothering you, Marie-Jeanne?"

Marie-Jeanne was looking over Elisabeth's shoulder at Anselme, who had stood up and was taking a few steps.

"Mr. Rochefort . . . "

Elisabeth turned around. And she, in turn, was shocked. "Anselme, you're walking!"

"By myself, my dear. I wanted to surprise you."

"How long have you been walking? So, Dr. Blanchard has been hiding things from me."

"Blanchard doesn't know, nor does any other doctor. This little miracle I performed all by myself."

Elisabeth had to admit that her husband was quite remarkable and more than worthy of the great Rochefort name.

The fighting continued for months. It seemed that each scrap of land purchased with blood was relinquished the next day at the cost of more blood. French soldiers dug in for the Battle of Verdun, which would prove to be the longest battle of the year. The French were determined to foil the Germans. Attacks and counterattacks followed each other. The war took on proportions never known before.

Jean-Christophe and Sebastien were in the thick of the fighting, although they were in different regiments and different locations and never saw each other. Each learned how the other was doing from their mother, who wrote regularly. She was careful not to worry them.

Neither one had been wounded since the beginning of the war. Elisabeth credited the numerous prayers and offering she sent to God and the Virgin Mary several times a week at Saint Castor Cathedral. Anselme credited his sons' bravery and intelligence in the face of peril. In combat, a man's life depended on his capacity to anticipate and react, qualities both had.

"When faced with trials, a Rochefort remains as hard as rock. Nothing can hurt us," he would boast with each letter from the front.

On those occasions, he set aside his differences with Sebastien and his dissatisfaction with Jean-Christophe, who had cost him a pretty penny. Anselme had quietly paid off his son's gambling debt after the sale of the silk mill equipment.

"I look forward to having us all together at the Clos du Tournel," he said one night when Elisabeth had approached him affectionately. He was surprised by his own words.

"Would you consider making peace with Sebastien?" she dared to ask.

"I'm not at war with my son."

"It's time to put an end to your discord, my dear."

"It is up to him to accept the fact that he is a real Rochefort."

Elisabeth pushed further. "Would you consent to your daughters choosing their own destinies?"

"What do you mean?"

Elisabeth hesitated. Elodie had taken her into her confidence several months earlier. She had fallen in love with a Russian expatriate who was a little younger than she was. Ivan Federovitch had lived in France since the beginning of the war. He was a Bolshevik opposed to the war, and he had fled his native land to avoid taking up arms.

Elisabeth decided to pursue the matter of Faustine first. "You know that Faustine has always gotten along well with Vincent."

"Rouvière's adopted son? I know that all too well, but I hope the young man understood what I told him the night I arrived in Anduze and saw them walking together."

"Those children love each other. I want Faustine to be happy."

"Faustine knows where her duty lies. She's a smart girl. I have already explained to her that there will be no second marriage with the Rouvière family, all the more so because Vincent is not their real son."

"You persist in being stubborn."

"No, I'm staying the course while the storm rages around us. In any case, the Rouvière boy will be called up in a few months. If my information is accurate, it will be at the beginning of next year. That will put things in order."

Anselme's response had been foreseeable, but Elisabeth was still disappointed. Just then Elodie came into the sitting room, thinking her mother had spoken to her father about the Russian boy she was in love with.

"Did you tell Father?" she asked before her mother could warn her.

"Tell me what?"

Elodie blushed. Realizing that she had been premature, she managed to say, "Mother was supposed to talk to you about me."

"About you? What about you?"

"About the young man Elodie met a few months ago," Elisabeth finally said.

"A young man? What young man?"

"Ivan Federovitch," Elodie said.

Anselme seemed disconcerted. "Well, this seems to be the day when all the secrets come out. I'm listening, both of you."

Elodie's decision to face life and even savor it had borne fruit. She remained somewhat fragile and still needed her mother's help and support, which she could count on. Elisabeth had lavished her with attention and denied her nothing. Sebastien and Faustine continually encouraged her to view the world with optimism. Responding well to all the doting, Elodie had chosen to look the other way whenever conflict erupted in the family. At the same time, she didn't take Anselme's inattention to heart.

One of Elisabeth's friends had introduced Elodie to Ivan Federovitch at a reception her mother had given when Anselme was away, and she had taken to him right away. They talked for a long time, as Elisabeth looked on. Elisabeth was happy to see her daughter finally come out of her isolation. She appeared to be captivated by the foreigner's words, his looks, and his charm. Indeed, he seemed to be getting attention from many of the young ladies that day.

That evening, Elodie couldn't hide her feelings. Elisabeth

cautioned her to be careful but promised to find ways for her to see the young man. So from encounter to encounter, Elodie and Ivan Federovitch took to each other. And Anselme was totally unaware of the reason for the radiance on his daughter's face. Ivan was four years younger than Elodie, but was mature and full of life. When she was in his arms, she forgot the depression and anxiety of her childhood spent in the shadow of her dead sister. A new future opened before her. She was even able to worry a bit less about her brothers, who were risking their lives every day.

Ivan told her about his grand country, with its powerful rivers that iced over in the winter and flowed full of promise in the spring, its steppes covered with flowers, and the melodious farming songs that rose in the hills during the harvest. He talked about Saint Petersburg, where his family lived, with its canals and large palaces and its streets and avenues bustling with life. It was a city where the working class rubbed shoulders with the princes of a declining empire, whose fall he dreamed of.

Ivan never hid his opinions from Elodie. And Elodie never hid the fact that her father had no liking for people whose politics were decidedly leftist.

"So what will he say when he finds out that I'm a Bolshevik?" he would ask, laughing and wrapping his arms around Elodie, who could not imagine a future without her knight in shining armor.

When she asked if he would return to his country one day, he said, "Revolution is brewing in the large cities. The people will soon overthrow the czar. It's a question of months or a few years at most. This war started by imperialist forces is very unpopular. It has to stop, because the working class is suffering. Lenin wants peace. When the Bolsheviks have taken power, I will go home."

"So, you'll leave me?"

Ivan always avoided answering this question. He did not

want to sadden or disappoint her. Then one day he put his own question to her. "Would you come with me if I asked you?"

Elodie did not show any hesitation. "I will follow you everywhere."

Anselme was totally astonished when his daughter announced that she was seeing Ivan Federovitch.

"A foreigner! A Russian immigrant? I hope he's at least white," he said.

"White?" Elodie asked.

"White Russian, of course. Czarist."

Elisabeth thought it better to change the subject. She didn't want to get into the young man's politics, as she knew it would only enrage her husband.

"Elodie would be happy to introduce you to him, Anselme. He's from a good family. His father is an imperial duke."

"So he's a noble. My goodness, daughter, at least you know how to honor your heritage. If this young man makes you happy, I'm eager to meet him and welcome him to our home."

Elisabeth was surprised that for once her husband had agreed to be open to a future for one of their children that he hadn't mapped out himself.

"I'm delighted," she said, hugging Elodie. "Elodie deserves to be happy. I'll take care of everything. We'll have Ivan Federovitch over for dinner."

Diplomacy, however, was an issue. Elisabeth wondered how she would handle the matter of the young Russian's political sentiments. As for Faustine and Vincent—that was another story.

31

Lassitude

1917

Vincent was enjoying his final days of freedom. After three years in vocational school, he had returned to La Fenouillère with the know-how that would allow him to modernize the farm's methods. He was eager to start, but Donatien thought it would be better to wait until he got back from the army to undertake the big changes that would make La Fenouillère the model farm promised by Vincent.

Knowing he would be called up in January, Vincent asked his parents for permission to spend weekends at Louise's house so that he could see Faustine. He would leave Tornac early Saturday and return Monday morning. Louise was thrilled to have him. Giving the excuse that she needed help with the children, she asked Faustine over every weekend. And so Vincent and Faustine were able to steal a few days together before he went off to war.

When Vincent returned from Nîmes at the beginning of

the week, already looking forward to the following Saturday, he would get right to work. Old Victor was still his companion and loyal confidant. One was never seen without the other. They were like two horses in the same harness. Donatien was proud of his son's enthusiasm for farming, He had feared that his studies would tempt him to pursue a more intellectual occupation. But in this regard, Vincent had never changed. He was in his element when he was working with the animals, feeling the soil with his hands, smelling the humus, inspecting the wheat to see if it was ripe, and pruning the vines and fruit trees.

"I made him a farmer at heart," Donatien boasted. "He really deserves to be called my son. He will say to his children, 'Thanks to the people who gave me a home, I became part of a fine family.'"

"You sound just like Anselme Rochefort," Constance teased.

"There is nothing more noble than the land. Our family has as much merit as the Rochefort family."

"Careful, Donatien, pride is a deadly sin."

While Vincent impatiently looked forward to the weekend and another two days with Faustine, Aline impatiently waited for Vincent to break up with the Rochefort girl and start giving her his attention. Since childhood, she had harbored secret feelings for her adopted brother. She had tried fighting them. Wasn't Vincent her brother? And wasn't his heart claimed by another? But her heart felt what it felt, and in reality, he was adopted. Anything was possible between them. The love that bound Vincent and Faustine frustrated and saddened her, but she was convinced that their relationship was impossible, and one day or another, Faustine would obey her family and say good-bye to Vincent. Aline was ready for that day.

After getting her school diploma, she had gone to the teaching college in Florac. Upon the recommendation of her teacher, Donatien and Constance had agreed, with some hesitation, to allow their daughter to continue her studies.

"She has a fine future in front of her. She is very good in school. It would be too bad if she stopped now. Let her go," the teacher had said.

But now Vincent had finished school, and Aline regretted her choice. "If I had stayed at La Fenouillère, I could have made him understand my feelings," she thought.

She returned to Tornac at the start of Christmas vacation with the intention of shaking things up. She knew Vincent would be mobilized soon, and she was going to open her heart to him.

She took advantage of a moment when Victor was taking care of three sheep with foot rot. Vincent was working outside by himself.

"You're going to get your pretty dress dirty," Vincent said when he saw her. "Now that you're a real city girl like Louise, you should be careful about your clothing. You are too elegant to be in places like this."

"Don't judge a book by its cover. I will always be a farmer. I don't deny my roots."

"That's good to hear."

Although Aline had prepared for this moment, she didn't know exactly how to approach the subject. Vincent was in love with Faustine, and she was afraid that he would not hear her out if she was too direct. Instead, she started by telling him that he had fulfilled his father's dearest wish—to have a son to carry on after him. It was her way of letting him know that she didn't think of him as a brother.

"What are you trying to say? You seem to be sad. Why? Are you unhappy in Florac, so far from La Fenouillère?"

"No . . . Well, yes, far from La Fenouillère—and also from you."

Vincent didn't understand.

"Vincent, haven't you noticed?"

"Noticed what?"

Aline burst into tears. She hid her face in her hands.

Vincent tried to console her. "Now, now, little sister, what is it? Go on, tell me."

"I'm not your sister! I don't want to be your sister!"

"But what did I do to make you so mad?"

"I'm not mad at you! I'm in love with you, Vincent. And you don't even see me."

Vincent was stunned. He had never suspected that Aline had such feelings for him.

"But Aline, that is not possible. You're wrong. I am your brother. Your parents are my parents."

"No, they are not your parents."

"How can you dare to say that?"

Aline couldn't get out the words that she had sworn she would say to make him understand that the love she felt for him was not sisterly.

"Aline, get yourself under control. You know I love Faustine, and she loves me. I've never hidden that."

Aline was devastated.

"But I love you too, and I always have. I can't help it. I'm so ashamed." Now that she had told him her secret, she felt remorseful.

"Come here," Vincent said, putting his arms around her. "I don't want you to be unhappy because of me. I love you too much."

"You love me?"

"Yes, the way a brother loves a sister."

They stayed like that for a long time, neither one of them breaking the silence. Aline didn't want to let go. She wished this moment in the arms of the man she loved would last forever. Here, there was nothing else in the world but the sweetness of the embrace she had yearned for.

The sound of Constance's voice brought her back to reality. "Aline, Aline. Where are you? Come quick. Louise just arrived with the children."

Vincent helped his sister smooth out her clothes. "Dry your tears. Put on a good face. Mom mustn't see anything."

Vincent received his mobilization orders the next day.

He spent a final Christmas with the family, and they celebrated the New Year together. Aline returned to her school in Florac without any enthusiasm.

Vincent joined his regiment a few days later, and to his great surprise, he found himself under the command of Lieutenant Rochefort.

With both Vincent and Aline gone, La Fenouillère felt very big and empty to Constance. She had never looked forward to this time in her life, when all the children would be gone.

Julie, too, had left La Fenouillère. For two years, she had been working as a waitress in a hotel restaurant in Alès. She had never liked working the land, and she had always rejected the idea of marrying a farmer, even if he was rich and from a good family. So she left her family for the city and seemed to be doing better, although she hadn't gotten completely over her sad adventure with Sebastien. Her bosses took good care of her. They hoped she would agree to marry their only son, Désiré, who had left for the front. Julie couldn't decide. She had seen him only four times, when he was on leave. He had courted her and quickly proposed, pressed by his parents to do so. Julie did like him well enough, but she was afraid of making another mistake.

"You were young then," her mother said when she mentioned her fears and Désiré's proposal. "You were both children. The mistakes of the past should not keep us from living our future."

Julie promised Constance that she would stop worrying and bring her beau to La Fenouillère on his next leave.

The sky seemed darker in this fourth year of the war. Troop morale was plummeting, and that of the civilians was hardly any better.

In the Rouvière and the Rochefort households, everyone was continually worried about their loved ones in the military. The anxiety was paralyzing. Bad news from the front made their hearts race. Talk of desertion and mutiny was spreading. Soldiers who tried to escape were shot as examples. The arrival of troops from the United States, however, gave them hope that military operations would speed up, and the war would end.

Vincent was shocked when he arrived at the front and found himself under the command of Lieutenant Rochefort. Thrilled to see a family member, he nearly hugged and kissed the man.

Jean-Christophe, however, didn't act thrilled in the least. He was just as haughty as ever. "Soldier Rouvière, you are under my command. Do not hope for any favors from me due to our family ties. I will not treat you any differently than my other men. So act like a soldier. Be brave and obey. The orders you receive from your sergeant will be my orders. You will follow them the same way your fellow soldiers follow them."

"I was not expecting any favors from you, Lieutenant," Vincent said. "I will do my duty like all other soldiers defending our land and country."

Vincent, who showed courage and a fighting spirit in combat, was quick to realize that his brother-in-law not only didn't show any favoritism, but also gave him the most dangerous missions.

"That brother-in-law of yours doesn't like you," one of his fellow soldiers said. "Why is he always sending you out to the barbed wire?"

"We were never too friendly. He didn't accept me as a family member. I was just his wife's adopted brother. He always treated me like some kind of orphan bastard. But the people who raised me treated me like one of their own and loved me the same way they loved their other children. So as far as I'm concerned, I'm as legitimate as he is, and my family's just as good as his."

"Whatever. He's got you in his sights."

"That's because his sister and I love each other. He knows it and disapproves, like his father."

"Who's that?"

"A big businessman in Nîmes."

"Damn! You've set your sights high. In the meantime, watch out for yourself. I get the feeling the lieutenant wants to push you too far. The slightest mistake can get you court-martialed and hauled in front of the firing squad."

As a seasoned farmer, Vincent didn't need his fellow soldier's counsel. Yet the reasons to rise up and disobey Lieutenant Rochefort's absurd orders and treacherous control multiplied. Vincent tried to focus on Faustine to make the best of it.

Just as the United States was entering the war, the Russian revolution was making the situation more chaotic. The Russian Empire collapsed like a castle made of cards. In November, the victorious Bolsheviks decided to lay down their arms and call for an armistice.

Ivan Federovitch was thrilled at this bad news for the Allies. He was only thinking about his country and his people, who had suffered greatly. Now the soldiers could return home, and civilians could look forward to better lives. Lenin was promising peace, land, and bread.

"I cannot remain far from my people in these circumstances. I must leave," he said to Elodie the day after the Bolsheviks took power.

Elodie hadn't thought the day would come so quickly. Deep down, she had hoped the day wouldn't come at all. "So, you're going to leave me," she said.

"I can't live without you, Elodie. But my heart is torn. Duty calls. And you are keeping me here. Come with me. We will live an exceptional life together. We will build our happiness in a great land full of new opportunities. We can share a life of exaltation and hope."

"Are you willing to give up everything your background has given you: your title, your wealth, and your connections? These are the things that tie you to your family."

"Hundreds of Russian peasants live under my father's authority. I want to be the one to free them from the yoke of servitude, to give them the land they have poured their sweat and blood into. I want to be the one who gives them equality."

Faced with such enthusiasm, Elodie couldn't find any arguments that would keep him in France. His words sounded so fair, and his heart was so full of the desire for justice.

He asked again. "Come with me. I will marry you, and we will build our family on the altar of happiness. The Russia of tomorrow will be a model for the whole world. Let's be there to build it."

Elodie was convinced. Naively, she thought her parents would accept her decision. Hadn't Anselme given him a warm welcome? Of course, she had not told her father about his political views. And her mother hadn't given the secret away either. In reality, Elodie didn't fully understand Ivan's revolutionary theories or how vehemently his father would have opposed his ideas, had he known. All in all, they were fine, generous ideas, broad idealistic principles that Sebastien himself defended. What could be so subversive? Didn't everyone want peace, equality, justice, and even the capitulation of imperial power? Hadn't France eradicated the monarchy and the empire? Wasn't the republic supposed to be governed by the people and for the people? That was what

Ivan had told her when she worried about her parents' reaction.

When she announced her intention to follow Ivan Federovitch to Russia, her father categorically refused.

"He is a traitor to his country! A dangerous revolutionary who was careful to hide his cards. If he were French, he'd be shot on the spot. I forbid you to see him again. From this day on, he will never set foot in our house. And he should be happy I'm not calling the police on him."

Faced with her daughter's despair, Elisabeth once again tried to temper her husband's anger. But it was futile. His threats grew even angrier. "If I hear that you saw him again or if he dares to come near our house, I'll inform the authorities. As for you, my daughter, you will stay in the house until the man has understood that he has made a mistake trying to take you away from your family."

Elodie was still fragile. This kind of shock had the ability to destabilize her. She brooded in her room for several days. Faustine tried to help, telling her that Sebastien had been able to fend off their father's excessive authority. But Elodie didn't hear, focused as she was on how hard her heart beat when she thought about Ivan leaving without her.

He had given her a week to decide. After that, he would climb aboard the first train for Marseille and try to sneak back into his country through Italy and across the Eastern Front, where fighting still raged.

Elodie secretly prepared a travel bag with a few changes of clothes. Then, one moonless night, while everyone else in the house was asleep, she tiptoed out of her room. She held her breath as she slipped down the stairs. Then, her heart pounding, she stepped out the door.

Ivan was waiting for her at the corner of the Rue Dorée. He held her for a long moment. Then he picked up her bag, and they vanished into the fog.

The next morning, Elisabeth discovered that her daughter was gone. Elodie had left a letter on her pillow:

> I am sorry to steal away like a thief, but I would be even sorrier to ruin my life by rejecting my love for Ivan. Father must understand that parents cannot keep their children against their will. Everyone must live the life they want to lead. My heart is torn, but I know what I must do. I am not leaving you. I am simply living. I love you. Your daughter, Elodie.

Anselme once again put on the face he reserved for his bad days. He felt overcome by a deep sense of lassitude.

32

Relief

1918

After Elodie disappeared, Anselme fell into such despair, Elisabeth feared he might do something that couldn't be undone. Nobody had ever seen him so depressed. He closed himself off behind a wall of silence and stopped all efforts to walk without assistance, even though the doctors said he was making remarkable progress. He wouldn't leave his wheelchair, except to go to bed, and he wouldn't go to work. Elisabeth didn't know how to get him to talk to her or simply show some sign that he was there.

"His mind is elsewhere," Dr. Blanchard explained. "He can't hear you. He couldn't handle the shock of your daughter's departure. You husband pushed his physical and mental capabilities to the limit. The efforts he made to start walking again depleted him mentally. This family incident was the last straw."

"Will he come out of it?"

"Perhaps when he finds inner peace. I have the impression

that your husband has been hiding behind a façade of infallibility. He wants others to see him as being solid as a rock. His pride keeps him from admitting when he is wrong. And he assumes he has the right to decide for others. But with age, the rock weakens. Elodie disobeyed him, and that was more than he could take."

Elisabeth informed Norbert Lesage at the factory, so he could take the necessary measures. Lesage had been Anselme's right-hand man for more than twenty years and had been promoted to the position of director. He knew his boss's plans for the business and was capable of running it alone.

"I can handle everyday business, of course, but with both Mr. Rochefort and Mr. Jean-Christophe gone, we'll need to consult with the board of directors."

Elisabeth didn't know what to do. She had never been involved in Anselme's business activities. She had provided her dowry, which had helped him rebound when he was nearly bankrupt. That was enough to make her feel that she had a stake in the business but not enough to immerse herself in the world of money, competition, and profit. Sebastien resembled her in this respect, and she was proud of that. Furthermore, at her age—she had just celebrated her fifty-eighth birthday—she felt incapable of making any informed judgment about her husband's business operations.

"I trust you, Mr. Lesage. As long as my husband is unable to take the reins, you can decide what is needed to ensure continuity. The war will end eventually. And then Jean-Christophe will come home and take charge if my husband is still unable."

Fighting was fierce in the North and East. With its troops freed up from the Russian front, Germany was on top at the beginning of the year, and American troops were slow to arrive.

Sebastien had often protested the abominable conditions he and his fellow soldiers were subjected to. And because of his subversive opinions, he had been put in a disciplinary battalion. That meant he was thrown into the heaviest fighting. A hundred times, he had seen his companions disappear, buried alive in shell craters or torn apart by buckshot. A hundred times, he had miraculously escaped the enemy fire. He even thumbed his nose at fate when his lieutenant commented on his luck. "What do you want, Lieutenant? Death doesn't want me. I'm too tough. It's scared of me."

This kind of sarcastic comment was the only way he challenged his superior officer. It was how he let him know that he was still a free man, despite everything. As tempted as he was to oppose his lieutenant, he followed every order. Some of his companions had mutinied the previous year. Most had been court-martialed. Others had been shot to serve as an example. Sebastien was determined to stay alive so that he could bear witness later on. More than ever, he wanted to work for a major newspaper after the war. He intended to use his writing to denounce injustice, defend the oppressed, and shed light on the truth.

Letters from Pauline boosted his morale when he thought the war would never end. He always kept her photo on him, along with their son's. The sepia images were shreds of peace in the chaos all around.

He received letters from his mother and sisters from time to time. That was how he learned that Vincent had been sent to his brother's unit. He was thrilled, unaware of what his brother was putting Vincent through. He was pleased that Elodie had dared to stand her ground and leave home with the young Russian he wished he could have met. Faustine had written to him about Ivan Federovitch. *We would have gotten along*, Sebastien thought. No one told him about Anselme's depression and silence after Elodie's departure. Elisabeth knew that despite their differences, Sebastien was concerned about his father's health, and she didn't want to add to Sebastien's worries.

In May, his regiment was sent to La Somme, where the Germans had stepped up their offensive. The Germans were trying to push the English army to the coast and cut off the French by breaking through the front in Picardy. They would soon open a breach in Saint-Quentin, advancing over thirty-five miles and taking nearly ninety thousand prisoners.

Sebastien fought fiercely, but like many of his fellow soldiers, he was forced to lay down his weapons. Taken captive, he vanished behind enemy lines.

Vincent was in the battalions that the German offensive had succeeded in pushing back. He also fought with courage. But his brother-in-law had not let up.

"He still wants to get rid of me," Vincent told his best friend, Sylvain Lafarge.

Before the war, Lafarge had worked in his father's vineyards on a small estate in the Corbières. In 1907, he had participated in winegrowers' demonstrations in Narbonne and Beziers, which the army had suppressed. He was arrested and sentenced to three months in prison for participating in what was termed a revolt.

"It's not right that he should be coming down on you so hard," Sylvan told Vincent.

Vincent knew that Jean-Christophe had it in for him because of Faustine. But he didn't know that Anselme had actually asked his son to make Vincent's life tough. In one of his letters, Anselme had written:

> Don't go too far, but make sure he doesn't come back unharmed from this war. Your sister must turn away from him. I don't think she would want

to share her life with a cripple. It would make her think and finally realize that she would be happier with a suitable husband.

Jean-Christophe agreed with his father and didn't hesitate to do what he had asked. He abused his authority and wouldn't let up on Vincent. Under daily fire the fighting men were ordered to make more and more sacrifices. Some were given the choice of following an order that led to certain death of facing the firing squad. Jean-Christophe thought it wouldn't take much to push the idiot Vincent into insubordination.

But Vincent was lucky. He returned from his perilous missions safe and sound. His sergeant, Ernest Legoff, was a good fellow who didn't agree with what his superior officer was doing, but he didn't dare oppose him. He would just warn Vincent of the danger he would be facing and offered him a double ration of liquor before sending him out. Vincent always refused so that he could keep a clear head.

At the end of May, Vincent's unit was called to the Aisne. He was injured as he tried to jump into an enemy trench.

When the gunfire ceased, Jean-Christophe asked Sergeant Legoff to report on the status of his men. Legoff went through the losses and then added, "Soldier Rouvière is unaccounted for. He may still be alive on the battlefield. We need to send some men out to find him."

"There's no point in doing that. With what we've just faced, I'm sure he's dead. I'm not going to endanger my men by going after a body."

"But Lieutenant, Lafarge saw him fall. He swears he's not dead, just wounded."

"That's enough, Sergeant. An order is an order!"

Legoff obeyed. But he told Lafarge that he would look the other way if he slipped out to help his friend. Lafarge didn't hesitate. When night fell, he and a medic slipped under the barbed wire and crawled to the spot where Lafarge had seen Vincent fall.

Vincent was still alive. He had started to despair that help would not come. "Finally. I didn't think anyone was coming," he said. "I made a tourniquet. I think the bone was hit."

The two men wasted no time taking their fellow soldier back to their trenches before the fighting picked up again.

The medic examined his leg more thoroughly and said, "The war is over for you, boy. We'll evacuate you to a military hospital. The doctors will probably send you home as soon as your recovery allows it."

Jean-Christophe Rochefort was furious as he watched his brother-in-law leave the front.

Vincent spent two months in the Compiègne hospital. He had been seriously injured, but his life was not in danger. The surgeon removed a two-inch-long piece of shrapnel lodged in his femur. The bone had a clean break, and the wound would heal.

"You were lucky. If you hadn't been retrieved so quickly, gangrene would have set in, and we would have been forced to amputate."

"If they hadn't come to get me, Major, I would have been dead."

"Well, now you'll spend two months in a cast, and then you'll go home. You'll be demobilized. You'll probably have a stiff leg from now on, but that's all."

Vincent would never be good as new, but he was a happy man. After fifteen months on the front, he was relieved to have his fighting days under Jean-Christophe's control behind him. *His plan to get rid of me failed*, Vincent thought. *When we see each other after the war, I'll have some words for him.*

Lieutenant Rochefort continued to hope that his brother-in-law's injury was serious. "If his leg is amputated, Faustine will turn away from him," he said to himself. "That little idiot wouldn't go so far as to kiss a cripple." His rage only intensified when he learned that Vincent had come through without any major consequences.

In August, Vincent returned to La Fenouillère, where his tearful family embraced him as though he were a savior.

"My goodness, what have they done to you?" Constance cried when she saw her son enter the farmyard on crutches.

The soldier, bearded and thin, had a hard time holding back his own tears as he let his mother hug him. He was so happy to be home.

Aline, still embarrassed, was hanging back. Vincent smiled, stepped away from Constance, and said, "So, little sister, don't I get a kiss? What are you scared of?"

Aline took a few hesitant steps and then threw herself at him.

"Whoa, gentle now. I'm not very good with these crutches yet."

"I'm so happy you came back alive! I . . . I . . ."

"Don't say anymore. I'm here now. It's all going to be fine."

Aline hadn't stopped hoping that Vincent would choose her. She calmed herself and felt relieved.

The pace of the war quickened, as the Allies were determined to keep the enemy from regaining strength. Fighting intensified under General Ferdinand Foch. In August, enemy lines were breached in Picardy. The Germans lost the benefits of the advances they had made in the spring. In October, French and English forces recaptured Saint-Quentin, Laon, and Cambrai. It seemed that victory was assured, especially because Germany was losing members of its coalition, one after the other, on the Eastern Front. Although the Reich army fought on with exemplary courage and still occupied part of France, its numbers were falling, and revolution was brewing in Berlin. The kaiser was forced to abdicate on November 9.

Finally, church bells pealed all over France. And this time, they announced victory.

Euphoria was everywhere, as people shouted the news out their windows, and those on the streets hugged one another in relief and joy. Farmers in the fields dropped their work and rushed to their city halls, churches, and temples to celebrate.

Vincent jumped with joy and nearly fell over. Donatien and Constance immediately called their servants to raise a glass of wine to victory. Donatien opened a barrel of his 1910 vintage, which he had been saving for a happy event. Julie returned from Alès, which was filled with jubilation.

Joy in the Rochefort household was more subdued but as real and genuine. Faustine had learned from Louise that Vincent was home. She was hoping she would soon see the man she had kept in her thoughts and her heart throughout the fighting. Although Elisabeth thanked God for keeping Jean-Christophe alive, she was still worried about Sebastien, from whom she had heard nothing. She knew only that he had been captured. In addition, she had no news of Elodie. A year had passed since she had run off. She had received only one letter from Warsaw. Elodie had said she was getting ready to go to Ivan Federovitch's hometown of Petrograd, formerly Saint Petersburg.

"I am sure she is happy," Faustine said. "When the war is over, and the mail is working again, we'll get news." Elisabeth was greatly relieved when Jean-Christophe returned home, and she learned that Sebastien would soon be freed.

To everyone's great surprise, Anselme began talking again in December, not long before Christmas. "We will celebrate the return of our sons and the glory of our country," he said. "Jean-Christophe and Sebastien fought valiantly and contributed to this victory. They have brought honor to their family. I am proud of them and will never forget it."

Anselme was also greatly relieved by the return of peace, and he decided to return to his business without further delay.

Part Four

APPEASEMENT

33

A New Era

1918–1919

The world seemed to be born again, even if daily hardships were still a sad reality, and everything felt somewhat precarious. Yes, Europe had emerged from the conflict in a state of shock and uncertainty. All sectors were unsettled: academia, politics, the economy, and society. But hope was omnipresent, as long as the major powers worked together to maintain the hard-earned peace.

Once released from the army, Sebastien couldn't rest until he was hired by a daily newspaper. He delayed his start date so that he could see his parents and siblings. He said good-bye to Pauline and Ruben and went off to Nîmes, where he quickly began to fight with his father again. Anselme was still refusing to acknowledge that his younger son had a family, albeit an unconventional one, in Paris. He had resumed his old ways and had used his influence to get Sebastien a reporting job at the local newspaper, *L'Éclair*, which one of his friends ran.

Sebastien learned this when he got to Nîmes and immediately rebelled.

"That paper's politics are the opposite of mine, Father! I cannot work for the right-wing press. And you seem to forget that Pauline awaits me in Paris. That's where my life is now."

"I had hoped you would return to your family, but I see the war has not changed your way of thinking."

"Did it change yours, Father? You have always tried to choose the lives your children lead, and soon you'll do the same with your grandchildren. Didn't Elodie's example teach you a lesson?"

Jean-Christophe tried in vain to soothe tempers during his brother's stay. He told Sebastien that his father was really putting up a front. He had lost some of his power and authority. But Sebastien would not back down or pretend to please his father.

"Jean-Christophe, I'm twenty-four now, and you are thirty-three. We aren't children anymore. We've been to war, and we've witnessed great suffering. Nothing will ever be the same—for me at least. I cannot bend to the authority of a father who represents what I find the most revolting: the power of money."

When it came to their father, the two sons were just as divided as ever. One had pledged his allegiance to the man. The other was still resisting.

In all the discord, Faustine was a ray of light. At twenty, she was a dazzling beauty. The war had not dampened her spirit, as she had experienced it from a distance and had not suffered much from it. Throughout the fighting, she had remained convinced that her brothers and Vincent would come home.For two years she had been studying architecture in Montpellier. She was a talented painter and also took classes at the École des beaux-arts, which she preferred over the school in Montpellier. Elisabeth supported her artistic bent but expected her to get a "serious degree," for Anselme, to ensure her status in society.

Unlike Sebastien, who confronted their father head-on, Faustine used her charm on the patriarch and always managed to soften him up. He would make concessions and even change his mind and allow her to do something he had opposed. When he ordered her to return to Nîmes every weekend because a young woman from a good family did not wander the streets of a big city alone, she managed to talk him into giving her permission to remain in Montpellier.

"I won't be fatigued from so much travel," she said. "And in my room, I can work without being disturbed."

Anselme gave in. "I'd rather have her alone in Montpellier than in the wrong company," he told Elisabeth, alluding to the period when Vincent had lived with Louise.

Anselme, however, wasn't overly worried about Vincent these days. According to Jean-Christophe, Vincent had been sent home after suffering a serious injury. Anselme thought his plan had succeeded.

In reality, Vincent was experiencing very few after-effects, other than occasional pain that would wake him up at night. He barely even limped. The doctor in Anduze who was following his recovery was surprised at how improved he was each time he saw him.

"It's nothing short of a miracle," the doctor said. "You should have lost the use of your leg and been on crutches for the rest of your life."

Vincent's recovery didn't happen all by itself. He had made a supreme effort to regain full mobility. He would walk for hours and work alongside Donatien and Victor. With the same determination he had shown in the face of the enemy, his mind won over his wounded body.

And his heart had never stopped beating for Faustine, who returned his feelings in kind. On the very weekend that

Faustine had convinced her father to let her remain in Montpellier, Vincent took a six o'clock train to meet her. He was exhausted from his week of work and physical therapy, but just the thought of Faustine reenergized him. She was waiting for him on the platform at the Saint-Roc station. She threw herself in his arms when she saw him and kissed him tenderly as the other travelers looked on.

They spent two marvelous days together, aware only of themselves, despite the crowds bustling around them in the narrow streets of the old town. They walked hand in hand or with their arms around each other in the shady parks, along the banks of the Lez River, and under the esplanade's plane trees. They dined in small restaurants on the Place des Trois-Grâces, which would later be called the Place de la Comédie.

On the first night, they returned to Faustine's small room and forgot the time. They undressed in haste and snuggled under the covers. Their senses slowly awakened as each explored the other's body and took in the other's perfume. Faustine pulled away for a moment to devour her lover with her eyes. Her gaze was full of happiness. She touched his lips, then leaned over and kissed him longingly. Vincent felt as though everything inside him was on fire. He pulled her close again and held her tight. He let her voluptuousness carry him. In one burst of light, he felt no pain, no fatigue, just sheer rapture. She belonged to him and he to her. Exhausted, they pulled apart and found peace in the warm sheets. They listened to each other's heartbeat and then slipped off to sleep, naked in each other's arms. When one of them stirred, the other responded, greedier than ever. They happily gave into their feverish desires all night long, until they fell into a deep sleep at dawn. They slept until the middle of the day.

"What will you do when you have finished your studies?" Vincent asked after they had gotten up. "Will you open an architecture firm?"

"Are you kidding? I'll never be an architect."

"I don't understand. Why go to school then?"

"To satisfy my father and give my mother peace of mind. You forget that I will be twenty-one in a year. So will you, for that matter. We will finally be legal adults."

"What does that change?"

Even though he was a practical man, he was sometimes less pragmatic than Faustine. She explained. "I will be able to decide what I do with my own life."

"You're going to go against your father's will, just like Sebastien."

"My brother is a rebel. I am not. But I won't have my life dictated by anyone, even my father. Until now, he hasn't refused me much."

"Other than allowing you to see me."

"Yes, and I will never bend to his will when it comes to you. But I am his daughter, and I love him. I don't want to hurt him. That is why I've always done what I could to keep him from finding out. In a year, though, I'll have to declare myself and tell him the truth."

"What's that?"

"Vincent, don't be such a numskull."

"I want to hear you say it."

"I'll tell him that the love of my life is a shepherd from the Cévennes who doesn't know where he came from but who knows where he's going."

"And school?"

"To hell with school. I want to paint. I want to be an artist. I'll set up my easel near you while you're working your fields or pruning the grapevines. The two of us will marry heaven and earth, dreams and reality."

"That's a fine plan, my love. But you are forgetting the most important detail."

"What's that?"

"We'll take the time to have some fine children, won't we?"

Anselme's business was slow to pick up after the defense orders stopped coming in. The slowdown followed three bountiful years, starting in 1915, when all the soldiers were supplied with uniforms.

Anselme had to find new markets if he wanted revenues to rise to anything close to their wartime high. Orders from the United States had dried up. Strong protectionist policies had made American textiles far more competitive than imports. American companies were now supplying the lion's share of fabric to US clothing manufacturers. And the Americans were inundating the rest of the world with their products. Clearly, wealth was moving to the United States, and America was becoming the new creditor for the Old World.

Anselme didn't let that scenario discourage him. "Until now, the Rochefort business has produced serge, part of which was exported to the United States to produce jeans," he told his board of directors. "I am proud to have contributed to the success of the Levi Strauss brand, even if there is nothing to prove that we played any part in it. Work pants don't have the status of clothing produced by the major clothing designers. I know that, and I regret it. I have always been a visionary, however, and I predict that our fabric from Nîmes—*de Nîmes*, or denim—has the potential to be a highly fashionable textile with a broad consumer base. Denim won't be used for clothing such as women's suits or dresses, for which the silk we were producing before the war was better suited. Cotton fabric, especially serge, is not as soft and smooth as silk or satin. Our challenge is finding the perfect application or applications for our product. I believe denim has the capability to revolutionize the fashion industry. I cannot tell you exactly when that will happen, but I know the day will come."

When Anselme gave his speeches, his board members

couldn't help but question him. Some criticized his excessive ambition and grandiosity, which caused him to make risky business decisions. In this time of economic downturn, many thought it was better to limit investment and adopt austerity measures by putting an end to wage increases or even lowering wages, laying off workers, and reducing other operating expenses. When Jean-Christophe presented a budget forecast, the board did, of course, approve it, but some members expressed reservations. Then Anselme announced his intention to take out a loan for a new production unit.

"To neutralize the impact of the drop in defense orders, I plan to open a unit to produce refined fabrics for women's clothing: muslin, organza, netting, and grenadine," he said.

"We'll need new machines and more workers," one of his dubious board members said. "Interest rates are not favorable at this time."

Rochefort had no intention of letting his board dictate his actions. He suspended the meeting before members had worked through the agenda, and he called Jean-Christophe to his office. "We need to get the board on our side. I want you to go see all the members who didn't say anything. Do it tonight, and do it quietly. They represent the majority. If we can't win them over, they'll wind up listening to those retired yellowbellies who want to hunker down and wait for the storm to be over. I think we should take advantage of the current economic troubles. We can be in a position of strength when the economy improves."

"Aren't you afraid the situation will worsen?" Jean-Christophe asked. "Inflation is running wild. The franc is weak. The government is in debt over its head, and that puts the country in a very vulnerable position. Taxes will just get higher, and business will suffer."

"Remember what I said before 1914: War would be good for business. When the economy is in ruins, as it is today, everything needs to be rebuilt. In the years to come, there will be a massive recovery brought about by the brave efforts made in all the countries that are now on their knees. We must be among the first to participate in France's economic recovery. In the days to come, we will see the return on the investments that we make right now."

Enthused by his father's speech, Jean-Christophe promised to convince the board members. "I'll put pressure on them one way or another," he said. "I guarantee that you will have your majority tonight."

"Be careful, Jean-Christophe. I don't want any shady business. I don't want us to be accused of abusing our power."

The second board meeting took place four weeks later, and two-thirds of the members voted in favor of Anselme's proposals.

He was jubilant. "The year 1920 will see the start of a new era for the Rochefort empire."

A few months later, the Credit Lyonnais Bank gave Anselme a substantial loan for the weaving facility that would produce the new fabrics. Anselme hired two sales representatives responsible for finding customers throughout France. Anselme knew he would be competing against behemoths in Roubaix-Tourcoing. Compared with those companies, he was Tiny Tim. But that didn't quell his determination to play in the big leagues. He wanted his name alongside the huge producers—Tiberghien, Motte, Masurel, and the others. He was barely aware of the peril he faced.

"I want to make Nîmes the textile capital of southern France," he told his family the evening after production got under way in his new facilities.

"Nîmes didn't wait for you, Father," Louise said. She couldn't bear his grandiloquence. "Our city has been known for its products since the Middle Ages. Shawl, hosiery, scarf, and even rug producers have been around a lot longer than your business."

"Louise!" Jean-Christophe said. "How dare you? You're involving yourself in something that is none of your business."

The discord in the couple's marriage was becoming increasingly apparent to others. Louise refused to hide her feelings. She was fed up with the hypocrisy and lying.

She had acquired some independence during the war years. Her husband's absence meant that she was free to make decisions about educating the children and running the household. Louise was forced to return to her subservient position when her husband returned. As haughty and smug as ever, Jean-Christophe quickly made it clear that he was in charge. And the disdain he had always shown toward the Rouvière family intensified when Anselme made him manager of the new production unit.

"You don't realize how lucky you were to marry me," he said, full of contempt during the family's celebration with the Rochefort board members. "You should thank me for taking you away from that farm and making you a member of this fine family."

With those words, Louise finally realized that there was nothing left between her husband and her. "I don't love you anymore, Jean-Christophe. You are revolting. You don't deserve the children I gave you."

"Did you ever love me? It's my family's money that you married, not me."

"How can you dare to say that when it was your father who plotted our marriage so that he could lay claim to my family's land."

Still, Louise felt torn. Her children were the only reason she was still in Nîmes—her children and social conventions, because wives rarely left their husbands.

Once again, Louise made the best of a bad situation and obeyed Jean-Christophe's order to stop her rude talk about her father-in-law.

Someday, mistreated women would rebel and seize their freedom. It would not be this day.

34

Dilemma

1920–1921

Sebastien had easily found his job reporting for the newspaper *L'Aurore*. He would have preferred working for *L'Humanité*, the paper Jean Jaurès had founded sixteen years earlier, but it was run primarily by communists. He did not adhere to that part of the left wing, which was on the verge of separating from the socialists and ultimately would in December 1920. In the end, *L'Aurore* was perfect for him. During the Dreyfus affair, the paper had taken a strong stand against anti-Semitism. Alain Dubreuil, an editor whom Sebastien had met on the front, had taken him on temporarily in 1919. He had been hired full time the following year. Sebastien was responsible for the Daily Life column and waited patiently for the day he would be assigned to a major story—a legal or political affair or a financial or social scandal that he could use to denounce injustice and defend people who had been victimized by those in power. He dreamed of seeing his byline on the front page and becoming a reporter who defended lost causes and people's rights.

Pauline worked at a woman's paper, where she covered health issues. It wasn't exactly what she had wanted, but she was less ambitious than her companion and was happy to find a position that would ensure she could provide for their child.

She was worried that Sebastien would ask her to sacrifice more than she could in his single-minded pursuit of a noble reporting career.

When he was hired at *L'Aurore*, they moved to the Rue de Vaugirard in the fifteenth arrondissement. Alain Dubreuil had found them an apartment with a reasonable rent. Ruben was seven and attended the neighborhood primary school. Because she couldn't leave the boy alone, Pauline had also hired a housekeeper, Linda, who cleaned for them and watched their son for a minimal amount. Pauline's heart ached that she couldn't spend more time with Ruben. In addition, she was becoming annoyed with Sebastien, who was often away when he was researching a column.

After meeting in 1915, Pauline and Louise had developed a friendly correspondence. Louise was suffering in her bad marriage, but instead of dwelling on it, she was giving others her attention. Little by little, the two women developed a genuine friendship. In every letter, Pauline encouraged Louise to spend a few days in Paris.

"The apartment is big enough," Pauline wrote. "Ruben would love to see his cousins. And Sebastien would be thrilled to have you. He has never forgotten how you took him in when he was a rebellious teenager and how you and Jean-Christophe opened your home to him."

Louise hesitated about visiting Paris without her husband. Seeing her parents without Jean-Christophe was one thing, but visiting the capital without him was another matter altogether. What would people say? She finally decided to make the trip during summer vacation. She got the children ready and told Jean-Christophe the day before she left. They took the first train for Paris the following morning.

Jean-Christophe welcomed the decision. He was glad to have her gone. He was no longer bothering to hide his mistresses. He spent extravagant amounts of money on them and kept an apartment for his dalliances on the Avenue Feuchères, not far from the train station. He took his women to the most fashionable restaurants in town and didn't care what people said behind his back.

"Vacation will do you good, my dear," he told Louise when she announced her plans. "I hope you come back with warmer feelings for me."

"I don't have any more feelings for you. I already told you that. Don't expect anything but my simple presence. I'm living with you only because of the children."

The split seemed final.

When Louise arrived at the Gare de Lyon station in Paris, Pauline was supposed to be waiting on the platform. She wasn't. While Pierre and the twins clung to their mother—they weren't used to the commotion of a busy train station—Louise called a porter and continued searching for Pauline in the crowd. As soon as the porter arrived, Louise was faced with a new worry. What if the porter took off without her?

"Should I take your baggage to the main hall?" the porter asked "Would you like me to hail a taxi?"

"That won't be necessary. I'm waiting for my sister-in-law."

Louise claimed her bags at the end of the platform and waited.

"We must have missed her, or she forgot to come and get us," she told her children after the last passengers had departed.

"What are we going to do?" Pierre asked, worried.

Louise was also fretting. Then her fretting gave way to all-out alarm.

"My handbag!" she cried out. "I left it on the train."

Her handbag contained not only all of her money, except what she had taken out for the porter, but also her brother's address.

She took a few deep breaths and tried to hide her fear. She took the children into the café and found a table where she could sit the children down and think.

"My goodness, if only I knew their phone number, I could call them."

"I know their number," Pierre said. "It's Odéon 10-14."

"Are you sure?"

"Absolutely. I know phone numbers for everyone in the family. You could ask the bartender to lend you the money for the phone call and ask Pauline to pay for it when she comes. She knows you'll repay her."

Pierre was very practical for his age.

"Thank you, Pierre. I hope that's the right number. Otherwise, I don't know how we're going to get out of this pinch."

Louise found a phone booth and called. Nobody answered. Louise paled. Her heart was pounding. She asked the operator to try again. And again, no answer.

She started to panic. "Goodness me, what am I going to do? People will think I'm totally inept."

She left the phone booth and headed toward the table where she had left the children. Panic became dread when she saw that they were gone. The bags were still there, but the children were nowhere to be seen.

"My children!" she screamed. "Where are they?"

Those at the neighboring tables stared but didn't offer to help. She darted around the café, looking everywhere. Finally, she got the bartender's attention.

"What are you looking for, ma'am?"

"My children! They were here a minute ago, before I went downstairs to make my phone call."

The man smiled. "Ma'am, nobody pulls one over on me. First of all, pay for what you ordered and your phone call."

"But sir, it's that . . . "

"You have quite a bit of nerve, using your children to wrangle your way out of paying what you owe."

Just as he was coming out from behind the bar to berate Louise face-to-face, she spotted Thibaud and Alix on the other side of the window.

"There they are! My children," she cried out. "They're right there!"

"I don't care. Pay me right now, or I'll call the police."

Louise pulled herself away from the man's grip and rushed to her children. Pauline, holding Ruben, was standing with them.

"Louise! We missed each other. It's a good thing your son is resourceful. He found us."

"Thank goodness. I was so scared," Louise said.

"Pierre has seen me only once, and he was four years old then. I'm amazed that he recognized me."

Louise explained her misadventure, and Pauline paid the bartender. She hailed a taxi, and together they headed to the apartment on the Rue de Vaugirard.

"Is Sebastien waiting for us at the apartment?" Louise asked in the taxi.

Pauline's face dropped, and she took her time to answer. "I'll explain later. We had a little fight."

"Nothing serious, I hope."

"I think we're going to separate."

As soon as they arrived, Pauline invited Louise into the living room to explain what had happened with Sebastien. "I want to tell you now, before he gets home. He went to Picardy for three days to do a story about those who died at Chemin des Dames in 1918."

"Vincent was wounded there and was almost left for dead."

"I know."

"And Jean-Christophe was his commanding officer. He said Vincent was dead and refused to send help."

"I know all that. It's such a distressing story. Vincent told Sebastien about it in a letter, and Sebastian told me. He was disgusted. That's why he took on the story. He wants to denounce the mistakes made by the people in charge."

"That doesn't explain why you want to separate."

"Sebastien wants all three of us to leave for Indochina."

"Indochina!"

"He's been offered a correspondent's position in Saigon. He says it's the chance of a lifetime, and we shouldn't pass it up."

"And what do you think?"

"It's too far. I'm not ready for such a long trip, not with a child. Ruben needs stability in his life. And Sebastien knows I want more children. But all he wants is to follow his dreams. He's still that idealist he was when we met. He hasn't changed. I thought that with time—and the war on top of that—he would mature and become more grounded. I was wrong."

"How long would he have the job?"

"There's no time limit. Knowing Sebastien, I'm sure he'd want to stay. I just can't see myself living there. It's too hot and too dangerous. I want a normal life, like yours."

"Like mine? If only you knew."

After the children were in bed, the two women talked all night about their problems. Pauline learned that Louise had been ready to leave Jean-Christophe but hadn't acted on it because of conventions, primarily concerns over what people would say. Louise, for her part, tried to reason with Pauline. But it was futile. She wanted no part of Sebastien's adventure in Saigon.

"I love him," Pauline finally said. "But if I don't agree to go with him, he will leave anyway. We are not married, which makes things easier for him."

"Is he determined to go?"

"I'm afraid so."

Sebastien confirmed his intentions the next day, when he returned from Picardy. "I cannot pass up this kind of opportunity. If Pauline doesn't change her mind, I'll leave alone."

"Have you thought about your son, Sebastien?"

"I'll return. I didn't say I would separate from Pauline permanently. But I'm going to follow my dream. Pauline knows I've always wanted something like this. She shouldn't try to hold me back."

"That is not what she's trying to do, but I fear that for her, this would lead to a permanent separation."

"She said that because she is sad. I promise I will come back."

"When? How many years later? You don't have the right to abandon your wife and son just to embark on some adventure. You have responsibilities to them."

Louise couldn't reason with Sebastien. He was the same rebellious boy she had taken in before the war, more determined than ever and willing to sacrifice everything to quench his thirst for life and liberty.

She tried to cheer Pauline up. But Pauline already seemed resigned to her fate.

At La Fenouillère, the Rouvières celebrated the day Vincent joined the family, March 26, as they did every other year. The family, Victor, and the full-time farmhands gathered for a meal to celebrate the young man. Louise was the only one not there. She had left for Paris the week before, without her children, to see Pauline, who had been devastated by Sebastien's departure six months earlier. Pauline had begged Louise to come visit her. Because Louise didn't know how long she would be in Paris, she had left the children with her parents, and they had put them in school in Tornac.

Jean-Christophe, who was very busy at work, was just as happy that they were gone, as he didn't want to be responsible for them. He wanted to be left alone to live the life he wanted.

Constance, on the other hand, was thrilled to have the grandchildren. And Pierre, who was eleven, and Thibaud and Alix, who were nine, loved spending time at La Fenouillère, where their grandfather showed them the animals, gave them chores to do, and explained his work. Vincent, who had grown fond of the children during his stay in Nîmes, also took them under his wing. Through them he could revisit his own childhood at La Fenouillère, a happy, promising time after seven long years in the orphanage. He had buried most of his memories of that place, not only because they were unpleasant, but also because they had nothing to do with his present life. When the children asked questions about that distant past, he said he didn't like to talk about it. To distract them, he showed them the goats and the sheep or had them pet a lamb or chase chickens.

Constance set the large table in the dining room, which they used only on special occasions. Spring was having a hard time settling in, and outside the north wind stung faces and darkened the sky. Donatien lit some wood in the fireplace. The blazing oak logs crackled and spread a soothing warmth throughout the living area.

March 26 fell on a Saturday. Julie had been able to get away from the restaurant. She arrived in the middle of the morning with Désiré Barthélemy, her boss's son. She had finally agreed to marry him, and she wanted to take advantage of the family celebration to announce their engagement. Constance sometimes teased Julie about winding up an old maid, but Julie knew her mother really was worried that she would never get married.

Before sitting down at the table, Donatien filled everyone's glass and toasted Vincent. "Today is a big day for our son," he began in a solemn voice. "I don't need to repeat why we always celebrate March 26."

"Oh Father, you can say it. I'm not ashamed of my origins."

"If you insist. Louise's children most likely don't know the whole story, that you joined our family exactly sixteen years ago today, when we brought you home from the Sisters of Charity orphanage. For us, March 26 was like your birthday, because that was when your life with us began. But it's not your actual birthday. Vincent, you celebrated your twenty-third birthday in January..."

"I was dropped off at the orphanage on January 22, Saint Vincent's Day, a few days after my birth," Vincent said for the benefit of his nephews and niece. "That is the date that was written down."

Donatien went on. "Today, you are an educated and experienced farmer. You know things that I do not. Your skills exceed mine, particularly in winegrowing. I know that is your area of choice."

Everyone was wondering where Donatien was going with his speech. He rarely talked so much.

Behind her mother, Julie was fidgeting, impatient to announce her news.

"Donatien, what is it that you want to tell us?" Constance asked.

"I'm getting to it: I'm fifty-six. I've decided to give my vineyards to Vincent so he can pursue his dream. I know he would love to establish a small winery producing quality wines. He is wasting his time at La Fenouillère, working at my side."

Vincent was shocked. He knew that Donatien was counting on him to take care of the farm when it was time for him to retire. He also knew that he would inherit part of the farm, as his sisters would. But he had never thought he would so quickly become the owner of a fine vineyard. He couldn't hide his joy and threw his arms around Donatien.

"Dad! You . . ."

"Don't say anything, my son. You'll end up making me cry. Just promise to make a wine estate worthy of our family."

"I'll call it Les Chais de la Fenouillère. I'll replace our grapes with noble varieties and make a quality wine that stands out, unlike the run-of-the mill Languedoc wines the region is producing."

"Don't you agree that great farming families can stand shoulder to shoulder with the families that lead industry and finance?" Donatien said. "We have no reason to think our life's work is inferior to any other pursuit. We should honor it."

Vincent smiled. He understood what his father was saying. "I have something important to tell you," he said.

Julie thought she would never get to speak.

"I hope it's good news," Constance said, giving Madeleine a wink.

"Yes, well, it shouldn't be a problem for you, in any case. Here it is: Faustine and I are planning to live together. We've been thinking about it for two years now, since we turned twenty-one."

"What did I tell you?" Constance said to Madeleine.

"So you knew!" Donatien said.

"I didn't tell anyone, Father. Mom just guessed. We wanted to move into the small outbuilding at the edge of La Fenouillère. I know you would welcome us here, in this home. But we want our own place. The fact that Father's handing over the vineyards shouldn't change anything. So is it all right with you if Faustine and I make a home in that little shed?"

"By all means. We'll even help you fix it up and make it bigger," Donatien said. "But do you intend to get married? You are both old enough."

"That is not entirely up to us. But that is another story. Faustine's father won't hear any talk of a second marriage in our families. Faustine is leaving home without his consent as soon as you agree to our plan. It's a real dilemma for her, because she doesn't want to make her mother sad or her father angry the way Sebastien did. But Anselme Rochefort won't budge."

"I know him well. He's stubborn, proud, and full of himself. I'll go talk to him."

"No! That will just make him even more hostile. Let time do its work. Faustine is counting on her mother to bring her father around."

In the excitement of the moment, everyone had forgotten to ask Julie what she wanted to announce. Constance was the first to remember that she had something to say. "Julie, what is it that you need to tell us?"

"Oh, nothing very important. Désiré and I have just decided to get married in Saint-Jean."

"You're getting married! My daughter! That makes me so happy. I had given up hope."

"Well, today is a big day," Donatien said, a huge smile on his face. He put his arms around both Vincent and Julie. "I propose that we raise a toast to these two happy events. Say what you like, but family is the greatest treasure a man has in this world."

35

Separation

1921–1922

Sebastien had left Pauline and their son in the late summer of 1920. He sailed to Saigon and settled in the colonial neighborhood where the majority of French residents lived. Before embarking in Le Havre, he promised Pauline that he would return to her if she didn't choose to join him later.

"Give me a little time," he said. "I haven't committed to this position for longer than a year. I hope you will change your mind and come join me. If you're still refusing a year from now, I'll come back."

Pauline didn't try to hold Sebastien back. Out of love for him, she let him go follow his destiny, knowing deep down that if she didn't, she would lose him forever.

"I'll wait," she said without much hope. "Take the time you need, but I won't be joining you in Saigon. You want to be free to pursue your dreams. Ruben and I would be burdens.

Go, but don't forget us. When you come back, if you come back, you will find me here, in our home."

As *L'Aurore*'s correspondent in Saigon, Sebastien covered all of Indochina. It was an important job that didn't give him much free time. He covered breaking news throughout the region and was often away from Saigon for weeks at a time. When he wasn't on assignment he spent his days at the paper, finishing off articles that he then sent to the Paris office.

He was always on the lookout for articles, and he quickly understood that tensions were intensifying between the colonists and the nationalists, who supported independence. France had called on colonial troops for backup during the war, and many young men had been dragged into fighting that had nothing to do with them. They made excellent recruits for the nationalist movement once they returned home.

Sebastien believed that people should decide their own future and thought colonial empires would one day be a thing of the past. He hoped the French government would come around to accepting self-determination for the people of Indochina, and his articles often betrayed his sentiments. This got him into trouble with his editor, who wanted Sebastien to be objective.

"The nationalists have ties with communist elements," Sebastien's editor told him. "They have gained considerable influence since Mao Tse-tung founded his party in China, and he's supported by the Soviets. You can see where this is headed. A communist revolution is brewing in Indochina. It is not our role to enflame any political passions. Our job is informing our readers in France with as little bias as possible. Just give them the facts."

Colonial rule had benefited very few indigenous people in Indochina. While foreign-owned rubber plantations were thriving, poverty was rampant. There was little industry in the cities and not much of a working class. Businesses were mostly small shops, many of which were owned by Chinese immigrants. The upper class, composed of intellectuals and shopkeepers, had gained a fair amount of power before the war and now hoped that France would give them a more important role in governing the country. But the reforms were slow in coming. This was pushing moderate thinkers toward radical opposition and heightening feelings of rancor.

"As a reporter bearing witness to the news, I cannot simply relate the facts without exposing the causes," Sebastien said, responding to his editor. "French readers have the right to know the whole story."

Sebastien disregarded his editor's instructions. He sided with those seeking self-determination and established relationships with influential nationalists. He made every effort to break into their inner circles. He organized secret meetings with their leaders in rice paddies and distant mountains, sometimes risking his safety without even knowing it. Although he made it clear that he did not support armed revolution, the nationalists came to accept him and hoped his articles would bolster their cause.

After spending time with the nationalists, he would request meetings with the governor general or his emissaries to relay their concerns and plead their cause. He was soon thought of as a French national with ties to the Viet Nam Quoc Dan Dang, a party that was aligned with the Chinese Kuomindang.

During a meeting with members of the Chinese Kuomindang, he met Hoa Mi, a young farm woman from Annam, whose parents had died two years earlier in an agrarian rebellion put down by the French Army. Hoa Mi was barely seventeen when her parents were killed, and she had gone to live with her uncle, a militant in the independence movement. She was an active member of the group he led.

Far from Paris, Pauline, and his child and impassioned by the cause he supported, Sebastien was feeling increasingly disconnected from his old world. It was true that every time he returned to Saigon from an assignment, he resumed his familiar life with French colleagues and associates. But as time went on, he became more and more impatient to join Hoa Mi again. Her life had touched his most inner self. Her fight against injustice reminded him of his own, and her youth and enthusiasm moved his heart.

Despite her impassioned beliefs, Hoa Mi had a gentle and quiet bearing. And Sebastien, who had always been inflamed by rhetoric, found himself seduced by a woman of few words. A single glance from this exotic beauty or a simple caress could convince him of anything and drag him into a whirlpool of sensual delights.

Sebastien fell so in love with Hoa Mi, he soon couldn't imagine life without her. He decided to leave Saigon to go live with her in her village in the middle of the rice patties, not far from Nha Trang on the eastern coast. He returned less and less to Saigon, where his bosses at the paper were starting to question what he was doing. His articles became infrequent and were so biased toward the nationalist cause, they were heavily revised. When he was reproached, he responded dismissively or disdainfully—sometimes even angrily. His love for Hoa Mi made him lose all sense of responsibility and reality.

"I'm expecting a child," she told him one day. "You will soon be a father."

Sebastien, who had not told her anything about Ruben or Pauline, was overjoyed. He decided to abandon his old life entirely and take up the life of a village peasant. He changed his clothes, grew out his beard and hair, and started working with the others in the rice paddies. He didn't bother to inform his bosses at the paper, however, and even though he hadn't been sending many articles, they were alarmed that they hadn't heard from him at all. They feared something bad had happened. Perhaps he had been kidnapped or had died in a skirmish with rebel groups.

Sebastien, oblivious to any concerns back in Saigon, was in heaven. He was living a simple life with the woman he loved. He had finally acquired wisdom and serenity. When he thought about his past, he had the feeling that he was not the same man. He had turned a page in his life and could never go back.

Hoa Mi gave birth to a girl. They named the baby Thu Suong, or Autumn Dew. It was Hoa Mi's mother's name. Little by little, Sebastien cut off all links to the past, including those to Pauline and Ruben.

His happiness was short-lived. Three months after Thu Suong was born, Hoa Mi's uncle warned him that the police were looking for him. Sebastien was suspected of being a revolutionary, and the police had a warrant for his arrest. Staying in the village would endanger all the other inhabitants, he said.

So Sebastien headed north, walking across Annam and then Tonkin. With the baby strapped to her back, Hoa Mi was by his side. He lived like a renegade, hiding in rice paddies, swamps, and mountain caves but never neglecting the woman who was devoted to him, the woman who had sacrificed everything for him and their child.

When they arrived at the port in Haiphong, they managed to get on a ship bound for Hong Kong. From there, Sebastien decided to leave for Polynesia, where he believed he could live peacefully with Hoa Mi and the baby. They settled on Maupiti island, where they rented a small, bare *fare*, or Tahitian house, in the middle of an island surrounded by a turquoise lagoon.

Lost in the middle of the Pacific Ocean, more than twelve

thousand miles from Paris, Sebastien had finally achieved his goal.

There, he started to write.

Sebastien's departure didn't surprise the Rocheforts. They knew their son would pursue his idealistic ambitions at any cost. When he was a teenager, hadn't he tried to take off to a distant land, totally unconcerned about how he would actually do it?

Elisabeth felt sorry for Pauline, all alone with her child in Paris. She wanted to get in touch with her son's companion, to console her and reassure her, to let her know that she really was a daughter-in-law, just like Louise, and Ruben was a true grandson, just as her three other grandchildren were.

But Anselme would not tolerate it. He would not accept Pauline and Ruben as part of the family. Nor would he allow any talk of Sebastien in his presence as long as his son's behavior continued.

"When you are a father, you assume your responsibilities," he said. "You don't run off to the end of the world to fulfill some fantasy."

Anselme Rochefort's children had refused to fall in line with his vision of a proud, united family. No one had heard from Elodie for some time. Now Sebastien had disappeared, as well. Faustine's disobedient decision to take up with an orphan Anselme had forbidden her to see was a final blow to his authority and arrogance.

Jean-Christophe was all he had left, the only one who had ever showed any interest in his business, the only one who could possibly carry on his life's work after he was gone. But Jean-Christophe was fickle and unreliable. Hadn't he already demonstrated his incompetence, thoughtlessness, and betrayal?

Anselme was about to turn seventy-three. Feeling that

he had nothing to look forward to, he closed himself off. Despite the progress he had made, he stopped trying to walk and remained in his wheelchair. Henry drove him to the factory on Monday morning and drove him home on Friday night. During the week, he slept in a room behind his office. A hired aide took care of him day and night. On the weekends, he stayed in the sitting room or his bedroom, where he took his meals and read the paper. The only person he would see was Elisabeth, and when she did come to his room, he berated her.

"None of that would have happened if you had given our children my values instead of all those lessons about liberty, fulfillment, and Christian charity. You see the result: Out of our four children, only one is married. The other three live in disgrace. We don't even know where two of them are."

Elisabeth didn't respond. She could not reason with her husband. Furthermore, his health was worrisome. He had been having heart trouble again. "Be careful, my dear," she advised. "You are overtaxing yourself at work. Let Jean-Christophe carry more of the load."

But Rochefort refused to give in. He was too proud.

When Louise announced her intention to leave her husband for good, it was clear that Anselme's fine, great family had never been anything but an illusion. Everything Anselme had worked so hard to build after the death of his father and his first marriage to Eleanor Letellier, everything he had carefully concealed to expedite his rise—it was all for naught. He had had great plans for his family, but his children had refused to bend to his will. And now he had nothing to show for his investment.

Although the company was benefiting from the economic upswing that the entire country had been enjoying for several years, and it was still recognized throughout the region for its denim, Anselme had not succeeded in his quest to rival the great textile dynasties of northern France. Rochefort's fine fabrics hadn't won the market share that Anselme had envisioned. Jean-Christophe was a poor standard-bearer for the Rochefort name, overcome as he was by his dissolute life. He didn't inspire trust in prospective customers, and he wasn't getting many contracts.

"If you continue like this, you will endanger the entire business," Anselme warned. "We've made a significant investment in the fine-fabrics line, and we must pay off our loans. You need to bring in more revenue."

Anselme also took his son to task when it came to Louise. "How could you hope to manage a company when you can't keep your wife at home?" he grumbled.

Jean-Christophe dismissed both his father's concerns and his wife's criticisms.

Louise had finally come to terms with the idea of a separation. It was during her second visit with Pauline, six months after Sebastien's departure, that she finally decided to split with Jean-Christophe. Pauline had convinced Louise that she deserved freedom and happiness.

"Your husband doesn't deserve you," Pauline had told her. "He cheats on you, pays no attention to you, and doesn't care about his children. Don't waste what is left of your life."

Louise spent four weeks with Pauline, the time needed to put some order in her heart and mind. Freed from the vise of her family in Nîmes, she shed her guilt over how the separation would affect the children. During the day, Pauline and she would take long walks along the grand boulevards and the Seine River. In the evening, Pauline would leave Ruben with Linda, and they would wander around the Champs-Élysées or Montparnasse. They spent hours in well-known Paris haunts, enjoying cocktails and listening to jazz, which was all the rage. Pauline needed the escape as much as Louise did. Together, they developed a new taste for life.

"I won't be the same person if Sebastien ever comes back," Pauline said.

"And me, if I meet another man, I won't marry him. Once is enough. I'll live with him like you and Sebastien or Vincent and Faustine. Free love. In the end, marriage is a false guarantee that love will last."

The two women were espousing ideas that were beginning to emerge among women of the time. They started smoking and cut their hair in bobs. They had no intention of shocking people or being extravagant. They just thirsted for liberty and wanted to satisfy their desires.

"Men aren't the only ones who have the right to do what they want!" Louise said, inhaling from the end of her cigarette holder.

"If our men could see us now," Pauline said, laughing.

The day before Louise left, they ran into Sebastien's friend Alain Dubreuil at a café. Pauline saw him first and pointed him out to Louise.

"Thanks to him, Sebastien got his job at *L'Aurore*."

"So it's his fault."

"I don't hold it against him."

Dubreuil spotted Pauline and came over to greet her. Introductions followed, and Louise felt a gentle warmth spread through her body. The reporter perceived her reaction and seemed to be feeling something similar. He ordered a cup of tea and spent the rest of the afternoon with them, never taking his eyes off Louise.

"I hope to see you again, Louise," Dubreuil said as they were getting ready to leave.

"I would like that too, but I'm returning to Nîmes tomorrow."

"She'll come back soon," Pauline said, thrilled to see what was developing between the two. "She needs to take care of a few things, and then she promised to come live with me for a few weeks, just until I find her a nice place to live."

"If you would allow it, I could take care of that for you, Louise. I know a lot of people."

"I don't know if—"

"Please don't say no. It would be such a pleasure to spend more time with you."

The next day, when Louise said good-bye to Pauline at the Gare de Lyon, she said, "I'll be back with my children. I'm leaving Jean-Christophe."

"Are you in love?"

"I don't know. In any case, I'm happy."

"So come back. I'll be waiting for you."

The day she returned, Louise waited for Jean-Christophe to come home in the evening. As usual, he got back late and wasn't expecting his wife to be up. Seeing the light in the living room, he thought it was the housekeeper and called out, "Cécile, my dear, are you still awake? You shouldn't have waited up for me."

Louise was sitting in an armchair. Its back was turned to him, and she spoke without getting up. "She didn't wait up for you, Jean-Christophe. She went to bed."

"Oh, it's you. You're back."

"Not for long, I assure you."

"But—"

"Don't say anything. I am not going to get mad at you tonight because you were out with another woman or because you are sleeping with our servant right under our roof. I've known about that for a long time. Before you go join your mistress, I want to tell you that I'm leaving for good. I'm going to Tornac, where the children are waiting for me. I am counting on you to have enough courtesy to do what needs to be done for a prompt divorce. We were married under separate estates. So we will see each other again with our attorneys. In the meantime, I will not wish you a good night."

Louise had wanted to talk to Jean-Christophe this way for many years. Her scruples, convention, and upbringing had kept her from doing so. Finally released from her shackles, thanks to her friendship with Pauline and her stay in Paris, she now felt like a woman in full possession of her own destiny—free.

36

Disillusions

1922–1923

The announcement of Louise's pending divorce did not surprise the Rouvière family.

Constance had known for quite some time that the couple did not get along, and she suspected that they would end up separating. She realized that couples from wealthy families whose marriages had been arranged for financial reasons sometimes divorced. But that wasn't something people like her did, and she didn't quite approve. Simple, honest people worked out their disagreements. And even if they couldn't do that, they never displayed their differences in public. It was better to stay in a bad marriage than be divorced.

Donatien didn't share his wife's opinion and regretted letting himself be influenced. The Rocheforts had seemed like a guarantee that his daughter would rise up in society. In addition, he had naively thought that her marriage would make him Anselme's equal. No longer would he be a simple farmer who rented a summer pasture from the Rocheforts. He would be a relative. Of course, Donatien had quickly seen how proud, self-important, and calculating the man was. But concluding that his daughter would never want for anything, he had set aside his concerns. Furthermore, hadn't Louise fallen in love with Jean-Christophe?

When Louise announced her intention to divorce and have her attorney demand that the property included in her dowry be returned, Donatien feared the worst.

"Do you really want to face the Rocheforts in court?" he asked.

"My attorney has to come up with the value of what you contributed to my dowry thirteen years ago, when we were married. Then he has to calculate the value of what we acquired together. Finally, we will negotiate with Jean-Christophe's attorney and split our estate."

"Rochefort and I will be going at it again. I really don't like the idea."

"This has nothing to do with you, Dad, or with my father-in-law. The divorce concerns only Jean-Christophe and me."

Donatien knew that Rochefort had a lot of connections and would not hesitate to use them for his son—and himself. He was most worried that the man would try to sully his daughter's reputation.

"Don't worry, Father," Louise said. "My estate is separate from yours. Nobody will expect anything from you. I even hope to get more than I put into the marriage basket."

Donatien and Constance weren't as confident. Anselme was already enraged over Vincent and Faustine's living situation, and he was capable of inflicting a great deal of damage.

While Constance and Donatien fretted, Vincent and Faustine were enjoying a carefree life together, with no concerns about tomorrow.

They had set up housekeeping a year earlier in a shepherd's hut at the edge of Donatien's land, on a parcel adjacent to the Rocheforts' estate. With the help of Donatien and his farmhands, they had transformed the hut into a country home. Vincent had made sure it had all the conveniences. He didn't want Faustine regretting that she no longer lived in a fine mansion. They planned an addition for their future children, along with a large stone cellar, where Vincent would "raise" his wine, as he liked to put it. He had already replanted the vineyards, and Victor was working with him full time. His knowledge and know-how proved as useful as ever.

As always, Vincent was learning from Victor. And as always, they worked side by side. Vincent and Victor replanted one parcel after another, so there would be no break in the harvest. A well-kept, promising vineyard slowly replaced the old vines. Vincent and Victor weeded, tended to the new rootstock, pruned the new shoots, and treated the vines with sulfates or sulfur, depending on the season.

After the phylloxera epidemic of the previous century, many farmers in the region had grafted high-yield grape varieties, especially Aramon and Carignan, onto disease-resistant American root stock. Everyday wine replaced the quality wine the region had once been known for. Like many other winemakers who had other sources of income, Donatien had been content with this mediocre product. And with the rise of cooperatives after the 1907 revolt, he had been selling the bulk of his grapes instead of making wine himself.

But Vincent dreamed of leaving his mark. He wanted to produce his own wine, under his own name, and to make a quality product. In school, he had learned about all the major grape varieties, including their histories. As he planted, he gambled on some varieties that were more widespread in the Bordeaux region, and some of them seemed to have a promising future. He had planted one parcel with merlot and was getting ready to plant another parcel with cabernet franc.

Donatien marveled at Vincent's knowledge as he explained

the gustatory and olfactory qualities of the wines that would be made with these new grape varieties.

"Merlot is smoother in the mouth, rounder and less tannic than Aramon and Carignan. Its hints of berries, cherries, and red currants are its trademark. It's nothing at all like the traditional varieties from this region. Cabernet isn't quite as smooth. It has more tannin but is much fuller than merlot. It also has more body and a deeper color. It leaves wonderful fruity aromas of strawberry and black currant in the mouth. By bringing these two varieties together, I should be able to make a fine, unique wine."

Vincent could go on endlessly about the wines he wanted to produce at his Chais de la Fenouillère.

"Faustine will do a painting for our labels, and I'll have them printed up when we bottle our first wine," he said.

"When will that be?" Donatien asked.

"Oh, you know as well as I do that we need to wait three years for the first harvest, and then the wine will have to age at least two years in oak barrels. I'm thinking we will be ready to sell our first bottles in 1927.

"I hope you will have made an honest woman of Faustine by then, if you know what I mean."

"We plan to get married. But Faustine would like her father's approval. And there is no guarantee of that. He doesn't even want my name spoken in his presence. He's contemptuous of both Pauline and me."

"Louise's divorce won't make things any easier."

"If Anselme Rochefort doesn't change his mind, Faustine and I will be married without his approval. She will make due with just her mother's blessing."

"It's true that Elisabeth is as good a woman as they come," Donatien said. "I don't know how she puts up with her husband."

"She loves him the way he is," Vincent said. "That's what Faustine says."

Elisabeth Rochefort spent more and more time at the Clos du Tournel. With Sebastien on the other side of the world, Elodie somewhere in the middle of the Bolshevik revolution in Russia, and Jean-Christophe in constant conflict with his father, who seemed to have no tolerance left, she wanted to be closer to Faustine, whose happy temperament and optimism lifted her spirits. She refused to deprive herself of seeing her daughter, regardless of her husband's feelings. Anselme had decreed that Faustine was no longer allowed in his house, so Elisabeth had to go to the Clos du Tournel to see her.

"If you don't come to terms with things, you will end your life angry with your children," Elisabeth said with her usual patience. "That is not how I choose to live. Do as you like, but you will never keep me from seeing my daughter."

"Your daughter! You are wrong! She has become a lousy peasant up to her knees in manure. And you still call her your daughter?"

In the autumn of her life, Elisabeth was deeply disillusioned and hurt. She had always believed in family, fidelity, and service to others. She had never failed in her duty as a wife, mother, and good Christian. The bishop often held her up as an example of generosity and altruism. She had always faced troubling moments with courage, humility, and piety. Her deep and genuine faith had never wavered in the face of doubt. Anselme was so different from her. She could have held a thousand things against him, but she didn't. Elisabeth had always respected the bonds she shared with Anselme. In their forty years of marriage, she had never questioned those bonds, even though she knew her husband had not shown the same consideration.

When she spent time with Faustine, she forgot the torment of her daily life. She felt refreshed and renewed as she witnessed her daughter's happiness in an unconventional life that she could have never chosen for herself. "Oh, if I were your age, I, too, would have tossed off the fetters," she said.

"Why didn't you, Mom?"

"Things were different then. And one's upbringing is a heavy burden. That is why I always supported you, more or less tacitly, when you aspired to live like a woman of your time. I refused to impose on my children the strict religious and moral standards that destroy one's spirit. That is what I experienced in my youth."

"Don't the qualities you are known for come from that kind of strict upbringing?"

"I suppose so. But sometimes I wonder if I would have been different, had I been raised differently. In any case, at least I've taught you to appreciate freedom. And no matter what your father says, none of you bring shame to the Rochefort name."

"What would Catherine have thought of all this, had she lived? You don't talk much about that sister I never knew."

Elisabeth's expression darkened. Mention of Catherine's name brought back bitter memories. She had never been able to tell her children what her husband had asked her to keep quiet at the beginning of their marriage, as if it were something that really needed to be hidden. She often wondered the real reasons Anselme wanted everyone to believe that Catherine was their daughter by birth. On the rare occasions that she had brought it up, he said he didn't want to talk about it. Elisabeth didn't even mention this lie in confession, and it was starting to weigh on her. *The children are adults now*, she thought. *We should tell them the truth.* But faced with her husband's obstinacy, she kept her word and obeyed, like a good wife.

She gave Faustine an evasive answer. "Catherine was eighteen when she died. She loved life. She was full of drive and loved liberty. She was a little like you. She respected her father but suffered from his excessive authority and his emotional remoteness."

"We would have gotten along."

"I'm sure of that. Of the four of you, you resemble her the most."

"But Elodie suffered so much when she died."

"She was eleven when her sister died, and they were very close."

"One day she told me that Catherine had told her a secret and had made her swear to keep it until they died."

"A secret?"

For a moment, Elisabeth suspected that Catherine had guessed that she was not her birth mother. But Elisabeth had raised Catherine the way Anselme had expected, as though she had carried the child herself. And considering Catherine's age at the time they were married, she would have had no memories of her birth mother. At least Catherine had never mentioned any memories.

"You've gone pale, Mother," Faustine said. "Do you want a glass of water?"

"No, thank you. It's nothing. I'm just a little tired. Talking about Catherine always hurts."

Faustine thought her mother's reaction was strange. She went on. "You'd think it would be better with time."

"There is pain that even time cannot erase, my dear, especially when it's tainted with disillusionment."

Faustine did not press, but she was convinced that her mother held a great sorrow in her heart.

Anselme Rochefort was clearly going downhill. He was increasingly silent and distrustful. Managers at the factory were worried about his judgment, and finally they turned to Jean-Christophe. Some even said it was time to demand that the boss step aside so that his son could take over and save the company, which hadn't yet recouped its investment in fine fabrics and was, in fact, bleeding money. Denim, the company's flagship, had seen a significant drop in revenues. Anselme had underestimated the growing American textile industry. In 1922, Cone Mills had become the sole supplier for Levi Strauss's 501 jeans. Despite all his efforts, Jean-Christophe had not managed to find new customers in America to offset the loss of Rochefort's biggest customer.

Jean-Christophe knew that Anselme would not be able to hold on much longer. Behind his father's back, he had already taken the necessary measures to replace him on a moment's notice. He assured the board of directors that he would overhaul the company's structure to do everything needed to bring about a rebound. In his father's absence, he gave a long speech to the board.

"We'll begin by closing our unprofitable operations and laying off workers. I intend to keep only part of our cotton mill, and I'll get rid of the dyeing unit. As for the fine fabrics, we'll stop producing organza and grenadine. We'll concentrate on mousseline. We've lost considerable business in America, and to compensate, I propose that we focus on countries that are close to us and are on the rise. Italy appears to have a promising future. Benito Mussolini's economic reforms are bearing fruit. As the economy continues to improve, there will be demand for our products. I see nothing but advantages in expanding our base in that country. After all, denim originates in Genoa. I also see opportunity in Germany—if not today, then tomorrow. The German economy is in serious trouble. And just as the Italians responded to Mussolini, the Germans will turn to a strong leader to bring them out of their economic shambles. Adolph Hitler has already led one putsch. He'll try again, and he will succeed. Once that happens, and the economy recovers, we should expect dynamic growth, along with demand for our textiles."

Jean-Christophe's assumptions seemed far too arrogant, as far as some board members were concerned. He didn't seem to understand that France's economy was still unstable, and a more cautious approach would serve the company better. Businesses were collapsing. Inflation was undermining the franc, and foreign competition was on the rise. Furthermore, social unrest was growing. The left wing was gaining strength and sharpening its arguments in view of the 1924 elections.

Weary and disillusioned, Anselme finally gave up. "It is time for you to take over," he said to his son. "I don't have the strength or desire to fight anymore. Everyone has abandoned me. I have no more authority."

"You're wrong, Father."

"My children don't listen to me. You are the only person who supports me. And how long will that last? My wife disapproves of me. My coworkers don't trust me. I'm no longer able to steer the ship. So I have decided to move on. I hand the destiny of the company to you. I have done my job. It is up to you to carry on."

His pride deeply wounded, Anselme handed over the reins to the only son he had ever believed in. But he did so without conviction, because hadn't believed in even that son for quite some time. He doubted that Jean-Christophe had the ability to deal with the difficulties the company was facing. And those hardships were certain to multiply in the years to come—if the company survived.

"I had hoped to build an empire, and I once aspired to make the Rocheforts a great family dynasty. What I give you today is a shadow of the company I dreamed of, and I enter my final years with the knowledge that I single-handedly managed to unravel the bonds that once held us together."

"Father, don't talk like that," Jean-Christophe said. "The business is a going concern, while others have failed. And you still have a family. The Rocheforts will stand strong in the face of any hardships that come our way. I will bring us all together again and prove that your efforts were not vain. I'll bring Faustine, Elodie, and even Sebastien back under your roof and prove that the Rochefort family is still great."

Although he didn't say anything, Anselme understood that Jean-Christophe was now the one who was harboring illusions.

37

The Mark of Destiny

1923–1924

Living far from any constraints, Sebastien was finally happy. Lost in the center of the Pacific Ocean, he had cut all ties to his previous life. He had not erased his loved ones from his memory or from his heart, of course, but he chose to focus on the present. With Hoa Mi and Thu Suong, life as a renegade was blissful.

He didn't try to work for a local newspaper. It would have meant living in Tahiti, and he didn't want to do that. The capital of French Polynesia did not appeal to him. Although Papeete was no bigger than a small city in the provinces, he didn't care for the bustle. Besides, he didn't want to associate with any French professionals or expatriates, who were sure to have the same preoccupations that had caused him to seek escape, first in a rice paddies and finally on a remote island.

Maupiti was a grain of sand in the ocean. A single road ran around it. The road was lined with *fares* occupied by Polyne-

THE ROCHEFORTS

sians with bright smiles, surprising kindness, and a laid-back attitude. Sebastien quickly made genuine friends. As he had in Indochina, he immediately adopted the local lifestyle and customs and did not try to impose his Western ways, as so many expatriates did. He had always rejected the notion of white supremacy, which most colonialists embraced.

To make a living, he found a job on a pearl farm run by a man from Brittany who had left France ten years earlier, as Europe teetered on the brink of war. He earned just enough to feed Hoa Mi and the child. Hoa Mi kept their home, raising Thu Suong in the tradition of her own country. In her free time she made palm-leaf panels used on the roofs of island houses, which brought in a modest income.

They would often explore the lagoon in their dugout. Or they would swim naked in the clear fish-filled water. Then they would linger on the white-sand beaches and let the tropical sun dry them off.

With Hoa Mi and the idyllic scenery serving as his muses, Sebastien was writing a novel based on his past and passions. "*The Rochefort Family* is the working title," he told Hoa Mi after reading her the first chapter. "But I can't really use it as the permanent title."

"Is it the story of your family?"

"Loosely, perhaps. In any case, it's the story of a great family that has known glory and decadence through the ups and downs of history. *The Rochefort Family* would be a perfect title, but exposing them would leave them open to too much criticism."

"You could call it *A Great Family*."

"Why not? No one would know the better. And I could write it under a pen name. I need one that is short and easy to remember."

"You could shorten your own name—something like Bastien Fort. It would be similar to your real name, but it wouldn't give you away."

"Yes, that would suit me perfectly."

After six months of writing every day, Sebastien sent a synopsis to a major Parisian publishing house. He knew an editor there from his days at *L'Aurore*. And because he understood how hard it was to get a first novel published, he also sent a synopsis to less prestigious publishers that were looking for new authors.

Several months went by. He had almost completed a second volume when he received several answers in the same week. To his great surprise, three of the five publishers had agreed to publish the novel, on the condition that his finished manuscript met their standards.

Filled with joy, Sebastien celebrated with his Tahitian friends. Fifty or so people gathered around his *faré*. As the sun slowly sank into the turquoise waters of the lagoon, he let himself go in Hoa Mi's arms. The melodies sung by the women, the ukulele music, and the rhythm of the pate drums became soothing lullabies as the night wore on.

They awoke on the warm sand early in the morning, in each other's arms. They were alone. Their friends had taken Thu Suong. The remains of the meal were scattered on the beach around them. Pieces of half-burned roots were still smoking in the warm ashes of the bonfire that had reached into the stars just hours earlier. The sun's rays were already heating the crystal-clear water. A few hundred yards away, the waves pounded the frothy coral reef.

Sebastien was the first to open his eyes. Hoa Mi shivered. Small dew-like droplets shimmered on her amber-colored skin.

"How beautiful you are," he murmured, caressing her long, thin legs.

She took his hand and pulled it to the secret place between her thighs. Her nipples hardened with pleasure. She opened her lips. He unbuttoned her shirt and covered her with kisses. He didn't let go until she had reached her final ecstatic moment. Then she climbed on top of him to take him on a passionate ascent into the azure sky.

Ten or so days later, Hoa Mi awoke paralyzed by pain. Her eyes were watering, and her face was burning. As soon as she stood, she was overcome with violent nausea.

Sebastien felt her forehead and said, "You have a fever. Don't go out. Stay in bed. I'll go to the dispensary to get a remedy."

There were no doctors on the island, just a nurse who provided first aid when plants and traditional remedies weren't working.

"No, don't go," Hoa Mi said. "I'll be fine. I just need some rest."

Sebastien listened and stayed by her side all day.

Her fever worsened that evening. He pulled out the thermometer he had brought with him and took Hoa Mi's temperature. It was 104. And now Hoa Mi was shivering and vomiting.

"It looks like the flu."

A neighbor came to Hoa Mi's bedside with remedies she had made.

"This isn't the flu," she said. "These are the symptoms of dengue."

Sebastien didn't know about this disease, which was transmitted by mosquitoes.

"Make her take the remedies. They should help. In general, it lasts a week. Then it goes away."

"Always?"

"Not always. If not, you'll need to take her to the hospital in Raïatea. Tahiti is too far."

Sebastien followed his friend's advice.

After a week, Hoa Mi was delirious with fever. Sebastien decided to take her to the Uturoa hospital on the island of Raïatea. But they needed to wait for a ship, as it wasn't safe to make the crossing in a dugout.

"There is a boat at the end of the week," the Maupiti shipmaster said. "It is bringing the usual cargo and then heading to Tahiti. It stops in Raïatea. The captain will take you on board."

"That's another six days of waiting," Sebastien said.

Hoa Mi's fever was still high, and she was quickly declining. She couldn't keep any food down, and her energy was diminishing by the day.

"It's affecting her liver," the nurse in the dispensary said. "This is a bad case. Dengue usually goes away in eight to ten days."

Hoa Mi could barely open her eyes but she still smiled when she felt Sebastien wipe her forehead with a cool cloth. He would prop her up to help her breathe and try to keep her focused by talking about his novel, which would soon be published by the big firm where his friend worked. He did whatever he could to encourage her to hold on until the boat arrived.

"You'll take care of our little Thu Suong, won't you?" she asked when her breathing became even more labored. "I think I'll soon be joining my parents in the land of the white lilies. Don't be sad. I'm not leaving forever. I'm just the first to go where we all must go."

"Be quiet, my love. Save your strength for the trip. The boat will be here tomorrow. The doctors at the hospital will save you."

"No, it's too late. I love you, Sebastien."

"Sh."

"Promise me one thing."

"What's that?"

"Do not let the sorrow take over. Go on with your life. What we lived together was short, but I was happy with you. Give that happiness to Thu Suong."

Sebastien's eyes flooded with tears as he promised Hoa Mi everything she asked for. He wouldn't let go of her hand. As the hours passed, and death loomed, he couldn't get out all the words he wanted to say.

Hoa Mi died in the arms of her first love at six in the morning, just as the cargo ship announced its arrival in Maupiti with a blast of the horn.

As grief was overtaking Sebastien, his brother, far away in France, was fretting over the economy. The left-wing cartel had won a majority in parliament, and then Gaston Doumergue had been elected president. This was bad news for business. Édouard Herriot, the newly elected president of the Chamber of Deputies, had announced draconian measures. The money powers had risen up, and now they were sending their capital abroad.

Jean-Christophe was one of those money powers. Like most others in his position, he was expecting even more dramatic government measures that would help the working class at the expense of business. In secret, he had transferred a large part of the company's assets to Swiss bank accounts. His loyal accountant, Robert Mazaudier, knew all the ins and outs of tax evasion. Together they had created shell corporations and doctored the financial records to hide what they were doing.

"As long as the tax officials don't ask us to provide proof that these companies exist, we're fine," Mazaudier said. "The money goes from one account to another, and then to another. It would take a very astute person to follow the trail."

The accountant appeared sure of himself and told Jean-Christophe that everyone else was doing the same thing. Financial collapse throughout the nation seemed almost certain.

Anselme didn't appear especially alarmed by the situation. He even shocked Jean-Christophe when, on the night that Gaston Doumergue took office, he said, "A president from the Gard region—that will be good for business. And he's a

Protestant who went to school in Nîmes. I see nothing but good coming from it."

"You're wrong, Father. Doumergue is a left-wing republican who only listens to the left."

"The right wing came out in force for him to block Paul Painlevé."

"His sentiments haven't changed. Let me quote to you from this morning's *L'Aurore*: 'I intend to govern from the left with a left-wing majority.'"

To tell the truth, Anselme was starting to forget things. His comments were filled with contradictions, and his attention was waning. He often asked people to repeat what they had just told him, and he sometimes took positions contrary to those he had once fiercely held. Elisabeth thought these were temporary problems. They would go away.

"He just needs some rest," she said. "When he's rested, his memory will improve, and his thinking will be clearer."

But Jean-Christophe had quietly seen one of his doctor friends and knew that was not the case.

"When the brain ages, the ability to think declines, and a person's behavior becomes unpredictable," the neurologist had said. Anselme Rochefort would eventually lose all of his memory.

Anselme, however, was far from gone. He could still read, and what he read often registered. When Jean-Christophe set down the newspaper with Gaston Doumergue's declaration, Anselme grabbed it and started reading an article in the culture section. He looked up, his eyes glistening with emotion.

"Listen to this, Jean-Christophe: 'A reporter from *L'Aurore* up for the Goncourt Prize. Our former colleague and correspondent in Indochina, who is using the pen name Bastien Fort, is a candidate for the Goncourt literary prize. Author of the novel *A Great Family*, he has just made a remarkable debut in the literary world. Fort is grieving the recent loss of his companion, with whom he lived in Tahiti for two years, but he has nevertheless accepted his publisher's invitation to Paris to meet his readers. He'll be signing his book at the Grande Librairie de Paris next Saturday. At his request, we have respected his anonymity, but there is no doubt that his pen name will soon be familiar to both critics and fiction lovers.'"

"I didn't know you were interested in literature, Father."

"Doesn't Bastien Fort ring a bell?"

"Maybe. I have to admit that I'm not too keen on novels. It's all I can do to keep up with the financial news. That's more important for our business, I'd say."

Anselme didn't insist. But he knew that Bastien Fort was none other than Sebastien. Hadn't Sebastien always dreamed of becoming a writer? Furthermore, he had been sent to Indochina as a correspondent for *L'Aurore*. Of course, Anselme had no idea of what had become of his son, and he hadn't tried to find out. When Elisabeth received his last letter from Saigon, he had pretended not to be interested. Still, he paid close attention when his wife had read it out loud.

> I'm experiencing a strange happiness here. I've abandoned all the principles of my education, which made my life a prison. I'm surrounded by simple people who want nothing more than the assurance that their children have a future. I no longer feel alone, and I am not alone. But I miss you a lot. You cannot cut yourself off completely from the past. There is something sleeping in the heart of every man who is stretching toward the limits of his possibilities that reminds him of where he has come from. Here, I write stories about events I witness, but I am not part of them. My opinions bother people. I believe that they won't be tolerated for long. The noose is tightening. I fear that soon I will have to slip into the crowds

and disappear. But I will reappear one day when I have accomplished the destiny I have dreamed of since childhood.

That letter was dated January, 1922. More than two years had passed with no further news from Sebastien.

Elisabeth didn't hide her worries and sometimes thought she would never see either Sebastien or Elodie again. "Something bad has happened to them," she would say. "They went to dangerous countries and were victims of the terrible events there."

Jean-Christophe had tried in vain to find out what happened to his brother and sister.

He had encountered difficulties getting information about Elodie, partly because of the anti-French sentiment in Russia resulting from the government's support of the counterrevolutionaries. In addition, the battered country was experiencing great upheaval and was completely closed. Jean-Christophe's contacts were only able to tell him that his sister had left Leningrad, where she had fled with Ivan Federovitch. They had lived in Leningrad for more than a year and then settled in Moscow. Ivan Federovitch was named a people's commissioner, despite his background, which had made him enemies. In 1921, he had dragged Elodie beyond the Ural Mountains to western Siberia for some unknown reason. Jean-Christophe supposed that the government had sent him. Then the couple disappeared. Had they been the victims of Stalin's first purges? Jean-Christophe had no way of knowing.

As for Sebastien, he feared the worst. Initially, he was easier to track, because he had not hidden his departure to Indochina, and he had sent several letters from Saigon. But then he, too, had disappeared. Indochina was in the throes of violence between the colonial army and nationalist groups that were armed by the Soviet and Chinese communists.

And Sebastien had never hidden his leanings. Could he have joined the rebels? If he had been killed in a skirmish fighting alongside the insurgents, the French authorities would not necessarily have been informed. That would have explained the two years of silence.

Jean-Christophe had called Pauline in Paris to ask if she knew where he was. She said Sebastien had agreed to return in a year but hadn't kept his word. She assumed he wasn't coming back.

Jean-Christophe picked up the paper his father had left on the sitting room table. He read the article about Bastien Fort.

"Father, you say this name rings a bell. What are you thinking?"

"That pen name, a former correspondent for *L'Aurore* in Indochina. Don't you see who it could be?"

"Are you thinking it's Sebastien?"

"Who else could it be?"

Elisabeth looked up from her knitting. "Sebastien! Do you have news about Sebastien?" Her eyes filled with tears.

"Control yourself, my dear. It's only a theory. Jean-Christophe will find out as quickly as possible. It can't be that difficult to find out who is hiding behind that pen name."

"It's true that Bastien Fort is a shortened form of Sebastien Rochefort," Jean-Christophe said. "And the biographical information in the article corroborates your theory."

Elisabeth's heart started beating hard. She was beginning to hope again. *Clearly*, she thought, *our family seems marked by destiny*.

38

Revelations

In November 1924, the Goncourt prize went to Thierry Sandre for his work *Le Chèvrefeuille*, *Le Purgatoire*, and *Le Chapitre XIII*. Bastien Fort's work had garnered some attention from the jury but not enough for him to take the prize.

Sebastien did not feel all that bad about it. He was happy that the novel's first two volumes—he was planning a third—had been published. It was the fruition of a lifelong dream: to write in complete freedom. And his novel was doing well. It could be found in bookstores all over France. In addition, the newspapers were writing about him. His publisher was disappointed but still happy, as his literary find had a promising future ahead of him.

Despite his grief over the loss of the woman he loved, Sebastien had agreed to meet his readers in Paris. He lined up book signing after signing. Before she died, Hoa Mi had made him promise not to give up and to focus entirely on his writing.

"I promise I will put all of my energy into it, in memory of you and your people's struggle to live free," he had whispered in the half-light of their room.

While he was in Paris—he had no intention of staying and planned to return to Maupiti, where he could enjoy the serenity that was conducive to writing—he couldn't resist visiting Pauline.

In reality, being in the capital was unsettling from the day he arrived. He found himself suddenly face-to-face with his past. It was no longer something he was writing about from a distance. And now the globe-trotting life he had led for four years felt unreal. Indochina seemed so far away, as did Tahiti and idyllic Maupiti. They were already another world. And yet he had promised to return as quickly as possible.

Around him, he re-encountered the reality that he had fled. He regretted having come back, leaving behind Hoa Mi's body under the paradisiacal skies of Polynesia. At the same time, he felt a strange calling from deep inside, like something vibrating in his flesh. His daughter, Thu Sucng, served as a relentless reminder now that he was back in France that another child was waiting for him. A child he loved and who couldn't understand why his father had left him to travel the world in search of his dreams.

His return to France brought him back to this reality. In his last letter to his parents, he had written, "There is something sleeping in the heart of every man who is stretching toward the limits of his possibilities that reminds him of where he has come from." Here, in Paris, he couldn't deny that truth.

So once his duties to his publisher were completed, he decided to see Pauline. He thought long and hard about what he would say. He looked for the words that could possibly justify his actions, and he knew there were none. He found no excuse for himself that could absolve him in Pauline's eyes. Furthermore, she herself had done nothing wrong. He had simply listened to the sirens' song, and like Ulysses, he had yearned to approach them. Unconsciously, he had known he would return one day. But for that, he had to become a truly free man. Hoa Mi had made him that free man. Now she had left his life the same way she had entered it, on tiptoe, leaving behind a gift, the fruit of their love.

Ultimately, the more he tried to persuade himself that nothing bound him to Pauline, other than their child, the more he felt love for her blossom again in his tormented heart. "How could I have forgotten what brought us together?" he asked himself. "Did I have to live my dreams fully to realize that I still loved the woman I abandoned? And yet I loved... I love Hoa Mi."

Sebastien didn't really understand what was going on inside. His entire being was torn.

As he headed toward his former address, everything he had experienced with Pauline flashed through his mind, from their meeting at school to their separation, when he had held her for a long moment, clumsily wiping the tears flowing down her cheeks.

He hesitated at the door. He almost turned away. But he pulled himself together and knocked—twice and then once, the code they had always used. Nobody answered. Yet he felt there was a presence in the apartment.

He turned the knob, his heart pounding. The door was not locked. He stepped inside quietly and glanced around the room.

He heard a familiar voice. "Come in. This is still your home. I was waiting for you."

The Rocheforts went to Anduze, to the Clos du Tournel, for the holidays and waited impatiently for news from Jean-Christophe, who had finally decided to go to Paris to meet the writer Bastien Fort. Jean-Christophe needed to know if it really was his brother. It was easy to find out where he would be. He looked in the daily newspaper to see where the author was signing his books. A little before Christmas, he went to the Grande Librairie de Paris. There, he ran into an impressive crowd of Bastien Fort fans. He made his way around the line and was not surprised to see his brother sitting behind a pile of books. "I knew it," he said to himself.

He took his place in line and waited his turn.

When he got to the head of the line, Sebastien took a book and without even looking up asked, "What's your name?"

"Rochefort," Jean-Christophe said.

Sebastien looked up, and the two brothers stared at each other. Sebastien was speechless.

"So sign my book, would you!" Jean-Christophe said with a smile.

"Jean-Christophe, what are you doing here? You knew?" Sebastien stood up and threw his arms around his brother. "You look exactly the same."

"You, however . . . How should I put it? You look a bit like an adventurer, which suits you."

The others in the line were growing impatient, and the bookstore manager reminded Sebastien of his duties. "Mr. Fort, the bookstore is closing in half an hour, and there is still a crowd."

Sebastien addressed his brother. "I'm sorry. My readers are waiting for me. Wait in the bookstore. I'll be finished soon."

After the signing, Sebastien took Jean-Christophe to a café he had frequented on the Boulevard Saint-Michel and began the long story of his adventures.

"There you go. That's how I became a writer. I owe it to Hoa Mi, Indo-China, and Maupiti. Three transformative influences."

"You always dreamed about being a writer. And Pauline?"

Sebastien hesitated a long moment. "I thought I had forgotten her. Now I believe that I had to leave to understand how much I love her."

"So you loved two women at the same time. To think that you always criticized my behavior regarding Louise."

"You said it yourself. I *loved* two women at the same time. My feelings for both were genuine. That is what makes us different. Life is complicated. I had to leave. I had to meet Hoa Mi. I had to love her to be reborn again and discover that I still loved Pauline."

"What do you plan to do?"

"Pauline waited for me. We have decided to live together again, picking up where we left off four years ago. The only difference is that now we have two children."

"Pauline accepts your daughter?"

"As if she were her own."

Sebastien took Jean-Christophe home. Pauline was waiting, as she did every other night now that he was back. She was surprised to see Jean-Christophe but didn't prolong her greeting. "I have some bad news for both of you," she said.

Sebastien's expression darkened. "What is it?"

"Faustine called. It's your father."

"What happened?"

"A stroke. He's getting worse. He's asking for Jean-Christophe. And you, Sebastien. He was hoping that Jean-Christophe found you."

The three looked at each other. In the room next door, Ruben was entertaining Thu Suong. He had taken to her immediately.

"We'll take the first train," he said.

At the Clos du Tournel, Elisabeth was beside herself. Anselme had hardly opened his eyes since his stroke. He could speak no more than a few words at a time, and he couldn't even hold the glass of water he asked for. He was paralyzed, and the doctor didn't hold out much hope.

"The nerve centers controlling his motor activity have been affected," the doctor said. "It's a real miracle that he is still alive. I won't hide it from you, Mrs. Rochefort. He hasn't much time left."

Everyone took turns at his bedside, including Louise, who was at La Fenouillère for the holidays. Despite the divorce—and her affair with Alain Dubreuil—she had come to help her former mother-in-law and sister-in-law. Constance and Donatien had also offered to do what they could.

Elisabeth and Faustine were overjoyed to see Sebastien when he arrived with Jean-Christophe. Elisabeth rushed into her younger son's arms and wept. Then it was Faustine's turn. Louise did her best to look comfortable with Jean-Christophe and greeted Sebastien warmly. She told Jean-Christophe that the children would be delighted to see him. They were with Constance and Donatien and hadn't seen their grandfather since his stroke. Louise thought it would upset them.

"Your grandfather is sick," she had said to the children. "We don't want to bother him and tire him out."

Once over her initial emotion, Elisabeth told her sons to go into their father's room. But she warmed them first. "He may not see you. He's lucid only a few moments every day."

Anselme was on his bed, propped up against large pillows so he could breathe easier. Even half sitting, however, he was breathing through his mouth. He was pale, and his cheeks were hollow. He opened his eyes but didn't appear to see either of them.

"I fear you may have arrived too late. He wanted so much to see his sons before he passed," Elisabeth said.

Sebastien stayed with Anselme all evening. Sitting near his father's inert body, he reviewed his life: what had driven him away and what had brought him back.

"Father, I'm here. My roots are here. I know that. I couldn't say this before, because I had to go away and become the man I am now. Despite everything that came between us, I have always been your son, and I have tried to honor the name you gave me in my own way."

Sebastien spoke to his father as if he could hear. Anselme's breathing became less labored, which was enough for Sebastien to believe that his father understood what he was saying.

A little before midnight, Anselme opened his eyes and leaned toward Sebastien. "My son, you have come back," he murmured.

"Yes, Father, I'm here."

"And your sister Elodie, as well?"

Sebastien, who had been told about his sister's disappearance in Russia, lied without hesitation. "She'll be here soon."

"I won't have the strength to wait. I'm going to die soon. But before I go, I have something to tell all of you. I don't want to carry my secret to the grave."

"Rest, Father. That can wait."

"No, it can't. Call your mother, brother, and sister. It's important."

Sebastien did what he was asked to do. "Father wants to see us all," he said.

"Is he conscious?" Elisabeth asked.

"Yes. He recognized me and asked about Elodie."

Elisabeth started to cry.

"Mother, control yourself. You must not show him your grief," Jean-Christophe said.

When they were all gathered around Anselme, he used his last bit of strength to say what was tormenting him.

He asked them to come closer. "Before I die, I owe you the truth. It's something I've hidden from you, a secret that has been suffocating me. I must tell you now, because I have only a few moments of life left."

Faustine, clearly distressed, interrupted him. "Father, you're hurting yourself. Please, you don't have to tell us anything."

"Let me speak, little one. I know that I have not always been a good father to you or your siblings. I was obsessed with raising you to honor the name I gave you. I expected you to make our family even greater. I committed the sin of pride."

"Faustine is right. There is no point going back over the past," Elisabeth said.

"I lied to you all my life out of vanity and self-interest."

Anselme gasped between each sentence, sometimes waiting long seconds before continuing. His words were increasingly disjointed, his breathing more labored, his voice weaker.

"Come closer."

His three children sat on the edge of the bed. Faustine, unable to hold back her tears, took his hand. "I'm so sorry, Father, that I disappointed you. I didn't want to hurt you."

"I'm the one who is sorry. For the lie I kept. My time has come. I need to tell you about Catherine."

Anselme couldn't go on. Elisabeth dabbed his lips with a moist cloth, and he started again. "Catherine wasn't sick. She was pregnant, and she died . . . She died giving birth to a child."

"My God, Anselme, why now?" Elisabeth asked, making the sign of the cross twice.

"The baby lived. I ordered him to be given up right after his birth. He couldn't carry our name."

"Given up! How could you?" Sebastien asked.

Faustine touched her brother's arm. "Let Father relieve his conscience. This is no time to be indignant. What's done is done. What became of that child, Father? Do you know?"

"It was a little boy. I don't know what became of him. He was placed in the orphanage. It was so long ago. I don't remember."

"The day after Catherine gave birth and died," Elisabeth said.

"You knew?" Jean-Christophe said.

Elisabeth seemed to collapse. "Dear God, dear God, what have we done?"

Anselme was panting. He squeezed Faustine's hand to draw her closer. She leaned her ear to his lips, and he whispered, "I want you to find that child. He's a man now. If he is alive, I want him to have his part of the inheritance. You must tell him."

Jean-Christophe stiffened. He had heard his father's last words perfectly. He couldn't control himself. "A bastard! You can't be suggesting that, Father! That's all we need."

Elisabeth rebuked him. "Jean-Christophe! None of that in front of your dying father. We must respect his last wishes."

Anselme's face stiffened. In a final effort, he opened his eyes one last time. "I also . . . "

He fell back, let out one final breath, and died in Faustine's arms.

They all made the sign of the cross and cried in silence, Faustine and Elisabeth openly, Sebastien and Jean-Christophe more discreetly.

Sebastien was the first to speak. "He was going to tell us something else." Elisabeth gathered her children in the sitting room. "I've known what he wanted to confess," she said.

They all focused on her.

"For my part, I've also hidden the truth from you," she said.

"So you've lied to us, too," said Sebastien, the most visibly upset by his father's revelation

"That's correct. Not telling you was, in effect, a lie. And I must take responsibility for my part."

"Do you know something more, Mother?"

She hesitated. It was too late to change the course of events, she thought. The fiction she had agreed to go along with had changed the course of an innocent being's life. There was no undoing that. What purpose did it serve to move heaven and earth now to find a man who was perhaps happy and had no desire to have everything he knew about his background and family turned upside down?

"You were young when it happened," she said. "Faustine, you weren't even born. Catherine was a very romantic young woman who loved life. But she suffered from her father's coldness toward her. It hurt her. When young men began to notice her beauty, she tried to make up for the hurt over her father's lack of affection. She responded to the attentions those young men lavished on her. And eventually she fell in love with a penniless man. Catherine was challenging not only her father's failure to love her, but also his wealth and pride. She became pregnant quickly. Crazy with rage, Anselme made her leave Nîmes to hide the shame that could blemish his name and honor. He sent her to the Taillades in La Bastide."

"I remember that. I must have been twelve or thirteen," Jean-Christophe said.

"She gave birth in secret and died giving life to a little boy."

"You're not telling us any more than father revealed just before dying," Sebastien said, impatient.

"What more do you want to know?" Jean-Christophe said. "It seems that everything has been said. The boy was raised in the orphanage. That is not our concern. It's the past."

"Are you forgetting your father's last words?" Elisabeth said, remorseful that the story had gone untold for so long.

"Mother, I thought you had something else to tell us," Faustine said.

"That is correct. You must also know that I am not Catherine's birth mother. I owe you the truth. Your father was married before we met. When I married him, he was a widower, the father of a four-year-old girl, whom I raised as my own child. Anselme asked this of me, and I agreed. He wanted us to build a great, unified, and honorable family. I kept my word."

Sebastien, Jean-Christophe, and Faustine were silent as they took in this second revelation.

"But the truth wouldn't have changed anything," Faustine finally said. "Catherine was our sister, after all."

"Our half-sister," Jean-Christophe said.

"What's the difference?" Sebastien said, rolling his eyes at his brother's arrogant and uncalled-for correction. "In any case, Catherine had a child who is probably still alive as we speak. Father asked us to look for him. We must respect his last wishes."

"You will always surprise me, Sebastien! You, the rebel son who always opposed your father's decisions. Now you are the first one to obey a dying man, who certainly was not entirely there anymore."

"That's enough!" Elisabeth shouted, appalled by what her oldest son had just said. "A little decency, children. Your father has just died. His body is still warm in the next room. This is no time to quarrel."

"Mother is right," Faustine said. "In any case, one should always respect a dying person's last wishes."

"Well, you'll do your searching without me!" Jean-Christophe said, leaving the room without any regard for his mother's grief.

Even on his deathbed, Anselme Rochefort couldn't get his children to agree. The great family that he had dreamed of was still far from united, and not just in spirit. Nobody knew where Elodie was. Her mother feared that she was lost forever on the dreary plains of Siberia.

39

The Will

1925

An impressive crowd gathered at the Nîmes cathedral for Anselme Rochefort's funeral. The mayor, his deputy mayor, the prefect, and many other dignitaries attended. A number of industrialists and important traders from the area were also there, and Rochefort employees were allowed to take two hours off to pay their respects. Elisabeth's society friends came in great numbers, as did others whom she had touched via her charity work. The new bishop of Nîmes, Jean Justin Girbeau, officiated.

Although Sebastien had always known that his father was influential, he was surprised at the number of people at the service. "I never would have thought that so many people would attend Father's funeral," he whispered to Faustine.

"Actually, I'd say that most of them are here because of Mother. She gives so much of herself through her charity work. Everyone, rich and poor, is aware of her generosity."

"She must have suffered greatly over the lie that Father made her live for so long."

"She loved him the way he was, and she honored her word. But her guilt might explain why she gave so much of herself."

"A penitence of sorts."

"Perhaps. But that doesn't diminish the good that she did."

Elisabeth's tears streamed down her face. She had never had an easy relationship with Anselme. She had endured his excessive pride, exaggerated sense of authority, and even, earlier in their marriage, his infidelity, which was no secret. But she had always forgiven and loved him. She had agreed to help him establish the family he dreamed of. In doing that, she had never lost her self-respect. She had always told him when he was going too far. She had countered her husband's heavy hand with a generous love for her children. Finally, she had kept the promises she made when they were married some forty years earlier.

Elisabeth was aware of Anselme's disappointment with the children, and there was little she could do about that. He had always relied on Jean-Christophe, the one who resembled him the most, but Sebastien was the son he really admired. He knew that Sebastien was more reliable and honest than Jean-Christophe. Sebastien, however, had always been a rebel. He rejected the world of money and privilege. He always stood up for the underdog. "If only Sebastien would agree to come work with us . . . " Anselme had often said to Elisabeth. She never replied, as she knew it would not happen.

Faustine had also disappointed Anselme by standing up to him. She had shamed him with the life she had chosen with Vincent Rouvière. Anselme had spent a lifetime buffing the Rochefort name. He had intended to hand down the moral and material inheritance he had received from his ancestors. But his daughter had taken up with a farmer—a farmer whose origins were unknown. She had demeaned him far more than Sebastien, who, passionate and idealistic, had ended up becoming someone.

In the end, Anselme's daughters had hurt him the most. That was what he told Elisabeth whenever she defended them. Catherine had been the first bad example, defying his authority with a penniless boy and getting pregnant. Then it was Elodie's turn. Oh, Elodie. He would have never thought her capable of waking up one day and cutting off her connections with the family. She had been the vulnerable one, always hanging onto her mother. What had gotten into her—disappearing with a Bolshevik adventurer?

Anselme had dwelled on these depressing thoughts, becoming increasingly aware of his failures as his health declined.

"He had been agonizing over things," Elisabeth explained to the doctor who had come to pronounce his death.

In the cathedral, only his family was aware of the emotional storm that had shaken Anselme's mind to the point of capsizing him. As far as everyone else was concerned, he was a great man, a captain of industry, the man who had made denim from Nîmes a celebrated product on every continent. He had fashioned a banner of denim that the city—and the whole region—could hold high.

"Anselme Rochefort has certainly contributed to the greatness of our city," the bishop declared. "For us, he will be remembered as the man who pulled a common fabric out of nothingness and made it great."

At the end of the funeral, those in attendance stopped to say a few words to the family members. Constance, who was with Louise, embraced Elisabeth. "Our heart goes out to you," Constance said. "Come visit us at La Fenouillère when you come back to Anduze."

Louise took Elisabeth's hand. "I'll come visit you before returning to Paris," she said.

"Thank you, my daughter," Elisabeth said.

Hesitant, Louise turned to Jean-Christophe. "I'm sorry for your loss. You know that I loved your father, despite our differences."

"Don't force yourself, Louise." Jean-Christophe hadn't changed a bit. "Your feelings for me are no more genuine than those you had for my father!"

Louise did not react. She moved on to Sebastien and Faustine, hugging them both and shedding tears.

"Excuse my brother," Sebastien said, offended by his brother's words. "He shouldn't say things like that, on this day especially. He'll come around."

Jean-Christophe cut him off. "That's enough, Sebastien. Louise is no longer part of the family. Stop treating her like your sister-in-law. And don't forget that I am now head of the Rochefort family."

Elisabeth gave her sons a pleading look. They fell silent, and the family continued to accept the condolences of those who had attended the funeral.

Before returning to Paris to attend more signings, Sebastien wanted to carry out his father's last wishes.

"Even if I'm not thrilled about it, I'm going to try to find out who this child our father abandoned is," he told Jean-Christophe. "I'm sure we can do that, somehow, if he is still alive."

"I'm warning you: giving him any part of the inheritance is out of the question."

"Father's notary wants us to meet to read Father's will. We'll have to accept whatever's in it."

"I'll fight it if I have to. I have friends who are attorneys, and if any mention of this child is in the will, I'll have them prove that Father was not of sound mind when he wrote it."

Eight days after the funeral—the new year had barely begun—the Rochefort family gathered in the notary's office. Elisabeth was in black, as was fitting; her daughter was supporting her.

Once the formalities were completed, the notary prepared to open the will that had been written, dated, and signed by Anselme Rochefort.

"Mrs. Rochefort, your husband filed this will with me just over ten years ago. He never expressed any desire to change its content."

"Ten years!" Jean-Christophe said.

"That's correct. On that day, Mr. Rochefort canceled his previous will, which he had filed several years earlier, and replaced it with this."

"So, at the time of this will and testament, our father was healthy. It was in 1915," Sebastien said.

"Not exactly. It was August 1, 1914. I remember the date very well. It was the day after Jean Jaurès was assassinated. We discussed that."

"The same day the French army was mobilized."

"Yes, your father feared the worst. He wanted to review his will to make sure everything was in order, were some tragedy to happen to one of his sons."

"So nobody can contest this will under any circumstances."

"That is correct. For that matter, Mr. Rochefort included a medical certificate proving that he was of sound mind and body. Everything is in the envelope that I will unseal in front of you."

Jean-Christophe shot a nasty look at his brother, who answered it with an expression that said: *You see, you can't fight it. Father's mind was fine.*

The notary unsealed the will and began reading it in a flat, ceremonial tone. It held no surprises. Anselme Rochefort named Jean-Christophe his successor and head of the company. Its worth, along with that of all the other assets and real estate, had been estimated ahead of time by an independent accounting firm, and he divided everything equally among his children and his spouse. His direct heirs would all receive shares in his company, along with vineyards he owned in Nîmes and the pastureland at the Taillades in Lozère, which he still rented to Donatien Rouvière. Elisabeth would have full use of the mansion on the Rue Dorée in Nîmes and the Clos du Tournel in Anduze until she died. In this way, Anselme had made sure that Elisabeth would have everything she needed, which was not essential, as she would also inherit from her parents, who were still alive.

"You are forgetting something," Jean-Christophe said when the reading was finished. "I didn't hear anything about who inherits the mansion in Nîmes and the Clos du Tournel. You mentioned that our mother has full use of them, but what will happen to them when she dies?"

The notary gave him a practiced smile. Pushing up his bifocals, he went on. "I'm getting to that. I did not forget anything. That, in fact, is the only change your father made to the previous will, which this one canceled. While Mr. Rochefort wanted the mansion in Nîmes to go to the aforementioned heirs, his final wish was that the land and the home of the Clos du Tournel—after the death of his wife—'be passed down to the child of Catherine Rochefort, who died in childbirth on January 21, 1898.' He doesn't name the child, but I suppose you know who it is."

Sebastien spoke up. "We learned of his existence from our father just before he died. We don't know anything other than what our mother recounted. He was a little boy who was abandoned at the orphanage."

"I can't tell you any more myself, because Mr. Rochefort didn't give me any explanations."

"He asked us to look for our sister Catherine's child."

"Our half-sister's illegitimate child," Jean-Christophe said.

"That changes nothing in regard to the will your father filed. We need to know who this mysterious heir is, and the Clos du Tournel will remain in limbo until we discover who it is."

"This is outrageous," Jean-Christophe said. "This will must be disregarded, and the previous will must be honored."

"Absolutely not! The medical certificate attached to the will specifies that Mr. Rochefort had all his faculties when he wrote it."

Too emotional to respond to Jean-Christophe's comments, which she deemed entirely out of place, Elisabeth stood up and said she wanted to go home.

"Thank you, sir," she said, leaning on Faustine's arm. "I now ask you to execute my husband's final wishes.'

Jean-Christophe stormed out of the office. "I'm going to have my lawyer examine that will. It's not going to happen."

Sebastien followed his father's last wishes and set out to find Catherine's child. Jean-Christophe could not stop him, but he did refuse to help. Only Faustine helped.

He had very little information about this nephew lost since birth, other than that he was born in January 1898, because his mother had died on the same day, and that Anselme had ordered the child be taken to an orphanage. Even Elisabeth could not provide more information.

"Your father was as quiet as a tomb about the whole event," she said. "He decided everything on his own in absolute secrecy and never mentioned it again. For him, it was done and over. I think, however, that he always blamed himself for Catherine's death. Of course, he was not to blame. But he must have thought that had he given her more love, perhaps she wouldn't have looked for it elsewhere. Or if he had been more attentive when she did get pregnant, she might have lived. As for me, I also kept the secret, out of loyalty to your father. I was an accomplice in abandoning Catherine's child.

And I should not have left her to deal with the pregnancy alone. That's when a daughter needs her mother the most."

Sebastien and Faustine tried to console their mother as her guilt intensified. Elisabeth had done as her husband wished and had put Catherine behind her. But now that her ghost was there, in front of her, Elisabeth was feeling more remorseful every day.

"We can't say whether she would have lived if anything had been different," Faustine told her mother. "Unfortunately, women sometimes die in childbirth."

Faustine swore she would do everything she could, along with Sebastien, to make up for the wrongs. She would try with all her might to find her sister's lost son.

Sebastien was convinced that Anselme wouldn't have looked far for an orphanage.

"If Catherine gave birth in the Taillades, we just need to look for the closest orphanage," he said. "Perhaps in La Bastide. There are sisters there, I think."

"They take care of invalids," Faustine said. "They're in Notre-Dame-des-Neiges. They don't take abandoned children."

"In Mende, then."

They immediately went to Mende and visited all the religious institutions in the city that could possibly take in orphans and abandoned children. They found nothing.

"Father must have placed him in Nîmes," Sebastien concluded. "We've focused on religious establishments, but perhaps he was a state ward."

They went to the state orphanage in Nîmes. The director met with them.

"You say that was 1898. At the time, our orphanage didn't exist. At the end of the century, there was only the Sisters of Charity orphanage on the road to Arles. They still have a large orphanage. They might be able to help. Of course, if the child was placed elsewhere . . ."

"Thank you, sir. We'll cover the whole region if we have too."

"Good luck, then."

Sebastien and Faustine didn't need to go far.

They headed to the Sisters of Charity and were welcomed by Sister Agnes, who had been the mother superior for two years.

"I was a novice in 1898," she said. "That was a long time ago. Another century. I vaguely remember that some unknown person dropped off a baby in the middle of the night. I have to admit that I was terribly afraid of the dark back then. The mother superior was always asking me to do things to overcome my fear."

"Can you describe the person?" Faustine asked.

"Remember, that was twenty-seven years ago! All I can tell you is that he was dressed in black, and he carried a kind of basket under his arm. Mother superior ordered me to go open the door to him."

"Don't you have records?"

"Yes, of course. I'll have to look into the archives. But normally, the information is confidential."

"Mother, this is our nephew!" Faustine begged.

"I know your family's reputation. I will make an exception."

Sister Agnes left the office and gave some instructions. A novice returned a few minutes later. She was carrying some large black-bound books covered with dust.

"I brought all the records from 1898," she said, dusting off the documents with her sleeve.

Sister Agnes looked for the list of registrations.

"You say the child was brought to us in January?"

"Yes, a few days after our sister's death on January 21. I don't think our father waited."

"Let's see. No, there is nothing on the twenty-first. Oh, but here, on the twenty-second, there is. A little boy dropped off by an unknown person and whom we named Vincent. Yes,

I remember now. It was Saint Vincent's day, in January. So we baptized him Vincent Janvier."

Faustine went weak. Sebastien barely had time to grab her before she collapsed on the floor.

"Is something wrong, miss?" Sister Agnes asked, looking afraid.

She offered to go get help, but Sebastien stopped her. Faustine opened her eyes again.

"The blood has drained from her face," Sister Agnes said.

Sebastien was feeling light-headed himself.

"Are you sure you don't need anything? Our nurse can help."

"That won't be necessary. It will pass," Faustine said.

"You know the child, don't you? Am I right?"

"That's correct. We've known him for many years."

Sebastien didn't say anything else.

"We raised the child until he was seven, and then—" Sister Agnes said.

Sebastien stopped her. "We know. Then a family from Tornac adopted him. Today his name is Vincent Rouvière."

40

The Tragedy

The world seemed to collapse around Faustine. She kept asking herself if her father knew that Vincent was Catherine's son, his grandson. The more she thought about it, the more convinced and distressed she became.

"Come now, Father couldn't have known," Sebastien said, trying to console her as they headed to Anduze "Once he dropped the child off, he had no further contact with the orphanage. Sister Agnes confirmed it."

"Someone paid for the child's board twice a year until he was seven. Father must have known when he was adopted."

"You're wrong. The sisters do not give any information to the people who abandon their children, especially once they have been adopted."

Faustine was incredulous. She had fallen in love with her half-sister's son, her own nephew. She had been having an incestuous love affair with him. The very idea that she could have committed such an act paralyzed her. In her mind, she had committed the worst of all sins.

Sebastien was appalled. As much as he tried to find excuses for Faustine, to find arguments that she had not done anything wrong, the very thought of it made his stomach turn. It was the stuff of novels, not real life—at least not their lives, he thought.

"How is Mother going to react when we tell her?" Faustine worried. "I'm sure Father knew the truth. That's why he was always against us being together."

"You're wrong there, too. He would have told you. He wouldn't have left you ignorant like that. He loved you too much."

"I don't think he loved me enough to admit his original sin, the one he committed by hiding the truth about Catherine and her child. He preferred to do what he could to keep Vincent and me apart. And you know he was unsuccessful at doing that."

Now Sebastien was beginning to doubt their father, as well.

"Whatever the case, we need to tell everyone the truth. I'll handle our family. Do you have the strength to talk to Vincent? Then he'll tell his parents and sisters."

Elisabeth could tell her son and daughter had bad news by reading their faces.

"The child died, right?" she asked, not giving them time to explain. "Your brother is going to be happy about that."

"No, Mother. The child lived. We found out who he is. He's a man now, and you know him."

"I know him? That's impossible. Did Anselme hide him away with our servants? Or at the factory? Talk to me. Don't leave me hanging like this."

Sebastien hesitated. He knew Elisabeth was fragile, and he was afraid she might collapse. Faustine was standing next to her. Although she was as white as chalk herself, she was ready to support her mother if her knees gave way.

"You seem to be very upset. Has the sky fallen in? I'm listening. There is no truth I cannot hear."

"It's just that, well . . . "

"No, let me speak," Faustine said. "I'll explain it all. Catherine's child, the one whose existence our father denied for twenty-seven years is none other than Vincent."

Elisabeth dropped the china cup she had in her hand, splattering tea on her percaline dress. She, too, went pale.

"Vincent?" She feigned disbelief, as if to put off the moment her fears would be confirmed.

"Yes," Faustine said, bursting into sobs. "Vincent Rouvière. Vincent is Catherine's son, my nephew. I have fallen in love my nephew! Can you believe it? I've been sleeping with my nephew."

"Faustine, you had no way of knowing," Sebastien said. "None of us did. Mother, explain to her that she hasn't sinned. She didn't know who Vincent was."

Elisabeth was too taken aback and stunned to comfort her daughter.

"You must put an end to your relationship," she finally said. "Does Vincent know?"

"Not yet. Faustine will tell him as soon as she feels up to it."

Faustine found the strength to face the unspeakable truth. She had never, since she was a young child, lacked the courage needed to overcome hardship with clarity and determination.

"She knew how to impose her relationship with Vincent on our father," Sebastien told Elisabeth. "She will know how to put an end to this impossible love. I'm sure she will manage to begin thinking of Vincent as a genuine friend, rather than her lover. Maybe not today, but eventually. She's a Rochefort, like the rest of us. She's got character. The Rocheforts always emerge from adversity with their heads held high."

"You sound like your poor father. This tragedy, I fear, will leave indelible marks."

The next morning, Faustine found Vincent in the vineyards. He immediately understood that there was something very wrong.

"I thought you were with Sebastien, looking for your sister Catherine's mystery child."

In the face of Faustine's obvious distress, Vincent tried to look cheerful. He was ready for anything. In fact, he had imagined all kinds of scenarios while she was gone. Perhaps Anselme's grandson had died in the war. Or maybe he was a hooligan, someone who would bring shame to the great Rochefort family. Or maybe he worked for one of his grandfather's competitors. Perhaps he had just disappeared without leaving a trace. And now he was hiding in the shadows, waiting to take his revenge, which he could finally savor because the man who had abandoned him was dead.

Vincent thought all of the theories were credible, but not one of them was horrible enough to upset Faustine as much as she appeared to be.

He led her inside their home. "You have some bad news for me, don't you?" he said.

Faustine couldn't bring herself to say the terrible words that would forever end their love.

Vincent poured her a glass of rosé. "Have a sip. It will help. It's from our first vintage. You remember, we called it Love Harvest."

Faustine fell apart.

"Darling, what's happening? Talk to me. Tell me. Whatever you have to say, it can never destroy our love. We've loved each other since we were children. Nothing can undo that."

Faustine managed to collect herself. She drew a deep breath, took a sip of wine, and said, "Everything is over between us, my love. We can no longer be together."

Vincent asked her to repeat herself. He couldn't believe

what she was saying. Then he said, "I don't understand. So you want to leave me? Who could keep us from loving each other?"

"Listen to me, Vincent. My half-sister Catherine's child is you, Vincent Janvier. That was your name at the orphanage. You are my nephew. I am your aunt."

Stunned, Vincent fell silent. He poured himself a glass of wine, which he swallowed in one gulp. He wiped his forehead with the back of his hand.

"That's impossible. Totally impossible."

From that moment, nothing could be the same. Faustine decided to move to the Clos du Tournel, despite Vincent's pleas to wait.

"There is no reason to hurry. Let's take some time to think this through."

"I don't want us to sleep in the same bed after what we've just learned. Do you realize what we've done? It's as though I made love to my brother!"

"Our relationship is not as close as brother and sister."

"We're the same blood. Your grandfather is my father. Oh, my God, what have we done!"

Faustine, who had always lived as she chose, regardless of her father's opposition, understood that freedom had limits, and she felt in every fiber of her being that she had unwittingly crossed the line. It was a line her religious upbringing had clearly defined.

"We can't see each other anymore. That is the only solution," she said.

Vincent also knew that they could no longer be lovers. Still, he couldn't face the prospect of letting her go. He asked her to consider living together as perfect friends, two pure-hearted people with no physical relationship. "Why don't we try? Let's live together like brother and sister."

"Thank God we didn't get married," Faustine said.
"You haven't answered my question."
"I wouldn't have the strength to hold in my feelings if you were constantly at my side, if I worked with you, if we lived under the same roof. It would be torture. I couldn't bear it."
Vincent finally came around to her point of view. His heart aching, he agreed with Faustine and let her go.
"It will be better if we don't see each other for a while," he suggested.
"I'll go back to Nîmes and will not come back to the Clos du Tournel. Let's hope that time erases the sin we have committed."

The Rouvières were devastated. Constance thought that God was punishing them for having allowed their children to unite with a rich and powerful family for no reason other than vanity.
"We pushed Louise into Jean-Christophe's arms," she said. "Their failed marriage should have taught us a lesson. We should never have allowed Vincent and Faustine to live together here."
"They've loved each other since they were young children," Donatien said. "We had no way of knowing that Vincent was Anselme's grandson."
"Anselme didn't want them to be together. He had his reasons."
"If he knew that Vincent was his grandson, he owed it us and everyone else to be truthful. If anyone was responsible, it was Anselme."
Of all the Rouvières, Aline was the only one happy about the situation. Of course, she wasn't mean about it, but once again, she was hoping to win Vincent over. At twenty-five, she had never been able to give her heart to another boy. She had had several opportunities, but had she rebuffed every young man who tried to court her.

"My heart is already spoken for," she would say to get rid of the most insistent suitors.

She taught at the public school in Tornac, where both her pupils and their parents seemed to like her. And she lived with Constance and Donatien, to whom she brought home her teacher's pay every month.

Constance had ended up believing that her daughter would remain single. Madeleine was more perceptive and had said, "Our little Aline is patiently awaiting her hour."

"If she keeps waiting for her prince charming, she'll end up a spinster!"

"The man she loves is not free. She'll wait until he is."

Madeleine had never dared to tell her cousin what she had sensed many years earlier, that Aline was in love with Vincent. So when she saw the change in Aline's behavior, she smiled and thought: I was right.

Yet Madeline kept quiet. Vincent and Aline were brother and sister by adoption. Constance and Donatien were still reeling from the news that Vincent and Faustine were nephew and aunt by birth. They weren't likely to be receptive to a relationship between Vincent and Aline.

Madeline knew, however, that Aline did not think of Vincent as her brother, and they shared no blood. So while Aline dreamed of opening her heart to Vincent, Madeline kept her thoughts and opinions to herself and decided to watch things unfold—if that's what they were meant to do.

Several months went by.

Sebastien returned to Paris, where he continued his writing. Pauline was responsible for educating their two children. She had left reporting behind, at least temporarily. Ruben and Thu Suong—who had been given the Christian name of Rose—took all her time. They often saw Louise, who seemed happy with Alain Dubreuil. Even with her three children, he had proposed marriage, but Louise hesitated. Pierre, Thibaud, and Alix, who were now fourteen and thirteen, were too young, she thought, to accept another man in their own house. Of course they knew that their mother and Alain Dubreuil were in love, but they couldn't imagine her getting remarried.

The two couples often got together with their children. Sebastien would think about Anselme. Seeing the five cousins playing together made him feel wistful.

"If my father is watching from above, he has to be overjoyed," he dared to tell Louise. "Whatever he thought of us, he would be proud that we gave him descendants. Pierre, Thibaud, Alix, Ruben, and Rose are the next generation of the great family he so wanted. Of course, they are the fruit of our stormy love stories, but they do carry the Rochefort name. Isn't that what counts?"

Louise liked Sebastien. He was like a young brother. "I'm really happy that my divorce hasn't interfered with our friendship," she said one night when Alain Dubreuil and she were having dinner with Sebastien and Pauline. "I know that despite all your differences with Jean-Christophe, you love him. You could have turned your back on me."

"How could you think that, Louise, after what you did for me when I rebelled against my father? Do you know what would make me happy?"

"No. What is that?"

"If one day we were all reunited. But I'm afraid that will never be possible. Elodie has vanished, and Faustine is in seclusion."

"She'll get over it with time. In the Rouvière family, Aline seems to be blossoming, which pleases me immensely. As for Julie, I don't hear as much from her as I would like, now that she's married."

At thirty-four, Louise was feeling nostalgic. The years had flown by quickly since her marriage to Jean-Christophe and the birth of her children. At the same time, she felt that she was at a crossroads. Should she cut her connection to the great Rochefort family by marrying Alain Dubreuil? Did she have the right to do that to her children? Did she dare head in an entirely new direction?

Alain Dubreuil was waiting for her definitive answer before accepting a position at the newspaper *Le Petit Méridional* in Montpellier. Not wanting to influence her, he hadn't told her about the job offer. But he knew he would soon need a yes or no from Louise. So on that night, he decided to take advantage of the friendly atmosphere and put everything on the table.

"You're probably aware that Louise and I are very fond of each other, and we've broached the subject of a future together. But tonight, I would like to make my desire to spend my life with Louise official." He turned to Louise and took her hand. "Louise, will you marry me?"

Pierre, who had been playing in the next room with his cousins, heard the proposal and joined the adults. His mother looked embarrassed and wasn't saying anything. He jumped right in. "Of course she accepts! Don't you, Mom."

Louise smiled at her son and called the two other children. "And what do you twins say?"

"We want you to be happy, Mom," they said in unison.

Louise looked at her lover, tears of joy filling her eyes. "So I accept."

Sebastien immediately took out a bottle of Champagne and popped the cork.

"That is the first happy event of the year 1925," Pauline said.

Faustine was living like a recluse in the Cordeliers mansion. Lurking in the half-light of her room, she didn't dare believe what was obvious. She hadn't had a period in more than three months. As much as she wanted to put it out of her mind, the memory of her final lovemaking with Vincent haunted her. It was just after her father died and before she left with Sebastien. She had been sad, and Vincent had consoled her. They had spent a night of tenderness and abandon. They had so wanted to have a child. Until then, nature had not granted it. So they took no precautions. Vincent thought he was sterile. Faustine thought she was.

When she had learned the truth about Vincent's identity, she had thanked God that they hadn't conceived any children. So why had her body betrayed her? When she missed her first period, she blamed the stress of losing her father and separating from Vincent. The second month, she began to worry, but she chased away the dark thoughts by telling herself that she was feeling the aftermath of the emotional upheaval. Now, however, there was no doubt. The morning sickness, her discomfort, the strange feelings in her belly: Everything pointed to what she had hoped for so long but now terrified her.

She went downstairs in her nightgown. She was sweating, and she could hardly see through all the tears in her eyes.

Elizabeth looked at her with alarm. "You are so pale. And you're sweating. Are you sick?"

"No, Mother. I'm pregnant."

41

Letter from Siberia

Every day, world events were getting worse.

While speculators were driving France to financial ruin, Stalin was putting an end to the hybrid policy that combined communism with capitalism, which Lenin had decreed for the transition period. Collectivism and repression were the replacements. Trotsky and his partisans had been chased from power and banished. Ivan Federovitch was among them.

Once again, suspicions were rising between the countries that had fought in the Great War. In Germany, the election of army leader Paul von Hindenburg to the presidency foretold international tensions. His supporters seemed bent on revenge. The French accused the Germans of renouncing the Treaty of Versailles and opening up their country to renewed nationalism. In France, the far-right movement Action française was causing a stir. Never before had the group attracted so much attention. Its leaders' Germanophobia fed feelings of resentment.

Jean-Christophe didn't hide his sympathy for the extreme

right. He found in their arguments something to feed the bitterness that had been eating away at him ever since his fraudulent transactions had caught the eye of tax officials, and he had learned that Vincent Rouvière was not only his father's grandson but also his heir.

"He'll never use what he inherited as long as I'm alive. That's if he actually inherits it," he told his mother before he met with the notary once again.

"Son, that bequest in your father's will was his way of making up for the mistake he made with your sister Catherine," Elisabeth told Jean-Christophe. "You must respect his last wishes. He named you his successor at the company; you are getting an equal part of his estate. What more do you want? Your attitude is not worthy of a Rochefort!"

Jean-Christophe had never liked Vincent Rouvière, whom he continued to call Vincent Janvier. In his mind, illegitimate children could never fully belong to their parents' families.

"We don't even know who the father is," he said, indignant.

"Yes, we do. Your father and I met him at a party we gave in our home. He was a very acceptable man. His only failure in your father's eyes was his poverty. His parents had lost their money when they were older, and they had left him with nothing."

"That is why he was after Catherine. He was chasing her dowry and taking advantage of a rich girl's naiveté. Besides, he disappeared, which proves it."

"He vanished because your father threatened him. She was still a minor, and Anselme had a lot of connections. The poor boy was afraid. But it was too late. Catherine was already pregnant."

Elisabeth did her best to reason with her son, but it was futile. Tired of arguing, she cut him short. "In any case, as long as I am Anselme Rochefort's widow, I will make sure that his wishes—all of his wishes—are respected, whether you like it or not."

Elisabeth was doing her best to face life as a widow with dignity and courage. Although her charity work kept her busy, she was as worried as ever about her children. She still hadn't heard from Elodie. Then, shortly before summer, a letter from Russia arrived. Her heart almost stopped beating when she saw it. She held the letter in a trembling hand, not daring to open it. *Dear God, it's Elodie*, she thought. The handwriting on the envelope was clumsy and in purple ink. It didn't look like her daughter's. She looked at the address again:

Mr. and Mrs. Rochefort
Les Cordeliers
Rue Dorée
Nîmes – Gard – France

No, Elodie did not write that. Perhaps it was Ivan Federovitch, she thought.

Fearing the worst, she sat down in an armchair. If that's the case, it's bad news, she thought. She started to shake and prayed. "Lord, please spare me more misfortune."

She sat for a good quarter of an hour with the envelope tight in her hand. Then she tried to make out the postmark to see when the letter was sent. It was smudged, perhaps rained on, and was illegible.

As she did every other day at teatime, Faustine came down from her room. She was having a hard pregnancy. At twenty-eight weeks, she was already experiencing painful contractions. She stayed in bed as much as possible and followed the doctor's advice.

"You need to keep your baby at least eight months," he

had told her. "A premature infant has a lower probability of survival."

In fact, Faustine was ambivalent about the child. She often wished she could miscarry—this child, whom she would have considered a gift from God in other circumstances. Now the pregnancy felt like a gift from hell. When she realized that the baby was developing normally, when she saw her belly growing day in and day out, she resigned herself. *This baby will be born, and I won't raise it*, she said to herself. But the idea of giving the baby up tore at her heart. Wasn't that what her father had done to Vincent?

Walking down the stairs carefully, she saw her mother slumped in the armchair. She had been prepared to tell Elisabeth what she had just decided, but seeing her, Faustine had second thoughts. Her pregnancy had also been hard on Elisabeth. The child's future was often the center of their discussions. Elisabeth kept saying that the baby had every chance of being born without any defects, but Faustine was sure of the opposite. She had quietly looked for information: Children born of incest often had physical and mental deformities.

She approached Elisabeth, not seeing the letter right away.

"I made my decision, Mother. It's the only decision that can bring me peace of mind."

Elisabeth started. "Your decision? What decision?"

"I'm going to enter a convent. I'll give birth there, and then I can say my vows. The sisters will raise my child, and I'll be right there. He'll never know. It's better that way. I don't want shame to follow him all his life, when he is innocent of the sin we committed."

"The sisters? The convent? You want to enter the order?"

"Yes, it's the only way for me to raise my child without him knowing I am his mother. He won't lack anything. I'll watch over him. He won't ask about his parents, because he'll think he's an orphan. Later, when he's old enough to understand, perhaps he should know, or perhaps not."

"That's crazy, Faustine. You don't have the right to sacrifice your life. You are young. You can start over again."

"I'll never be able to erase Vincent from my heart. I'll never find happiness in the arms of another man. The only way to forget is to give my life to God."

Elisabeth was crying now. Still holding the letter, she removed a handkerchief from her sleeve.

"You got mail?" Faustine said.

"Oh, I forgot. Yes. A letter from Russia. I was getting ready to read it when you came in."

"A letter from Russia! Oh, it's Elodie!"

"I haven't opened it yet."

"What are you waiting for?"

Faustine rang the housekeeper for tea and sat down next to her mother. She took the letter and asked if she could read it for her.

"I was going to ask you. I'm afraid to do it myself."

The letter was dated October 20, 1924, and had been written in Tomsk, on the banks of the Ob, in Siberia.

"It took nine months to get to us," Faustine said. "That's strange. It looks like it wasn't sent at the same time that it was written."

"Is that Elodie's writing?"

Faustine went right to the signature. "Yes and no. It's also signed by a Pietr Boroslav."

"Pietr? That's a Polish name. Who is that?"

"I'm sure we'll know by the end of the letter."

Faustine, paralyzed with emotion, began to read:

> My dear parents, and my brothers, and sweet sister,
>
> When you receive this letter, I may no longer be in this world. I am so weak, I cannot write this myself. I have asked our comrade Pietr Boroslav a devoted

friend, to write for me and make sure my news gets to you. You must be wondering what has become of your daughter. You might have thought I was dead. So much has happened since I wrote while we were in Leningrad—that is what the Soviets call Saint Petersburg, but you must know that already. I won't be able to recount everything in a single letter.

I have been having an exciting and terrifying adventure alongside Ivan Federovitch, who was and will always be my one great love, the one my being seeks out in times of adversity. The life we have had together has been filled with intense joy, boundless hope, a thirst for ideals, but also terrible torment, immense disappointment, and deep regret. How could I describe the passion of all these people who, like Ivan and me, believed that everything was possible and that a few decrees would be enough for the word "communism" to become a reality, a tangible reality, a synonym for the people's happiness.

The Bolsheviks imposed the dictatorship of the proletariat so that the well-off could no longer steal the fruits of the working masses' labor, so that nobody could grow rich off the backs of others, so that each person could enjoy the benefits of life without being deprived of anything. These ideas inspired us so. Ivan was enthusiastic, always ready to sacrifice himself—hadn't he set aside his noble background to espouse the cause of the people and the revolution? Everything seemed possible as long as Lenin held the reins of the country. But ever since his premature death a year and a half ago, ever since Comrade Stalin took over, the dictatorship of the proletariat has become a personal dictatorship. Ivan had been wrong to support Comrade Trotsky, Stalin's sworn enemy. He was run out of his job as people's commissioner. I followed him into his exile in Siberia, where poverty and sickness got the better of his already weak health. We lived in a work camp, digging up the earth like the peasants did before us. Ivan's social background didn't play in his favor. He was accused of betraying the revolution, treated like an enemy of the people—and to think that he sacrificed so much for the happiness of the Russian people. They wanted to destroy him without making an attempt on his life, to eliminate him without killing him, as if to make him suffer more. Until his final day, Ivan believed in his ideals and never understood how the regime he had so hoped for could turn against him and sentence him without appeal to such a tragic end.

Ivan died. Of cold. Of hunger. Of fever and mistreatment. I stood by him in his terrible despair. I accompanied him to the end of his ordeal. Where did I find the courage and the strength? Me? The most vulnerable one in our family? In the love that Ivan gave me every day and that I gave back. When Father reads these lines, I hope that he will forgive me for having left you simply because my heart was guiding my steps. Nothing is nobler than love.

Today, I am alone in this village—if you can call it a village—lost in the middle of the taiga. Will you see me again one day? I'm afraid not. I am a poor peasant who doesn't have the right to leave the place where I have been assigned to live. My sole companion was a friend of Ivan's, Petr Boroslav. He managed to escape from here, taking this letter that I dictated before his departure. He promised to send it from a safe place as soon as he could. I do not know where he has gone. He has my full trust and all my hopes so that you can learn that your daughter Elodie is still alive on this twentieth of October 1924. She will never forget you.

I think of you every day that God grants me life in this land of redemption. I hope to see you again, but we would need a miracle. I know I can count on Mother's prayers, so I am not ruling out this miracle.

Your loving daughter, Elodie.

Faustine had a knot in her throat, and didn't say another word. Elizabeth collapsed in tears.

"My Elodie, my dear child! What became of you? What misfortune befell my fragile girl? Is she still alive?"

Faustine was not feeling good. Her contractions were multiplying. She covered up her own discomfort to help her mother.

"Mother, I'm sure that Elodie is still alive."

"That letter was written nine months ago."

"Nothing is impossible."

"Even if you are right, we will never see her again. They won't let her go."

"Don't despair. All hope is not lost."

Nothing and nobody could get Faustine to change her mind.

In August, she went to the convent of the Sisters of Charity and asked the mother superior to accept her as a novice. She couldn't hide her state, but she didn't dare confess the bond between her and the child's father. The sin was weighing so heavily on her.

"Have you thought this through, my child?" Sister Agnes asked. "Your commitment to serve Our Lord and Savior Jesus

Christ must not stem solely from remorse. The baby you carry comes from love and deserves better than the orphanage."

"I already explained, Mother, that this child must never know who his parents are. But I want to remain close to him. My place among you will allow me to do that. It will also allow me to ask God for forgiveness for the sins I have committed."

"God has already forgiven you, my child. Your repentance is sincere. He does not need your sacrifice if this is not your vocation."

Faustine would not reconsider her decision. Sister Agnes admitted her as a novice and agreed that she could quietly give birth in the convent.

Faustine had the child at the beginning of August, three weeks early. The doctor who delivered the child offered to transfer the newborn to the Nîmes hospital for better care, but Faustine refused.

The child was a little girl, scrawny and surprisingly calm for an infant.

"What do you want to call her?" Sister Agnes asked as soon as Faustine had regained her strength.

"To tell the truth, I hadn't thought about it."

Sister Agnes was surprised. "It's been nine months, or nearly, and you never thought about it?"

"I did not want this child, Mother."

"So what would you say if we called her Elena?"

"Elena? Why not?"

"The name evokes light. She will bring light into the darkness where you find yourself now."

And that is how Elena Rochefort was born. She couldn't have any other name, as the father was entered on the birth record as unknown.

Since Faustine had left him, Vincent had not tried to see her or find out what she was doing. He also wanted to put their life together behind him. He dived blindly into work. He rose at dawn and was out in the vineyards until nightfall, exhausted and empty-minded. Despite his rheumatism, Victor went out with him, but he was unable to get him to ease up.

"Your determination will not erase what happened," Victor said repeatedly, urging Vincent to go a little easier on himself. "How many times do I have to tell you that you didn't do anything bad? You didn't know."

But like Faustine, Vincent was inflicting a penance on himself.

"I can't forget her," he admitted. "As long as I stay here, her memory will haunt me. I tore out all those vines and replanted them for her. It's because of her that I created the Chais de la Fenouillère. I can't find peace working in my vineyards anymore. They smell like her; every time I touch the leaves, it's like I'm touching her hands. Everything reminds me of her."

"With time, you'll forget. The memories will fade."

"I don't think so, Victor. I only see one solution. I have to leave. I have to go far away."

Vincent had thought about it for a long time. So when Elisabeth told him that Faustine had gone into the convent and given birth to a child, he became even more committed to his decision. His pain also deepened.

"I'm a father and didn't even know it. Our child will never know her parents, just as I never knew the people who conceived me. Clearly, history repeats itself. Still, I will not oppose Faustine. Her decision is a wise one. That child would be more miserable if she were to learn the truth."

"Vincent, you must know that although I respect my daughter's decision, I do not approve of it," Elisabeth said. "Yes, you shared blood, but you were not brother and sister. You did not have the same mother and father."

"Of course, but we are close relatives. And our child could

have physical or mental problems because of it. Faustine has done the right thing."

Vincent demonstrated as much determination as Faustine. Constance, Donatien, Julie, and Aline were all unable to get him to change his mind. Vincent told them he would become a shepherd and go live in the mountains.

"I won't be leaving you entirely," he said. "You can come see me up there. I'll live by myself with only the sheep to keep me company. I hope to clear my mind and perhaps even be reborn as a new man."

Donatien gave him part of his flock and promised to maintain the vineyards. It would be temporary, he said, because he had every hope that Vincent would return one day.

"It doesn't matter what you think today, son. Know that your home will always be here, at Chais de la Ferouillère."

Vincent left for the highland pastures at the end of the summer, when the first flocks were already coming back down to the plains.

As he settled into his sheepfold in the mountain, ready to face the first cold weather like a hermit who had retired from the world, Faustine was beginning a long life of renunciation in the shadows of the convent walls.

As for Elodie, the Siberian winter was an even harsher existence.

42

The Years of Winter

1927–1929

For the Rochefort and Rouvière families, winter seemed to last all year. The seasons came and went, but in their hearts, it was cold and gray.

More than two years had gone by since Faustine and Vincent had separated and gone their own ways, each living a reclusive life of meditation and renunciation. They had cut themselves off from the world and turned inward.

Not wanting to add to any friction between Elisabeth Rochefort and her son Jean-Christophe, Vincent had not answered the notary's summons. The man had invited Vincent to his office to go over Anselme's bequest. When he got no response, the notary froze the transfer of the Clos du Tournel. Elisabeth would continue to have full use of the manor house and would maintain the estate.

"This estate belongs to my husband's grandson," she told

the notary. "I will make sure it is maintained. And as long as I'm alive, nobody will dispossess Vincent Rouvière."

Faced with his mother's resolve, Jean-Christophe was all the more determined to get his hands on what his father had given his illegitimate grandson. Jean-Christophe's hatred for Vincent became vicious.

Aline visited Vincent often. The youngest Rouvière did not despair in her efforts to persuade him to give up his penitence and focus on her. She was twenty-seven and aware that the years were passing quickly. The longer she waited, the more risk there was of winding up alone. But despite her mother's warnings and what she herself knew, Aline continued to rebuff all her suitors and dream of a day when she and Vincent would be together.

"She is convinced that Vincent will turn his attention to her," Madeleine told Constance.

"You don't really think that, do you? They are like brother and sister."

"Everyone but Aline thinks of them that way. Believe me, that young one has had a thing for Vincent for years. She has been waiting for her time to come, and she must have lost hope at one time or another. But she's much more confident now that Vincent and Faustine have separated. Why do you think she goes up to see him every chance she gets? Just to keep him company like a kind sister who pities her elder brother? They aren't children anymore. Believe me, Aline knows what she is doing."

Madeleine understood perfectly well what was in Aline's heart. But she wasn't privy to Vincent's thoughts and feelings. She didn't know that he was still keeping Aline at arm's length while at the same time trying not to hurt her.

Then an event shook Vincent's fragile tranquility. Donatien had joined Vincent in the highlands, where he was pasturing the rest of his flock. He told Vincent that Faustine intended to take her vows. Until that point, she had not made a full commitment to monastic life. Sister Agnes had recommended that she wait and give the child her attention, if only from a distance.

"Elena doesn't know that you are her mother, but she is thriving, thanks to what you are giving her," Sister Agnes had told Faustine. "Wait until she is older and independent before making an irrevocable decision. As long as she is not aware of the real bond between you, there is no reason to hurry."

Faustine initially followed Sister Agnes's advice. But two years later, when Elena began to babble her first words and understand that Sister Faustine was not like the others in the convent, she announced that she wanted to take her vows. Again, Sister Agnes asked her to wait, and again, Faustine agreed.

Faustine told her mother that she was serious about taking her vows, even if she couldn't do it right away. Elisabeth told Constance, and finally, Vincent learned the news from Donatien. Faustine had not changed her mind.

With his heart forever broken, Vincent acquiesced to Aline's tender words. As the year was coming to an end, and winter was settling into his soul for good, Vincent opened his arms to Aline. She had come to spend Christmas with him in his shepherd's lair. Alone and surrounded by vast stretches of snow, they wandered the paths of forgetfulness, dwelled in the present, and delayed envisioning a future. Aline was discreet, gentle, and understanding. She was too attached to Vincent to risk losing him by being overly eager. She was thrilled that this moment, which she had awaited so long, had finally arrived. But at the same time, she was afraid of being compared with Faustine. When his lovemaking was rough, she wondered if he was imagining Faustine. Who was he really holding in his arms?

Yet they avoided talking about Faustine. Skillfully, Aline

reminded Vincent that she had loved him since she was a teenager and that her feelings for him were always far from sisterly.

"You treated me like your little sister," she said. "But deep down, you've understood that I wasn't really your sister, just as I've understood that you weren't really my brother. I always knew you would end up loving me."

Vincent smiled. Aline saw in his eyes, though, that he was still thinking about Faustine. *With time, maybe he'll only see me*, she said to herself.

In the Rochefort family, the years followed each other. One after another. As with Vincent, the winter seemed to have settled in their hearts. The cold crystallized the bleak landscape of their lives. Although Anselme had been far from an easy man to live with, he had been the central, commanding force in the family. With him gone, and everything else that had happened, Elisabeth felt that her family had fallen apart. Faustine had renounced everything in the world. Sebastien was gone. Jean-Christophe was more insufferable than ever. And Elisabeth didn't even know if Elodie was still alive. She felt that her fate was being drawn on a cloud-filled sky that even the most intense rays couldn't pierce. The only distraction from her worries was her charity work.

Anselme's former competitors were thrilled to see Jean-Christophe's setbacks, which they thought would end up bankrupting the company. The previous year, Jean-Christophe had been fined heavily for failure to pay all the taxes he owed the government. His accountant had not been able to adequately explain the money that had been diverted to Switzerland. To pay the fine and make up for his back taxes, Jean-Christophe had been forced to reduce operating costs and let employees go. This, in turn, had forced him to cut back production.

Meanwhile, the economic recovery that most of Europe's

industrialized countries, including France, had enjoyed since the beginning of the nineteen twenties was losing steam. Germany was fighting inflation and had stopped paying reparations. Germany's World War One allies had followed suit.

It now seemed likely that the rest of the decade would be especially difficult for those who, like Jean-Christophe, had made poor investments and weakened their companies. But the Rochefort son—as his critics and competitors called him—refused to see what was becoming clearer every day. He continued to err and squander.

Far from Nîmes, Sebastien still had no interest in the family business. He was, as ever, a foreigner in the world of business and money, and he was indifferent to the news about the company that Elisabeth shared in her letters. Even as the owner of a quarter of the company's shares, he did not concern himself with their value and was not aware that his brother's reckless actions were causing his personal fortune to melt away like snow in the sun.

Since his return from Polynesia, he had been living happily with Pauline and his children and was totally focused on his writing. The success of his first novels had opened many doors in literary circles. No, he was not making a lot of money, but he still refused to cash in the dividends on his shares of the business. In reality, he trusted his brother to manage the company. For that matter, Jean-Christophe would occasionally visit and reassure him that everything was fine.

Eventually, however, Elisabeth's news about the company's state of affairs began to resonate. Sebastien decided to return to Nîmes. He visited the Rochefort factories and immediately realized that they were not operating at full capacity.

As he had before, Jean-Christophe glossed over the company's troubles. "It's the times," he said. "You must know that, since you live in Paris. But the economy will soon take off again. Then I'll hire people back, and we'll get all the machines running again."

Sebastien insisted on going to the next board of directors meeting so that he could meet the members. He had every right to attend, as he owned a quarter of the company's shares. Sebastien couldn't help but notice the board members' gloominess at the beginning of the meeting. Jean-Christophe spoke first. He was cautiously optimistic. Although he expected the economy to remain sluggish, he predicted better-than-average earnings for the company.

When it was time for the board members to speak, Sebastien heard something altogether different. Many were threatening to pull out "before the ship sank," as they put it. When Sebastien questioned them, they accused Jean-Christophe of keeping shady accounts, investing in unreliable companies, mistreating his workers, and failing to keep his word with the unions. Sebastien ended up understanding that the family business was on the road to ruin.

He did not say anything at the meeting, but the next day he met with Jean-Christophe and threatened to demand his resignation if he didn't change his ways.

"Mother is managing Elodie's shares in her absence," he said. "I'll go see Faustine in the convent. The three of us will have a majority, and we can force you to leave."

"You never once showed any interest in our business," Jean-Christophe said, indignant. "I was always the one who worked with our father while you, sir, lived it up in the tropics. And now you dare to threaten me because a handful of senile, yellow-bellied board members shared their unjustified fears!"

"I'm going to ask for a review of our company's full situation."

"Our company! Don't you think it's a little late to become interested?"

"Sorry, Jean-Christophe. I trusted you. But everything I've seen corroborates our mother's fears."

"What fears?"

"She's been telling me about the business in her letters. I didn't think the situation was as dire as she suggested, but now I see otherwise. In my sisters' interest, I must act. You don't have the right to think that you're the only one with a stake in this business. Even if I don't matter to you, we have two sisters, and you have children!"

Jean-Christophe left his brother that evening with a venom-filled heart. "Clearly, everyone is abandoning me," he said to himself before returning home to his mistress.

At the end of the year, the world shook at its core. The Great Crash in the United States reverberated around the world. France felt somewhat protected, thanks to the devalued franc. But French companies that traded with the United States encountered financial difficulties right away. As the Great Depression took hold, the difficulties deepened. Rochefort had been losing market share in the United States for some time. The final blow came with the near-total closing of American borders, a protectionist measure designed to help US companies get back on their feet. Jean-Christophe had also invested heavily in the US stock market, and that money was quickly lost. Jean-Christophe's accountant, Robert Mazaudier, was in total despair.

"This is an unprecedented catastrophe," he said. "We'll never come back from it."

The last meager orders from American textile firms were soon canceled. Industries the other side of the Atlantic were ordering from each other—that is, those that had escaped total ruin. Companies in Europe were wobbly, as well. Jean-Christophe wasn't getting much business anywhere.

"We've managed to keep some of our capital in Switzerland hidden," Mazaudier said. "We'll have to use it. Otherwise we won't last long. We won't be able to pay our wages. We're on the edge of bankruptcy."

"We can't dip into that money," Jean-Christophe said. "The tax officials will nab us. We'll have to pay what we owe, plus the penalties. That money will go straight into the government coffers, and it won't help us at all."

"So what are we going to do?"

"Wait. We'll only operate the machines we need to fill our remaining orders. France is not yet in real danger. Starting today, we will work exclusively for the domestic market."

Jean-Christophe still hoped that the Great Depression would spare France, which still seemed to be holding up.

Sebastien decided against executing his threat. The upheaval of the capitalist world sickened him, and he wanted no part of that world. When Pauline worried about the future of his family business, he gave her a detached response. "When you have exploited people for too long, consequences are inevitable. This storm will allow for a deep cleansing. If that means that the Rochefort business must vanish, along with our great family, I accept that."

43

The Great Secret

1930

Faustine lived like a recluse in the Sisters of Charity convent. To be as close as possible to her daughter, she cared for the young orphans, to whom she demonstrated remarkable devotion. Sister Agnes never tired of praising her new recruit, but deep down, something was telling her that she had made a terrible mistake. The period she had set for Faustine to reconsider her decision was coming to an end. Elena would soon be five. If Faustine was insistent on taking her vows, now was the time to cut the cord with the child.

"Have you fully thought out the meaning of the pact you are sealing with Our Lord Jesus Christ?" the mother superior said. "Not only are you committing your entire life, but also you are deciding on your child's destiny. Elena will never know who you are. On that point, I consulted with the bishop. For your daughter's own good, it would be preferable that you move away from our convent for a few years, the time

Elena needs to grow into a fine young lady and start her adult life. Then, if you wish, you can return to us. Elena will never know that you were her mother."

Faustine, in her white novice habit, hesitated. She moved to the window and stared at the children playing in the yard. Her eyes blurred over. Elena looked so sad in the middle of a small group of girls. *She understands what is going to happen*, Faustine said to herself. For a moment, Sister Agnes thought Faustine would change her mind. She walked to the window and stared at the children with Faustine. Touching her shoulder, she said, "We get attached to them, don't we? We can't help it. But we must not forget that we are here to make sure they get on the right path, the one that their parents refused to or cannot show them. That is not your situation. You can still take your daughter and give her what every child wants: a mother's love."

Sister Agnes spoke from the heart. She was convinced that Faustine would go back on her decision. She loved her child. "I gave you a lot of time to find the light inside you. Now you have to decide, for Elena's good. But I must repeat once more: If you join our congregation, you will give up your daughter forever."

To the mother superior's surprise, Faustine said, "If I must move away from the convent after pronouncing my vows, I will."

"So you've decided to take your vows."

"Yes, Mother. I have."

The ceremony was set for August 15, Assumption Day. Faustine had two months to prepare to leave secular life forever. She decided to slowly distance herself from Elena. Another nun took over her care, and Sister Agnes asked the nun to give the child special attention.

"The time it takes to soften the transition. Elena always felt her mother's presence, even if she didn't know who Sister Faustine was."

For the remaining few weeks, Faustine focused on reading the Scriptures, praying, and doing manual labor. It kept her mind and body occupied. She asked to be assigned to the vegetable garden.

"I know the earth," she said to Sister Agnes.

"Yes, your father was a large landowner."

"That is not what I meant. I worked the land like a real farmer with Vincent . . . "

She didn't finish her sentence. It was the first time she had said his name since she had entered the convent. She felt a lump in her throat. She couldn't hold back her emotion.

Sister Agnes continued for her. "With Vincent Janvier. You were happy with him, weren't you? Real happiness, a man who loved you, humble, honest work, a child—"

"Stop, Mother. You are torturing me. I ask you not to make any further reference to my past. I decided to give my life to God. Today, I'm starting another life in which those I loved before cannot have the same place. Didn't Jesus himself renounce his family when he began to preach?"

"There, my daughter, you are committing a sin of pride by daring to compare your situation to that of Our Lord Jesus Christ."

Faustine felt reprimanded. "I will never speak to you about them again. Help me, Mother, to grow strong and no longer sin."

"Being strong does not mean having an empty heart, my daughter. Be careful not to sin further by being too intransigent."

While Faustine continued to pull away, the world was plunging into disaster. The crisis was spreading, and companies were falling like dominoes. Many businesses in France were still standing, but the economy was showing serious signs of vulnerability. Banks were refusing to lend money to all but the most rock-solid businesses. And connections weren't working for anybody anymore.

THE ROCHEFORTS

Jean-Christophe Rochefort, like many others, was beginning to fear the worst. He had already laid off half his employees, and he was getting ready to let even more workers go. His orders were dangerously thin, and he was losing money.

"We're operating at a loss," his accountant, Robert Mazaudier, said. "At this pace, we'll be shutting the doors before the end of the year."

Despite everyone's warnings, Jean-Christophe had never thought the crisis would take down his business. To him, Rochefort was an indestructible citadel. He found himself with his back against the wall, facing the tangible reality that he had, out of carelessness and incompetence, refused to acknowledge until that moment. He had so loved to imitate the American president Herbert Hoover by telling his workers, "Prosperity is just around the corner." It was now clear that disaster, not prosperity, was lurking just around the corner.

Every day, he had to make serious decisions that considerably weakened the possibility that the company would survive. He had already realized—a little late—that he had squandered his resources on poor investments. He finally agreed to dig into the money he had hidden in Switzerland, at the risk of raising the suspicions of the government tax officials. It was either risk that or file for bankruptcy.

His father would have known what to do. But now an embittered Jean-Christophe found himself alone as he faced disaster. His relationships with his colleagues and family had become poisoned. For that matter, he wasn't seeing much of his mother or his society friends. His associates were shunning him like a wounded animal left to the predators. The arrogant, vain, show-off Rochefort was demeaned to the point of begging his business creditors for more time and selling off the vineyards he had inherited from his father.

Elisabeth criticized him. "You see what your foolishness has gotten you? Your poor father is probably rolling over in his grave."

Jean-Christophe hated being compared with Anselme. He controlled himself in front of his mother, but it angered him. His father had never been without fault.

"You forget, Mother, that Father married you for your money. Everybody knows that. It was a marriage of convenience."

Elisabeth's health had begun to waver, and she didn't want to argue with her son. She knew his failings too well to try to make him see reason and admit he was wrong. At seventy-one, she suffered in silence. Every night, she prayed that her son would change his ways.

Similarly, she continued to pray for Elodie's return and Faustine's happiness. Sebastien was the only one who didn't worry her. He called from time to time with news about Pauline and the children and his literary successes.

"I'm proud of you," she would often say.

But that bit of happiness was not enough to banish the shadows creeping into her remaining days. "What have we done to our great family?" she asked herself bitterly.

At the Sisters of Charity orphanage, Sister Agnes spent long hours looking through the archives. She was in a hurry. Faustine would take her vows in a week.

Ever since Faustine had made her final decision, the mother superior was giving the orphan Vincent Janvier all her attention. She vaguely remembered the night when a man in black had knocked at the door. He had dropped off a basket with the baby who would soon be baptized Vincent Janvier. She had been very young at the time, and her visceral fear of the dark had dulled her senses. To help her overcome her fear, Sister Angela, the mother superior, had asked her to go open the door and lead him to the office. Sister Agnes had not been there when they spoke and had not made out the stranger's features, as they were hidden under the brim of his hat. No other details of the scene came back to her.

The next day, she was told to care for the newborn, and she had given him special attention. He was especially young and vulnerable. Nothing else about that event came back to her, and in other circumstances she would not have remembered it.

Of course, the baby had been recorded, as stipulated by law, and declared on the civil registry. But there had to be some other trace of his existence in the orphanage. She knew that twice a year, for seven years, the convent had received money to cover the cost of the child's care. That was rare. Most parents were too poor to pay for any children left at the orphanage. So it made sense that Vincent Janvier had come from a wealthy family.

These were the thoughts that disturbed Sister Agnes's sleep at night. She wouldn't let them go and continued searching. Finally, she found a large envelope in the back of a drawer in an old cabinet that the nuns had stored in the basement. Intrigued, she opened the envelope and took out a bunch of receipts, each indicating a sum of money given to the orphanage for Vincent Janvier's care.

Sister Agnes gasped. *It's proof of what I remembered*, she said to herself. But the name of the person who had paid the money was not on the receipts. She emptied the drawer, which was full of papers. A short letter with angular writing attracted her attention. She started when she read the signature: Anselme Rochefort.

She walked over to the wall lamp, adjusted her glasses, and read aloud so she couldn't be mistaken:

> Mother Superior,
>
> > The man you saw tonight must remain totally anonymous. Similarly, the child must never know his origins. He is the son of Catherine Letellier, my first wife's daughter. My first wife was expecting

when I met her, and she has been dead for many years. Today, I give you a large amount of money to cover the cost of the child's education. I don't want him to lack anything. As long as he is not adopted by an honorable family, you will receive an equivalent amount twice a year. I know I can count on your silence. The child lost his mother at birth and has no father. I am sure you will raise him to follow a righteous path, one his poor mother, unfortunately, did not find."

Sister Agnes read the letter again to make sure she hadn't missed anything and then sat down in a chair.

"That changes everything," she said aloud.

She was bothered by one thing: Why did he sign the letter rather than make it anonymous?

"It didn't matter," she said. "He knew that nuns were like priests in confession and would keep it confidential."

Her heart pounding, Sister Agnes hurried to Faustine's cell. Preparing for the big day, Faustine was on her knees in prayer. Tears were streaming down her cheeks.

"What's wrong, my daughter? Why such sadness? Is it because your vows are nearing?"

"I'm sorry, Mother. It's just the emotion."

"I understand. Are you sure you want to go through with it?"

Painful thoughts were preying on Faustine. The more she tried to forget the past, the more it surfaced in her prayers, as if God Himself was keeping the memory of her love for Vincent alive.

"Here. Read this. It concerns you, my child."

For a moment, Faustine thought it was something related to her vows.

"Read it. I think it will make you change your mind."

Faustine wiped away her tears and skimmed the letter. Her face brightened as she discovered what was in it.

"So then . . . "

"You read that correctly, Faustine. You and Vincent are not related. Your father carried the secret to his grave. Catherine was not his daughter, just his step-daughter, his first wife's child."

Faustine was stunned. "But why did Father hide the truth from us? Why did he lie? Even to Mother!"

"He alone could tell you. But it is pointless to dwell on that now. What is important, my child, is your decision. You still love Vincent, don't you?"

"I can't seem to forget him, Mother."

"That is the Lord's way. You must not go against his will. Your life is with Vincent and your daughter."

Sister Agnes spoke at length with her young protégé, urging her to do what was in her heart.

"Vincent must have forgotten me and found a new life by now. It's probably too late."

"Believe, my child. Faith can move mountains."

Faustine took a few days to get her thoughts in order. In the end, she let herself be convinced by Sister Agnes that it was better to break off her commitment and return to the life she had left behind.

Elena went with her and didn't hide her joy at going out into the city. A taxi dropped them off at the Cordeliers. Elena now called Faustine "mom" and wasn't surprised when she carefully revealed the truth. Elena had always had a special bond with Faustine.

"You've always been my mom," she said. "But why don't I have a dad?"

Faustine hesitated to tell her the whole truth and didn't give her a straight answer. "You will meet him soon, my dear. We'll go see him together."

That answer satisfied the child.

Before getting out of the taxi, Faustine said, "This is where I lived when I was young. My mother, your grandmother Elisabeth, still lives here. Your grandfather Anselme went to heaven a few years ago."

"Is he dead?"

"Yes."

"Is this where we will live now?"

"For a few days. Then we'll go see your father."

At the Cordeliers, where grieving had reigned for so many years, the housekeeper shrieked with joy when she saw Faustine at the door. "Madame, it's Faustine! Lord . . . Miss, it really is you! I'm not dreaming. You've left the convent?"

"Yes, Marie-Jeanne, it's me. And this is my daughter, Elena."

The little girl kissed the servant.

"You've come at a bad time, miss. You should have warned ma'am that you were coming. She would have prepared you."

"What's happened?"

"A terrible thing, miss."

"Spit it out, Marie-Jeanne!"

"It's sir, miss. Mr. Jean-Christophe. He tried to end his life."

"Jean-Christophe? He tried to commit suicide! Is he . . . "

"No, miss, he is not dead, thank the Lord. But the doctor said he barely made it."

"Where is my brother?"

"In your father's room. That's where your mother found him just in time. He tried to hang himself. I helped get him down. Oh Lord, it was horrible, but we saved him."

"Why did he do that?"

"Mrs. Rochefort will explain."

Faustine handed Elena over to the housekeeper and rushed to her father's bedroom. Elisabeth was watching over her son, who was lying on the bed. Elisabeth heard the door open and looked up. Seeing her daughter in the simple dress she had worn to the convent, she cried out, "Faustine! You are back!"

"Yes, Mother. I've come home."

Faustine's return helped Elisabeth overcome the distress caused by Jean-Christophe's desperate act. The doctor confirmed that his life was no longer in danger, but he would be paralyzed.

"He broke a cervical vertebra. His spinal cord was affected," Elisabeth explained.

Faustine thought about her father. "Paralysis didn't keep Father from running his business," she said, trying to give the newest family tragedy a note of optimism.

"Your father's business is in poor shape, my dear. Jean-Christophe is bankrupt. That's why he attempted suicide."

"Is there no more hope?"

"I called Sebastien. He should be arriving on the last train tonight. He promised to help. I don't know what he can do. He just said he had a very competent friend who could help."

"So all is not lost then?"

"Only the future will tell."

Faustine remained with Jean-Christophe. Just being in the room reminded her of the happiness she had experienced in this home with her brothers and sister, the whole family united and strong.

When Sebastien's train arrived, he rushed to the Cordeliers.

"Sebastien! It's you," Faustine cried out when she saw him in the doorway to the bedroom.

"I came as quickly as I could. How is he?"

"He's not talking. His larynx was injured. But that is not the most serious problem."

"Yes, I know."

"He'll come through, but what a price to pay."

"That idiot. How did it come to this?" Sebastien said.

"What's done is done. Now we need to help him pull through."

"That's why I came."

Having her children around her comforted Elisabeth. *If only Elodie were with them*, she thought.

During the following days, Jean-Christophe began talking again and regained some strength. Unlike his father, he did not storm against his fate and even seemed resigned to spending the rest of his life in a wheelchair. He felt finished and had no desire to fight.

"I made serious mistakes. I admit it. I was a bad husband, a poor father, and a terrible boss. I ruined everything. How can I hold a grudge against fate? I got what I deserved."

Elisabeth, however, encouraged him. He was her son, and she loved him. She lavished him with attention. At the same time, she turned to Sebastien to do what he could to save what was left of the family business.

Sebastien asked for an audit to get an accurate picture of the company's finances.

"Then we'll see what needs to be done," he told his mother and siblings. "But we know these things for sure: We must listen to our partners, clean up our finances, and move carefully into safe areas. The crisis is not over. We'll have to continue austerity measures until the economy improves."

Sebastien surprised those around him. This family member who had never shown the slightest interest in his father's business was now talking like a real business manager on a campaign to reboot the company.

"Do you intend to come on full time and run the business with me?" Jean-Christophe asked.

"Full time, no. I'm a writer. I want to remain one. But I think you need my help. After all, I am a Rochefort, aren't I?"

Epilogue

44

A warm autumn sun lit up Mount Lozère. The slopes wore a carpet of violet heather. The beach trees were slowly turning gold, and the prairies were once again green. A long-awaited rainfall had broken the long months of summer drought.

Most of the sheep had been taken back to the lowland plains. No farmer wanted to be stranded with his animals when the snow began falling. Everyone was preparing for winter. The wood was stacked, and the equipment was put away. On the farms, the sheep were herded back to the stables every night. Only hardy cows, not bothered by the first cold, remained outside after dark. Their owners would bring them in later in the fall, thus conserving hay stored during the summer.

Vincent was preparing to face his fifth winter cloistered in his mountain sheepfold, with only his animals and his dog, Goupil. Of course, Aline came to see him when the school holidays gave her time off, but those visits hinged on the roads, which weren't always passable in the winter. This seasonal relationship with Vincent was all that she had managed to achieve. She was satisfied for the time being but still harbored the hope that he would change his mind one day and return to Tornac to live with her. She also hoped to have a child, but Vincent refused.

Constance worried about the situation. She had hoped that her daughter would put this impossible love behind her and find happiness in someone else's arms.

"You see that Vincent can't forget Faustine. You're wasting your time with him," she kept saying.

But Aline wouldn't let go. And for his part, Vincent did his best to please Aline. People called them the "lovers of the Taillades." Those people smiled when they said it. But they had also called Vincent and Faustine the "lovers of the Taillades." Vincent remembered that all too well.

When the first flakes started falling, he hurried to gather his flock and bring them back to the fold. They weren't in a rush, and Goupil had to nip at their hooves to get them to move faster. Once the flock was sheltered, Vincent sat down with Goupil on the threshold of the only room he occupied. It was next to the stables. The only sound was the bleating of the sheep—until the dog raised his head and began barking.

"Quiet," Vincent said.

But the dog didn't stop. Ears perked, he looked into the distance and barked with all his might.

Vincent finished rolling a cigarette, lit it, and stood up to get a better look at what was getting the dog's attention. He spotted a slight figure coming his way. He could barely see it through the snowflakes that were now falling heavily.

"Someone is coming," he said to his dog. "You were right to bark. In this weather, it must be a lost walker."

The shape approached slowly. Vincent saw a second, smaller person next to the first.

"A woman and child. Go to them," he ordered Goupil. "Don't scare them with your bark."

The dog rushed off.

Vincent followed. He stopped a short distance from the stranger, who was wrapped in a thick wool cape.

"I thought I'd never find you," he thought he heard.

He hesitated. He tried to see who was hiding under the thick cape. Then his heart felt as though it would explode in his chest.

"Faustine? But what are you doing here? And in this weather!"

Faustine let go of her daughter's hand. The child was shivering from the cold.

"Elena, I promised you. This is you dad," Faustine said.

Vincent was dumbstruck. "That's your . . . That's our?"

"Our daughter, Vincent. Her name is Elena, like the light. We named her at the convent."

"But why aren't you there?"

"Why don't you invite us in, Vincent? I think we'd be more comfortable there."

"I'm sorry. I'm just so surprised. Follow me. Ignore how rustic it is."

Vincent couldn't take his eyes off the little girl, who was already captivating him. He was speechless when Faustine finished telling the story.

"I never could forget you, Vincent," she said. "In my convent cell, I kept asking God to forgive me and bring me the peace my soul needed. I was ready to sacrifice myself if that was the price I had to pay to erase you from my memory. But now everything is possible."

Vincent listened without moving.

"You're not saying anything. You don't love me anymore, do you? Is that why you're so quiet?"

Elena was playing with Goupil at the back of the room. She heard her mother's last words and walked over to Vincent. "Are you really my daddy? Are we going to live together?" she asked.

Vincent lifted her to his knees and held her tight against his chest. His eyes filled with tears. "I've waited so long for this moment," he whispered in Elena's ears. "I didn't dare believe it would happen."

Then he opened his arms to Faustine and said, "I love you so much. I never stopped thinking about you either."

Vincent and Faustine spent several days at the Taillades. They experienced the most wonderful moments of their lives. They discovered each other as if it were the first time. Elena brought the light into her parents' hearts that had been so lacking during the years of renunciation and confinement. She quickly became the greatest source of their happiness, the living proof of their love.

Vincent didn't keep his relationship with Aline a secret. He promised he would talk to her as soon as they got back to Tornac.

"I'm sure she will understand. I think she always knew I was waiting for you to come back. She offered me her love so that I wouldn't suffer as much from not having you. But she knew I belonged to you. I saw in her eyes the last time she left that she understood I would never make her totally happy."

Vincent decided to take the animals back to La Fenouillère. There were no more shepherds left in the highlands, other than Victor's cousin, Antoine Chabrol. He always went back down the mountain with his son during the last part of November. Vincent had known him since he had moved up to the Taillades.

"If Chabrol goes back down this time of year, we might as well, too," Vincent said.

His decision surprised Faustine. "Wouldn't it be best to wait for good weather? We could spend the winter here, the way you usually do."

"I prefer to go down while we still can. I can't wait to

announce the end of my retreat. A new life is starting for the three of us, Faustine."

"No, not a new life! Our life is simply resuming. And we'll make it even better. Don't forget that you inherited the Clos du Tournel. Together, we'll ensure that it prospers, along with our vineyards at the Chais de La Fenouillère, which your father kept up while you were gone."

Vincent's flock took five days to return to Tornac. At the way stations where Vincent had always stopped with Donatien, Vincent, Faustine, and Elena were welcomed warmly. Everyone was thrilled to hear that Vincent would soon marry Faustine Rochefort.

Donatien and Constance soon learned that they were on their way down. Elisabeth had told the Rouvières that Faustine was back and had gone to see Vincent. But they hadn't expected their son's early return.

Aline accepted the news with equanimity. She told her parents that she would let Vincent go and that she would love him like a brother from that day on. Constance was relieved but couldn't help feeling sorry for her daughter. Madeleine tried to console her cousin.

"Now she has a free heart, and she'll feel ready to accept the love of an honest man. And believe me, I know one who is just waiting for a look from her to declare his love. I'm sure he'll be more than a consolation prize for her."

In the days that followed, Elisabeth arrived at the Clos du Tournel with her family. Jean-Christophe had agreed to come with her. Sebastien, who had not yet returned to Paris, asked Pauline to join them with Rose and Ruben. Louise was expected too. She wanted to introduce her parents to her fiancé, Alain Dubreuil.

They all wanted to celebrate Faustine and Vincent's

reunion and hoped to be together for the wedding, which was set for December 27. Aline, looking radiant, showed up on the arm of a young man Vincent recognized. It was Antonin Porte, one of his best friends from school. He was the son of his former teacher, Roland Porte. Like his father, Antonin was a schoolteacher.

Finally, Julie arrived with her husband and children.

Everyone gathered around the table for a fine meal to celebrate Faustine and Vincent's engagement. Emotion could be read in everyone's eyes. Joy filled their hearts.

Donatien wanted the celebration to take place at La Fenouillère. Elisabeth had readily agreed to have it there instead of the Clos du Tournel. And although she was happy for Faustine, she couldn't stop thinking of the daughter who wasn't there.

At the end of the meal, as the Rocheforts prepared to return to the Clos du Tournel, a car pulled up to the gates of La Fenouillère. The driver, dressed in black, left the engine on as he got out to open the back door. A frail women got out unsteadily. The man in black held her until a second man emerged from the car. The second man took her by the waist, and the driver returned to his place behind the wheel.

The woman pulled the cord to the bell hanging from the gates and then entered the yard with her companion. The two strangers climbed the stairs to the front door. The woman knocked on the door.

Sebastien was the first to hear the knock. He quietly got up and went to open the door. The two visitors took a few steps inside without being invited. The woman lifted her face to meet Sebastien's eyes. He was speechless.

"I have returned to live with my family if you will have my husband and me. This is Pietr Boroslav."

Elisabeth let out a cry of stupefaction and joy and fainted.

When she came to, Elodie was leaning over her. "They let me go, Mother. I'm alive. Very much alive."

Little Elena wasn't quite following everything that was happening in front of her.

"What's going on, Mom? Is grandmother okay?"

"She fainted, sweetheart, because she is so happy that your Aunt Elodie has come from far, far away to be with us after a very long time."

Faustine turned to Vincent. "You know, my father used to call us a great family because of our wealth and power. But it's our perseverance, our loyalty, our willingness to admit our foolishness and forgive each other, and, finally, our love that make us what we are. My heart is filled with joy today. All of us here together—we are a truly great family."

Saint-Jean-du-Pin, September 10, 2009–July 14, 2010

ABOUT THE AUTHOR

Christian Laborie was born in the North of France but has lived in the southern region of Cévennes for more than twenty years. *The Rocheforts* is his first novel to be published in English.

Publishers Square, a subsidiary of Place des éditeurs, a publishing group based in Paris, is dedicated to bringing commercially successful French authors to American readers. Its list covers a wide range of genres, with an emphasis on women's fiction, thrillers, and historical fiction, and includes authors such as Françoise Bourdin, who regularly hits the French bestseller lists. Publishers Square believes that the best stories have a universal appeal, and hopes to break down the barriers between American and French readers in the digital age.

FIND OUT MORE AT
WWW.PUBLISHERS-SQUARE.COM

Publishers Square is one of a select group of publishing partners of Open Road Integrated Media, Inc.

Open Road Integrated Media is a digital publisher and multimedia content company. Open Road creates connections between authors and their audiences by marketing its ebooks through a new proprietary online platform, which uses premium video content and social media.

Videos, Archival Documents, and New Releases

Sign up for the Open Road Media newsletter and get news delivered straight to your inbox.

Sign up now at
www.openroadmedia.com/newsletters

FIND OUT MORE AT
WWW.OPENROADMEDIA.COM

FOLLOW US:
@openroadmedia and
Facebook.com/OpenRoadMedia